D0959427

A NEW LIFE

SHE was a different person in the daylight hours, without her makeup and with her eyes like slits and her skinny frame wrapped in an oversize robe. I tried to hide my surprise, which reappeared when she emerged from her rooms an hour later, primped and wide-awake and put together. She peered in the library door, squinting.

"There you are. Hiding. It's time we put you right," she said as I stood up, and then she looked down at my old black shoes. "Good grief. First order of business is new shoes. And for pity's sake, take off those awful stockings before we leave the apartment."

"I'm not a flapper," I said.

"Yeah? Well, we can fix that," she responded. "Come on."

SIREN

BOOKS BY JANET FOX

Faithful
Forgiven

SIRENS

JANET FOX

speak

An Imprint of Penguin Group (USA) Inc.

COUNTY LIBRARY

DISCARD

TILLAMOOK, ORE.

SPEAK

Published by the Penguin Group

Penguin Group (USA) Inc., 345 Hudson Street, New York, New York 10014, U.S.A.

Penguin Group (Canada), 90 Eglinton Avenue East, Suite 700, Toronto, Ontario, Canada M4P 2Y3
(a division of Pearson Penguin Canada Inc.)

Penguin Books Ltd, 80 Strand, London WC2R 0RL, England

Penguin Ireland, 25 St Stephen's Green, Dublin 2, Ireland (a division of Penguin Books Ltd)

Penguin Group (Australia), 250 Camberwell Road, Camberwell, Victoria 3124, Australia
(a division of Pearson Australia Group Pty Ltd)

Penguin Books India Pvt Ltd, 11 Community Centre, Panchsheel Park, New Delhi – 110 017, India

Penguin Group (NZ), 67 Apollo Drive, Rosedale, Auckland 0632, New Zealand
(a division of Pearson New Zealand Ltd.)

Penguin Books (South Africa) (Pty) Ltd, 24 Sturdee Avenue, Rosebank, Johannesburg 2196, South Africa

Penguin Books Ltd, Registered Offices: 80 Strand, London WC2R 0RL, England

First published in the United States of America by Speak, an imprint of Penguin Group (USA) Inc., 2012

3   5   7   9   10   8   6   4

Copyright © Janet Fox, 2012
All rights reserved

LIBRARY OF CONGRESS CATALOGING-IN-PUBLICATION DATA IS AVAILABLE

Speak ISBN 978-0-14-242430-8

Printed in the United States of America

All rights reserved. No part of this book may be reproduced, scanned, or distributed
in any printed or electronic form without permission. Please do not participate in
or encourage piracy of copyrighted materials in violation of the author's rights.
Purchase only authorized editions.

For the two men who rule my heart, Jeff and Kevin,
and for my sister Mary, who is my own sassy Lou

PROLOGUE

THE *Titanic* taught us that there are no unsinkable ships. The Great War taught us that there are no deathless heroes. The influenza taught us that there are no places to hide.

We were done with darkness, so we shed our old skins. And some of us drank that wild brew called abandon.

The other girls, they came from everywhere: from the small towns with their quiet commons, from the city tenements with their honking mayhem. They wore their hair short and their skirts shorter. Followers of Bacchus, devotees of Pan, heedless of the old rules, yet they wanted to be all the same, the same—they were Zelda, they were Clara, they were Coco. They were flappers.

And when I shed my old skin, what soft and tender flesh did I expose? The heart does hold secrets, and is itself an unruly thing.

CHAPTER 1
LATE SEPTEMBER 1925

First you will raise the island of the Sirens,
Those creatures who spellbind any man alive,
Whoever comes their way. Whoever draws too close,
Off guard, and catches the Sirens' voices in the air—
No sailing home for him . . .
—Homer, The Odyssey, Book 12, 44–48

JO

The wharf stretched over the water, a black slab like a prone tombstone. Across the river the lights in Jersey cast shimmering reflections that bobbled and broke, the only light by which I could see since I'd pulled the Nash sideways and the car's headlamps cast their lights south. With my right hand I tucked my collar up under my chin; the night was crisp and the stars threw a hard brilliance.

In my left hand I clutched the scarf, the metal tucked inside biting through the silk and into the leather glove, sharp points digging into my palm.

"Okay, Teddy," I whispered to the chilly dark. "This is what you wanted. This is for you."

I pulled my fist from my coat pocket and opened the scarf, the silk weeping over my open hand. I couldn't see the poppies in the dark, those big scarlet splotches on white. I couldn't see the three medals with their grosgrain ribbons, their insignia, but as they shifted and clinked they grew heavy in my palm—some figment of my imagination—and I plucked them out of the scarf one by one and tossed them, my best Teddy-taught ball throw, into the water, which they hit with a soft splash, one, two, three.

The water shivered, just the smallest ripple, then stilled.

I hustled back to the car, hobbled by my coat and the uneven ground, shivering as I climbed in and pressed against the leather. I glanced through the glass knowing that he wouldn't be there.

I let out the brake and stomped on the clutch and put the thing in gear and made off with a roar, spitting stones, navigating out of the maze of warehouses and dockside loading bays and back to the dark streets of the Lower West Side. I thought about Charlie, and my heart skipped a beat, and my foot pressed harder on the accelerator. I thought about Lou and what she'd say about Teddy and the medals. She'd probably think it was a shame.

But I'd made a promise. I did what Teddy asked me to do. I didn't need his medals anymore. Because as I looked at everything I'd learned, at everything I'd found and lost in these five months past, this was my northern star: I still had Teddy.

* * *

LOU

So boys. Am I a witness, or a suspect?

As I cross my legs I can see the detective's momentary distraction. I savor the moment.

You mind exhaling your smoke in the other direction, Detective?

It's not the cushiest chair ever, either, though I don't go on about that. The detective in the suit perches on the desk in front of me. The guy taking notes sits right behind me, where I can't see him. We're in a tight little office with glass walls, and a bustle goes on in the precinct headquarters around us. Every so often some joker stares in at me like I'm a museum specimen or something. I fan my face. A gal can hardly think in here, especially considering.

Fine. I'm gonna start at the beginning. That way maybe you guys can fill in the rest of the blanks yourselves and stop pestering me. I'll give you the whole kit and caboodle. Me and Danny. Me and Jo. Jo and Charlie. What happened that night. What happened to take us to that point. It's quite a story, and I'll give it to you straight, especially . . .

I pause for effect.

. . . how I'm an innocent victim.

I can see the smirk starting to form on those skinny lips, and I think, Don't laugh, buster.

And Teddy, you want to know about Teddy, don't you? It doesn't all start with Teddy, but yeah, it sure ends with him. Yeah, right there in the water. Such a shame.

Jo thought she had him. A crying shame, that. But . . .

Then I see that the detective—Smith, isn't it?—he shifts like he's impatient, and I think, Settle down, sweet pea. I'm not gonna get ahead of myself.

CHAPTER 2

Lies are essential to humanity. They are perhaps as important as the pursuit of pleasure and moreover are dictated by that pursuit.
— Marcel Proust (1871–1922)

JO

Tonight Pops was in a foul mood. He'd been that way ever since Teddy had disappeared—dead, they said, but I knew the truth. I was not grief-stricken like Ma and Pops, because I'd been privy to the lie.

Pops chewed on a bitterness so sharp and keen it gave him a permanent frown. But this was worse than usual.

"Fanny!"

I winced, yanked out of my fictional world, and I bowed my head over the story I was working on and tried to concentrate on that last sentence I'd written, tried to block out Pops's bark and Ma's scrambled response.

"Fanny. Where's that ledger? I need those numbers."

I heard Ma's soft voice, though not her words, and I gave up on the sentence and rested my forehead on my palm and shut my eyes. My turn next.

With a thud, the ledger landed on the table, burying my paper and nearly smashing my right hand, which still clutched a pencil.

"Josephine. I need those numbers," Pops said. He was gone before I looked up.

My skill with numbers was more important to him than anything else. Certainly more important than my fledgling desire to write.

Ma hovered in the doorway, and her eyes met mine before she slipped back into the kitchen, hiding behind the flower-infested apron and the clattering of pots. The gauze curtain that hung over the dark window lifted, a round belly, then dropped; the breeze riffled the loose hairs across my cheek. A distant dog's bark drifted in on the spring night air. It was warm for May, the breeze fragrant with lilacs.

I shifted the heavy bound black ledger until I could open it to the page with its marker showing where I'd left off. I sighed at the columns citing cases of whiskey and rum, gin and mixers.

Pops had to be so upset tonight because of what had happened the night before. Danny Connor's men had been at the house and were looking for something of Teddy's. I'd overheard the conversation, and wished I hadn't.

Teddy. It was like I could feel his hand on my shoulder. Séances were all the rage with my friends at school, but I didn't need any old séance to manifest my brother. He'd told me he'd gotten into a jam and had to lay low. He'd said he'd come back and made me promise not to tell. I might not know where he was now, but I held fast to that promise. I held to it even after we'd placed an empty coffin in the ground, even when everyone else was sure Teddy was dead.

I worked the figures totaling the profits that the black market liquor had brought in over the past week. My Pops, bootlegger for the biggest gangster in New York, Danny Connor. It was all wrong.

Pops said he was in the business for the family. Our sweet little grocery next door to the house had been a fine thing. Once. Now the old dry-goods section hid a false wall, and midnight deliveries of crates from Canada disturbed my sleep. The business had grown lately, and the figures in the ledger had swelled, too. Bootleggers made a lot of money as middlemen between the Canadians who imported the booze and the swells down in the city who drank it despite the Prohibition. But bootleggers like Pops who made deals with gangsters like Danny Connor were always one step away from danger.

Before Teddy disappeared a year ago, Pops had kept his bootlegging to small-time deals. But after Teddy disappeared, Pops assuaged his grief by making a bigger deal with the devil. It didn't matter. All the money in the world wouldn't cure what ailed him. As far as I was concerned Pops had forgotten about what was right.

And here I was, helping Pops's misbegotten work by keeping the books. Helping him try to drown the memory of Teddy when I wanted to shout, He's not dead! Except that I had made Teddy a promise.

A hard, hard promise to keep when I watched my ma and pops. But I kept it, for Teddy's sake.

The clock chimed ten when I leaned back in the chair. I rubbed my eyes with the heels of my hands. My hair had fallen out of its pins and lay like a blanket hanging down my back, hot and heavy.

Last week Moira had her hair bobbed. The other girls all crowded around, touching and admiring. Moira said she felt a million pounds lighter and, with her voice low and thrilling, told us that a man on the street had stopped and asked her if she was the real Colleen Moore. Colleen Moore, whose smiling visage graced the posters at the moving picture theater just about every week, who was touted as the perfect flapper with her short skirts, heart-shaped face, and bow lips.

I didn't want strange men stopping me on the street or, heaven forbid, thinking I was a flapper—daring and naughty and foolish. But it was already warm and the steamy summer loomed, and my thick curls weighed on my neck. Shorter hair would be nothing more than a convenience. A simple haircut wasn't enough to turn a girl into a flapper, right? Modern and smart, sure. But not a flapper. The last thing I wanted was to be taken for a fool.

Ma was still in the kitchen, hanging the damp wash. Her black skirt grazed her ankles as she bent over the tub to pick out the next wet shirt and position it to run through the wringer.

"What would you think if I cut my hair short?"

She started and straightened and put one hand up, touching her own gray-streaked hair, which was piled in a rolling crown on top of her head.

I lifted my hair off my neck, peeling clinging moist strands off my skin. "It sure would be cooler. And easier. It's just a practical matter." I waited. "That's all."

"Cut your hair. I'll think on it." Ma wiped her hands on her apron. "I've been wanting to tell you. There's something important come up. Your father put a call in to your uncle this morning."

I let my hair drop. "About?"

"Things." She shifted her eyes away. "Your father and I, we want you to go stay with your aunt and uncle for a time."

"In New York? What?" I was stunned. "Why?"

She met my eyes again, her cheeks dark. "That's the decision." The worry in her voice made my heart pound.

I said, "But after school ends, right? Exams are over in three weeks."

She shook her head, said with finality, "Sooner."

"But, Ma. I have to finish school. I won't graduate."

Pops's voice came hard: "School's for boys, not girls. Last time I looked you weren't a boy."

I jumped. "Pops!" I hadn't heard him come up behind me.

His face creased with a frown. "You're to go down to the city and stay with your aunt and uncle." He paused. "And meet someone proper, a proper guy. Your aunt and uncle can see to it. It's high time you get married and get on with your life."

A proper . . . what? The color rose up my throat. "Pops. I'm not getting married." I would've laughed, but Pop's expression choked the humor out of me.

"You'll do as I say." No question, he was not just upset tonight but cornered-animal upset.

I kept my voice steady. "I have to finish my schooling, Pops. I'm only seventeen!"

"Your ma was seventeen when we married. You're better than her?"

I bit my tongue so as not to hurt Ma's feelings. She shifted, and the shirt she had hanging halfway through the wringer dripped into the rinse water, a soft *plink, plink* in the warm night air.

The warm night air that rippled with undercurrents of confusion and worry and threat. And all of it focused on me.

I had dreams, though Pops didn't know about them. I wanted to become a writer—like that Agatha Christie. Teddy'd told me I had talent. He read the little things I wrote, and he liked them. Lots of girls were working now. It was modern and all right and didn't mean you were bad. Teddy'd said he'd help me, said he'd talk to Pops so that after I graduated from high school I could set out on the path toward my dreams.

But Teddy wasn't here.

I stood as straight as I could, hanging on to those dreams. "I have to graduate high school. I've got plans for when I graduate. I want to go to college. And then make something of myself."

You could've cut the air with a knife.

Pops's voice was low. "Teddy was the one should've gone to college. He went to war instead. Sacrificed his brain to that good cause. At least he was a hero." Pops now stared at the floor so hard I thought he might bore holes right through it. "I spoke to your uncle. You're darn lucky he's got the goods and the willingness to take you in. He can introduce you to society types. You can make yourself useful by getting married to a guy who has some dough. Then there's one less thing to give me a headache."

What was he thinking? Marriage? I talked back, made bold by the warm temperature and the worry. "I can help the family by getting a job once I graduate from college."

"Job." Pops paced the floor, spouting, my back talk unleashing his anger, all his pent-up arguments. "First they get the vote, and now women think they can go around taking jobs from men. Worse thing that ever happened to this country was when women got the vote. Dumb politicians."

I'd heard it all before—Pops's raving about the suffrage—but this time was different. This time it was about me.

He turned on me. "There's no job except where you ought to be—at home, taking care of your family. Like your ma, who takes care of things around this house. You don't hear her complaining, do you?" Behind me, Ma shifted, a soft murmur in her throat. Pa's voice rose, quick. "You're going, and you'll find a husband. And no nonsense about cutting your hair. Women who cut their hair short are floozies."

My voice trembled. "I'm not ready to get married. I want to finish out the school year. I have plans. And my plans don't include becoming a floozy."

Pops narrowed his eyes. "I'm your father. You'll do as I tell you. You're to go to New York, to stay with your aunt and uncle."

My throat grew tight, and I heard Ma behind me, felt her rest her hand on my shoulder. "Of course she will. Won't you, Jo?"

Pops's eyes slipped between Ma's and mine, and he turned on his heel and left us in the kitchen, the air weighing damp with the clean clothes that smelled of Ma's lavender soap.

I turned. "Ma." Now the tears welled. "This is all wrong."

She shook her head. "Don't. Don't, Jo. It'll do no good."

"But why? Why can't I stay here?" Even as I said it I could see it in her eyes: she and Pops both wanted me out of the house, to disappear behind a curtain. Something was surely wrong. Frustration edged in again behind my fear. "He sells spirits illegally and I can do his books, but I can't finish school and get an honest job?" I folded my arms over my chest, tucking myself in.

"If he's worried about floozies, he should take a look at the places that sell his liquor."

"Josephine." Ma's voice was hard now. "You will not talk about your father that way in this house." She took a breath. "Especially not when he's only thinking about you."

I dropped my head.

She went on, "You know, Mary landed on her feet with Bertram. My sister was clever that way. He's done well. They've got a big beautiful place on Park Avenue now. They tell me it's all the rage, living in a Park Avenue apartment. Plenty of privacy there, and lots of protection. They even have a doorman to keep you safe."

Safe. The word stuck in the air like a dab of glue on paper.

"Aunt Mary and Uncle Bert hardly know me. Why would they want to take me in?"

"They're family. We're family." Ma didn't lie well. *Safe* hung there, thick. *Protection.* Pops's anger was out of bounds. Ma pressed the shirt through the wringer, squeezing the life out of it.

"Mary said you don't need to bring anything but underclothes. Your cousin Melody has dresses she's dying to give you."

"Ma? What's really going on?" I reached for the shirt, hung it for her while she picked out the next.

She shrugged. "I don't ask for details. I don't question your father." She worked the wringer with a vengeance, snapped the next shirt hard, then handed it to me to hang it over the drying rack. She said as she turned away, in a voice so calm it was chilling, "We just couldn't bear to lose you, too."

The argument went out of me as I heard the tremor in her voice. Lose me, too. Like they lost Teddy.

She moved back to me then, placed one hand on my shoulder,

lifting the hair away from my face with the other. "You're a smart girl. I know you can take care of yourself in New York. Your aunt and uncle aren't unkind. They live high, but they won't treat you poorly. Please. Do this for your father. For me."

"All right, Ma. When should I be ready?"

"Your father said over the weekend."

"This weekend?"

"Best not to finish out the school week and have the other students knowing where you're off to."

I rubbed my eyes with my fingers. Not finish out the week. And not finish out the year. "Do you need my help here?" I asked from behind my knuckles.

"No. You go do what you need to." Her voice was soft.

I turned away fast so Ma couldn't see my face.

I left the kitchen, back to the dining table where I dropped into the chair, my eyes stinging. Pops's books were done. My story wouldn't be finished tonight; I was in no mood for it. Besides, now without school and Miss Draper, there'd be no one to read it.

Pops had never mentioned marrying me off before. I thought again about that conversation in the alley I'd overheard the night before, the one between Pops and Danny Connor's men. There was a threat hanging over this house, and he wanted me out. Fumbling for answers, I went over in my mind what I'd heard of the argument in the dark alley outside my bedroom window.

Close to midnight the noises had started. I'd gotten so used to noises like those that usually I slept through. But not last night. Behind the clatter of bottles and from the depths of sleep I heard Teddy's name.

And then, ". . . something Mr. Connor's been looking for. You know anything?"

"No." Pops's voice was sharp.

"You wouldn't be lying now, would you?" The voice was a low growl. "'Cause Mr. Connor, he wants us to tell you he's got reason to believe there might be something Teddy . . ." Here the clanking of bottles drowned the next words.

After a few minutes, Pops said, "We're done."

"Done for now, Billy-boy, but if Mr. Connor suspects you're hiding—"

"Nothing. I'm hiding nothing," Pops interrupted. "My son has been dead and gone these past eleven months, and we have nothing." They might not hear it, but I could: Pops's voice shook.

"Mr. Connor says to tell you he's paying you a visit in the near future. If he thinks you know something, our next pickup might not be the usual."

"Yeah," said another voice. "Liftin' boxes is tough when your knees don't work."

Car doors slammed; a car motor started; the sound moved off. The back door shut with a thump and the lock clicked. Murmurings issued from my parents' bedroom, and I lay there listening until I couldn't hold my eyes open any longer.

Now as I reflected on that conversation it still made little sense. New York gangster Danny Connor was looking for something of Teddy's, here in this house. Pops was sending me away as fast as he could, and had Ma talking about losing me. I didn't know the specifics, but this was something so dangerous or so important that the threat to Pops, to Ma, and even to me was serious. And then there was Teddy's Houdini-like disappearance. He left us—he left me—for a reason.

I could see now that Pops wanted to get me out of the house for my own good.

If Teddy's troubles were wrapped up with Connor, Pops's line of work had put all of us in a devilish spot. Pops had been wrong to swallow his grief by working with the likes of Danny Connor.

I would never blame Teddy for this turn of events. No, I would not.

CHAPTER 3

LOU

So who knows right from wrong straightaway, anyhow?

I adjust my posture, folding my hands in my lap.

Look, Detective, I know what you're trying here, but it ain't working. That light is glaring straight into my baby blues, so would you mind? That's better. Now, where were we? Oh, yeah. Me and Danny Connor. And right and wrong.

I never pretended to be sure about what was right. I never pretended to know anything but this: I did what I did to survive. Me, Louise O'Keefe, as tough as nails on the outside, but all I truly wanted was some guy to take care of me.

So sure, it was all about keeping us safe, at least at first. It was about me not having any more dough and us being down on our luck and Danny being in the right place at the right time. That he was from the old country? That was extra. I was pretty sure a boyo like him would have a soft spot for the likes of me since we were both only a step away from home.

I hear the *clack* of the steno from behind my back as I talk.

I met Danny Connor back in 1921. When I saw him that day on the street, I was just about on my last dime. There he stood: handsomest guy I'd ever seen and oh so swanky in that three-piece and those spats, a cane with what I thought was a polished brass knob—I later learned it was solid gold. And his eyes, gray like a spring storm. Sure, he was the best-looking swell I'd ever seen. But that wasn't what took me there. It was that other thing, that smell. Expensive aftershave, the kind you can buy only uptown in a shop where they know you by name. He reeked of it. That, and dough. Because money has a smell, too, you know?

And he was doling out the goods to the neighborhood: food, booze, money. Gave special attention to the elders and the littlest. I liked that.

I asked one of the boys, some jerk standing there, who the guy was and what he was about, and I learned he was a palooka who'd fought his way to the top. That he took care of his own around town. Every week he'd truck in stuff for the community. He was the biggest benefactor the Irish community had ever seen. Daniel Connor.

"So he's decent," I said, watching Danny work the crowd. I figured that he wasn't born rich, and that he was trucking in liquid goods most of the time so as to make his dough, but by that time everyone and his mother was a rumrunner. "That's pretty swell."

"I'll tell you what's swell," the jerk answered. Then he tried to put the squeeze on me, but I'd already set my sights higher, right straight to the top, to Danny, and I slugged that jerk smack on the kisser.

Detective Smith laughs out loud, and I smile. Back those four-plus years ago I was an eighteen-year-old with moxie. Enough moxie that I turned right around to Danny and stuck out my hand.

So I says to Danny, "Heyo. I'm Louise O'Keefe. My parents came from County Cork, but they're now both dead and gone, and I'm looking for a job."

Yeah, Danny laughed at first, but I could see it in his eyes when he looked me up and down. I might be short, but I've got curves in all the right places, or so I've been told.

"What did you have in mind?" Danny asked.

I stiffened my shoulders, folded my arms. "I can cook, clean, wash, iron. I can do it all."

He looked me up and down again. This wasn't anything new, but I was hopeful. Because one true guy was better than what I thought I was gonna have to put up with, being clean broke like I was.

"A girl like you doesn't need to be ruining her pretty hands with that kind of work. Can you read and write?"

"Sure."

"Can you learn to speak properly, and manage a household?"

I had no idea what he meant by that, but I said, "I'm willing to manage anything."

When he smiled this time, he showed all his pearly whites.

A few weeks later he told me I was his dame, and that he'd take care of me. I took him at his word.

I watch that detective smirk now as I think again about right and wrong. That's the only kind of right I knew back then, the kind I got from Danny. That he'd treat me right, yes, sir. As right as rain.

CHAPTER 4
MAY 18–19, 1925

Moll: noun, informal (also, "gun moll"): a gangster's female companion.
—Oxford Dictionary of the English Language

JO

The dream of fire, of flames, of heat—my recurring nightmare—that's what woke me, that terrible consuming desire of fire reaching for me that woke me this night or that out of a sound sleep so that I lay panting in the dark. Fire and being trapped in the fire in that small playhouse and the smother of smoke and snap of the wood around me: those were the memories that fed the nightmare that woke me. And made the scar on my back tingle with remembered pain.

And then any number of other things would keep me lying there, awake, in the dark.

This night, after the nightmare, what kept me awake was the obvious lie about sending me to New York City to find a suitable husband, and what was going on that had Pops and Ma so worried about me being safe.

I got up and turned on the light. Sleep had left me; I might as well put my time in these wee hours to some use. I had to pack for New York. For Pops's magic trick: making me disappear.

I'd likely never return to White Plains High. Not say good-bye to Moira, even if we had so little in common anymore with her eyeing the senior boys all the time, looking for a catch. No one else would miss me; within a couple of months kids would be scratching their heads trying to remember the name of the girl who read and wrote every spare minute, that quiet girl who disappeared like the mist that made up her dreams. Only my teacher, Miss Draper, who encouraged my writing, would worry over my absence.

Since from what Ma had said I didn't need many clothes, I filled my suitcase with books. All my novels—the old ones by Austen, the newer ones by Eleanor Porter and Zane Grey, and the latest by Forster and Fitzgerald—they'd come with me. And I slipped in as many as I could of those masterful stories about clever Mr. Holmes, the ones Teddy'd given me. I'd carry the suitcase myself, even if it weighed a ton.

"It isn't fair," I whispered to the air in my room. "You were the hero, but I have to obey his orders."

Life isn't fair, Josie, I would've heard Teddy say. You've got to make what you make for yourself. Watch yourself, Josie-girl, because life can be downright dangerous.

As I looked at the last bundle to add to my suitcase, I wondered if Ma would notice that the things that had sat on Teddy's dresser for the past year had gone missing.

I doubted it. Ma suffered in silence. She was too knotted up with her ongoing grief over Teddy to want to spend time in his room. I was the one who'd set up and maintained the little shrine, who'd spent nights in the dark, staring at the boxes, at the medals, those shiny, shiny medals, that reflected what little light came in from the streetlights, the moon, the stars.

I lay the contents of that little shrine on top of the silk scarf, the one with the red poppies, the heavy silk square spread out flat. I rubbed the silk between my thumb and forefinger.

Teddy had brought that scarf for me when he came home from the war.

Like he'd promised before he left, that day in the early summer of '17. He already had his uniform. His hair was still curling over his ears, blond and thick like sheep's wool. He still flashed that beautiful smile, the one that made all the girls melt and made Ma and Pops proud—and made me proud, too, because I knew Teddy had a smile just for me.

"I'm gonna bring you something back from France, Josie-girl," Teddy said. "Something real special that a body can't find except only in Paris."

"What?" I asked, excited, bouncing a little, not understanding what it meant for him to go to Paris then. "What, Teddy?"

"Oh, it'll be a big surprise," Teddy had said, and winked.

And when he came back only half a year later and handed me the fancy box with the scarf, I still didn't understand. His hair had become short and stiff, and his back and his eyes had turned stiff, too.

"Like I promised" was all Teddy said as I opened the box and unfolded the scarf and draped it over my shoulders.

I stroked it and thanked Teddy, but he turned away and disappeared into his room before I could tell him how happy I was that he was home, how much I had missed him, how many new secrets I had to share with him, how many new words I'd written during that half year he was gone. . . .

I never really got Teddy back from that war. Not really. And all I had now was this scarf and the precious things that lay atop it.

I touched them one by one. The medals in their hinged boxes. One, two, three of them, those medals, all points and hard edges and high-sounding words.

"Keep these for me, Josie-girl," Teddy'd said when he left almost a year ago. "I've got to go away for a while. Got to lay low."

Then he'd asked me to cover for him. That business that still gave me a chill.

"It should only be for a time," he'd said. "Then I'll be back."

"Why wouldn't you be back?" I'd asked. "You will, won't you?"

Teddy had chewed his lip, not looking at me. "This is a secret you've got to keep. Not tell Ma, not tell Pops. It's life and death."

I began to tremble. "How can I keep this from Ma and Pops?"

He took both my hands. "You can't let on to anybody. Not anybody. Especially not Ma and Pops. You've got to pretend. Swear it, Jo."

I tasted a bitter tang; the misery we would put our parents through was gall. But I swore, and now it was almost a year, and I had to believe that any day now Teddy would come back and everything would be all right again.

I put the medals back on the scarf and folded it over them and tied the corners into a tight knot and tucked the bundle deep in my suitcase under the books so that even the red poppies disappeared beneath the weight of leather and parchment.

Yes, Teddy was right. Life can be downright dangerous.

* * *

Pops came into the kitchen while I was eating breakfast. Worry worked at his mouth. "I got a telephone call. It's best if Jo stays up in her room until I can get her to the train."

Ma and I exchanged a quick look. She nodded at me, and I rested my fork on my plate.

I rose and started to my room, but a slight cough by the front door stopped me. The door was open to let in the spring air, the screen door keeping out the flies. A man stood on the other side of the screen.

Our eyes met, and he held mine like he was a hypnotist. I'd seen him in the flesh only once before, but I knew who he was. His picture was in the paper often enough. Mr. Daniel Connor. Boss man of the East Side, heir to the throne left vacant when Big Al Capone went to Chicago. Boss of my pops now, too.

Without turning away, I said, "Pops?"

Connor's eyes were gray, the color of steel. He was young for someone with such power, maybe not even thirty. His eyes held mine, and something twisted inside me. I was alone on a steel-gray sea, and he was reeling me in, much against my inclination. He was a devil of a man

My heart slowed, and then time slowed. His lips formed a small smile that vanished in an instant. I didn't like him. But he had my attention.

Pops came in behind me. "Go to your room, Josephine." As I turned away Danny Connor tipped his hat.

I left the door of my room ajar and leaned against the wall next to the jamb. Daniel Connor had a soft, pleasant voice for someone built so square. I supposed he didn't need to use his voice when, from what I'd read in the paper, his fists could do the job. Though he looked like he hadn't hit anyone himself in a while—his tailored suit, spats, felt hat, and gold-tipped cane were not fighting gear. No, he had men around him, like the men from the other night, who were not such sharp dressers and who looked like they could break a guy's arm as if they were snapping a chicken's neck.

For a minute or two it sounded like a social call. Pleasant conversation about the weather. Inquiries after the health of Ma and me.

I'd seen Connor that once at Teddy's memorial service, about two months after Teddy's disappearance. Connor had sat in the back at a respectful distance. I'd wondered at it then, why he was there. Later I put two and two together: it was right about that time, more or less, that Pops had started in on the bootlegging.

But now I heard: "Billy, my boys told you why I'm here."

"I know, and I can't help you."

"Have you made a thorough search?"

"Teddy left nothing behind. Just his clothes. And his medals."

"Yes. Of course." A bee batted lazily against my window screen. "His medals. Your son was a true hero."

"Yes."

"It is such a shame, not to be able to bury him properly. It's a shame that you and your family can't say good-bye." Someone paced around the room. "You don't think he might still be alive?"

My heart thudded.

"No." Pops's voice was flat.

"From time to time I imagine I see Teddy, here and there. I remember him well. He was such a pleasant young man," Connor said. The blood pounded in my ears. "Why does someone commit suicide, I wonder? Just up and disappear in such a fashion, only his

25

clothes left on a beach?" Connor paused. "Well, Billy, here's the point of it: if Teddy told you anything about his involvement in certain affairs, things he might have been mixed up in, in particular anything that might reflect"—and here he coughed—"reflect on me, I'm sure you would let me know."

"Teddy was not himself after he came home," Pops said, his voice shaking a little.

Silence, except for a tapping—I imagined Connor's cane on the floor—and then, "You have not addressed my question."

Pops's voice came out low and rumbling. "Teddy didn't confide in me."

"Who did Teddy confide in, Billy? His sister, perhaps? Didn't she find his clothing on the beach?"

The bee parried, feinted, moved on. My mouth was dry as a desert.

"Josephine was very close to her brother. But he'd never mix her up in anything. Never."

"No. Of course he wouldn't. Not a hero like Teddy."

I was so parched I couldn't swallow, as if I'd tried to drink that salt water while the hook in my mouth reeled me in, steel, gray, sharp.

"I would appreciate it, Billy, if you could look again for something he might have left behind. And should you find anything, you would inform me at once, wouldn't you." It was not a question.

Pops said something I couldn't make out.

"My respects to your family." I heard the screen door squeak open and shut, heard Connor's footsteps, heavy and sure, on the wood porch and stairs, heard the slam of a car door and the engine start and the car pull slowly over the gravel and away. Then, silence for a moment before I heard Pops's heavy tread as he mounted to the second story and approached my room.

I scrambled to my chair, grabbing a book and holding it before my face.

He knocked.

His face was pale now, that rough anger drained away and replaced by something else. "I'm getting you a ticket for the noon train tomorrow to your uncle's. Be ready, Josephine."

"Pops . . ." I held the book in my hand like a shield. "Do you need help with anything before I leave? You know, any last calculations?"

His eyes met mine, and then he shook his head once. "Tomorrow, noon. Be ready."

I nodded, and he left.

Pops might not know it, but Teddy had confided in me, all right—although not anything about Danny Connor. And if Teddy had left anything hidden, surely he would have told me.

New York City was a special place for Teddy and me. I should be happy I was heading there; of all the places on earth, it was the one in which he was most likely to reappear. And I wanted more than anything for him to come back and help set things right.

But at the moment all I heard was the humming of the bees outside my window and the distant shouts of children out in the fine weather, and my pops in the kitchen talking to Ma in a voice low and rumbling like the thunder that rolls across the Hudson before a summer storm.

CHAPTER 5

LOU

I was so proud to be with Danny Connor—yes, Detective Smith, whatever you might think of him, I was proud—that I held my head up like a queen.

Danny bought me an entire wardrobe. Took me right over to Herald Square to Macy's and outfitted me from head to toe in the latest styles. Right from Paris and only the best. Slinky velvets, chiffons, and silks—even silk unmentionables—and a swell coat with fur at the collar and cuffs and even around the bottom. As if my calves needed to keep toasty. And such shoes! Sweet little patent pumps with straps and heels, and silk pumps, too, that were to be dyed to match the two gowns he bought me. Gowns! I was putting on the Ritz.

I walked into Macy's one girl and came out another girl altogether.

I thought it was kind of sweet when Danny asked the saleslady to burn my old shirtwaists and wool skirts, for fear they carried nits or fleas or such.

"We aren't bringing anything from that dump"—he meant the apartment I had downtown when I met him. "We aren't bringing old trash with us, Louise. Leave it all behind."

I confess it made me a little teary when I had to leave my ma's wedding portrait because the paper might carry bookworms, but Danny was a stickler for cleanliness, and I wasn't about to argue with a guy who gave me everything. A guy who made me over, like new. Who made me feel like I was floating above the clouds.

He took me to the finest hair salon and had my hair done just the way he liked, bobbed and curled over one eye. Had the ladies show me makeup. Eyeliner black as ink. Lipstick in a shade called Killer Red.

"You look lovely, honey," the hairdresser whispered when Danny's back was turned. "You take care, now."

"I'm the happiest girl on the planet," I said, in a voice that brought Danny around.

I thought he'd smile, but instead he frowned and said, "Feelings are best kept inside, Louise. See you remember that."

That hairdresser's eyebrows went up, but I wasn't going to let that wet blanket spoil my day.

He set me up in this hotel, the Algonquin. He'd been looking for a proper house and wanted something grand, he said, but in the meantime, while he was still on the hunt for the right place, we had a whole suite to ourselves on an upper floor so high it made me giddy to stand at the window. So high I was truly floating. A suite with walls as white as snow and fresh sheets daily and fluffy white towels and a monogrammed robe.

And he took me over to Tiffany's and bought me a diamond necklace and earrings, although he never let me wear them except when he took me out. He'd unlock his little safe and clasp that necklace on me, and I wanted to faint at the touch of his soft, manicured hands on my neck. Of course, in my heart I kind of hoped for a ring to go with that necklace, but I wasn't about to say anything like that to Danny.

Yes, sir, Danny treated me like I was the Queen of Sheba, and I was sure we were set forever and always.

CHAPTER 6

MAY 20, 1925

New Grand Central Ceiling Has the Heavens Turned Around
—Headline from The New York Times, *March 23, 1913*

JO

Pops dropped me at the train station at noon the next day. It was a forty-minute ride in to Grand Central. "I'll see you in a couple of weeks," he said as we stood side by side on the platform.

"Listen," I began, but he held up his hand.

"No arguments." He dropped his eyes, examining his hands as he stretched and clenched his fists. "I'll try and bring your ma."

I flattened my lips and then said, "That would be swell."

"Okay, then. Mind your aunt and uncle." He coughed. "You can make something of yourself, Jo, if you find the right guy. These are good times. There are lots of rich guys out there, looking for a pretty wife like you to show off. Lots of lonely war heroes making some dough now, the way things are." He looked away, pursed his lips. "I know I'm not a perfect father. And I've gotten mixed up with people that aren't . . ." He rubbed his fingers on his forehead. "Take a tip from your aunt. Don't marry down like your ma did."

"Pops . . ."

"Get on that train." His eyes were bright, his voice like rough gravel.

I sat by the window facing back so that I could see him. He stood on the platform, watching, not moving, and I kept my eyes fixed on him until the train picked up speed and leafy branches whipped by and Pops and the White Plains station disappeared like they were spinning into a green tunnel.

As the view out the train window opened toward the west, toward the distant, hidden Hudson, I remembered that week when I was ten—the good parts—when I fell in love with the river and wanted to watch it forever, watch it ripple by below the high banks where my uncle's summer house perched. I'd sit on the bank, the tickle of cool grass on the backs of my knees, and read and daydream, safe in my books, while Teddy helped Uncle Bert with chores. I had dreams about the river after that, dreams in which I could swan dive down into the cool water, lift out of that water like a tiny nymph, and then cling to a leaf that had drifted down from high in the Adirondacks. I'd float toward Dobbs Ferry and past Hastings, drift by Spuyten Duyvil, passing Harlem and Midtown, until I floated right past the tip of Manhattan and butted up against Liberty Island. I'd fly on my magic wings up to Lady Liberty's crown and sit and watch the sun set, and the lights come blinking on, the bright white and yellow incandescents, all through the stretched-skyward buildings of the city of dreams.

New York City was magic. I should be happy I was headed that way. Happy at the possibility that Teddy might return to me there.

Happy that although Pops had commanded me to go, I was, in fact, free. Instead, my belly clenched with nerves. I fretted over what was happening at home and over leaving Ma and Pops.

And what of my plans? Without Teddy, could I see them through? Teddy, he knew. I wanted to do more with my life than run clothes through a wringer. To do more with myself than hang on the arm of some rich fellow.

I felt tiny, all right, floating down the Hudson and wishing I knew that my voyage stretched toward liberty.

The train screeched into the underbelly of the city and right into its heart, and I climbed down the narrow steps from the train and lugged my suitcase bumping along the platform, the air around me stinking of metal, and up the ramp into Grand Central Terminal.

Even though I was barely a kid before Teddy left for the war, he'd bring me to the city to see a show from time to time. Now as I moved with the crowd into the station itself, and remembered those earlier trips, I looked straight up at that ceiling that was dotted with painted constellations as if someone was trying to say, You wanted to see New York stars? There you go. Even beyond the glow of the lights of Manhattan there's a heaven above, traveler.

Stars.

And the swirl and the bustle, too. Gee, I liked that, the people heading this way and that, going upstate or to Connecticut or coming in to New York for the first time, most in a hurry, but some, like me, taking the time to admire the place, the echoing marble, the high, high stars.

It had been great being there with Teddy, who took me down to the Oyster Bar, where he'd order a dozen and I'd have two of his and then a bowl of chowder. All the girls in the place had eyes for Teddy, and I'd sit up straight with my braids and ribbons and best dress and hat and I'd feel special.

The stars. I set my suitcase down and looked up. Teddy. What was it about those stars?

Well, for one thing, the constellations were painted backward.

Teddy had told me that the artist painted them as if we, the little people below, were, in fact, looking at the constellations from the outside. As if we were gods, looking down from the heavens, from the vast universe looking inward to the tiny globe of earth.

"Like you're sitting way out in space," Teddy had said, when I shook my braids and told him I didn't follow. He knelt down so that his blue eyes were level with mine, and he tugged the end of one braid. "Like you're way out in the middle of the universe, Josie-girl. Sitting way up with the angels." And Teddy smiled. "Which is where you should be, my little angel."

My suitcase full of books weighed a ton, and when I hefted it again and lugged it across the noisy echoing hall to the exit onto Forty-second Street, it felt like it had picked up a few extra pounds. Pops had given me enough money to hail a taxicab, but it was only a bit more than ten blocks uptown to my aunt and uncle's new place on Park Avenue. I wanted to save every penny I had in my pocket, just in case. I could walk even if I had to stop every half a block and switch arms.

Which I did. The suitcase was hard, and it banged against my calf and shin with each step, as the handle strained, squeaking on its hinges. It was yet another warm day, and I wore Ma's old linen summer coat—shortened to a more modern length, thank goodness, but still a decade out of fashion—so by the time I arrived at my aunt and uncle's Park Avenue apartment building, sweat ran down my spine in a stream. It didn't help any that my long hair was tied back in a ribbon and not pinned up, and that the floppy hat I wore—also way out of date—was made from wool felt.

I stopped on the sidewalk and looked up in wonderment at that brand-new pale stone building, with its sparkling glass windows and its dark green canopy, its carved fluted ornamentation. I thought I must've looked like Dorothy, gazing up open-mouthed at the Emerald City.

Oh, this magic city, this New York Oz, this city that never sleeps. That keeps one eye always open. That prowls like a beast and growls with life. With hum and buzz and memory. And Teddy, who haunted her streets, he loved this island of a million eyes. He said that despite all those eyes and all that movement, the city could hide secrets.

I so hoped that was true. That that's where he was hiding now.

The doorman coughed and looked me up and down, but Aunt Mary, now out and about, had left word and I was expected. I let the doorman haul my suitcase; I had to bite back a smile when he picked it up with a grunt of surprise. The elevator boy, in his smart red suit and cap, was years younger than I was, and he stared at me wide-eyed and open-mouthed, as if he'd never seen a country girl welcomed as a guest in these quarters.

The elevator cage opened with a clang directly into the foyer of the apartment, so it was no surprise to see Melody emerge from the living room, right behind the butler.

I hadn't seen Melody since Teddy's memorial. She was seven years my senior, and I'd always thought her a sophisticate. To say she'd changed in the last year would've been an understatement. She'd gone from sophisticate to worldly.

"Cuz!" She held me at arm's length. Her forehead wrinkled as her thinly plucked eyebrows lifted. "What a quaint little outfit!" She turned to the Negro butler, who hovered over my suitcase, appraising, having tried to lift it once. "Go ahead, Malcolm. Take it to the guest room." She waved her hand. "Shoo."

"Hi, Melody." I touched my hair. Hers was short, about chin length in front and shorter in back, and fell in thick blond waves across her left cheek, a diamond barrette fastened high on the other side. "So. Here I am."

"Yes. Here you are." She tapped her index finger against her berry-red lips, and seemed to come to a conclusion. "Let's just get rid of that, shall we?"—she pointed at my coat—"And that"—she motioned at my hat. I shrugged out of the coat, unpinned the hat, and handed them over. She tossed them on a chair without giving them a second glance, then folded her arms. "Oh, dear."

I surely wasn't the fashion plate she was, in her sleek peach silk dress with its beading along the hem, and with her silk stockings and pale-colored low heels. I tugged at my middy blouse and fiddled with the waistband of the navy wool skirt.

"Cuz, you must let me advise you. You can't go around New York dressed like that."

The flush crept up my neck. She looked terrific, I had to admit. "Honey, no big deal. We'll have you square in a jiff."

"Gee, thanks." I folded my arms across my chest as if to hide the oversize blouse. Then I changed the subject. "Look, I need your help. Pops sent me here on a pretext, I'm sure of it. He said something crazy about my meeting a man."

Melody burst out laughing. "Yes, my dear, that I can arrange."

I waved my hand now, impatient. "No, Mel. There's another reason for this sudden excursion to New York. Something Pops wouldn't tell me. What am I really doing here, do you know?"

She looked surprised. "Staying for a time. Beyond that, I haven't a clue. No one tells me anything." She smoothed her brows with one finger. "Now, listen. I'm on my way out, and Mummy is off doing whatever it is she does, and Daddy is still at work and heaven only knows when he'll be home, so it's just you and Chester." She paused. "And the help, of course."

"Oh, great." Chester. Three years younger than Melody. To say he was not one of my favorite people would be, well, an understatement. The scar on my back burned at the thought of spending time with him.

Melody read my mind. "Cuz. It was an accident. This you know."

"Yes, Mel. I know." That he hadn't meant to start the fire was really beside the point.

She moved, impatient. "Look, I have to go. There's all the alcohol you could want in the hidden closet in the library. You just have to press the hutch door, you know, push on it like this, 'cause it's a fake—"

"I don't drink."

Her perfect brows furrowed. "Josephine."

"Jo."

She waved her hand. "Whatever you like to call yourself. Jeepers, you're seventeen. Almost eighteen. Everyone drinks. You don't? Well, fine. You want to know why you're here?" She leaned toward me. "I would guess it has to do with your daddy and the business he's in." She pulled back, and her eyes went distant. "Too bad Teddy isn't here. He always knew what to do." She snapped upright, turned on her perfect heel, the beaded hem of her dress splaying out around her knees. "Tomorrow, first thing—well, later, first thing, because morning is not my favorite time of day—we'll tend to your hair."

"I'd like that," I said. And I would, too, as the unpleasant weight of my hair draped against my damp blouse. Just a purely practical matter. That it would be modern was secondary.

But Melody paused and smiled. "There. I knew there were a few outrageous thoughts in that smart brain of yours."

*   *   *

I stood at one of the tall windows in the apartment's living room and watched the day draw toward slumber while the city below woke as if from a long nap. The windows of this room looked east, and the sky I could see between the buildings opposite already had a purple hue, while the sun reflected burnt orange in their windows. The avenue below growled with life. Nighttime was not rest time here but another facet of New York's glittering magic.

I thought again about my uncle's other house, the one way up the Hudson, where the river ran below. That week when I was ten. I inched my hand up under my blouse and felt the scar that stretched across my back. The skin had seared to a sandpaper roughness. I thought about the playhouse.

How the playhouse was, and then wasn't. How what was left after they cleared the rubble was a blackened stone square. How I had been inside. How I'd run in for my doll, to save her. How

Chester had been punished even though he hadn't known that I'd run in for her, after he set the fire. How he set it for no reason. How he had been punished but not enough to my liking.

How much I loved the river, and how much I hated the flames.

* * *

Chester showed up in time for us to eat dinner together.

I shifted in my chair at the table. "Where are you in school?" I tried to make polite conversation, even if I didn't like meeting his eyes.

"You mean, this year?" He smirked, leaning across the table over our soup. "School number four. In four years."

"Ah!"

"Just left the last place. Seems I was cheating. Or failing. Or something. They packed me off without a wave or a bye-bye."

I thought about my own classroom in the school that had housed me for three years, and how Miss Draper would surely wonder why I was missing, even if my classmates gave it no more than a passing thought.

He shrugged. "School is fine, if you like that sort of thing."

I tried not to slurp. Chester, because he was a boy, and a wealthy one at that, had every opportunity, which he tossed off without a second thought.

"I've decided it's high time I moved on anyhow." He lifted his glass of wine and took a noisy sip.

I couldn't look at him. "Move on to what?"

"Why, business. Banking looks good, since my dad can give me a position downtown. But heck, why not take up a little bootlegging on the side? Might as well. Your father's in on it." He paused, and our eyes met. I saw the light in his eye, and my stomach turned so that I couldn't swallow my food. "Right, Josephine?"

The blood rushed to my face.

Chester sat back, watching me, his brown eyes narrowed, his smile thin, hair slicked back and parted in the middle with careful precision, his wineglass raised. "Come on, Jo. It's the best way to make a mint. No taxes, just straight-on profit. A man can become a millionaire in no time."

"It's illegal," I muttered into my soup. It was the only thing I could think to say.

Chester snorted. "As if that matters. Are you that naive? There's a speakeasy on every block in this city. The police are on the take. The biggest bootleggers ride around in bulletproof limousines. Illegal? Who cares?"

I cared, at least as far as my pops was concerned. My moral compass pointed toward the straight and narrow. And Chester, the last time we'd spent together, his moral compass was skewed by a desire to be reckless. I cared, but what could I do about it? If Teddy was here, he would've cared, too.

Teddy, if only you could be here, would be here . . .

Malcolm brought in the main course: a bloody filet in béarnaise sauce with sides of potatoes and snap beans dressed with almonds.

When Malcolm left, Chester leaned across the table toward me, a glint in his eye that made me draw back. "I know what's going on in that sharp brain you've got. You're thinking about Teddy and wishing he was here. Perfect Teddy. He wouldn't have done anything illegal, now, would he? No, sir." Chester grinned. "Why,

Teddy was destined for great things, wasn't he. Senator, governor, maybe even . . . yeah, maybe even president. Yes. President Winter. Being groomed and heading for stardom. Perfect Theodore Winter, ready to become king." Chester snorted. "Right."

I sat still, my eyes now fixed on my plate.

"But the king has no clothes, does he?"

"What do you mean?" I whispered, lifting my eyes, my back stiffening.

Chester waved his fork in the air. "I mean, old Teddy went and disappeared, didn't he? Kings die and become dead heroes. End of story." Chester leaned over, punctuating his next words with his fork. "He should've thought that one through." He turned his attention to his plate, sawing away at his filet.

I let the air out of my lungs. Bluffing. Chester was bluffing, which I should have expected. But for a moment, I'd thought Chester knew about Teddy, knew our secret, what I had done for—how I had lied for—Teddy. But no. I kept Teddy's secret. I held on to the belief he'd be back. I'd promised Teddy.

After dinner Chester and I retreated to our separate rooms. I had my own private suite here—with a door I could lock. Melody had tossed a pair of pajamas on my bed, a thoughtful gesture. They were navy-blue silk with white pin dots, and came with a matching robe.

And the closet was packed with clothes, as promised. Pretty things, classy and smart, if more than a little revealing. Short dresses, slim and silky, in pale colors and trimmed in handmade lace or long beading or wispy frills. If they weren't the very latest fashion, I wouldn't have been able to tell. I looked at those dresses for a long time, rubbing the silk between my fingers, admiring the details, but also feeling the blush creep across my cheeks as I imagined my near-nakedness when wearing them. They were nothing like the full-sleeved middy blouse and midcalf skirt I was wearing, and I looked down at myself with a rueful twist of my lips.

I actually couldn't wait to try some of them on though I'd have to pick the ones that didn't reveal too much, or expose that ten-inch scar.

My bedroom here was twice as big as my room at home. High ceilings, carved moldings, tall satin-draped windows that opened high above the noisy city so that the air they admitted was cooler and sweeter than the air down on the street. I had a private bath done all in black-and-white tile, and a medicine cabinet stocked with all the latest in personal items: deodorant, mouthwash, their smells spicy and antiseptic.

And Melody had left me a small bottle of perfume—CHANEL NO. 5, read the label—that smelled divine, along with a note: "Enjoy!"

I'd landed in a grand luxury. It was enough to turn my head. So why did I feel like I'd stepped behind bars?

An empty bookcase waited, and I unloaded my suitcase, setting the books in place by author. I took the silk scarf with its sacred contents out of my suitcase and sat for a long time with it cradled in my lap. I had to keep faith with Teddy; he'd return. I tucked the scarf and its contents away deep inside my bottom dresser drawer.

I pulled one of my books off my shelf as I tucked into bed, and smiled. A perfect choice, under the circumstances.

"About thirty years ago, Miss Maria Ward of Huntingdon, with only seven thousand pounds, had the good luck to captivate . . ."

* * *

Sirens

I woke in a cold sweat to the sound of a fire engine. The high-pitched wail echoed through the concrete canyons, tearing down the avenue and disappearing into the nighttime.

I lay in the bedroom and watched the play of lights from the street below as they moved across the ceiling. Flash and fade. Red, then white. My back itched with the memory of pain, and I rubbed the rough skin, an old habit. The fire engine was gone, into the night, into another fire, not my fire, but it was a long time before sleep crept over me again.

CHAPTER 7

Lou

One of the first things Danny took me to see after we'd become an item was Miss Liberty out on her little island. I'd seen the lights since I was small, that torch lit up at night like it was truly on fire, and how the Lady with the Lamp glowed across the water after Mr. Woodrow Wilson turned on the new lights in '16, and how we four—Ma and Da and my brother and me—had watched it from the Battery when we were still one big happy family.

But I'd never been there, right up close, unless you count me riding in Ma's belly from Ellis Island not that far away. My ma and da didn't take us around much to see the sights, especially if it cost time or money.

I felt like a little kid when Danny said we should go and take a tour. I had to hold in my giddy feelings so as not to make Danny cross.

Danny had a thing about that statue. He explained to me about how it had been made in France and carted all the way across the ocean and set up here, a gift to us Americans from the French people.

I was so excited I couldn't help it. I opened up and said, laughing, "I think French champagne is the best gift the French people gave us."

"This is America," he said, his voice a razor. "I won't have you speaking like an ignorant paddy just off the boat. You understand me, Louise?"

"Of course, Danny. I didn't mean . . ."

He looked at me then, eyes to match his voice, and I shut up.

That was when I really learned about Danny's sense of humor. And when I learned to keep my mouth shut, except when I was saying something he'd think was smart. Which was usually something he'd taught me. I tried hard to be a quick learner, but I did wish he liked to laugh more.

We took the tour, but I don't remember much about what the guide said. I was busy watching Danny.

Now, don't get me wrong. Right after that little excursion we walked the neighborhoods, and Danny gave me sacks of candy to hand out to the kiddos, while he glad-handed their das.

You know, he liked that Lady Liberty so much, but he couldn't forget where he came from. He couldn't forget his Irish roots. He was in America now, but he hadn't been able to leave behind the feeling that he wasn't good enough. And that made him both the most generous guy in town, and the most . . . well, I gotta say it: dangerous.

Yes, Detective, it's true. Even though I would've walked through wet cement for Danny, that's what he was. Dangerous.

CHAPTER 8

MAY 21, 1925

They were friends, and began rounding in there every noon for lunch.
—From "New York by Day" article on the writers
composing the Round Table at the Algonquin,
The Miami News, May 19, 1928

JO

The following morning I had the apartment to myself. If my aunt and uncle had come home during the night and departed again before I stumbled out of bed, I'd heard nothing. I found a white rayon sheath in the closet, the least revealing article I discovered, though it was a skinny silhouette that just hit my knees. It was at least practical and suited to the unseasonable heat; happily, Melody was only a little bit shorter than me and not too much smaller through the hips.

The sun blazed through the open windows of the living room, and the cacophony of the city rose with the hours. After a lonely breakfast I wandered from empty room to empty room. The bookshelves were lined with books whose spines had never been cracked. The walls were white and hung with paintings that were modern, impressionistic, stark and linear. In the library were dozens of small replicas of statues; most were modern but for one striding Egyptian prince, modern in his own offbeat way. I stared at the painting in the foyer for long time, thinking I'd seen it somewhere, but its soft blue squares were so abstract as to be both familiar and foreign at once. The few tables in the apartment were bare. The floors were polished to a high shine.

Rarely had I spent time alone in such a vast and new-minted place. It made me uneasy, this impersonal, empty luxury. I thought about my own home, with its scuffed floors and threadbare armchairs and scattered objects—the little vases Ma collected, the antimacassars, the folded newspapers left at the fireplace by Pops. I missed my ma, my quiet little room, and Felix, our mouser cat who mostly hissed in my general direction but sometimes acquiesced to a soft ear rub.

Here I stood in someone else's clothes in someone else's room, and new fears crept through me: fears that I would never find my dreams or my brother. Whatever Pops had gotten himself into he'd dragged me into it as well, and I'd have to find my own way out.

The only room in the apartment in which I felt comfortable was the windowless library off the foyer. Books lined all four walls, and the chairs were dark leather, the lighting just enough for reading. I settled in and opened one of the books and read until Melody roused around eleven, heading to the kitchen for a cup of coffee.

She was a different person in the daylight hours, without her makeup and with her eyes like slits and her skinny frame wrapped in an oversize robe. I tried to hide my surprise, which reappeared when she emerged from her rooms an hour later, primped and wide-awake and put together. She peered in the library door, squinting.

"There you are. Hiding. It's time we put you right," she said as I stood up, and then she looked down at my old black shoes. "Good grief. First order of business is new shoes. And for pity's sake, take off those awful stockings before we leave the apartment."

"I'm not a flapper," I said.

"Yeah? Well, we can fix that," she responded. "Come on."

I heard Pops's voice in my head berating flappers—and then I felt a tiny thrill of rebellion, so I let myself be led by Melody. She treated me to a shopping trip that changed me from top to bottom.

We started at the hair salon.

When the hairdresser took hold of my thick dark locks, she said, gleeful, "Snip, snip!" And with a few bold cuts she held twenty-four inches of my former glory in her hand. As she worked, shaping and thinning, she spun me away from the mirror. Melody nodded approval, and when the hairdresser spun me back so I could take a good look, I gasped.

I looked older. Heart-shaped face with blue eyes. Dark hair that now formed pleasing angles to frame my face. I sat up and lifted both my palms against the blunt-cut ends, feeling as if a weight that had tied me down had been lifted.

I wondered what Moira would think, what the other girls would say. I wondered if I might see them again next fall and whether they'd treat me differently, whether the boys might notice me for the first time. I smiled at that thought, then promptly shot it down. Modern was fine. Turning into some silly, moony flapper swooning over boys was not.

Still, I couldn't help it; I was happy with the bob. Thrilled, in fact.

As if to echo my reaction, the hairdresser said, "Honey, I'd swear

I was looking at the next big moving-picture star." She smiled, shook her head. "Just dreamy."

"It sure is a change," Melody said.

It was a change, all right. I was shedding some old skin that I'd outgrown without knowing it.

I touched my hair again. One of Teddy's favorite things to say about me had to do with my stubborn determination. Tenacity, he said; I had it in spades. Like the ornery mule he'd had to buck around that summer out at Great-Aunt Elizabeth's, or maybe like old Aunt Lizzy herself, whom Teddy claimed I took after. When I wanted a thing done, Teddy said, that was the end of it.

Although that tenacity fought with niggling doubt. Hair was just hair, right? Or in this case was hair a link in a long chain? A long chain leading me to foolish thinking and foolish behavior? I bet Teddy would approve. Even if Pops would give me the business.

Well, too bad. I put that thought straight out of my mind.

Melody took me to Macy's next. Shoes first—sweet, pale little pumps with straps—and flesh-colored stockings, of real silk, rolled up above my knees. I already had the closet full of her cast-off dresses. After buying me a soft green cloche, a pair of gloves, and what she called "the right clutch," she plunked me down at the cosmetics counter, where, over my feeble protests, a salesgirl painted my cheeks and colored my lips and eyelids. Melody held up the hand mirror, and again I was taken aback, but I did kind of like what I saw, even as my cheeks grew pinker all on their own. Good thing Pops wasn't here; when the salesgirl and Mel weren't looking, I wiped off the worst of it.

We left the store with a bag of cosmetics, and Melody dropped me back at the apartment in the midafternoon before she went off on some private errand.

So silent and so white, this space. I thought again about my home, my room with its flowered wallpaper, my chenille bedspread, Pops's creaky old chair, Ma's rhubarb pie, the landscapes cut from magazines and hung in Pops's homemade frames, Grandpa Joe and Grandma Ellie in their finery in the round portrait over the fireplace. There was nothing homey here, nothing but still, clean newness. And me, plunked down in the middle of it, already a changeling, and wondering what was to happen next.

I buried my queasiness in a cup of tea and a plate of fresh biscuits smothered in butter and made by my aunt's capable cook.

* * *

But I didn't linger indoors for long, and decided not to wait until Melody returned. The day was warm like a promise, and New York beckoned. Teddy and I had walked the streets together enough that I knew where I was and felt at home. In the late afternoon I ventured out, my new shoes surprisingly comfortable.

I made my way back down to Herald Square to Macy's again. This time I paused to survey the fashions arrayed behind the glass windows. The mannequins gestured at each other accusingly, their pouty lips shiny with brilliant carmine, the long strands of pearls draping their necks iridescent in the glaring hot window lights. I wandered back to Fifth Avenue and headed uptown, passing the library, where I waved to the lions like a kid, the way I had when Teddy had brought me there so many years before. Autos rumbled down the avenue; horse-drawn carters hauled empty, clattering milk bottles for cleaning; boys, their voices singsong and unintelligible, hawked the evening papers.

I walked west across Forty-fourth. The setting sun washed down the street, and I lifted my hand to my forehead and squinted against the glare. As I passed a set of heavy doors, they burst open and a group of men and women tumbled onto the sidewalk, all laughing and chattering, surrounding me in such a swell of enthusiasm and banter that I froze.

"Oh, pardon me!" The man who'd almost trod on my shiny new toes lifted his hat in apology. The book tucked in the crook of his arm tumbled toward me, and I caught it; as I handed it back to him I saw the cover: *Fanny, Herself.*

"I've read that," I blurted.

He paused. "Really? You mean it? You've read it?"

"Yes, of course." The warmth crept into my cheeks. It had been a favorite with Moira and me when we'd discovered it in the library. The heroine, Fanny, was a girl with a gift for drawing—why, I spent many nights rereading passages, savoring her search for freedom and success and imagining myself in her shoes, but with a pen substituting for a paintbrush.

He looked me up and down. "So did you like it?"

"I . . . yes, I did."

He turned to his companions. "Hey, Ed, listen to this. This lovely young thing has read your book."

The woman behind him said, "Really? One of the few," and she laughed as she was tugged on up the street.

"She liked it, Ed!" he called. He shrugged. "Oh well, they're off.

So, then, must I be, darling." He tipped his hat to me and made a little bow. "Cheers!"

And they were gone, leaving me in their wake.

The doorman stood a few feet away, his hands behind his back. "You know who you were just talking to, don't you?"

I shook my head.

"That was the membership of the Round Table."

"The Algonquin Round Table? Oh, my stars!" I gaped up at the awning. The Algonquin Hotel. Of course. Everyone knew about the Round Table at the Algonquin, set up in the back of the dining room. Since shortly after the war it had become the gathering place of New York literary types. Playwrights, novelists, journalists—they came together to talk about books, politics, and art. Early on the management had encouraged them, given them a reserved table, no doubt eyeballing a grand publicity ploy as well as the steady luncheon check.

"I know them all by now." The doorman wagged his finger. "I bet you don't know who that was. The lady that Mr. Connelly spoke to."

Then I realized. "That wasn't . . ."

He nodded, looking mighty pleased. "Edna Ferber. Author of that book you had in your hands."

"She's one of my heroes." I gazed up the street in the direction they'd gone; the party had disbursed.

"They're here every day, though the members aren't always the same. You might see her next time, or maybe Dorothy Parker. And Mr. Connelly, he's a playwright. I know them all, yes, indeed." He leaned over me. "I'm writing my own book, see. I plan to make it as a big-time writer, one of these days." He moved away to mind the door.

I looked up again at the awning, at the elaborately lettered name. New York was the city of all possibilities, of dreams come true. Even a doorman knew that.

Whatever I was doing in this town, maybe my dreams didn't have to die. Maybe they could just change, with luck.

I pictured myself, a little journal in one hand and a pencil in the other, my cloche pulled low over my face, at a table just within earshot of these heroes of mine. I'd be taking notes. And then writing my own stories. Or I'd be a well-heeled editor in a smart suit working in one of the grand publishing houses. Or a librarian or teacher, writing in my spare hours from a cozy garret on the Upper East Side. A job, my own job. My own life.

Girls like me, we had possibilities now, in this new decade of the twenties. We had the vote. We had our freedom . . . just look at Melody. My future was not so grim. New York City was the land of dreams.

I touched the tips of my hair that peeked from under my cloche, tossed my head a little. I hadn't realized how much those long locks had weighed me down. I was a modern girl now, living in the city that never sleeps, living in the decade of dreams. . . .

"Hey, watch it, babycakes! You're interrupting the flow of traffic!" A woman coming out the door of the Algonquin barged straight into me, standing as I was in the middle of the sidewalk and looking up at the canvas awning, my moony eyes still fixed on my imaginary future.

"Miss Louise!" The doorman greeted the woman with a hearty bark. "How's the boy?"

"Oh, he's coming along, thanks, Pete. Didn't drop any trays today, anyhow." She had a husky voice, rough like sandpaper, gritty with cigarettes and experience. She turned to look straight at me. She was pretty, maybe about Melody's age, with large, dark round eyes and hair curly and thick and red-tinted auburn, wearing a silky blue dress with a dropped waist and a hat with blue velvet trim. "Well? You alive? I didn't trample you, did I? You're standing there looking like you've just seen a ghost."

"Sorry," I said. "Ma'am."

"Oh, doll, don't give me 'ma'am.' Good grief. Makes me feel way too old." She looked at me hard, but friendly. "Name's Louise O'Keefe." She leaned toward me. "But my friends call me Louie." She shrugged. "Or Lou."

"Hi." I extended my hand, growing bold. "It wasn't a ghost I was looking at. It was my future."

She threw her head back and laughed, and it was a joyous thing to behold, her laugh. "Future? Well, careful now. The difference between seeing your future and seeing a ghost is just a matter of time." She smiled as she shook my hand with a firm grip. Her smile and that laugh were so infectious I had to smile right back.

I liked her. Her eyes had a spark, a kind of fire, even when her face was unreadable. "Are you a writer?"

"Me?" Her round eyes grew rounder. "Heavens to betsy, no. I can barely hold a pencil." She thumbed back toward the Algonquin's dark interior. "But that's why you're here, huh? Stargazing."

"Stumbling, really," I said, feeling sheepish. "Or being stumbled into."

"Gotta start somewhere." She looked up at the awning. "I guess this is as good a place as any. Well, I gotta run, kiddo. Great to meet you, um . . ."

"Jo."

"Great to meet you, Jo. Maybe we'll run into each other again. This city only looks big. In reality, it's just another small town on a tiny little island." And she gave another laugh, and tripped off, only to slip into the back of a shiny limousine up the block, the door held open for her by a gray-uniformed chauffer.

My mouth dropped open, and I turned to Pete. "Is she famous?"

He shrugged. "She's connected." He turned away, calling for a taxi for another client emerging from the hotel.

I slipped behind him and through the great glass-and-brass doors and into the dark lobby, feeling like the commoner stealing into the magic castle.

Inside, the wood and thick carpeting gave the place a hush, and massive furniture, clustered in arrangements for quiet conversation, hulked. Enormous square pillars supported a coffered ceiling. Even though the lobby bustled with activity, it was more like a library than a hotel, as the patrons in their rich attire moved in stately parade, sharing whispered confidences, knowing looks.

I moved toward the restaurant, the entry guarded by a podium manned by a stiff employee who surveyed me over his half-glasses.

"Help you, miss?"

"I'm just looking, thanks."

He rolled his eyes and turned away, studiously ignoring me.

I could see into the restaurant but had no idea where the Round Table might be, especially now that it was empty.

But I saw a boy. The best-looking boy I'd ever seen.

He stole my mind right away from Round Tables and stars and ghosts and swirling New York. I was a commoner, the beggar girl, inside the magic castle, and I was spying on a dark-haired prince.

Except that he was a prince in disguise. He was a waiter, clearing up, moving among tables and chairs, his white shirtsleeves rolled up above his elbows, his black half apron double-tied over dark slacks. His thick black hair curled over his forehead, and he had a powerful build with an aquiline nose and eyes black as night. Even working hard as he was he fit right into that hushed and magical place, with his quick-sure animal movements and dark, dark eyes.

I was a girl who'd given little thought to boys, except the unobtainable romantic heroes of my books. Now I felt as if one of those figures had sprung to life right here—and that was a first for me. Josephine Winter, the practical girl with the honest dreams, turning into a silly stargazer. Had I lost my common sense when I lost my hair?

At this moment I didn't care. He was what I'd dreamed about, a young Mr. Darcy, all dark eyes and smoky intensity. A drumming beat picked up in my chest.

Echoed by the drumming of someone's fingers on wood. "Miss?" Mr. Podium—Jacques, from the name on his badge—looked tired. "Would you like a table?"

"Um, no. No, thanks."

"Then will you kindly step out of the way?"

That was when I heard the couple murmuring, impatient, behind me, and I scuttled sideways, casting my eyes down and pulling my cloche over my forehead. And this gesture may have saved me.

For in a corner of the grand lobby where I hadn't seen him earlier, engaged in conversation with a group of men who seemed to attend to his every word, sat Daniel Connor in a thronelike chair, his boxer's hands folded over his middle, his hair slicked back, his piercing stone-gray eyes flitting from the group he was with to the lobby at large, searching, reminding me of a cat, those narrowed eyes ever aware, ever watchful. He oozed power. I didn't think he'd seen me, what with my new look and close-drawn cloche.

I ducked lower and slipped behind one of the square pillars, my heart now beating a loud thumping percussion.

What was it about Daniel Connor that made my throat burn? He wasn't the dark prince; he was more like the prince of dark forces. He frightened me in a way I couldn't explain, made me weak in the knees. It was as if he knew some secret about me.

He was dangerous.

I heard one of the men in his circle laugh, and peeked, and saw Connor leaning forward now, his head down; I took my chance to escape through the glass doors into the brilliant sunlight of the May afternoon. I walked as fast as I could up the street toward Park Avenue and the safety of my uncle's apartment, my mind a whirl.

So many new things had come in such a rapid clip. From my physical transformation to stumbling into my personal heroes to seeing a boy who seemed to have stepped right out of a romantic novel to nearly running into the very man my pops wanted to keep me away from . . . In only a few hours New York City already seemed a place where magic is real and where dreams—or nightmares— come true.

I wanted all my dreams to come true. And my nightmares? I wanted them gone.

CHAPTER 9

LOU

I met her—Jo—not too many days after she landed on the island of Manhattan. She seemed like such a kid compared to me. And for some reason the thought came to me, right off. Gosh. I'd met Danny when I was her age. Could it have been that long ago? And I'm not even that old, honey. Not that much older than Jo.

Here's the thing. I saw right off that she could become the next Louise O'Keefe. Pretty as all get-out, and I could tell she was smarter than me. But more important, she had that look. She wanted things. Not the usual things, maybe she wanted things I don't care about, but does that matter in the end? It's the *wanting* that matters.

It was one of those two goons who said it first. Way back when it all started with Danny and me, back when I was Jo's age, back when I had those same stars in my eyes. I wasn't supposed to overhear them, and I dunno if Danny ever did hear them, 'cause if he had, he wouldn't have been happy about it.

But it was what he said, that Ryan or Neil or whichever. Talking to some guy who saw me sitting alone in the lobby of the Algonquin, waiting for Danny. They didn't know I could hear them from behind that pillar.

"Get a load of that! Some gams on that babe." The guy gave a low whistle. "She a hoofer?"

"Bank's closed, buster. That's Louise O'Keefe. She's Danny's moll. Touch her and you'll end up at the bottom of the river."

"Too bad. His moll, huh? Too darn bad. Sings to me like a goshdarn siren. Too bad."

Me, Louise O'Keefe, that's who they were talking about. I sat up a little straighter. No rough dishwater hands on me ever again, no; I was a siren. I was Danny Connor's *moll*.

I hadn't heard the word before, since even growing up on the rough side of town, I was still kind of innocent, you know? Like Jo was when I met her.

Back when I met Jo, that's how it was. Me, a jealous moll. Jo, a sweet little kid who seemed to know right from wrong, who seemed to have it figured out, innocent or not. But the wanting, that's where it comes from; it's all about the wanting. When you want something bad enough, you'll do anything to get it. Anything.

Danny taught me that, along with just about everything else I know.

CHAPTER 10

MAY 21, 1925

Zelda could do outlandish things—say anything. It was never offensive when Zelda did it, so you felt she couldn't help it, and was not doing it for effect.

—Lillian Gish, on meeting Scott and Zelda Fitzgerald in the 1920s

JO

The shadows were long by the time I stepped out of the elevator and into that spare white foyer, lit now by the sleek deco table lamps. From the living room at the end of the hall I heard music, a gramophone playing Bessie Smith, sultry and slow. I slipped down the hall into my room.

I combed my hair and put some of my new lipstick on my lips— and then wiped it off again as best I could after I looked at myself in the mirror and saw that glaring crimson—Killer Red, it was called—and made to head for the living room. As I turned into the hall, I ran smack into my aunt, who was emerging from her own rooms.

"There you are!" Aunt Mary wrapped me in a hug, then launched into a mile-a-minute monologue. "I'm sorry I was out last night, couldn't be here to greet you. The museum fund-raiser, you know—far too important to miss—we're trying to purchase the Monet. . . ."

A pair of sisters couldn't be more different. Aunt Mary was small boned and blond, with a chirpy laugh and a ready smile. No wonder Uncle Bert had been so taken with her. My ma, on the other hand, was tall, thin, solemn, and dark haired—or had been dark haired before the gray had brushed it with ever-widening streaks over the past few years. And if my aunt wasn't hip to the latest styles—her skirt was on the long side—she made a glamorous statement in black silk and a single long strand of pearls, and her hair fell over her ears in softly marceled waves.

"Hi, Auntie. Ma said to send her love."

"Oh, sweetie, I'm just so happy you're with us. Let's go find your uncle." She tucked her arm through mine and walked me into the living room. "Bert? She's here."

The living room seemed to hold a crowd, suddenly silent, as Bessie and the gramophone stalled to a *scratch, hiss, scratch,* and all eyes turned toward me.

In addition to cousin Chester, who lolled on the love seat with a smile that looked predatory, there were two men in the room: my uncle, Bertram Cates, round and red-faced and wearing a three-piece suit with a watch chain stretched across his ample middle; and a tall man with a beaked nose, his elbow resting against the mantel, leaning back so that the light of the room lit his face in profile but hid his eyes, the single thread of smoke from his cigarette spiraling into the air.

Chester rose and moved to the phonograph and lifted the scratching needle from the recording.

"Ah!" Uncle Bert beamed. "Josephine. So happy you're here. I'd like to introduce a business acquaintance and good family friend. John Rushton, this is my niece, Josephine."

The man, Rushton, crushed his cigarette as he stepped forward and extended his hand. "Miss Winter." I guessed him to be in his late twenties. His eyes revealed nothing; he didn't release my hand for some seconds, so that I had to pull away from him. There was a gloom about him, a sadness tinged with desperation. He was an uneasy presence.

"Please, excuse me. I must check with Cook," my aunt said, and left the room. In the awkward silence that followed I thought to slip back out myself, but my uncle intervened.

"I hope you're settling in, Josephine?"

"Yes, thanks." To fill the silence, I began to blurt. "Melody took me shopping. And I went for a walk."

"Splendid." My uncle clapped his hands together. "Lovely afternoon for it."

Another silence followed, this one even more loaded. I fluttered, trying to fill it. "I ran into some literary types coming out of the Algonquin Hotel. You know, the one with that group, those writers, the Round Table. Edna Ferber was there. Right there, on the street." I made a small noise. "I'll confess. I was flustered."

My uncle laughed, a bit too hearty. "Those literary types. They love to talk, talk, talk."

Warmth flooded my cheeks. "They're heroes to me."

Rushton turned away.

Anxiety filled the air, like a vibrating string. I looked at Chester. His eyes gleamed, a half smile on his lips, as he now leaned on the wall, legs crossed at the ankles. Honestly, I disliked that boy.

My uncle cleared his throat. "Chester, please excuse us. We have something to discuss." I made a move, but my uncle held out his hand. "Stay for a minute, won't you, Josephine?"

Chester passed me and whispered, "Have fun," as he headed off.

Rushton examined a painting on the wall.

Uncle Bert cleared his throat. "We have a question for you, my dear. It's about Teddy."

I stiffened. "Yes, Uncle?"

"You see, John, here, thinks that you might know something about Teddy, something important. Something he might have done before he, well. You understand."

I bit the inside of my cheek. Here it was. The reason for my quick expulsion from home.

Uncle Bert rubbed his chin. His face was flushed, beads of sweat dotting his forehead. Fear: I could smell it. "We should like to know, that is, we would—"

"Did your brother tell you anything, Miss Winter?" Rushton asked without turning, his voice pressing through my uncle's stammer. "Any information? Did he say anything about his activities in the months before he . . . so tragically . . . disappeared?"

I remained silent. This was nearly the same question Danny Connor had asked. Yes, I had a secret to keep, the one Teddy *had* sworn me to. But he'd told me nothing—I didn't even know why I'd helped him disappear.

"Josephine." My uncle's voice trembled. "You have to understand that with Teddy gone, any information you may have regarding some of his experiences—"

"I can't help you, Uncle. I'm sorry." No, not with this, I couldn't.

"You see, there are some people who might need information, or want information about Teddy's last days, and if you have access to anything, anything at all, letters, perhaps . . ."

"I really don't, Uncle." My fists were clenched behind my back. Teddy didn't have last days, was what I thought. He'd said he'd be back, and when he returned, he could answer for himself.

"Ah. Well." Uncle Bert rubbed his chin again, not meeting my eyes. "That's that, then. Yes. That's it." He looked up and smiled broadly, clapping his hands together. "I think it's time for a drink. I'll be right back, John."

Uncle Bert left the room before I could move out ahead of him. I was left alone with Rushton and his uneasiness and the shadow of my uncle's fear and that inquiry about Teddy. I had to try to make an escape. I started to slip toward the door.

"Why are they heroes to you?" Rushton asked, his back toward me.

"What?" I froze in my tracks.

"Those people you saw at the Algonquin. You use the word *hero* so lightly. Why do you think they are heroes?"

"Oh!" I wondered how to answer; I settled on the plain truth. "I'd like to become a writer myself."

He turned until his eyes met mine. "Really. So that makes them heroes."

I was speechless.

He went on. "And what would you write?"

"Stories," I stammered. This man Rushton made me feel foolish. I could feel the blush creep over my cheeks. "I've written a couple of things that have been printed. Locally." In a high school paper, but I wasn't about to tell him that.

He turned his back on me again. "I'm sure you could paint quite the portrait of a flapper. Like that fellow Fitzgerald." I heard his mocking tone.

He thought I was a flapper? I covered my lips with my fingertips; I must not have erased all of that Killer Red. "I happen to like his work." My voice came out a near whisper.

He didn't respond, and I fidgeted. He turned back to face me, and the cloud of his despair was so dark I sucked in air. His eyes were wells of sorrow. In spite of his mocking manner, he was a man suffering. He opened his mouth to speak again when a commotion erupted in the hallway, the clang of the elevator, loud laughter, stumbling footsteps.

Melody came in, her arm looped through the arm of a young man wearing a broad smile and a sharp suit, with another couple tagging behind them, all giggles and feints. Rushton drew up, pulling himself inward. I watched Rushton as he looked at Melody, then at her beau, Rushton's expression pained and something else—condescending?—before he turned away.

I took him for a snob, passing judgment on my cousin the flapper just as he'd passed judgment on me. I couldn't wait to be out of the room.

I slipped away and stopped in the hall, where I leaned back against the wall, listening to the noise from the crowd and the gramophone as it restarted, a tinny upbeat of jazz bubbling through the apartment.

What was I doing here? Pops didn't honestly expect me to be hunting for a husband among this crowd. No. And what thing of Teddy's was everyone looking for?

I wish Teddy could tell me. I wish he'd come back and straighten out this whole mess.

Who was that miserable Rushton? He had been making fun of me. Making fun of Scott Fitzgerald and his stories. I touched my new-shorn hair. Rushton judged me, assuming I was just another flapper with nothing on my mind but dancing and drinking and finding my next beau. Yet something lay beneath his scorn, something dark and desperate. I saw the way he'd looked at Melody. Anger, I thought, barely veiled, and something else more elusive. What was it?

Uncle Bert emerged from the library bearing a tray with glasses and a decanter and saw me leaning against the wall. "Join us, Josephine?"

"No, thanks, Uncle."

He'd taken a handkerchief to his face, but the flush remained.

"Suit yourself." He disappeared into the living room, and the chime of the voices of Melody and her crowd lifted with the clink of ice on glass; I vanished into my room and closed the door.

Despite the pretty clothes and new hairstyle and brush with my idols at the Algonquin, once again I felt a rush of homesickness. I wished I had my ma to confide in. I missed my bedroom with the blue bedspread and yellow-flowered wallpaper. I missed slipping into Teddy's room as I often did late at night, slipping onto his empty, made-up bed and staring at those boxes on his dresser, at his things arrayed like a shrine. Lying there in the dark and hoping he'd come home soon.

Teddy had promised me.

I pulled open the bottom dresser drawer and parted the few sweaters, then took out the scarf and its contents that lay buried beneath.

He'd made me swear. "On Ma's gray head," he'd said. "No one can know where I am."

I'd nodded. But my eyes must have betrayed my confusion.

Teddy had leaned close. "Look, Jo. Some people might . . . some might be looking for me. So you can't let anyone know what we did." He'd looked away, chewing his lip. "I don't want anything to happen to you. You're my special girl. Okay? You swear?" He'd touched my forehead.

As fast as I could I'd lifted my hand, scout's honor, and said it. "I swear. On Ma. On Pops, too." As much as I knew it would pain them to think Teddy was dead, as long as I knew he wasn't, I could protect them all.

He was still here, I was so sure, and maybe that was why I was in New York. It couldn't be just chance. I was meant to come to the city. Meant to be here. Because here was where I'd find Teddy again, and once I did, everything would be all right.

And then I jumped: someone knocked hard on my bedroom door.

CHAPTER 11

LOU

I've got this belief: there are no pure coincidences.

Oh, for pity's sake, Detective. Hear me out.

It's not like we're all being herded by Fate or anything, not like some Supreme Being is playing a gigantic game of chess and we're all pawns—no, nothing like that. It's that things happen for a reason, and chance isn't a reason.

Maybe I have some special gift. I get these tingly feelings that tell me, Whooee, honey, look out.

Like when Danny took me to the show with the magician, that Howard Thurston, that's what I'm talking about. The minute I looked at that poster of his, standing out on the sidewalk in front of the theater, brother, I got goose bumps all over. Thurston's looking all mystical while little red devils and wispy white ghosts dance around his head, reaching for him, whispering in his ears, trying to make him see. See what, you ask?

THURSTON, THE GREAT MAGICIAN, the poster read, and then, DO THE SPIRITS COME BACK?

I turned to Danny. "Whatcha think? Do the spirits come back? You think there might be ghosts and such? Like, are there angels and devils and, you know, an afterlife and all?"

Danny stared at that poster like he would bore holes through it. "No. No."

"You sure? 'Cause I'd like to believe. It would be nice to know there's something out there."

"It's all a trick," he said. "Fakery."

"Too bad, 'cause—"

And Danny gave me the look. By that time I knew enough to shut my mouth. But believe you me, my tingly feelings were alive. Almost as if there were devils dancing around us right there on the sidewalk as Danny grabbed my elbow and steered me inside.

During the show, when Thurston levitated that girl—lifted her right into thin air and made her float like she was smoke—I got the tingly feelings again, deep in my gut. And lo and behold, his next move was to pack her into a box and make her disappear. She disappeared, pure and simple. The box was empty.

Don't know if you guys have seen this show, but believe me. Goose bumps. You will have goose bumps.

After the show Danny and I talked about it for hours, trying to figure out the trick. Actually, we got into kind of a fight about it, but Danny, he didn't mean it, and always apologized nice after. With flowers and jewelry, and that time with a real nice diamond bracelet that didn't go into the safe. Anyway, Danny paid some guy to find out how Thurston did it, but no dice, the magic man wouldn't give up his secret, which didn't please Danny.

Any guy who can make a girl disappear into thin air without actually, you know, killing her, well, that's a neat trick. In my opinion, that Houdini fellow that everyone talks about, he's got nothing on Mr. Thurston. Houdini gets out of traps. Big deal. I've gotten out of plenty of traps myself. But that Thurston, he sets off tingly goose bumps all over the place, talking about spirits and life after death and stuff like that.

So, anyhow, there we were that afternoon, Jo and me, on the sidewalk in front of the Algonquin, and I got that tingly feeling right off, and I knew. I was supposed to bump into her. She didn't know it yet, but she was all mixed up with something that would require a neat trick, like levitating or disappearing. She stood there, starstruck, talking about ghosts and staring up at the awning like it held a secret message that she couldn't make out. I knew it right off, that our destinies were intertwined. Sweet kiddo Jo and jealous moll Lou. We were mirrors, reflections, like in a Coney Island funhouse. One of us would levitate, and one of us would disappear, if you get my drift, and the twist was which of us would do what.

They say truth is stranger than fiction, and that is no joke. There are no pure coincidences, and when I get my tingly feelings, I'm usually right.

CHAPTER 12

MAY 21–22, 1925

The low-cut gowns, the rolled hose and short skirts are born of the Devil and his angels, and are carrying the present and future generations to chaos and destruction.
—*Albert A. Murphree, president of the University of Florida, 1920*

JO

"Yes?"

Someone fumbled with the doorknob. I had to get up to open the door, only to find Melody on the other side, a cocktail glass in one hand and a package in the other. Her eyes were bright.

"Jo! Well, honey, you look fantastic. I'm a swell makeover artist, if I do say so myself."

"Yes, Melody, you are." I touched my bob again, still adjusting to the short hair, but pleased. I gave her a smile.

She gave me a big grin in return. "Swell. Listen. I have this package." She wobbled into the room, lowering her voice. "Was told to give it to you. No one but you. I forgot entirely about it 'til this evening, but since I wasn't supposed to let you have it until . . ." She paused and held the package up before her eyes, squinting. "It says here . . ." She thrust the package at me. "What does it say?"

"'June 1, 1925,'" I read, and my hands holding the package began to tremble. The pinched handwriting was Teddy's.

"Well, close enough, doll. I have no idea what's inside. He made me promise not to look, and I owed him, so . . ." And she held up two fingers in the pledge gesture. "It's yours now. To do with as you will," she added, leaning toward me conspiratorially. "Because we both know about Teddy, now, don't we?"

My mouth felt like it was full of sand.

"Okeydokey! Back to fun and games!" She looked at me straight in the eye and said, "So, whatcha think of him?"

"Who?" I asked, my voice warbling. "Teddy?"

"No, no, no. John. You know. Rushton." She waved her free hand.

Mean, I thought. Cold. Irritating. But I lied. "Oh. He's, um . . . He's, well, he's nice enough."

She pointed her finger at my face, the glass in her hand. Fumes from the alcohol wafted to my nose. "Exactly. He's a bore." But her eyes shone. "But a nice bore, doncha think? There's something kinda sweet about him. He's all right. I mean . . . I don't know what I mean." She drifted out the door. I closed it behind her.

I stared at the package for all of ten seconds before I ripped it apart to see what was inside.

It was a journal. I sank onto the bed with the journal in my lap.

Soft, worn leather, tied with a cord to keep the loose contents from spilling all over, the journal was about two inches thick. I ran my fingers over the cover, knowing that it must have been Teddy's, knowing that he had left it for me. Left it for me, to be opened a year after he'd disappeared. A year after I'd helped him fake his death, pretending to find his clothes on that Long Island beach, and said good-bye with the promise that he'd return.

Was this journal what Danny Connor and my uncle and John Rushton wanted? Well. They wouldn't have it from me.

My hands shook as I tugged at the leather cord that tied it shut. I pulled the cord apart and leaned forward with the journal in my lap, and opened it.

His tiny, cramped handwriting with the tight vertical slope tugged at my heart. Oh, Teddy. How I wanted him back right now. The journal was full and well used; every line was covered with print; the words and the writing were hard to make out. Most all of the pages were loose; I had to take care not to let the entire journal fall apart and scatter into a mess. Some of the sentences crawled up the margins; some had little stars and led to thoughts at the bottom. It would take me a long while to read the entire thing, to be able to decipher it.

The first entry was dated just after he'd shipped out to France.

> August 20, 1918
> Off to fight in the noblest of causes . . . am both
> excited and nervous. Pops wants me to come home
> a hero. I just want to come home.

The next few pages were, as near as I could make out, about arriving overseas, being assigned to his unit, learning where he'd be deployed. Then some waiting, and then Teddy and his troop were off, and then the following:

September 11

I lay in the dark trying to remember the sky at Lizzy's. It was so big, so blue that summer. Here there's nothing but gray, and rain. It rains every day. I've got foot-rot, and the medic has given me something for it. But Lizzy's place, the ranch, it was so dry, and I want to remember how the dried-out grasses poked me in the back when I lay down on the earth and stared up at that blue. I sure wish I was there now.

Seventy-seventh. That's my battalion. Hope it's my lucky number, too.

Lizzy's. That was the summer he'd gone to Great-Aunt Elizabeth's, out in Montana. I was way too little to know much about it. But he talked about it all the time, how he wanted to go back someday.

The pages after that recounted his arrival at the front. They were filled with entries so grim that I felt sick. Entries that began when Teddy arrived in the field and what awful things he saw. More than once I skipped through the notes, picking up bits and pieces from the words I could read clearly.

September 15

We're all alike here. No rich, no poor. Just a bunch of fellows fighting for our country, fighting for what we believe in. For our families, and our honor.

Fighting for our lives.

September 20
Lay in the trench all night. Gas—and fear—making us all vomit. Constant barrage from guns. Ground trembling beneath my stomach. Stench of vomit and excrement and blood is suffocating.

His hand grew shaky and the pencil thick, worn to a nub.

September 29
Think I must be dead. Raining for two straight days, so the trench filled with water. Haven't eaten since I can't remember when. Feeling light-headed.

October 1
Wishing I would die, be done.

October 2
Whatever happens, I can't take any more. This is rotten and useless. Watched a bullet go through the eye of the guy sitting next to me. Willie O'Shaunnessy, from Chicago. We were smoking, taking a break. Just got a meal, first time in days. Feeling good. Willie, a character, a red-headed Irishman with a sense of humor, made me laugh. Bullet ricocheted off a shovel—a shovel!—propped against the trench. Right in the eye. Done.

   Thinking I might've been the one put the shovel in that spot. will hate myself forever.

Stop. What was I doing? I had to stop reading. Teddy's war memories were killing me. My chest was tight, my heart hurt to breaking.

Will hate myself forever. Forever.

A sudden knock at the door. "Jo?" My aunt's voice.

I jumped to hide the journal beneath the scarf.

"Yes?"

"Dinner, sweetheart."

"Be right there."

I wrapped the journal in the scarf that lay on my bed, tying the scarf around both the journal and Teddy's medal boxes. The misery of his words almost burned my fingers. This journal was a terrible account of his war experiences. Why had he left it for me?

I tucked the scarf and its contents deep in my bottom dresser drawer. I didn't know when I'd have the strength of mind to pull them out again. Maybe, I prayed, maybe Teddy would return before I had to read more.

At dinner my aunt tried valiantly to hold the party together. John Rushton spoke only when spoken to, his eyes frequently lighting on Melody with what I read as disdain as she filled the awkward spaces by chattering loudly with her friends about the latest gossip, movie news, wedding announcements, and social engagements. My uncle made stabbing efforts at disjointed patter and drank until he finally slipped off to bed, teetering down the hallway. And through it all Chester maintained his persona as the grinning Cheshire cat.

The day caught up with me during dinner, when I had to make polite conversation and as the food filled my belly. By dessert I could barely keep my eyes open. When dinner was over, I went to bed quickly and sank into an exhausted sleep.

* * *

I caught Chester at breakfast the next morning, just the two of us. "I need to talk to you."

Chester tugged the napkin from his shirt collar and downed a swig of coffee. "Jo, Jo. How many times do I have to tell you it was an accident? I was a kid. I had no idea you were in there. I would never have started the fire if I'd thought you were. Okay?"

My skin went cold. That was not what I'd meant; I didn't want to remember the playhouse, much less discuss it. The skin of my scar tightened involuntarily, as I recalled the pain. My voice came out low. "I'm talking about what's going on in the family."

"Ah! You mean you want to know why you're here at glorious chez Cates."

"For a start."

"Honestly, Jo?" Chester leaned across the table. "I only know it's something to do with Teddy. With stuff that happened right before he disappeared." Chester waved his hand. "Maybe you know more than you think. Was Teddy mixed up in any funny business?"

I sucked in air. "I don't know what you mean."

"That whole thing that went on in 'twenty. You know, the bombings. That's what they were talking about last night, before you arrived. Was Teddy involved with people who were talking anarchy? Anything like that."

Bombings? Anarchy? What in the world? "What are you talking about?"

"Jo. Don't you read the paper? Listen to the news? Well, okay, you were only twelve when it happened. September something, 1920. Bomb blast on Wall Street. The target was J. P. Morgan's bank, but, as usual, the people killed were mostly messengers and clerks. Not the important bigwigs. The police never caught anyone and blamed the Bolsheviks. Though everyone thought the culprits were Irish. Which takes me back to Teddy." Chester leaned toward me, eyes shining. "I've got a nose for conspiracy. Your brother went to a bunch of meetings around that time, all so mysterious. He used to talk about the Irish, how they were so downtrodden. Talked about how unfair everything was in this country. The unfairness of the situation bothered him like crazy." Chester paused. "Maybe crazy enough that he got into some funny business, in over his head."

This was new and unexpected. My stomach clenched, and I put down my fork. "Teddy would have hated that stuff."

"Sure he would." Chester's mouth twisted. "We all do. Especially you, so dreamy and innocent. Right, cuz?"

My aunt's voice drifted in from the foyer. "No, I don't know what you're talking about." By the way she paused every so often, she must have been using the telephone.

Chester pressed on. "So when your perfect brother disappeared, he was up to something, wasn't he? Up to his shins, or maybe his eyeballs."

I shrugged, not meeting his eyes. I was sorry I'd asked Chester anything, now.

He continued. "He'd had a pretty bad time of it over there, from what I could see."

This was true enough. In the years after he'd come home from the war and before he disappeared, Teddy hadn't been himself, despite the honors and the medals.

"It was an ugly war."

Chester choked on his coffee, snorting out a short laugh. "They all are."

Teddy had had bad dreams, ugly memories, bigger than the war. Something else had haunted him. Something he couldn't let go.

Something that I might now find in his journal. I would have to read on, like it or not. He'd meant for me to read it.

Chester went on. "My father said Teddy couldn't give up on some scheme to make money, either. He wanted to do something that would finally make your pops proud." He sat back. "Must've been hard for old Ted."

My stomach twisted. "What? What was hard?"

"Being perfect. Having to be the family savior." He leaned forward again. "Looks like you're about to find out how tough a spot that is, Josephine Anne. Think you can save your family?"

My aunt's voice rose. "I will not. Those are all malicious lies. My daughter is not mixed up in anything of the sort." Tension thickened the air like a brooding storm.

I said, my voice shaking, "From what do I have to save my family? And just how would I do that?"

"Ah, now. My questions exactly. Mysteries abound." That grin again.

"Yes, they do." I was losing patience with Chester. I prodded at the remains of my breakfast. "The least you can do is to tell me what was going on last night." I thought about Rushton, his aloof condescension. "Who is John Rushton, and why was he here?"

Chester withdrew, lowering his eyes and leaning back in his chair. "Rushton. An old family friend. New York money, old New York. He comes from a long line of robber barons, and for all I know he's one, too. Lives just around the block on Fifth in one of the big old New York mansions. Lots of floors in that place. Lots of ghosts, too. Just him and his servants and the kid." Chester chewed his lip, still not meeting my eyes. "Can't stand him, myself. Too high and mighty."

I was surprised; for Chester, this was revealing, and I had to say I agreed with him. "So what does Rushton have to do with Teddy?"

Chester leaned toward me, pointing his finger. "The very reason I asked about your brother. Figured that if we put our heads together, we could come up with a few of the answers."

Putting our heads together was not something I wanted, though it could be useful. I said, "He was prying into my private business with Teddy."

"Oh?" Chester sat up, staring at me hard. "You have private business with Teddy? What kind?"

I stared back. I knew better—I should never open up to Chester.

He regarded me carefully, then looked away. "John Rushton does have one reason to be prickly. His brother was working down on Wall Street when that bomb went off. Frank Rushton was killed, and John's never gotten over it. So," Chester said, smooth as silk, "what's this about Teddy's private business? Come on, spill."

My aunt's voice broke into our conversation again. This time her shrill shout echoed from the foyer. "I've told you, and I'm done telling you. I have no idea what you're talking about. Now leave us alone." The receiver hit the cradle with a *thwack*.

Chester raised his eyebrows as we regarded each other across the table.

Aunt Mary stormed into the dining room, stopping short when she saw us. "Oh!" She brushed back her hair and straightened her shoulders. "I didn't know anyone else was here." She gestured toward the foyer. "That switchboard operator must have crossed the lines."

Chester tossed his napkin onto the table in a heap. "Well, I'm off. Career beckons. Miles to go and all that. Later, Mumsie. See you, cuz. I'm sure we'll talk more when I get home. Dying to finish this conversation. Wall Street. Such a blast." He winked at me and kissed his mother's cheek as he blew by.

I rose to follow, but my aunt took my arm. "Jo, I need to ask you a favor."

"Sure, Aunt Mary." I gave my aunt my full attention, trying to put on a smile, my stomach lurching with uneasiness. "What can I do for you?"

She lifted her eyes to mine. "I'd like you to keep an eye on Melody."

I had to stop myself from revealing my shock, so I bit my lip. "Um, Aunt Mary, I don't see how—"

Aunt Mary waved her hand in the air. "I know she appears to be grown up, but I can assure you, she's made some very bad choices. You're a steady, smart girl, Josephine. You know right from wrong. If you go out on the town with her, you can be a good influence."

"Really, Auntie, I'm not sure I can influence Melody at all."

"Nonsense." Aunt Mary pushed her hair back in what was becoming a familiar gesture. "I know all about the flapper doings. I know all about the . . . boys. She drinks too much alcohol—

they all drink." She paused, her eyes troubled. "Do you drink, Josephine?"

"No."

"There you are! You're sensible and smart. Not likely to get into trouble with boys and the law and such."

I shook my head. "Aunt Mary, Melody is pretty strong-willed. If she gets it in her head to do something, I don't think I can stop her."

Tears popped into my aunt's eyes, and her voice trembled. "Just be there, Jo. Please?"

I put my hand on my aunt's arm. Whenever I'd seen my aunt in the past, she'd seemed breezy and free, not like this, shaken. "I'll do what I can."

If Teddy was here, he could keep Melody in check. But me? She'd blow me away like yesterday's cigarette ash.

"Where is Melody now?" I asked. I had the feeling that my aunt was worried about more than she was letting on.

"She's still asleep. She's rarely up before noon." My aunt shook her head. "I just don't understand. When I was her age, I wouldn't have even considered behaving so. Bertram would never have given me a second glance if I'd acted out like you all do today. Dancing all night, smoking cigarettes, pulling silly stunts like sitting atop poles, dressing with no regard to decency . . ." Aunt Mary looked me up and down. "At least you're wearing something that isn't see-through."

I blushed; there were a few dresses in my closet that I'd considered and rejected for that very reason, and because they'd expose my ugly scar. But maybe that made me old-fashioned. Old-fashioned enough that I was being asked to play nursemaid to my reckless cousin.

"I'll be in my room," I said. I would have the chance to read more of Teddy's journal, if I could steel myself to it. "I'll find her when she wakes up."

My aunt nodded, her eyes drifting to the floor.

But my room was being cleaned by talkative Adela, the maid, and it was clear she wouldn't be finished for a time; there was no way I would fetch Teddy's journal under anyone's curious gaze. After shuffling around impatiently, I decided to go for a walk to clear my head.

The weather had turned from warm to downright hot, and now the air had that ominous feel of threat that preceded thunderstorms. The sun baked the streets through a humid haze. The city was in its morning rush, and businessmen in their hats and suits with umbrellas looped over their arms marched forward, chins thrust out like the prows of steamships. I stood under the awning watching the ebb and flow for so long that Ed, the doorman, asked if I'd like a taxi.

"No, thanks. I'm just standing here watching the city go by." And trying to let my unsettled emotions calm.

Ed nodded, and I felt bad. I wondered at how he must be suffering in that heavy coat and those pristine white gloves that were part of his uniform. His whistle hung across his chest on a long brass chain.

"I'm sorry about that suitcase the other day," I said to him.

"Excuse me, miss?"

"That it was so heavy. I should have warned you."

He shrugged. "It's my job, miss." He glanced up and down the busy street, always at the ready. "But if you don't mind my asking . . ."

"Books." I smiled. "Just books."

"Ah, no gold bricks then. Or," he dropped his voice, "bottles of you know what." He shook his head. "Not that you'd need to hide that in a suitcase. Everyone looks the other way. Why, there was a delivery right to this door last week, cases of the stuff, broad daylight, and nobody blinked." He bounced on the balls of his feet. He lowered his voice further, talked out of the corner of his mouth. "Not that I forgo the stuff myself, mind you." Then he stepped back. "Sorry, miss. Don't know why I'd say something like that, speak to you like that. My apologies."

He was a decent guy. "Ed, I assure you I can keep a secret."

"Thank you, miss. Much obliged. Our secret." A woman pushed out the door, and Ed moved off to help her to a taxi.

I could keep a secret, couldn't I? I could keep the deepest of secrets.

The air was heavy and my heart was heavy and my mind full of doubts. Spying on Melody, and my aunt's deep worry, and Teddy having something to do with bombings.

Teddy, war hero, my hero, would never, could never . . .

Cars rushed by honking and weaving, and people threaded the sidewalks in the shimmering heat, and I thought about the last time I had seen Teddy, in similar shimmering heat, and about that promise that I had made to him, that I kept even as it haunted me, wormed through me, tortured me, and showed the crack in my fastidious belief in all things right.

CHAPTER 13

LOU

I think, if I'd known, I would've told Charlie, don't do it. Don't take that job. I don't like you mixed up in this stuff. But then, where would we be?

Danny was always doing stuff like that, stuff that drove me crazy. *He* drove me crazy. Yeah, I knew about the others. I knew what he did for a living. I knew there was a part of him that was dangerous.

You boys getting the picture?

'Cause, if not, here's a clue. That time in '23. We were in the mansion on Long Island by then. Business was really picking up as Danny had taken over most of Big Al's operations. I walked in on something I shouldn't have. How was I to know?

Danny and his brother Pat, they were out in the greenhouse. I went out there, 'cause they'd been at it so long and Cook had prepared a nice dinner, quail, for pete's sake, and when I knocked, they didn't answer, so I opened the door.

"Danny?"

Up they popped like a couple of rabbits, covered in dirt. I couldn't help it; I started to giggle.

But Danny, he didn't think it was funny. He came at me so fast it was like watching a bull charge down a field, horns first. He shoved me back out the door and slammed it so hard one of the glass panes cracked.

"Don't you ever surprise me again," he said, right through his teeth.

I didn't say a word, just nodded.

He took a deep breath. "Patrick was helping me unload some fresh soil. That's what you saw. You understand?"

I nodded again. I wasn't a dummy; I saw his clenched fist.

"Get back to the house."

I did. Danny, he didn't talk to me for almost a week, and he went out every evening, which was worse than anything else he could've done. It was downright hurtful. Oh, I could've left him, sure, since I knew he was up to no good.

But I didn't. I was stuck on Danny, like lint on wool. I was goofy over him. Danny was my one and only, even if I wasn't his.

So maybe it was a good thing I didn't know about Charlie's little job until after. 'Cause if I'd stopped Charlie, asked him not to do it—and I would have, thinking the wrong thing altogether—then none of it would've happened with Charlie and Jo, and me. And you boys probably wouldn't be talking to me. No, the story would've had a different ending.

So there's your proof. Nothing happens by chance.

CHAPTER 14

MAY 22, 1925

Body of King Tut Is Found in Sarcophagus
—Headline from The Washington Reporter, February 12, 1924

JO

I walked over to Fifth, intending to head uptown through Central Park toward the Metropolitan Museum. The new Egyptian discoveries were all the rage, but that wasn't what I had in mind. It had to do with Teddy. I went to the Met to revisit a series of paintings.

Between receiving Teddy's journal out of the blue, Rushton's peculiar interest in Teddy, and Chester's insinuations, I was feeling my way through a labyrinth. All I could do was try to follow the thread as I waited for Teddy's return.

After the war Teddy hadn't taken me to see shows so much. It was as if he couldn't laugh or let his hair down or even sit still that long. Instead, we'd go see other, quieter sights in the city, one of which was the Met. There was one particular set of paintings that he liked. It was clear that they meant something to him. If I could figure out what, maybe I'd know enough so I could find the thread that would lead me to him.

Because I believed in Teddy's promise to me. I believed he'd be back, and would be here any day now.

I struck out up Fifth Avenue. Buses, cabs, and automobiles hurtled along, past the tony brownstones that rose imperiously above the sidewalk. A few horse-drawn wagons stood waiting or sidled into alleys; deliverymen carried baskets of flowers, stacks of boxes, crates of food into service entries. Polished limousines in bright colors—a fern-green Packard, a maroon Daimler—lined the curb, waiting, while doormen in stiff coats surveyed their domains. One matron emerged from her building, her tiny dog on a gem-encrusted leash, her silk dress shimmering, her diamond necklace glittering, her eyes sharp and focused, the door to her limousine held for her by a Negro driver who was outfitted in an immaculate uniform complete with gloves, his eyes tracing the ground. It even smelled rich here: swept, damp sidewalks and the scent of car wax and jardinieres overflowing with petunias glittering with moisture. This was the upperest crust of New York society, and it made my aunt and uncle's lavish lifestyle look plain.

The day grew ever more sultry. I walked at a slow pace, taking in New York, trying not to work up a sweat. I was close to the intersection at Sixty-fifth, where I'd cross the avenue to the park, when I stopped, midstride and midsidewalk, the other pedestrians streaming around me.

A silky black limo had pulled alongside the curb. The driver was at the wheel, his eyes fixed on the space in front of him. Stepping out the door of the limo, his gray pinstripe immaculate, was Daniel Connor. And he was looking right at me.

He nodded. "Miss Winter," he said. "I've been following you. I was hoping to catch up with you."

My tongue was a clunky thing, unable to form words.

"May we speak?" He stepped aside, and held the car door open, gesturing.

I found my words now, although my voice shook. "You may speak to me right here. In the open."

He smiled. "I understand your concern, but for your family's sake, you should get inside." He spread his hands. "You have my word I won't spirit you away." His smile sharpened.

I had no choice. I slid into the backseat, my palms sweaty, tacky on the leather, as Connor closed the door behind him. As I sat back, facing him, the skin of the scar on my back prickled.

"Your father," he began, "I think he's hiding something. Do you know what I'm talking about?"

I shook my head. A bead of sweat formed on my forehead.

"It's not important. Suffice to say I don't tolerate secrecy in my employees."

I couldn't move.

"Now, under certain conditions, I'm a forgiving man."

My mouth went dry as a desert as I said, "Conditions?"

"I'll be blunt. I'm looking for your brother, Miss Winter." He paused, held out a cigarette case. I shook my head again, eyeing the lighter in his other hand. He put both away. "Do you know anything about Teddy? Where he might be? Because we both know he isn't really dead, don't we?"

I tried not to betray my surprise, tried not to show my terror. He waited.

He said, "I think you know where he is."

"No, I don't." This, at least, was the truth.

"But you do know something. It will be better for your family if I can speak with Teddy. Better for everyone. Do you know anything about him?" He paused. "Anything he might have left behind?"

I sat as still as I could.

He leaned toward me and lowered his voice. "I don't tolerate deception or betrayal. Information about Teddy would make me . . . hesitate to punish your father." He leaned back. "Here's my card. That's my phone number. I'm always available to you." He took out a cigarette, tamping it on the case. "But I'm not terribly patient. I will give your father two weeks. That's two weeks for you to think about my question, Miss Winter." He reached past me and opened the limo door to let me out. But before I could slip past him, he stopped me, his arm barring my way. "You're an attractive young woman. Perhaps there's something I can do for you. To sweeten the deal. I can help you, you know."

My thighs stuck to the leather. My dress clung to my back, to the skin of my scar. "I don't think so," I said.

"No? Not thinking of becoming an actress?" He paused. "Or perhaps a writer? I know lots of people in the publishing business. Someone who could give you a job tomorrow. Here, in the city. A nice high income."

Sweat streamed down my back. How could he know? I shook my head.

He removed his arm. "You have two weeks."

I peeled and pulled myself off the seat in an awkward jerk; I couldn't get out of the car fast enough.

Once out I moved up the avenue at a real clip now, away from the limo, hearing the engine roar to life. I saw from the corner of my eye as it pulled away, and I could exhale at last.

Daniel Connor didn't think Teddy was dead. But what did he want with him? What did he want enough to threaten Pops? To threaten me?

One thing was clear: the paintings would have to wait. However much it pained me, I had to go back home and read Teddy's journal.

* * *

The day had turned suffocating. I moved into the shade of the trees in Central Park, just to cool off before I turned back to the apartment. Children ran across the grassy lawns, oblivious of the heat; nannies in starched caps and gray uniforms fanned themselves as they sat watching their charges and gossiping. A young couple lay sprawled face-to-face on a blanket, her dress thin as tissue, his bare arm draped over her back, their ankles locked, their faces close as they whispered, in my imagining, sweet endearments. Pigeons strutted, cooed, then flapped as they were disbursed in a melee of flight and feathers by a dog that ran at them, wild-eyed, tongue hanging.

I paused to let my nerves settle. I bought a vanilla ice cream from a vendor and sat on the bench across the path.

That was when I saw I was still being followed, but not by Danny Connor.

This boy had been behind me since I'd left the limo. He stood out—wearing a white shirt with sleeves rolled up, rather than a suit and tie and hat. And now I recognized him.

It was the boy from the Algonquin, the dark-haired boy, my

waiter-prince. Seeing him sent ripples through me, making me feel weak-kneed. He stared at me for an instant, then looked away, fixing his gaze on the children running in loops through the park.

He was just as striking as I'd thought when I'd laid eyes on him in the restaurant. He wasn't good-looking in the usual sense: his nose was a bit too large, his cheeks too flat, his lips too full. But he had a mesmerizing quality that makes you want to watch and watch, see what he does, follow how he moves. He had an animal quality: broad shouldered, heedless, bullish, even a little awkward. And his eyes. Large and round and dark, like wells. Just a teeny bit scary.

And he was following me, which made my heart thump.

I held the ice cream as it melted in the cup and watched him shuffle his feet and pretend to be occupied with something up in the branches of the oaks overhead, all the while avoiding looking at me.

I rose from the bench, tossed the ice cream in the trash, moved up the path with a faster step, and kept walking until I reached Fifth, where I saw a policeman strolling along the avenue, his nightstick swinging from his left hand. Then I stopped on a dime and turned right around, and yes, there he was, my shadow with the animal gait, following about twenty feet behind me.

I covered the distance between us before my footpad could fully react, and his eyes widened even farther and he froze.

I spoke fast. "You've been tailing me. Now, don't try to deny it. If you do anything, I'll scream bloody murder, and that policeman will come running. Am I clear?"

He swallowed and nodded, then stepped back and narrowed his eyes and folded his arms across his chest. "So what's the problem?

I'm following a pretty girl. Even he"—and here he thumbed toward the policeman—"would see that was no crime." Those eyes brightened to a sparkle, and a small smile crept onto those full red lips.

Which attracted my attention such that I almost had to pinch myself to keep from staring.

I folded my arms, too, and then imagined that we looked a sight, a matched set of stubborn figures. Though, I'll admit, those lips and dark eyes made me shiver.

"All right." He dropped his arms and shrugged. "Fine, then. I was hired to tail you."

I dropped my arms. "By whom?" Although I could make a pretty fair guess, after what had just happened in the limo.

"That's for me to know."

I raised my eyebrows. "That's not fair. If you're going to follow someone and you're caught, you have to come clean."

"Have to?" He smiled again, which, considering how nice he looked when he smiled, was really and truly not fair. Cheating, in fact. Then he shrugged. "I can't tell you who. I can only say that I was asked by an acquaintance. 'Follow her,' he says. 'I'll give you ten dollars a day to find out where she goes and who she sees.'"

I snorted, choking back a laugh. "You're not much of a detective, even if you are commanding such a high fee."

His eyes turned darker. "What do you mean?"

"Have you ever read any Sherlock Holmes? First of all, I caught you. You were so obvious. And second, you've now told me you know the guy. And that it is a guy. And finally, you've lost the edge of surprise. Now, whenever I see you, I'll know to keep my private business private."

"It doesn't matter. I'll get paid whether you do something or not. I'll get paid just because I followed you." He pulled a watch from his pocket. "Or until I have to get to my next job. Which gives me three more hours of following you."

I bubbled with laughter now. It felt good to laugh, and I let out the tension that had been haunting me for the past twenty-four hours.

"What?"

"You've given me your entire itinerary. I'll work around it. There's not much you'll learn from me." I didn't dare add that I even knew he worked in the Algonquin; those dark eyes told me he was already humiliated enough.

"Like I said. I only have to watch you. Which isn't hardly a chore." His face cleared, and he smiled. "In fact, I should be paying him." He surely was a pleasure to gaze on, and that smooth line made my heart thump.

This was a new experience. I was the shy student in White Plains, always in the background, not wanting to be taken for a silly girl. Some combination of my new clothes and hairstyle, my exiled state on the island of Manhattan, the deep, leafy green of Central Park, the hovering threats, and this boy's deep, dangerous eyes made me brave.

I stuck out my hand, grateful for the change in my mood. "My name's Jo. But you already knew that, I expect."

He reached out and shook my hand with a firm grip. "Charlie. Charlie O'Keefe."

O'Keefe. Why did that ring a bell? I shook my head. "Well, Charlie O'Keefe, you can run along." I hesitated before I lied, "I'm just out for a walk. I was about to turn back for home, anyway. Not much to see here."

"I'll walk you back that way. I've nothing else to do before the afternoon."

Which made my heart fairly race, and I was not at all unhappy. "You're hopeless. Suit yourself." We began to walk, staying on Fifth, just in the shade of the trees. He had a loping, wolflike gait. "Three hours until your next job? Not another bit of detective work, I trust."

"I wait tables." His cheeks grew rosy. "But what I love is music."

I knew he waited tables, but . . . "Music?"

"That's what I do mostly. I play jazz. At night, at different places, wherever they want me."

I figured he was talking about speakeasies.

His manner was open, his talk rambling. "Just a little while ago I worked at this joint called the County Fair."

"Excuse me? The County Fair?" I began to laugh all over again, thinking that this Charlie had the ability to make me laugh, something I hadn't done in a while.

"It's a club. A theme club. It ain't enough, you know, to serve liquor. Everybody who's anybody can do that. The latest thing is to have a club with a theme, and this one's a county fairgrounds, complete with a white picket fence and kiddie cars and even a kissing booth, which, let me tell you, the flappers fight over the chance to be part of. Folks come from all over to dance the night away at a place that makes them feel almost like they never left their hometown." He gave a large grin. "Doesn't that beat all?"

I had to stop walking while I laughed, holding one hand over my stomach. To be frank, I had a hard time keeping my eyes on the sidewalk. Those full lips and dark eyes of Charlie's drew me like a magnet. And his transparency: he was not a secret keeper. That's what I liked best.

Teddy would like this guy. I think he'd like anyone who made me laugh, but there was something about this one.

When I stopped laughing, I felt suddenly shy. I searched for conversation. "Do you live in the city?"

"I've got a small place downtown. It's not much, but the neighbors don't mind hearing me practice, long as I quit before ten P.M."

"What do you play?"

"The cornet." When I looked puzzled, he said, "It's kind of like a trumpet."

"And you wait tables at the Algonquin?"

His face grew dark again, and he stopped walking. "How'd you know that?"

"Mmm," I bit my lip. Admitting I saw him there would be admitting I'd watched him. "Didn't you say . . . ?"

He rubbed his chin. "I don't think I did."

I could see that I'd embarrassed him. Would he hate me for showing him up, for my own sleuthing skills, which were far better than his? I sought to change tacks again, and I put my hand on his arm. "Do you know the Round Table?"

He eyed me for another minute before he shrugged. "Sure, I do. Everyone does."

"What I wouldn't give . . ." I started, and then stopped. My hand lay on his arm, and every nerve in my fingers vibrated. His skin was warm, and his forearm sinewy and strong. My cheeks grew hot as I lifted my fingers away.

The birds had stopped calling, and the trees hung overhead, still and drooping. Somewhere in the distance thunder rumbled.

"Hey," he said, and his dark eyes went soft. "If you ever want to come by, I'll point them out. Those famous folks."

The air was full and heavy and moist. Thunder rumbled again, closer. I could smell the rain. And then we both heard it coming.

I looked at the sky, dull gray now. "I think we'd better find some shelter, or we're in for a drenching."

Charlie lifted his face and looked around. "How about there?"

It was a coffee shop across the avenue. Just as we started to move, fat raindrops fell in slow warning. Charlie grabbed my hand, and we ran across the avenue, making it through the honking autos and buses, through the door, and into the shop just as the rain came down in sheets.

We laughed, shaking off nerves at the near miss of both traffic and rain, and as he released my hand I realized that I liked it, the way that his warm hand had enveloped mine as he'd pulled me through the danger. I smiled at him and he grinned at me, and my heart fluttered.

"Cup of coffee?" he asked.

I nodded, and we found a pair of stools at the counter; Charlie ordered two cups of coffee and two pieces of apple pie, warm, à la mode.

We ate our pie and sipped our coffee in silence while the rain battered the window, then slowed, then stopped altogether, as the storm passed and the clouds split to allow a brilliant stream of sun that mirrored off the wet sidewalks and cars. I stole sidelong glances at Charlie, at that profile that looked like he'd stolen it from a Celtic warlord. Passersby lowered their umbrellas, shaking off the rain.

"I need to get home," I said.

"Sure thing. The coffee and pie are on me. You know, for tailing you." I started to protest, but he stopped me. "I'll still get my ten bucks. Plus expenses." He grinned, raising his cup of coffee in salute before bringing it to his lips.

Oh, those lips. I looked away, staring into the depths of my own cup.

The air was cool and fresh now, and we walked the blocks downtown in silence. When we reached the corner of Park and Fifty-sixth, Charlie stopped. "I think I'd better leave you here. No sense letting your doorman see me when I'm supposed to be invisible. Even if you are twice the detective I'll ever be." He gave me another of his grins; I couldn't help grinning right back.

I reached out to shake his hand. "Nice meeting you, Charlie. Thanks for the coffee." As we shook hands, my fingers tingled.

He turned away, then turned back. "Hey. I'll be downtown at a joint for two weeks. Why don't you come on down? It's in the lower west. You can hear me play."

"To a speakeasy? Me? Good grief, no!"

"Well, if you should change your mind." He took a pencil and a slip of paper from his pocket, moistened the tip of the pencil with his tongue, wrote something, and handed it to me. "That's the address."

It was a street number; I tucked it into my purse. "I'll think about it."

"Okay, then." He gave me a two-fingered salute and moved off. I watched him weave into the crowd of pedestrians, hands jammed in his pockets.

And then, as I watched him, there was someone else in the

crowd, someone else watching me—blond hair, eyes flashing blue watching me, watching Charlie—watching . . .

I raised my hand. "Teddy?" My voice came out in a croak, and my heart raced. But even if Teddy could have heard me, he was already gone, disappearing into the wave of pedestrians who jostled and pushed along the sidewalk. I stood there for the longest time, hoping to catch sight of Teddy again, but he'd vanished into thin air.

But I'd seen him. He was here, in New York. Alive and here and still laying low.

I walked back to my aunt and uncle's, trying to sift through the tangle of feelings.

Everyone wanted something from me. Connor, Rushton, Pops, my uncle, Charlie, even my aunt . . . that was when I remembered. I stopped to ask Ed, "Has Miss Melody left the apartment yet?"

"Yes, miss. Right after the rain stopped."

I groaned. I sure wasn't acting like Miss Draper's "A" student, nor like the detective I thought I was. Already I'd let my aunt down by not being home in time for Melody.

Ed lifted one finger. "Oh, and miss. Your aunt and uncle and Mr. Chester are also out, but there's someone waiting in the apartment. I let him up because I know he's a particular friend of your uncle's."

"Who?" But I already thought I knew the answer, and the very idea of it carved a hollow in my middle.

"Mr. John Rushton."

CHAPTER 15

LOU

Not too long after we moved into the Long Island mansion, Killimor—Danny named it after some place he knew in the old country; can you beat that, Detective? He wants to leave his past behind, and the first thing he does is settle on a name . . . oh, never mind. Anyhow, not too long after we moved in I learned how Danny felt about me consorting with the help.

He'd gone off to the city, like he did near every day, and I was hungry, that's all. Cook made me a lamb sandwich and, I ask you, why should I eat all alone at a table for twenty in that drafty old dining room with its gloomy tapestries and empty armor, with the feeling there were eyes in there watching me, when I could eat in Cook's cozy kitchen? And it was a cold and rainy day, too, so the kitchen fire was nice.

I told Danny once that I thought modern was much nicer than all this old stuff—used furniture, I think I said—and he lectured me for near an hour on the value of antiques. On history and how rich people all have antiques. I still didn't like them, all those creepy, dark, old things, even if he did make the help clean them till they glowed. But by then I'd learned to keep my trap shut.

Anyway, I'm eating my sandwich, and Cook starts in with stories about Danny that I hadn't heard before. About how he'd arrived as a kid on Ellis Island with nothing on but an oversize dress shirt and a ratty pair of knickerbockers. How he started out on the Lower East Side picking pockets before moving up in his early teens as a boxer. How he earned a boxing nickname right off: Dapper Dan O'Connor.

"Wait," I said, between bites. "O'Connor?"

"Aye," Cook said. "He dropped the 'O' when he got important. Some say he dropped it because he didn't want to be taken for someone right off the boat." She made a noise in her throat that sounded like "harrumph."

"Go on," I said. "And by the by, this lamb is very tasty."

"Why, thank you, dearie. So, anyways, he was Dapper Dan because he valued his pretty face so. I heard tell he never let a fist near it. Never got a black eye nor a broken nose, not Dan."

I laughed. "He couldn't have been in too many fights, then."

"He picked and chose his fights, and he was small and fast. He dodged the sluggers and knocked them out. Some say he only fought with drunks. Be that as it may, Dapper Dan fought enough to win some influential friends, who bet his way and won." Cook pronounced it "in-flu-en-tee-al."

"How influential?"

"Let's just say Mr. Daniel Connor is no stranger to all sorts of shenanigans. He made himself important to Mr. Alphonse Capone, I'll tell you that. He was one of Al's boys. He'd learned to keep his face pretty and his hands clean, even when his hands were deep in the muck. From running the booze to getting people out of his way, your man there knows how to take care of business."

"Getting people out of his way?" I put my sandwich down, no longer hungry.

Cook looked at me. "Here, now. How do you think an Irish lad—I don't care if he hears me say it—how do you think a lad off the boat gets all this?" She waved her hands around the kitchen before fisting them on her hips. "What do you think he does all day out in that greenhouse of his, and why do you think them plants grows so big?" She pointed one large finger at my plate. "I thought you liked the lamb."

The kitchen door swung open with a thud so hard I jumped near out of my skin. "Danny!" I said.

He stared at me, his eyes like diamond points. "What are you doing in the kitchen, Louise?"

I sucked in air. I pointed to my sandwich.

In two strides Danny was at my side and swept the sandwich off the table and onto the floor. He took my wrist. "You will never eat in the kitchen again."

I wanted to tell him he was hurting me, but I knew better by then. "Okay. I won't. I promise."

He dragged me from the room, and just before the door swung shut he turned to Cook. "Clean that up. Then pack your bags."

His next cook wasn't near so nice, nor could she make such a lamb.

CHAPTER 16

MAY 22, 1925

Clara Bow, Paramount star, is the flapper turned "moll"' and the title of this drama of the underworld, which bristles with action and suspense, is Ladies of the Mob.
—From "Clara Bow, 'It,' Stars at State,"
Reading Eagle, July 24, 1928

JO

On the way up in the elevator I considered my options. I could pretend I didn't know he was there and slip into my room; or I could ask him to leave; or I could engage him in meaningless conversation. Whatever I did, I wasn't about to tell him anything about Teddy.

The elevator doors opened, and I stepped into the foyer. Light from the library told me that Rushton was in there. I decided to face him.

He had his back to me when I entered, but he turned at once, and when he saw me he shut the book he was holding and nodded a terse greeting.

"Mr. Rushton," I said, uneasy.

"Miss Winter."

"Is there something I can do for you?"

"Yes, you can." He returned the book to the shelf. "You know already that I'm here to see you."

We stood in silence. He scrutinized me. Again, I felt some awkward combination of disdain and desperation in him. He wanted something from me, but he didn't want to ask.

"So?" I asked, not even trying to hide my frustration now. "What is it you want?"

"I knew your brother."

This was a shock. "You knew Teddy!" I took a step back.

"Yes. We met during the war. We served together. We spent the better part of a year in the same unit. We became quite close. You could say we were friends."

I wasn't sure what to say. Teddy had never mentioned him. Nothing of Teddy's life over there came up in conversation after he'd returned home. But then, Teddy wasn't very well after he came back. He didn't talk about his war experience, whether pleasant or not. If a friendship with John Rushton during the war was, in fact, pleasant. How could Teddy make a friend of this obnoxious man? I thought of Teddy's journal, whether Rushton would appear in its pages.

"You don't believe me," he said.

I shrugged and moved to sit on the arm of a chair. I worked hard to appear calm, unruffled. "I don't disbelieve you. I don't know you."

"I'd like to tell you something about your brother. There is some unfinished business between us. I hope you can tell me something that will finish it."

I was the keeper of my brother's secrets; I wasn't about to discuss Teddy with this man I didn't like. I stiffened and stood again, clenching my fists. "Thanks, Mr. Rushton, but I have to go get ready for the evening."

He glanced at the clock on the wall. "Yes, I suppose it does take you girls some time to prepare."

"You girls?"

"Girls like you. You and Melody."

"Now, just one minute." That did it. "What kind of a girl do you take me for?"

"I assume you're like all the rest. Like your cousin. A flapper." As he spoke he turned away. "I thought I could count on your help, but I see now that you're as shallow as they are."

"Well, I'm not," I snapped.

"Then the appearance is deceiving."

His comment made me seethe. There was something about him that reminded me of Pops, that close-minded disapproval. I touched my hair. "I happen to like my short hair. I happen to think a girl shouldn't have to fuss with long tresses anymore. I happen to think a girl should be as comfortable in her clothes as a man is in his. She shouldn't have to wear long entangling skirts and confining corsets." My voice rose with each sentence. "I also think a girl has the right to vote, and the right to work for a living." I took a breath and tried to sound the cynic. "I assume you want all women to be slaves to their husbands." Just like Pops.

Rushton was now looking straight at me. "I didn't mean—"

"I suppose you believe that a girl like me can't think. That I don't know what it means to be a slave. That I don't know about Mr. Darwin and that upcoming trial down in Tennessee that I bet'll prove just what apes men are. That I don't know how the Prohibition works, and all the sneaky little business dealings that my pops and maybe even you, yes, you, Mr. High and Mighty, are engaged in."

"Miss Winter, that's not—"

"I'm a thinker, Mr. Rushton. I want to be a thinker, not just a doer. And I certainly am not a flapper, or a floozie, or a . . . or a . . . or anything else cheap and insulting!"

"I never—"

"You think you know everything by just examining the surface. Scratch a little deeper, Mr. Rushton. I'm not leaning on my gangster boyfriend for every little thing like some dumb moll."

There was a movement at the door, and I turned my head. It was the same girl I'd met in front of the Algonquin. That Louie something, who'd slipped into the back of a limo like she was slipping onto a chaise longue.

How long she'd been standing there, I had no idea. I'd been so caught up in my argument with Rushton that I could only assume she'd come into the apartment unheard.

She raised her hands and gave a slow and deliberate *clap, clap, clap.* "You tell him, honey. No dumb moll, you." Her eyes were sharp, narrowed at me, and she smiled with her lips only.

I unclenched my fists and lowered my shoulders, slow and easy, trying to breathe.

Melody came up behind her. I guessed now that the two had come into the apartment together. "So Lou, you've met my cousin Jo? Josephine Winter, fresh from White Plains." Then Melody turned to Rushton. She frowned, but it was an attempt at charm. "John Rushton, speaking of fresh, are you giving my naive little cousin a hard time?"

I looked at her, wide-eyed. Melody was flirting with Rushton.

He pulled himself up, then acknowledged her with a slight nod of his head, his cheeks flushed. "Miss Cates. I think I should take my leave."

"So soon? Wouldn't you like to stay for cocktails? Why, I can make a wicked highball. Or an even tastier Orange Blossom." She moved toward Rushton, silky.

He flushed dark. "Thank you, Miss Cates, but no."

What was going on here, between the two of them? Because there was no question: Melody wanted Rushton's attention, and he was working hard to avoid giving her even a bit of it.

Louie watched the scene with apparent amusement, leaning against the doorframe like she owned it. Then she moved into the room. "John Rushton," she said, extending her hand. "We meet again."

Rushton hesitated before he took her hand and bowed his head. "Miss O'Keefe."

O'Keefe! That's where I'd heard it. Charlie's last name was O'Keefe. I shook my head. It was a coincidence. O'Keefe was a common Irish name.

Yet those eyes . . .

"Oh, how sweet," she drawled. "You remembered." Her eyes skimmed away from Rushton and to me. "That's right. Louise O'Keefe. I'm Daniel Connor's *moll*." She emphasized the last word as if it was distasteful. Which must have been the way I'd pronounced it.

The blood rushed to my cheeks. "I didn't mean . . ." I mumbled.

"What, hon?" She came around Rushton to me. Then she laughed. "Oh, sweetie, no hard feelings. I mean it. It wasn't fair to spy on you like that. I am Daniel Connor's girlfriend. Absolutely right, and I don't deny it." She leaned toward me in a feigned whisper. "I had a feeling when we met the other day that we'd meet again." She gave me a smile, warmer now, but cautious.

I gave her a tentative smile back. But . . . Daniel Connor's girlfriend?

Rushton made to move toward the door. "Please excuse me."

Melody leaned on his arm. "Oh, do stay." She smiled up at him, her head cocked to one side. Her short blond hair fell in becoming waves.

He pulled away, separating her arm from his, his face beet red. "No, thank you. Please give my respects to your parents." He nodded toward her, not meeting her eyes.

At the doorway he turned back to me, clearing his throat to recover his composure. "Your brother, Miss Winter. I didn't finish telling you. He saved my life during the war. I owe him everything. I think you should know that." He paused. "There's more, but I'll save it for another time."

I could say nothing; I'd said all the worst things already, and it was time for me to shut up.

After the elevator door clanged closed behind Rushton, Louie said, "Honestly, Mel, what are you thinking? Listen to how he talks. He may be young, but he's stiff as a board. Like he dropped in from some other century, at least. How could you fall for such a dull knife?"

Melody drew up. "I haven't," she snapped. "He's an old family friend. He's done a great deal for us. I was just being polite." Melody turned. I could see her face; Louie couldn't.

Mel was lying.

"Hah!" Louie laughed.

"Louise O'Keefe, you know nothing," Mel said. "Nothing." Her words were icy.

Even Lou looked surprised at her tone. She exchanged a glance with me; I shrugged.

"Sorry, doll," Lou murmured.

I thought I'd stumbled into a farce, one of those stage plays that I'd watched with Teddy on one of our early excursions into the city, when I had looked at the constellations in the plaster firmament of Grand Central and dreamed of stars. I'd heard all the jokes and innuendoes that mostly went right by my head while the audience reeled with laughter. I looked from Louie to Melody, flummoxed.

Then out of the blue I remembered my promise to Aunt Mary. "Melody."

She looked at me. "Yes?"

What in the world was I to say? Your mother asked me to look out for you. I'm supposed to spy on you. Be a good girl, Melody. Don't drink. Don't smoke. For pity's sake, cover up those knees. Walk the straight and narrow. Come to a temperance meeting with me. Leave the boys alone. Leave John Rushton alone.

Instead, I blathered. "What are you up to tonight? You know, what's going on, and such. . . ."

Melody looked at me as if I was out of my mind. I was, after hearing Rushton's last comment, and then after sensing whatever it was between him and Mel.

I floundered in this unfamiliar water. Teddy liked John Rushton enough to save his life. And Melody: Was I getting the feeling that she liked—more than liked—John Rushton, too?

I started in again, trying to sound casual. "Maybe I'd like to try one of those highballs."

"Well, okeydokey! Coming right up," Melody said.

"That's the spirit, doll," said Louie. She opened a cigarette case and thrust it in my direction. "Ciggie?"

Good heavens. What had I just done? And why? When what I needed to do was go into the privacy of my room and read Teddy's journal, now I'd trapped myself here, with these two and a glass of alcohol.

What an idiot I was. Wrong, wrong, wrong.

*　*　*

Melody showed me how the hidden liquor cabinet worked. Push here, slide there—a false wall of bookshelves slid away and revealed bottle after bottle. It looked like enough alcohol to run an entire speakeasy. The cabinet was a dark place, a hoard, a great place for hiding secrets of any kind.

Giggling, she pulled out a small flask and showed me how she stowed it in her garter for excursions on the town. And she mixed my beverage with an expert hand, telling me how soda water provided the base and when you ordered soda water it was a wink-wink clue that you carried a flask.

My first taste of alcohol, in the form of a highball, was so unpleasant that I let the ice drift in the glass and pretended to sip, while Lou and Melody gossiped away. The concoction I held in my hand made my throat burn and my eyes water. Honestly, it tasted like ammonia.

I'd heard that some alcohols were, in fact, not far from cleaning fluid. That in the early days of the Prohibition, when desperate folks took matters into their own hands and built homemade stills, some of the resulting potions could kill a body. Crazy people distilled all sorts of stuff: rubbing alcohol, camphor, bichloride of mercury, embalming fluid. Innocent young girls from the sticks drinking liquor lost all inhibitions and all decency. They drank until they were stupid. Some went blind. Some went mad. Not a few died.

Melody then opened a bottle of champagne for herself and Lou, popping the cork so that it hit the ceiling and the champagne foamed out of the bottle so that she had to guzzle. She held the bottle by the neck and laughed like crazy as she swiped her mouth with the back of her hand. I watched as she drank more than her share, and watched as Louie took a more circumspect approach. Lou's glass was never empty, yet she guarded herself. She was clever, that girl.

As I had expected, there was nothing I could say or do to stop Melody. I could only sit and watch and bite my tongue, feeling for my aunt, who was so full of worry and, I thought, for good reason.

The afternoon skimmed past. Melody turned on the radio, searching until she found a station that played slow jazz, then she swayed around the room to the rhythm. The setting sun cast a rosy glow down the hallway from the living room windows into the foyer, and we switched on the library table lamps. Melody and Louie gossiped about some club up in Harlem that played a wild kind of jazz; Melody wanted to take me there, although Louie seemed to have other ideas.

Once, while Melody and Louie were deep in gossip, I went to the bookshelf, where I'd marked which book Rushton had been reading. Why did I feel surprise at Proust? Surprise and a twinge of satisfaction.

At some point I began to smell the dinner that my aunt's cook prepared, savory smells drifting through the apartment that made my mouth water. Melody may have smelled it, too, but not with pleasure; without warning she stood. "Must go potty." She staggered out of the library.

Louie murmured, "Probably time to be sick." I put my drink on the table.

Lou said, "So, you're Teddy's baby sister? Sorry about what happened to him."

I stared at my hands.

Lou leaned over toward me. "Reason I'm here? I've been told to invite you along tonight, take you out on the town."

"By whom?"

"My guy. Daniel Connor."

My hands lay folded in my lap, fingers laced tight. "Why should Daniel Connor have an interest in me?" I thought I knew, but wasn't about to let on to her.

"I have no idea. He's a nice guy, that's all."

Not so nice to my pops, I wanted to say, but didn't. Connor's hateful, I wanted to say, but couldn't. Especially not to her. Because I did like her.

She looked at me with those large eyes. "Danny doesn't tell me everything, doll. But I gather you're important." She gazed at me for a minute. "What'd you do, get ahold of some dope on some high roller?"

"I don't know what you're talking about."

She stared at me, her eyes narrowed. "Danny's taken an interest in you. He wants to introduce you around, or so he tells me. Wants to show you the town, you being a pretty thing and all."

I was so startled I picked up my drink and took another sip, avoiding her eyes. I stared into the glass, the half-melted ice cubes floating like small barges. "My pops sent me here. Pops said he was hoping that Uncle Bert and Aunt Mary would help me meet the right people, help me find a husband. I know that's not true—well, maybe partly. But that's not why I'm here, really." Maybe that one little sip had loosened my tongue. I couldn't tell Louie the truth, not her, since I was really here so that Pops could keep me away from Louie's guy, Daniel Connor.

What would Pops say if he knew that I was making friends with Daniel Connor's moll?

"So. Your old man wants you to find a husband?" Louie laughed. "Well, he's a good father, then, looking out for his little sweetheart."

"No, you don't understand." What didn't she understand? I stammered. "I have no interest in getting married."

"Ah," Louie said. "You looking to score a good guy but not get married?"

I looked at her. Those eyes were big and round, but they weren't innocent. They were like giant drill bits, piercing me. And that voice, like gravel. I had the feeling she was testing me.

"No," I said.

"'No' what?"

"No, I don't want to get married. I mean, I'd like to fall in love with someone who loves me, someday. Have a family, all that. But I have other things, other dreams, plans, you know." Goodness. Now I was unloading my thoughts on Louie as if I'd known her all my life, for the second time in a matter of days.

"Do I know?"

I rushed on, more and more heedless. "I want to be a writer. Maybe a reporter. Something to do with words and books, anyway. I want to be independent. Have my own place. I want to work. Not like my ma, who's slaved away all her life taking care of the family." I looked at my hands, twisted them in my lap. "And there are other things I want to do, need to do, some things I have to take care of. Like Teddy . . ." I stopped myself. Yes, that little bit of alcohol had surely loosened my tongue.

Louie sat back. "If I could offer a bit of advice."

I nodded, pinching my too-loose lips together.

"Don't go saying anything about your brother around Danny." She pursed her lips as her eyes grazed the floor, as she seemed to retreat in thought.

I nodded again, swallowed hard. "Okay."

She lifted her chin toward my drink. "You're smarter than your cousin."

Good, a change of subject. But I thought, Are you sure? I sighed. "I'm supposed to watch out for her."

Louie snorted with laughter. "Good luck. Melody's on a bit of a tear. Been that way for a few years now. Doesn't know what she really wants—unlike you, doll—so she dives into the sauce. I suppose it's her way of escaping." Louie sat forward, put her elbows on her knees, rested her chin on her fists. "It's tough, these days." She was looking away from me, musing, talking almost to herself. "A girl doesn't know what to do anymore. We have it all free and easy, right? Can do whatever we want. Wear whatever we want, smoke, drink, stay up all night, go necking with some stranger, have it all. There are no more scandals: why, we're all scandalous.

Even nutty Zelda Fitzgerald can dance in a fountain and drink like a sailor and everybody thinks she's charming. Your pops is wrong. It's not about finding the right husband. It's about finding yourself. Isn't it?" Louie looked up at me, her eyes bright. "What do you really think, doll?"

Maybe my openness had unleashed her own. I shook my head.

She watched me. "You said it yourself, about finding love someday. Is it all about the happily ever after, even if you do make something of yourself? I dunno. What do we want, really? Don't we all want the happy home? The nice little hubby and the couple of sweet kids? And the freedom, the independence? Happily ever after. Yeah, we want it all." She leaned back again. "You do, dollface. You just said so."

I tucked my hands beneath my knees and leaned toward her. "What about you?"

Louie stared at me for a minute with those big eyes, then she reared back in a laugh. "Sure, I do. Of course. I want a nice happy home."

"With Daniel Connor?"

She stopped laughing and looked at me sharp. "Daniel," she said in a slow drawl, "is not the marrying kind."

"Then, why? Why stay with him?"

For the first time, Louie seemed vulnerable. She looked away from me, fidgeted, tugged at the curls that hugged the nape of her neck, then stuck her index finger in her rope of pearls and wound the necklace around and around. She shrugged. "Lord knows."

But she sat right up and smiled, the act back in place. "I must love him something wicked." And she peered at me. "You wouldn't try to steal him now, would you?"

I heard the edge in her voice; I shook my head and made my voice firm. "No. Never."

"Good, then. We can be friends." And she flashed me that smile with only a hint of wariness.

I heard the elevator door clang and the voices of my aunt and uncle as they entered the apartment. Melody came back into the library. "Well. That was titillating." She looked better, freshly made up, her lips a dangerous red. "Everyone's home, and the limo'll be here at eight." She looked from Louie to me. "I'm starved. What are you waiting for? Shall we eat?"

CHAPTER 17

Lou

She had this funny thing going on, Jo Winter. She was innocent but savvy. She thought she knew what she wanted, but it was stuff right out of a fairy tale. I wanted to shake her and say, "Wake up, baby."

But I also wanted to believe. I wanted to believe in happy ever after. I wanted to believe Jo was as innocent as she seemed. I was that innocent, once upon a time. I'd traded up.

John Rushton, he believed only in what he'd lost. I'd heard about the bombing; we all did. It was the time of the "Red Scare"—the "Reds" were coming to set off a revolution here in the good old U.S. of A. Whoever they were, they didn't get very far. You fellows put out a reward for the Wall Street bombings: $20,000. You boys have some money in the bank, right, Detective? Gosh. That reward is almost as much as Danny paid for the mansion.

But then you arrested those Italians, Sacco and Vanzetti, and now they'll hang, so everyone's saying, even though there's no good reason to believe they were part of it.

It's interesting how no one ever claimed that reward. Who knows who the bombers really were? Maybe we won't ever know. But blaming a couple of Italians? No different than blaming a couple of Irish. Or a couple of Negroes. Or blaming me—oh, don't put on that face, Detective. You know what I'm saying.

And in case you don't, here's a taste. It was like that time when Charlie and me were out on the town and we ran into one of Charlie's friends, some guy he'd played in a band with. Okay, so the guy was a Negro. So what?

There we were, on the street, having a nice conversation about the latest nightclubs, when some goon walks up and spits on the other fellow's shoe.

Charlie, his face went sour. I got real fearful there would be a fight.

But Tooley—that was his name, the Negro bass player—he just bends down and wipes that spit off his shoe with a bright red hanky he pulls from his pocket.

"Some folks have a hard time seeing in this light," he said, squinting at the sun.

"I'd be happy to go break his neck," Charlie said. His dark eyes lit on the spitting guy, off laughing with his pals liked he'd scored something big.

"Now, what you want to do that for, son?" asked Tooley. "You've got a gig tonight, and a fat lip won't help your tuneless playing improve." And he laughed, at least with his teeth, and tossed that spoiled hanky in the nearest garbage can.

And we moved on, then, Tooley in his direction and we in ours, and Charlie, I had to rein him in when we passed those boys so he wouldn't take revenge for Tooley's insult.

There are people who would rather take revenge than claim any amount of fortune. John Rushton, when he lost his brother, he kind of lost his soul. He didn't believe any more than I did that it was the Reds that pulled that bombing, but I could tell he wanted to find out who it was. John Rushton was out for revenge.

Oh, revenge. It drives the world, you know? From the first time some kid pushes you down on the playground, or some flirt steals your boyfriend, you think about revenge. About getting even. It's the Hatfields and the McCoys, all over. It's always the same: step up by stepping on top of the guy who once knocked you down.

Little did I know back then how mixed up we all were—Danny, Charlie, Jo, Teddy, Rushton, me—with revenge. Or how that would all turn out.

But I sure watched Jo like a hawk, especially right after we met, 'cause I could see what might happen to her. Heck, it happened to me. All that sweetness. Danny liked sweetness, even if he didn't like me appearing to be dumb. He could easily like that sweet Jo Winter, which made me want to shake her, but hard.

Yeah, buster, I was sweet once. So I knew. Life has a way of burning the sweetness right out of you and setting you up to take revenge.

And don't think for one second, Detective, that that was a confession. I'm just telling you a story.

CHAPTER 18

MAY 22, 1925

About the spectacular dry raids of last week. There is nothing special to be said except that a number of naughty cabaret owners just won't be allowed to sell liquor any more.
—From the column "Lipstick," The New Yorker, January 1, 1927

JO

I'd ridden in a limo only once, when Ma and Pops and I crowded into a big black thing that took us to Teddy's memorial service. Now I lounged with Melody and Louie in the Daimler sent for us from Daniel Connor, being driven by a quiet dark-skinned fellow named Sam who was wearing a gray uniform and hat. I was buoyed by the other girls' high spirits.

That is, until Louie leaned across the empty space between our seats and said to me, "You know, you could be the next Lois Long."

"Pardon me?"

"Lois Long. She's that smart young gal over at *Vanity Fair*. She parties all night and writes theater reviews during the day. You even kind of look like her." Louie regarded me, her head tilted in appraisal.

I had no intention of partying all night, but writing theater reviews sounded interesting. "She gets paid for writing?"

"Oh, boy, does she. And she's one heck of a writer. She's the new woman, all over." The new woman. Now Louie's observation made me uneasy.

I thought about Danny Connor's offer. My dream future in exchange for Teddy.

I sat back against the leather. Louie looked out the window of the limo as it cruised downtown, lights of the city flashing by. Melody reapplied her lipstick with the aid of a small compact. The night was cool; a front had come in behind the rain. Melody and Louie were done up in fur jackets, and Melody had lent me a fur caplet. I dug my chin into the soft mink, the first I'd ever worn.

Ma had a beat-up old fur coat—raccoon—and Pops swore he would one day buy her a "real" fur. And, he said, he'd drape her in real pearls. Before Teddy disappeared Pops would say to him, "When you're a big shot, we'll have everything we ever wanted." When Teddy didn't become a big shot, Pops changed his tune to "Prohibition's gonna make us rich."

The only thing the Prohibition had done was to get Pops mixed up with Danny Connor, and a convoluted web of secrets, a web in which I felt more and more entangled.

One week ago I was Josephine Anne Winter, high school student, whose ma had a ratty old raccoon coat and whose pops dealt bootleg liquor under the cover of his small grocery shop. I was an old-fashioned girl in a middy blouse and a too-long skirt, with dark hair that reached her waist. Now I was Jo Winter, riding through the streets of New York at night in a chauffeured limousine with a couple of honest-to-goodness flappers and sporting a mink and a bob and a short silk dress.

I twisted; the scar on my back itched. I wanted to help my family. But I didn't want to marry some rich guy I couldn't stand. Wouldn't it be better if I got a real job, like that Lois person? Went back, finished school, went to college? I twisted a curl of hair around my finger, pursed my lips.

The lights of lower Manhattan flashed by; we were in a sweet cocoon, riding in this limo. I was closing in on my dreams. I was having fun. I liked my new look. I could be a "new woman" and make my own way, make scads of money, enough for me and my ma and pops.

What would Teddy say if he could see me now: bravo, or boo?

For the first time, I didn't want to know Teddy's answer. Because, looking over to the front seat, to where Sam's dark eyes were fixed on the road ahead, never once glancing back—that would be too forward—I knew what Teddy would say. I knew.

"Here we are," Louie announced.

We double-parked in front of a brick town house, and Sam hastened around the car to let us out. The street was empty. You wouldn't have known there was any kind of club around here, it was such a dingy place. A few streetlamps glowed like orange balls, reflecting in the puddles. The street smelled like wet cement.

I stood on the sidewalk waiting for the other girls, watching Sam as he moved back around to the driver's seat, then pulled the car down the street to find a spot to park. My eyes followed the car, and then I saw something—saw someone, not Sam, but someone else—standing on the sidewalk opposite.

The light, casting shadows, hid his face; but it had to be. Just like earlier that day, on the street after I'd met Charlie, the blond hair. Those eyes. I was sure it was Teddy. My muscles all went tight. I stared into the chilly dark, straining my eyes, but he was so deep in the shadows, could it be? And then as the thrill filled me I thought, Yes, it is, just like earlier, only this time he was wearing his familiar jacket and hat, and it was the way he stood with his legs splayed; it was him, standing just outside the circle of light. It was Teddy. My hand flew to my mouth as I tried to suppress a cry. I wanted to run to him.

"Doll? What's up?" Louie touched my shoulder, and I whirled to face her. "Whoa. You look like you've see a ghost."

I turned back and pointed, but the street was empty.

Melody arranged her wrap, fussing with the catches. "Can we go in? This street is giving me the creeps."

I stared back at the shadows, searching, but they were empty.

"Come on, Jo."

I trailed them, glancing back. Nothing. No one.

Louie led us down a flight of stairs to a door behind an iron fence that looked for all the world like a basement entrance to the tailored brownstone above it. We went inside and walked down a narrow, dim hallway to a single wall lamp that cast an anemic glow next to the only other door.

Louie knocked, and the door opened a crack and then swung open all the way, the beefy man behind it sporting a broad grin.

"Evening! Nice to see you again, Miss Lou. And ladies." He eyed us as we shuffled, awkward, behind Lou. He looked us up and down, seemed to think that we passed some kind of test. He stepped aside. "Welcome to Walter's place!"

"Who's Walter?" I whispered to Melody.

She shrugged. "Don't know his last name. Does it matter?"

We were ushered into a joint so swank, it was hard to imagine it belonged to the hallway through which we'd entered.

"Only been set up a couple of weeks. Would you believe it?" Louie waved her hand around the dim room. "Some swell guy with a wad of dough and a whole lotta friends."

Plush velvet banquettes lined the walls; scattered round tables with soft chairs filled all but the dance floor; recessed in the far wall sat a stage on which a small band played, accompanying a blond woman who was wearing a dress the color of a ripe tomato and singing "All Alone." Cigarette girls in skimpy outfits and jaunty caps paced the floor between tables, and couples leaned toward each other over their iced drinks. Smoke rose in spirals; the ceiling was adrift in clouds of smoke. The smells of tobacco and whiskey mixed with perfume and aftershave and hair tonic. Six or seven couples fox-trotted on the dance floor, their bodies so close together I had to take a breath.

A speakeasy.

"All alone, I'm so all alone
There is no one else but you. . . ."

"Come on, girls." Louie led the way to a far corner booth, already occupied. Three men in tuxedo jackets slouched in the booth, all of them smiling, teeth gleaming in the semidark.

Louie slid into the seat next to one man, who drew his arm over her shoulder and gave her a kiss, right on the lips.

Daniel Connor. He looked up at me, those gray eyes sharp as steel daggers. "Miss Winter. Such a pleasure to see you again." His black hair was slicked off his forehead with brilliantine. Louie stiffened as he spoke, watching me.

What would Pops say now, if he knew I was here, with this man—the very man he'd sent me to New York to avoid, and who had already found me, twice now? I could be stepping into a trap, or I could be helping Pops. Should I tell Danny Connor that it was all a lie—that Teddy wasn't dead, that Teddy and I, we'd faked his death a year ago? I twisted my fingers into the fur around my neck.

Uncertain of the right move, I felt uneasy and alone.

Connor's steel eyes fixed on mine, and again I felt that lurch inside me, as if he reeled me in on a tight wire, as a slow smile crept across his face, a smile Lou couldn't see because she was watching me.

Melody slid right into the booth next to the other men and promptly crooked her finger at one of the serving girls, who brought her ice in a glass and a bottle filled with brown liquid.

I fidgeted with my wrap, standing by the table, the eyes of the men on me, their too-broad smiles, feeling the weight of the room and the people all around me and their moody desires snaking through the chair legs and table legs and roping around me in invisible coils, drifting up my torso like the smoke.

Louie said to me, "Honey, you can't stand there all night. Besides," she leaned around me to glance at the stage, "you're blocking the view." She waved her hand.

I turned to see. And there he was, Charlie O'Keefe, playing a horn with those dark eyes of his closed, his broad shoulders straining with his effort to make the music, and make it he did. He pitched that horn high and low; he turned to face the other musicians and then back again to the crowd; he matched the crooner and her full-bodied voice. I stood mesmerized until the song ended and the crowd burst with applause.

Then I ducked my head and plunked down on the nearest chair,

JANET FOX

because I didn't want Charlie O'Keefe to see me in the midst of this fast crowd. I wanted him to think of me as the nice girl he'd met in the park who didn't go to speakeasies.

"Good girl, cuz," said Melody. "Now all you need is a little ammunition." She slid a glass across the table at me. I stared at it.

"Danny, you weren't just flapping your gums," said one of the men, who sat to my left. He had a nose like a badger, long and sharp. "She's a sweetheart. A real looker."

"Quit it, Neil," Connor said, his voice a low growl.

That was when I realized that badger-nosed Neil was referring to me. His grin had broadened, appearing carnivorous. I looked him square in the eye. "I'm right here. You can speak directly to me."

"And she's got spark!"

I sensed, rather than saw, Connor's surprise. It didn't matter; I could stand up for myself. I went on. "If you want to speak to me, speak. Because I can spark that silly grin right off your face." My own face flushed with the heat of my emotion, and I moved my eyes away and stared down at the white tablecloth.

Louie leaned toward me over the table and said, her lips against my ear, "Sister, you have just become my personal hero. I've never liked that guy."

But the two men laughed as if I was the funniest thing they'd seen and heard in a long time. "Sweetheart," said the one called Neil, "you could be the next It Girl. The future Clara Bow. You've got the looks, and you've got the spunk. You could be a star."

It was the second time in an hour that I'd been told I could be the next someone else. Except that what I wanted was to be the next me, Jo Winter. If only I could figure out who I was.

And then Charlie O'Keefe was there, standing at the table, standing right by my side.

"Hey, Charlie!" Louie tapped Charlie's arm, and then my earlier suspicions were confirmed. O'Keefe: they were sister and brother.

"Hiya, sis. Hello, Mr. Connor." Charlie nodded, deferential.

I wasn't supposed to know Charlie, and I hoped he played the game, too. Because now I was convinced I was right on another score: Danny Connor had hired him to follow me.

Introductions were made all around, and I discovered that the other man's name was Ryan. When Charlie and I shook hands, I said, pretending, "You play the saxophone quite well."

"Why, thank you, miss," he said. His eyes had the glint of mischief. "But it ain't a sax. It's a cornet. Kind of like a trumpet." He winked. So I could keep a secret, but he struggled with the concept. It shouldn't have surprised me. "How are you enjoying the place here?"

I pulled my wrap tight around my shoulders; I hadn't been willing to give it up. It was as if I hadn't committed to staying. "It's fine. Nice."

"Well, we'll try to give you something real nice to remember it by," he said with a grin.

I liked Charlie, even if he did work for Connor. He was sweet and innocent. I bet he had no clue why Connor wanted me followed. I wished, in that instant, I could jump into Charlie's arms, safe and secure from this menacing man sitting opposite me, one arm trailing over Lou's shoulder, but whose eyes were fixed on me. I wished I could run right out the door with Charlie, run away and never look back. Except I would look back. Those gray eyes of Connor's were like big steel traps, and he was not about to let me go.

Charlie was a sweet guy. Danny Connor, he was . . . something else again.

"There is no one else but you. . . ."

Louie slid from the booth. "Charlie. Come with me. I gotta talk to you about something." She turned to Connor. "Be right back, honey." Then she glanced from Connor to me as she grabbed Charlie's arm and dragged him away.

"So long!" Charlie called over his shoulder.

Melody was deep in conversation with Ryan and Neil, flirting, giggling, touching. The men were mesmerized. She tossed her head and dropped her eyes and pouted her lips, and left them no doubt as to her intentions. I couldn't watch. I stared at my still-untouched drink, at the table, at my fingernails, at anything except Melody—and the only other man at the table, whose steel eyes were now fixed on me, boring holes right through me.

Glasses clinked with ice; smoke drifted overhead; chatter and laughter filled every corner. I wouldn't meet his eyes, because I feared what I'd see there. I feared him, and what he wanted from me, because I wasn't about to give him Teddy, even if it would help save Pops. Even if he offered me all my dreams on a silver plate.

The ice in the glass in front of me slipped and melted, sending waves of water through the alcohol. I wouldn't look, no, not into those mesmerizing eyes.

"Miss Winter, it is truly a pleasure," he repeated, and I couldn't help it.

I looked.

CHAPTER 19

LOU

I hated Danny when he started eyeballing her. I hated her, too, but I can be forgiven for that because I didn't know what was really going on. I guess I didn't have any of my tingly feelings at the time because I was too busy having other ones.

Like a movie star already, that's what she looked like. And I was sure I knew how she felt. I'm not an idiot. And gosh, I could hardly blame her.

I pulled Charlie aside to talk to him about his rent money, to make sure he had enough and all, but I was stuck on what was happening back at the table. "You see that girl? That Jo Winter?"

He grinned. "You bet I did. She's the bee's knees."

"Yeah? Well, she better keep her mitts off Danny."

Charlie looked like he'd swallowed something big. "Why would she be interested in Danny?"

"Look at him."

Charlie looked. He nodded, real slow. "She's real pretty."

I stuck my elbow into his ribs so hard he wheezed. "Not her. Him."

It took him a second. "Lou, I know he's a charmer. Everyone knows that. Gosh, I've been trying to be like Danny Connor since I was fourteen years old."

That shook me. "You don't want to be like Danny. You don't." I looked back at the table and found my eyes stinging. "You think she's pretty enough to steal him?"

Charlie put his arm around my shoulder. "Sis, I think you are too pretty and wonderful to even worry about stuff like that."

Charlie's a saint, I'll give him that. But me?

I was ready to kill someone when I thought something started happening between Jo and Danny. I wanted to find a way to make him suffer. Or make her suffer. Sure, why not? I thought about that. Thinking, Detective, is not a crime.

But one thing for sure: I'm no saint. And no, that is not a confession.

CHAPTER 20

MAY 22, 1925

I lean to the belief that these [psychic] effects are produced by an intelligent force, which can manifest itself mentally and physically to some people under certain circumstances. . . . I do believe in spiritualism.
—Letter from Howard Thurston to Harry Houdini, 1922

JO

Daniel Connor leaned toward me. "Neil may be brash, but he is correct in his assessment." He took a sip of his drink, moistening his lips with his tongue. "That's a most attractive new look, which I neglected to remark on this morning. Your new hairstyle is quite becoming."

I had a hard time breathing. And it was impossible for me to look away. Daniel Connor's steel eyes had hooked me again.

"You know, Josephine, I was a friend to your brother. To Teddy."

I stopped breathing altogether. "You? A friend?" Connor had come to the memorial, but I'd thought that was because he and Pops were in business together. First Rushton, now Connor. It seemed that Teddy had a number of surprising friends.

"I believe he would be happy if he could see us, right now." Our eyes were locked; I couldn't look away. "Perhaps he can. What do you think, Miss Winter?"

"I . . ."

"As I said earlier, I believe he is still with us in the flesh. I don't believe in the spirit world, myself." He smiled. "But then, Teddy was exceptional in so many ways." He leaned back again, then pulled out a cigarette case, opened it, and extended it toward me. I shook my head. He took a rolled cigarette from the case and lit it with his lighter, turning his head, exhaling. "I'd like you to come see my greenhouse out on Long Island, Miss Winter."

"Your greenhouse?"

"Yes. Not at the moment, of course." He laughed, a smooth and satiny laugh that matched his slick hair. "Sometime soon."

I had to speak, because it was the only thing that afforded me a breath. "What do you grow?"

"Orchids," he said, and smoothed the napkin on the table between us, a delicate gesture.

"Orchids." I hesitated. "I know what they are, of course. But I've never seen one other than in a corsage."

"We will remedy that." He watched me with narrowed eyes. "I have a passion for them—their smell, their form. Orchids are difficult to grow. Tricky. They must be kept at the perfect temperature, perfect humidity. They won't bloom under any but the most auspicious conditions." Connor leaned across the table toward me again, and his eyes shone in the reflected light from the stage, from the candles. "I'm fascinated by puzzles. By things that are tricky to handle. Orchids are puzzles, and must be treated with a delicate hand." He paused again. "You are a puzzle, Miss Winter."

I froze, my fingers curved onto the table, fingernails resting, ready. "Really."

"You like books. You like intellectual endeavors. You like solitude." He paused. "I believe you like mysteries, as well."

How did he know so much about me?

"Ah, mysteries," he went on, gazing toward the stage, where the musicians were gathering again. He stretched out his hand, taking in the room. "But you don't care for this, this kind of a place. Do you, Miss Winter?"

I held still.

"You don't like all this, and yet"—he leaned closer to me, across the table, his arms resting between us—"you are not your brother, are you? You are not perfect Theodore Winter. If, that is, Theodore Winter was—is—actually perfect, which I believe is debatable. You have some quirks of your own. As I said, you are a puzzle."

Connor was close enough to me now that I caught the brilliantine shine on his hair, smelled his expensive cologne. "Remember what I said this morning. I'm looking for Teddy, or for something he might have left. It's most important to me. I can make all your dreams come true, Miss Winter. And help your family in the bargain. Or rather, keep your family from harm. All you need to do is say the word." His lips curled up in a smile that showed his teeth. "Two weeks, Josephine. You have two weeks."

"Hey." It was Louie. She looked from me to Connor, and for the second time since meeting her, I sensed her vulnerability. She sat down next to Connor as he made room for her. But her eyes were on me, accusing.

He offered Louie a cigarette, and when he lit it, the lighter flashed. I jumped, and Lou saw my reaction.

"Don't like fire?" she asked, inhaling, the tip of her cigarette a red dot.

"I don't care for smoke," I lied. My back burned, and the scar chafed.

From the darkness behind me a man grabbed my shoulder, and I jumped again. "Wanna dance, sweetie?"

Connor bristled.

I shook my head. "No. Thanks anyway."

"Aw, come on, honey. Just one!"

In one swift and leonine movement Connor was out of his seat and had dragged the man to the other side of the room, placing him in the clutches of the doorkeep; Connor returned before I could blink.

"My apologies," Connor said, adjusting his jacket and tie.

"Thanks." I sat back in the chair, flattened.

"Well," said Louie. Her eyes looked bruised now as she watched me. "How noble of you, hon."

I breathed hard; I stood. I wanted out of there. I had to get away from him, from her. I felt as though I was sinking into a pit. I abandoned my promise to my aunt; Melody, drowning in the liquor and the men, was on her own. I'd lost all curiosity about speakeasies.

Without another word I turned and marched across the room, now throbbing with the beat of a new tune, Charlie's cornet gracing the high notes and keeping synchrony with the singer. Then I pushed past the beefy doorkeep and shoved into the gloomy, dank hallway and straight on out into the night.

The street was black as pitch as my eyes tried to adjust.

I feared that he—Daniel Connor—would follow me. I had the

feeling that, in the same swift and leonine fashion he had dealt
with the stranger in the speakeasy, he would follow me, his prey,
out into the dark.

I pulled the caplet tighter around my shoulders and looked up
the street. There. At the far end, close to the avenue with its noise
and lights, I saw our limo waiting. I started down the sidewalk, the
click, click of my heels on concrete the only sound.

But then I heard another, a different sound. Footsteps, heavy,
behind me. Connor? I stepped a little faster, my heart keeping
time, and clutched my arms tight around my chest. The sound
behind me drew closer, the footsteps faster.

The limo was far down the street; it seemed a million miles
away, and I walked as fast as I could walk without running, hearing
the footsteps behind me, gaining.

I broke into a trot.

I reached the limo, found it locked, pounded on the window,
praying that Sam hadn't gone off to his own joint; but he was
sleeping at the wheel, and I saw his wide eyes as he started and
turned toward me, just as a hand grabbed my arm.

I yelled, surprise and fear mingled.

And then came chaos. Sirens blared, and police cars, paddy
wagons—a whole string of them—roared from around the corner.
As the lights swept over the limo and me, the hand that gripped
my arm let go. I turned to see the back of a man sprinting into the
darkness away from me, while the noise of the raid—the shouts and
slamming doors—swelled around me. I looked at the brownstone,
and it was as if rats were abandoning a sinking ship. People poured
from windows and doors, running in all directions away from the
speakeasy while the police shouted orders and grabbed whoever

came within reach, which really meant whoever was drunk enough to stagger within reach.

Sam came around the car. "Get in, miss. Now."

I sat in the car and stared out the window. The hand on my arm hadn't been Daniel Connor's. I knew that grip.

It had been Teddy, I was certain. Like Connor, I didn't believe in spirits, either. I believed in Teddy.

I huddled, shaking all over, in the backseat while Sam waited with the engine running. The door popped open and Melody and Louie tumbled in, laughing hysterically, followed by Daniel Connor, silent and slick.

Connor rapped on the inside window of the limo. "Not too fast, Sam. We don't want to draw attention."

We pulled away from the curb, slow, and I looked out the back, at the street teeming with drunken people, police, lights fanning the building, and I let myself shake, now, still feeling the grip of a hand on my arm.

"Such a shame," Melody said with a pout. "That was a swell joint."

* * *

I remembered the fire, the flames reaching for me and me helpless to stop them, my voice choked with smoke as I tried to scream but could not. It had been Teddy, Teddy's hand on my arm that had pulled me to safety from the flames that afternoon. He'd rescued me, had been my hero.

Teddy's hand on my arm.

I locked the door to my room and turned on a light. The quiet was deep, even the city noises hushed. We'd arrived home a few minutes earlier; Melody had stumbled off to bed, while I knew what I had to do now.

I had to find out what Teddy had to say about all of it. Maybe I could intervene for Pops. Save my family from Danny Connor by giving him Teddy's journal entries, without giving him Teddy.

I threw my wrap and clutch on the bed and dug into the bottom drawer, and pulled out the journal. I sat cross-legged on my bed with the journal in my lap. I untied it, fumbling with the leather cord. But before I could open it, a frightening new idea took shape in my mind.

I could save my family another way, couldn't I? Make myself attractive to Danny Connor, make him like me. He already did; I wasn't stupid. And then, when he liked me enough—what? Beg? Or not give him Teddy at all, but give him me.

I shuddered. Goose bumps freckled my skin, and a sour taste rose into my mouth.

This personal sacrifice would be my last resort. I'd have to uncover as much information as I could, but in the end . . .

The more I learned, the more danger I'd be in; but the more I knew, the more I could help. I prayed I'd uncover some bit of information, just enough to send Danny away from my family. And away from me.

I'd left a ribbon to mark the page where I'd stopped reading the night before, Teddy's writing so cramped that my eyes watered.

> October 3, 1918
> I keep dreaming about Willie O., how that bullet
> went into his eye. One minute I'm looking at him

and we're laughing, and then the next thing I know he's only got one eye and it's fixed on a place I don't want to see.

All I want to see are Lizzy's fields, brown, green, yellow, purple.

October 4
What are we fighting over? It makes no sense. Surrounded. Many dead. This is a bad deal.

October 4
If I don't get out of here, I'll go mad. I'd sell my soul to get out of here.

October 5
I've decided. It doesn't matter anymore. Nothing I do makes any difference—except to get someone killed.

I've done it—make any bargain I can make. Come take my soul. I'm dead already.

We've been in the same trench for what seems forever. I know every rock, every root, every hunk of wet dirt. My feet and hands are rotten. So many dead. We're about done in. Nothing matters. Nothing except getting home. Home to Ma, to Pops, to Josie.

I stopped reading and sat back against my headboard. I lifted the journal again, my eyes blurring.

October 5
I see my opening and I'm taking it tonight.

October 10
Going home. Pops will be pleased. Actions deemed
heroic. Saved 5 fellows including Rushton, my CO.
Really, didn't mean to. Was trying to get out, run,
and I took a wrong turn. German guy never had a
chance, I was moving so fast, came up behind him,
gut instinct took over. Later shown he had grenade,
would've killed them all and me, too.

And I think about that German guy, how I knifed
him. Did he have parents, a sister?

I'm a coward, not a hero. But Rushton thinks I
am. Says he owes me. Says he'll make it up to me.

So this smart rich guy? Think he means it?

Heck. I've got to take him at his word. What else
do I have? I've lost everything else. Gave it away. My
soul, everything.

I sat back again and rubbed my eyes. Rushton. Rushton had
been telling the truth, as he saw it. Now I understood why Teddy
was so lost after he came home. He felt a failure, a fake. That
would never do for Teddy. That was not honorable or right. That
was not the hero's way.

Maybe this is why he didn't give me his journal right away. He
didn't want me knowing that he wasn't a true hero.

I got out of bed and went to my dresser, sat on the floor, and
pulled out the medal boxes.

Purple Heart.

Silver Star.

Victory.

Teddy didn't feel worthy of these honors. I touched each of the medals, which he'd never worn, never removed from the boxes once they'd been awarded. Pops had been all over town about Teddy, bragging and puffing. But never with Teddy. Now I knew why.

But I still believed he was a hero. Teddy had pulled me from the fire. He'd rescued me when no one else knew I was even in there, but somehow he knew. He saw the flaming tar paper drift down to land on my back as I huddled there, screaming but not screaming. He knew and ran to me and grabbed my arm and pulled me out, rolling me over and over to put out the fire, saved me just when the flames blew up into a frenzy, just before the whole thing was a conflagration. Chester standing by with that lighter and looking, for once, shocked at something he'd done. Teddy had heard me even when my voice could not be heard by anyone else.

Teddy was *my* hero. He was my heart, my victory, my star. Nothing else mattered, except that he was my hero and I would keep my promise to him.

I could no longer force my stinging eyes to stay open; I'd have to read the rest of his words in the morning. I stuffed the medal boxes and journal and scarf deep under the sweaters in the bottom drawer and crawled back into bed. I turned out my light and lay back against the sheets. As I drifted into exhausted sleep, I thought I heard Teddy's voice.

Something else matters, Josie-girl. And because of that, I must still protect you.

CHAPTER 21

LOU

I didn't say one word in the car. Not one, all the way home. I thought
that would make him suffer, but no. Because he didn't say one word,
either, and the silence was killing me.

When Sam pulled the car up to the door and hopped around to let
us out onto the wet paving, Danny turned. "It's late. I'll see you in the
morning." And he walked right in that front door, leaving me standing
there with Sam and my wide-open mouth.

"May I get you anything, miss?"

"No, Sam, thanks." I hoped that over the soft splashing of the fountain
behind us he wouldn't hear the sob that caught in my throat.

Later I lay in the dark, wide-awake in my own room, alone, for hours.

Once upon a time there was this poor young Irish girl who met a
handsome prince who swept her off her feet. But when the Irish girl grew

older, the prince's roving eye began to light elsewhere . . . until a new young girl arrived to steal the prince's heart.

I took out my diamond bracelet, the one thing he didn't make me lock up, and snapped it on my wrist there in the dark room, the light from outside sneaking in and making those diamonds flash like a million suns. Those diamonds would fetch a pretty penny. But what would Danny say when he didn't see it on my wrist? I left it on, in the dark, in my room, the diamonds biting at my wrist.

As you can see, Detective, those diamonds were not the issue. I'm getting to that part.

CHAPTER 22

MAY 23, 1925

Almost since girlhood, beautiful Mrs. Philip Lydig has been an unquestioned leader of New York's ultra-smart society. Now for the first time Mrs. Lydig proceeds to turn the spot-light on that society— telling in great detail why she finds it futile, false and corrupt.
— "Mrs. Philip Lydig Reveals Secrets of New York Society," <u>The Deseret News</u>, September 10, 1926

JO

Next morning I rose later than usual. My aunt was home, so I wouldn't be able to avoid her, nor could I get back to the journal until my eyes could focus.

She joined me at the breakfast table, as I poured a fourth round of coffee into my cup, trying to snap my system awake. I couldn't meet her eyes.

"Well," she said, her voice weary, "it must have been quite an adventure."

"We weren't out that late. The place was raided." I saw her alarm and strove to calm her. "Daniel Connor was there. He got us all out." I didn't want to tell her about that hand on my arm.

"Josephine? What about Melody? Were you able to talk to her?"

I shook my head. "Aunt Mary, I don't know what I can do. Melody's got a mind of her own."

Aunt Mary sighed, her shoulders slumped. "If she'd only meet the right man. Settle down."

Pops's voice echoed in my head. As if marriage would solve everything, even if the guy had money. "I'm not sure she's ready for that. She's having fun."

My aunt rested her hands before her, folded, on the table. "I think you might be wrong. She might not be having as much fun as it seems."

Nor was I. I took a gulp of coffee, not sure what to say. At this moment, all I wanted was the sweet comfort and quiet of my own home. The traffic noises outside were aggravating. The smell of diesel exhaust rose up through the open windows, and dust and debris filled the air; New York City right now was getting on my nerves. I supposed anything would get on my nerves at the moment, frayed with sleep deprivation as they were.

Everything in this city happened too fast. And some things in this city hinted at a larger darkness. I wanted my old-fashioned simple life back. My flowered-wallpaper bedroom and my ma.

My aunt reached her hand out, placed it on my arm. "I'm at my wits' end. I have to ask you for one more favor."

I nodded, trying to overcome my irritation.

"I want you to find out where Melody goes in the afternoon."

"What?" Good grief. First Connor puts a tail on me, and now I'm expected to haunt Melody. Either I was really in a bad way this morning, even though I'd hardly had a sip of alcohol the night before, or this whole episode was evolving into a warped Sherlock Holmes scenario. "Follow her? Why?"

"Melody is mixed up in something. Something that will hurt

her. I can't help her. She won't speak to me. If I tried to follow her . . . Well, it's impossible. Please, Jo?"

I pushed my half-eaten breakfast away. What could I do? "I'll try." At least I knew I'd be a better sleuth than Charlie O'Keefe.

Aunt Mary left, off to do some of her charity work, while I mused on my awkward situation. There was no reading Teddy's journal again now; Adela was, once again, busy cleaning my room in a most thorough fashion. I almost thought she was there on purpose, like a spy. She was so nosy whenever I went into my room, gabbing and looking over my shoulder.

I gave up and I fetched a novel and made myself at home in the library, although my eyes kept drifting from the page and my thoughts wandered all over.

Around noon the phone rang. Melody hadn't yet emerged, Malcolm had gone out on an errand, and Adela was singing from my bathroom. I answered. "Cates residence."

"Mrs. Cates?" A woman's voice. "Or could this be Miss Melody Cates herself?"

"No, this is Mrs. Cates's niece. May I take a message?"

"Hey, there." A pause. "Her niece, huh?"

I stiffened. "Who's calling?"

"Listen, mind if I ask you a couple of questions?"

"As a matter of fact, I do mind."

"Don't hang up. I've got just a couple of questions about your cousin Melody. What do you know about the pickle she's in?"

Now I recalled my aunt on the phone yesterday and her words of only hours earlier. "I can't help you."

"Look, sweetie. I'm working on the society column for _The Times_.

How'd you like to appear in the pages? Nice photo, the works? You'd be the toast of the town. . . ."

I lowered the receiver into the cradle.

So Mel was in some kind of "pickle." Her mother thought she was mixed up in something that might hurt her. Now there was no question that I needed to find out what was going on.

Melody stirred right after the call. It never failed to amaze me how fast she could pull herself together. I sat in the library reading, watching as she passed back and forth from her room to the dining room, from her room to the living room, from her room toward the elevator.

"Bye, Melody," I called.

"Oh!" She came to the library door. "I didn't know you were in here. I'm off to do some shopping."

I made a stab at it. "Want some company?"

"It'll be boring. Have to find some hose." She tugged on her cloche, moved at a clip down the hallway, stabbed the elevator button three, four times. "Later," she called.

I waited for the door to clang shut before grabbing my own cloche, gloves, and purse, and ringing for the elevator.

"Afternoon, miss." Joey, the elevator boy, was a gap-toothed kid who should have been in school. "How are you this day?"

"Just fine, thanks." I pretended to check my purse. "You didn't happen to see which way Miss Melody headed, did you?"

"She turned left, miss. Uptown."

"Thanks."

"Want me to try to catch her for you?" His eagerness suggested his desire to get out of the elevator, anything for a mad dash along the sidewalk.

I felt bad, but there was no help for it. "No, thanks. I know where she's going. I'll find her there."

"You sure?" Poor kiddo. He looked so disappointed.

"Maybe next time." I pressed a dime into his palm, and he grinned.

Ed saluted as he held the door for me. I greeted him and paused on the sidewalk. There. Melody was about half a block away, walking briskly. I followed her, keeping a mindful distance.

She didn't pause or vary her pace, stopping only at the intersections, heading first uptown and then across to Fifth. She was following the same path I'd walked yesterday, over to Central Park.

"Miss Winter?"

Oh, honest to pete. I'd been so intent on tracking Melody, I'd been paying no attention to passersby. John Rushton appeared at my side out of nowhere.

"Mr. Rushton." I made to move on, but he stayed by my side. I fidgeted. "I'm in something of a hurry."

"I'm still hoping to finish our conversation." His eyes met mine.

I scowled at him. "Are you following me?"

He raised his brows.

Then I remembered. Chester had said he lived nearby, only around the corner. My cheeks burned. What was it about him that bothered me so? I didn't even try to be polite. "Why are you always hanging around the Cates's building?"

Now it was his turn to look flustered. He adjusted his hat, then his jacket. "I have business with your uncle."

He was lying. I could feel it. There was more to him and his relationship with Uncle Bert than met my eyes. Or was it some other relationship? I looked down the avenue in the direction

Melody had disappeared. Rushton's sense of desperation pooled around him and threatened to sweep me in its undertow.

"I really must speak to you about Teddy," he said.

"Look, I can't tell you anything. There's nothing to tell. Teddy's gone, and that's that."

He said, "I don't think that's that."

I shifted, looking off again toward where Melody had disappeared. I almost growled with frustration. "Teddy is gone, Mr. Rushton. Leave him in peace. And me as well."

Pedestrians circled us, the rush and pulse of traffic passed behind me, and I couldn't meet John Rushton's eyes. He tipped his hat. "Miss Winter."

I nodded. "Mr. Rushton." I pushed off and made my way as fast as I could along the sidewalk.

Fast, but to no avail. I'd lost Melody. I was no better a sleuth than Charlie after all. I stood at the edge of the park, where the path diverged from the street sidewalk; she was nowhere in sight. She might have followed the path, or she might have stayed on the avenue. I couldn't be sure.

What I could be sure of was that she hadn't gone out to buy hose. We were well away from the shops. Aunt Mary's suspicions were good: Melody was up to something. So. I was not the only one with a secret. Melody had one, too.

I sat down on a park bench, defeated. Pigeons fluttered around me, searching for a handout. Traffic passed in waves. Smells of soot and exhaust and garbage overwhelmed the sweeter smell of green grass from the park behind me. The dull, distant rumble of the city filled me from the ground up.

SIRENS

As far as I was concerned, it was a miserable day. I hunched my shoulders and folded my arms, trying to puzzle it out.

Melody and I were about as different as night and day. One a flapper, and the other . . . A shadow fell on me, and I started and looked up, squinting and shading my eyes. Well. I relaxed again; maybe the day was looking up a little.

"You look pretty gloomy for someone out on such a nice day," Charlie said.

"Don't get me started. Are you still following me?"

"You're my only job other than waiting tables at the moment." Maybe Charlie was getting better at his detective work. At least he kept track of me, unlike my wretched sleuthing of Melody.

"Did they arrest you last night?" I scooched over on the bench to make room for him to sit next to me.

"Nah. They give the musicians a break, most of the time. Cops figure we don't get paid enough, just like them." He grinned at me. He was a sweet guy, and those dark pools of his eyes, I wanted to drown in them. I smiled back, feeling my irritation drift away. He nudged my arm. "Want to take a walk?"

We ambled deep into the park, the street noises receding behind us. The breeze lifted and fell; I heard the squeals of childish laughter ripple over the grass from the other side of the meadow.

"So, you are Louie's brother," I said. "That's how you know Daniel Connor. And that's who employed you to follow me."

"Yup."

"Louie is pretty sweet on him."

"He treats her right. Gives her whatever she wants. He's got a swell place to live, buys her nice clothes, jewelry. . . ."

149

"Everything except a wedding ring," I said.

Charlie laughed out loud. "Lou, married? Nah. Especially not to Danny Connor."

Danny Connor. I needed him to like me so I could help Pops. I shivered. I said without thinking, "What is it about him?"

"Connor?" Charlie took my question differently, thank goodness. "He's a tough cookie, but clever. He's the boss of a gang that controls most of the East Side. Came out of the Lower East Side as a boxer, and must've knocked off a few bruisers in order to rise to the top. Runs the speakeasies and jazz joints up and down town. Had some mix-up back in 'nineteen and 'twenty when people were all scared of the Reds. Connor may be a Red, for all I know. For sure, he's a supporter of the Irish community. He's been pretty nice to me and Lou." Charlie hesitated. "He can be a little peculiar. He's got this thing about collecting."

This gave me pause. "Collecting?"

"Stuff. Artifacts, artwork. He buys all these antiques, things from Europe, has them all over his house. You should see the museum he's got there, his own private museum. It's like he needs to have all this stuff. Not that I wouldn't like living that way. Surrounded by all that nice stuff. His biggest thing is plants."

"He mentioned something about his greenhouse. About orchids."

Charlie nodded. "He gets these shipments in special crates from all over the world. He knows a thing or two, I'll give him that. The orchids, they're really delicate. Can only be sent at certain times of the year. Then he breeds his own, too. Even has one named after him, supposedly." He paused, rubbing his chin. "It's kind of spooky, that greenhouse."

It was as if a cloud had covered the sun. I stopped walking and folded my arms across my chest. "Why?"

"It's locked, and he's the only one with the key. Even Louie's been inside only once or twice. And those incidents spooked her pretty good." We'd reached the edge of one of the ponds. Ducks paddled in our direction looking for us to toss them a treat, and the water rippled in the breeze. Charlie laughed, but he sounded uneasy. "Maybe he buries his bodies under the dirt."

"Bodies!" I hugged myself tighter, feeling a chill creep up the back of my neck.

Charlie shrugged. "You can't be a tough guy and not be tough."

"How tough? Like Al Capone tough?"

"Yeah. Capone. I read some article where Capone says he's not a killer, but . . . well. Everyone says Capone's a gangster, no matter what he says." Charlie examined his hands. "Connor filled in the void here when Capone left New York for Chicago."

I shuddered. Connor was Capone dangerous. Capone thought nothing of murder. I thought about Connor's invitation to see his greenhouse. He'd let me in . . . would he let me out? "So Connor's a murderer?"

Charlie looked away, then back again. "There's no proof of that. But it's pretty wild, if you look real close. Connor's just doing what anyone wants to do in a free country. Make money and be powerful."

"Charlie, if Daniel Connor is that bad, why do you let your sister . . ."

Charlie moved away; I sensed his impatience. "Look. What Louie does is her business. I can't stop her. She's got to make her choices. All I can do is hang around and keep an eye on her. She's

Connor's moll, and that's that." Charlie turned away from me, bent, picked up a small rock, and threw it far across the pond, where it splashed and sent the water away in great circles. He stood with his back to me, silent for a couple of minutes. Then he turned back toward me with a grin. "But heck. Because of Lou, he keeps setting me up with gigs. He got me a new job for a couple of nights from now. I'll be playing in a joint up in Harlem." Charlie watched me. "And whether he knows it or not, he made it so I could meet you."

The flush crept up my face, my cheeks flaming. "I guess he did."

"You know, with help like that, I could really be something someday. A great musician. Famous. Rich, even." He paused. "I know that a girl like you . . ."

"What?" I asked as his words trailed off.

"Well, a girl like you wants a smart guy. You, you're different. You don't want just any joe. You want someone special. Someone who can give you pretty things. Someone who can make things happen." Charlie's cheeks were dark. "I know you don't just want some guy who waits tables. I want you to know that I'm gonna make it as a musician. Be the best. Who knows?" He stubbed his toe at a clump of grass. "Danny Connor can help me make it. I do a few things for him . . . he makes things happen for me. No big deal." He shrugged. "Then maybe even a girl like you would like a guy like me."

My heart was flapping like butterfly wings in my chest. "I think you've got enough talent to make it on your own," I murmured.

"You think?" Now his eyes were bright. "Gee."

We stood there in the shade of a great oak. Charlie was a sweet guy. Those dark expressive eyes of his were like windows. He couldn't help showing me his heart, everything he thought, or so

I believed in that moment. I said, "So Charlie. Want to walk me home?"

The rest of the walk was filled with noises of the city as we walked without talking. I'd never even had a guy friend, much less a crush. Molly used to rib me about turning into an old maid before I was even old. Now here I was, talking with Charlie as if I'd known him all my life. We paused on the sidewalk a couple of blocks from the apartment. Charlie shuffled his feet. "Probably see you tomorrow, if Connor wants me back on the job."

Despite Charlie, a dark feeling stole over me at his words. "Why do you think he's having you follow me?"

Charlie shrugged. "I'm just glad he asked me, and not one of those other two."

"Other two?"

"Ryan and Neil. His right-hand men."

"Well, I'm glad he asked you, too. But I still don't get it."

Charlie looked up the avenue. "I overheard something. Connor was talking to Ryan. Saying something about you and your family."

"Saying what?" The wind was knocked out of me.

"Something about how you might know where Teddy is. That maybe you were meeting him. That Connor wants to find him."

I looked across the street.

Charlie shuffled. "I mean, I thought he was dead, but Connor, he seems to think otherwise. Do you know where Teddy is?"

I looked at Charlie with a creeping suspicion. "You knew Teddy?"

He shrugged. "A little. Not well. Is he? Dead, I mean?"

I swallowed hard. I wouldn't answer that. "Why do you think Connor would want to find him?"

"I don't ask Danny Connor why."

"Even when it involves me?" I felt like I'd swallowed a golf ball. Only minutes earlier I'd thought I could see into Charlie's heart. Now, he was a closed book.

"Look, long story. Forget I asked." Charlie stared at the sidewalk.

That chill came over me again, bitter and sharp. Charlie worked for Danny. Danny was looking for Teddy. I kept Teddy's secret. Was Charlie being nice to me just so I'd take him into my confidence?

It may have been a nice spring day for some, but for me it was clouded and bruised and portended storms. The city air smelled rancid and bitter.

"I'd better go," I said. I couldn't keep the anger out of my voice.

"Right," Charlie said. He stabbed his toe at something invisible. "Listen . . ."

"Don't," I snapped.

"Okay." His voice was wounded, sour. "Okay. See you, then."

I watched him walk away from me, waiting until he'd darted across the street, until he walked on down the avenue, head down, that now familiar wolflike gait, with his hands jammed deep into his pants' pockets. Only then did I turn toward the apartment.

I found it empty except for the staff—Adela still rummaging around the bedrooms, fetching and distributing clean linens and laundry; Malcolm setting the dining room for dinner. I still didn't feel comfortable fetching Teddy's journal from the drawer in my room; it would have to wait until I didn't feel someone's sharp eyes on me.

The apartment, for all it had, was a vast white space, luxurious and lonely and sad. I wondered at that, at my aunt and uncle living in a place with no heart, having a life with no soul. I sat in the library as the afternoon slipped toward evening, but for a change I wasn't reading.

CHAPTER 23

LOU

Yeah, I remember when Teddy came into our little world. Teddy's uncle recommended him to Danny. Said Teddy was discreet.

Danny took a liking to him right off the bat. He was a good hard worker. But I had to be real careful, 'cause Teddy was a good-looking kid and older than me and younger than Danny, and he'd been a war hero and all that. I had to make sure Danny never found us alone together, even having a simple conversation, 'cause I hated to think what Danny would do to either one of us.

It was Paddy who liked to yak about the greenhouse. Danny didn't seem to mind when Paddy talked to me in private, though I sure did. Especially after that time Paddy followed me out to the beach. When all I wanted was a little sun after a long, cooped-up winter.

The shadow fell on me, and I sat up. "Hey, Louise."

"Patrick." I pulled on my robe.

"Aw, you don't have to cover up on my account. That new bathing costume sure looks nice on you."

I could see him looking at my legs. I drew the robe tight around me. "Time I was getting back."

He sat down next to me, too close. I tried to scootch away, but he put his hand on my arm. "Why are you in such a hurry?"

"Patrick, take your hand off me."

He did, but not as fast as I wanted. "Say, I know you've been dying to see what's inside the greenhouse. How's about we go exploring?"

"How about I leave now?" I made to gather my things and stand, but Paddy put his hand on my arm again.

I eyed him hard. "Danny'll kill you," I said through my teeth.

"Not if I tell him you came on to me," Paddy said with a grin. "Come on, little bearcat, just one kiss for your boyfriend's brother."

I tried to twist my arm away, but he held me tight. And it would've ended badly except for Teddy.

We both heard him pushing through the roses, and Paddy removed his arm just in time.

"Hi!" Teddy came down the path with a big warm smile, so big it made my heart ache with thanks. "Hey, Paddy, we've got to move some boxes. Hi, Miss Louise."

"Move 'em yourself," Paddy grumbled.

"Hi, Teddy. Say, would you be a sweetheart and help me up? I'm about done roasting out here."

Teddy helped me to my feet, and I beat it for the house double time.

Yes, I would've agreed with Teddy's uncle Bert. Teddy was discreet. And that war hero stuff—even with the mutterings, I knew that Teddy had the hero's touch.

CHAPTER 24

MAY 23–24, 1925

Houdini, who has a genius for contriving, and then getting out of dangerous situations, was in the most ticklish position of his eventful life yesterday afternoon.
— *"Houdini in Sealed Coffin 91 Minutes,"*
Youngstown Vindicator, August 6, 1926

JO

The elevator door slammed open, and Melody walked straight into the library and right past me without missing a beat. She opened the hidden cabinet, yanked out a bottle and a glass, poured some of the brown liquid into the glass, and knocked that drink back without a second's hesitation; then she refilled.

"Mel . . ."

She whirled on me, pointing her index finger at me while she still held the bottle by the neck. "Don't." Her face was twisted, contorted, all that pretty girlish charm lost to some inner demon. She knocked back the second drink.

This was not the Melody who'd welcomed me to New York, who'd outfitted me from head to toe, who'd partied at the speakeasy.

It hurt just to look at her. Tears sprang into my eyes, and Melody turned away, putting the bottle back in the cabinet only after topping up the glass yet again. Then she settled into a chair opposite, watching me, swirling the scotch around and around.

"I bet you think I'm really sick," she said.

"I think you have a problem," I whispered. "And not just with the booze."

"Yeah, well, Miss High and Mighty, you've got no idea." She watched me with narrowed eyes. "What makes you so special? How come you think you're so right?" She took a gulp. "Why do you think you've got it rough and you alone, you little Goody Two-shoes?"

That hurt. "I don't think that way at all."

"Oh, sure. Perfect Teddy up and disappears, and it all falls on you now, doesn't it? Which must make you bloody annoyed."

"That's got nothing to do with you." I felt angry now. I wanted to give her my sympathy, but she was making it hard.

"Are you sure?" She leaned toward me. "You asked me a few days ago why you were sent here. You have no idea why you're here, in this apartment, right now, do you?"

Something in the way she said it made my insides freeze. I lied, "Pops thinks I should find a husband. He sent me here because he thought your parents would help me meet the kind of man . . ." I couldn't finish. It was all a cover, a lie.

She snorted. "Something like that." She took a sip, staring hard into her glass.

I leaned forward, sliding closer. "Something like what, Mel?"

"Find a something, that's for sure." She nodded. "Women got the vote, right? We've got all this freedom? Sure thing. Let me fill you in on a small surprise. Nothing's really changed, Jo. We're still property. We're still being laced up good and tight. We're still being told what to do, how to think, what to feel, and oh, by the way, put on a good show, girls. 'Cause if you step too far out of line, look out. Somebody's gonna take away everything you care about. Somebody's gonna tell you you can't have what you want. Somebody's gonna break your heart."

"Mel." I didn't know what to say.

"Aw, honey. Maybe I can just get over it, huh? I bet all it'll take is me reciting that line, you know, the cure from that Frenchie psychologist. Coué, or whatever his name is." Her voice went up a notch as she parodied. "'Every day in every way I'm getting better and better.' Hah!" She tossed back the last of her drink, slammed down the glass, and stood and stalked out of the room.

I sank back, stunned. Somebody had broken Melody's heart, no doubt about it. And she'd kept all that emotion locked up good and tight, so that I hadn't seen it until now.

The shadows were long and I would have turned on a light, but I kept thinking, trying to piece it all together. It was dark in the library when Chester came home. He turned on a lamp, looked up and saw me, and started.

"Cuz! Sitting alone in the shadows?" He grinned, then shook his head and put up his hands, wiggling his fingers as if he was conjuring evil. "The Cates family has already gotten to you."

"Stop." I couldn't put up with Chester's obnoxious behavior at that moment.

"Whoa, sorry. What bit you?"

Maybe Chester could enlighten me, at least about Melody. "Your sister has a serious problem."

Chester turned and paced away from me before answering. He sat down and drew his hands behind his head. "Yes. She does."

"What do you know about it?"

He shrugged, but kept his eyes cast up, addressing the ceiling.

"Chester, come on. Don't you want to help her?"

"Jo, nobody can help Mel now. She made her bed, and now she's got to lie in it."

I snorted. "What does that mean?"

He moved his eyes to meet mine. "It means Melody made a mistake. One she's going to pay for the rest of her life. And that's all I'm gonna say about it."

I shook my head. He didn't want to help his sister; he refused to tell me anything but wanted to know what I knew. I disliked him for what he'd done when we were kids; now I was beginning to detest him. Only one thing might make him open up. I thought about how helping Melody was worth my taking a risk. "Okay, Chester. Have it your way. You can forget about learning another thing about Teddy." I bit my lip. If he called my bluff, I might have to tell him something.

We watched each other in silence. It was so quiet I could hear the *tick, tick* of the small brass clock on the bookshelf across the room.

"I'll think about it," he said. Then he got up and left.

There was no family dinner that evening. Uncle Bert was working late; Aunt Mary had to attend some social function or other. Melody and Chester stayed put in their rooms. I ate alone at the great polished dining table, served by Malcolm, who did his best to make me comfortable even when he was clearly feeling the brunt of the awkward silence. I went to my room, uneasy with the weight of the sadness that hung over my aunt and uncle's house.

And at last I had my room to myself and knew I wouldn't be disturbed or spied on. Teddy's journal was waiting for me, maybe to give me answers to my questions. I closed my bedroom door and sat on the floor next to the dresser as I unwrapped the scarf and opened to the page where I'd left off.

The next entries were made after Teddy'd returned home and were short and filled with gaps.

> December 12, 1918
> They all look good. Ma and Pops and Josie. Makes me feel like I did the right thing. Went to war to take care of them.

> January 5, 1919
> Marched in the parade. All those folks cheering for me. Felt like a fake. I am a fake. A fake who wanted to get home and got lucky.
> Some guy said, "Seventy-seventh. Sounds like it was a lucky number for you, mate."
> Yeah. 77. My lucky number.
> They're calling it "the lost battalion," the 77th.
> Little do they know.

> January 20
> Will I ever feel normal again?

> April 10
> Went to Coney Island. Love the beach there, even

when it's cold. The sea, especially when it's calm, reminds me of the prairie, reminds me of that summer, of the time before.

Made me feel better.

May 1

Rushton's made good on his promise. Gave me a heck of a nice position. Moving to New York to start up. Sad to have to leave Josie, but seems to me I'm making her sad all the time, anyhow. Maybe the city will pick me up.

May 15

Job with Rushton going okay, now I've settled in. Uncle Bert and Aunt Mary are genereous to let me live with them. Rushton's okay, even if he's rich.

Which is the hard part. Everything's changed. I've changed. I think about Willie O., who talked about how his folks were spat on when they arrived from Ireland. How his pop couldn't find a job, how they called him a dumb paddy.

You know, that son of a dumb paddy took a bullet—for what? For freedom? Whose freedom? John Rushton and his rich-guy friends?

May 17

I'm concerned for Melody. Tried to tell her not to grow up too fast, but she's a looker and knows it. She flirts and carries on. Sneaks out at night. Chester too young to be a help; I've taken to following her when I can, keeping an eye on her.

June 2
Josie came into town. Took her to the museum, to my favorites. I felt sorry later that I was such a wet blanket, but memories crept up on me.

I gripped the cover of the journal tight, remembering that day.

June 5
Went to a meeting today. Liked what I heard. About time these guys made themselves heard.

Bolshevicks? Nah. Just poor blokes needing a job, a voice, any voice.

July 20
Not sure I agree now with everything that's being said. Feeling like I need to lay low, 'cause some of what they want to do I can't buy into.

Still . . . it's rough out there for the Irish, the Italians, the Jews. "Give me your tired, your poor. . . ." Sure, right. Just shut the door behind you, and be sure to lock it and keep out the riff-raff, those funny-accented blokes.

September 10
Everyone's astir with Melody's situation. I should've been there. The one time I wasn't.

November 1

A solution has been found, but Melody will pay
the consequences forever. And I will, too, because I
made a deal that cost me. But I had to. She's family.
I thought I was turning it all around. I thought I'd
never have to play that role again.

This other business has gotten dangerous. I'm
beginning to suspect their plan will hurt people.
Don't like it and have decided not to play that game
any longer. I may sympathize with these guys, but
I'm not willing to do what they're asking.

And if John Rushton ever found out what I know,
how I'm—

The page ended, at the bottom, in midsentence.

What was this? I flipped back and forth, trying to decipher what
had happened, careful not to let the loose pages fall and scatter. The
following pages looked like they had been removed, so the rest of
the entry and those that followed for some months were missing.

I felt the sweat bead on my forehead as I searched, and then it
caught my eye, a note in a different ink, written sideways in the
margin on the last page before the missing ones. The note read:

J. Loved those library lions. First time.

What?

I leaned back against the dresser. What was this? What happened
to Mel? Who was going to find out what? What business had he
gotten mixed up in?

And what was with the note that was clearly addressed to me?

The library lions: Teddy had to mean the New York Public

Library. He took me there on one of our first trips into town. We had such a time, and afterward we went for ice cream and then a matinee.

He wanted me to go back to the library.

I lifted the journal and turned to the next written page. The entries went to odd things, tallying personal accounts, items of clothing purchased. Nothing else was revealed in those pages about Teddy's "deal," or the consequences, or Melody, or what plan Teddy disapproved of that had "gotten dangerous."

I closed the journal. What had happened to Melody? What did Teddy have to do and what was he hiding from Rushton?

The missing pages that held the answers. The library lions were a clue.

I sat on my bed and looked around these lovely quarters. My aunt and uncle were invisible, keeping their status as upper-middle-class respectables; I thought about others around me who were invisible, busy with labor, slaving after the likes of the Cateses. And me, now.

I thought about what Teddy had said about those who needed a voice.

Like Malcolm, who served me and tried to make me comfortable when he himself was not. Or Joey, who should be in school, not filling his days with the mindless, endless up and down, up and down in a vertical carriage for wealthy clients. Or Ed, who braved whatever weather just to open a door and act pleasant, no matter what abuse he suffered. What did I know about them, these three, about their dreams and hopes?

What did I really know about my own? Rich man, poor man, beggar man, thief: everyone's equal in joy and sorrow. Melody's misery could not be assuaged by all the pretty dresses Manhattan could provide. Money does not buy happiness.

I was now of a mind to think that whatever the missing secret in Teddy's journal was, it had put him in some real danger, and that's why those pages were missing.

I put the journal aside, wanting to find those missing pages. A trip to the library was in order, but it would have to wait until morning.

* * *

When Ed buzzed from the lobby, I was alone at the breakfast table, planning my library trip. Malcolm called me to the intercom.

"It's Mr. Charles O'Keefe, miss." Ed's voice came through all tinny; I had to strain to hear when he lowered it to a near whisper. "I think he works for that Mr. Connor."

"You're right, Ed, he does. I'm surprised he's here, honestly." I tapped my foot. "Well, I've just finished breakfast, so send him on up."

I greeted Charlie as he stepped out of the elevator. Joey, his large ears sticking out from under his cap and his wide eyes watching me, peered around Charlie. Poor thing, he was dying of curiosity. Me, nearly alone in the apartment with a young man my age? Quite a thing to gab about, even if Joey had seen Melody's doings all these years. Joey slid the door shut slowly, leaning over farther and farther, until I was afraid he'd catch his nose in the gap.

Charlie stood in the foyer, shifting from one foot to the other.

I put my hands on my hips. I hadn't forgiven nor forgotten that he might still be Daniel Connor's stool pigeon. I said, my voice caustic, "Well, you can't be spying for Danny Connor now, can you? I mean, you're out in the open, coming here."

He sounded unhappy as he blurted, "I won't be following you like that anymore. Forget all the secrecy. I'm here to invite you to his house."

"Invite me!" I dropped my hands. "When?"

"Right now. This minute. The car is waiting."

My stomach clenched right along with my fists. "And if I don't want to go?"

Charlie shrugged, his eyes on the floor, his hands playing with his cap. "Mr. Connor said I was to come and pick you up."

"Honestly, Charlie." I shook my head. "Connor may be your boss, but he isn't mine."

His eyes met mine. "Please, Jo. He'll have my head if I don't bring you round right now." He shifted again, sounding miserable as he said, "I'd never see you again, that's for sure."

I heaved a big sigh. I couldn't let Charlie get into trouble on my account. And the thought of never seeing him again brought a lump to my throat, despite my suspicions. I thought about my new idea, the one that made me shudder: I had to make Connor like me. Wrap him around my little finger, if I could. And then beg him to leave my family alone.

I felt a cold chill at the thought, and this time I shuddered visibly. Charlie looked up at me with those dark moon eyes.

Maybe I'd been wrong in my suspicions about Charlie. I hoped I had been. But that didn't mean I had to be warm, especially when I was scared to death. "Fine. Let me get my things."

I combed my hair and applied lipstick, then stepped back and regarded myself in the mirror. No, that wouldn't do. It would send Daniel Connor too far in the direction of the wrong idea. For a second I wondered what idea I'd like to send to Danny

Connor. I still wasn't sure myself. But I rubbed the lipstick off as best I could, pulled on my cloche and a lightweight summer jacket that covered my shoulders and otherwise bare arms, and found Charlie, who was standing awkwardly right where I'd left him.

If I'd known Connor lived on the north shore of Long Island, I would've put up more of a fuss. The drive to Great Neck took about thirty minutes. As we crossed the Queensboro Bridge the sunlight sparked off the water, and boats plied the river, gulls hovering and diving. Charlie insisted on sitting up front with Sam; I guessed it was because he didn't want to talk to me, or maybe he was nervous about what Connor would say if he saw the two of us together in the back of the limo. I tried to relax into the leather seat, even though I felt like a prisoner. I kept wishing Charlie'd sat in the back with me; I think I would have clutched his hand, if I'd been able to forgive him.

Once we reached the island the road narrowed to almost a country lane, and we wove in and out along the shoreline. Scrub roses clambered around the edges of the dunes that were festooned by bunch grasses standing up like tufts of hair on an otherwise bald pate. The water of Long Island Sound beyond rippled with whitecaps.

This was not a place I wanted to be.

Connor's estate was fenced and gated in iron. Sam opened the gate, and we drove up a winding drive. Statuary lined the drive: marble fawns, nymphs, elves, plus plinths and urns. Along one stretch a series of columns stood like somber sentinels linked by a chain of carved ivy garlands. Marble whatnots were crowded along the entire length of our passage.

I couldn't imagine anything more garish. Until I saw the house.

It was brick, with eight three-story white fluted columns along the front. Vast wings of rooms angled back to either side, away from the curving drive. A fountain in the middle of the circular drive sported grinning cupid upon leering cupid pouring water in endless cascades from buckets and bowls. The fountain rose so high I arched my neck; it was half again as tall as the house.

"Oh, good grief," I said.

Charlie came around and opened the back door and extended his hand to help me out of the auto. He stood back. "Pretty amazing, isn't it?"

"It's more than amazing." I couldn't blame Charlie for being awed, but I was appalled.

I followed Charlie up the steps to the main entrance. The butler answered the door—at which point I was treated to further extravagant displays.

The door opened into a great hallway, and the butler left us standing in the middle of the hall, at the foot of a broad stair. More statuary. Paintings from floor to high ceiling, and where there weren't framed paintings, painted murals covered the walls. And flowers decorated every available surface—fresh flowers, with scents so heady I thought I might be sick from the sweetness.

It was the most awful house I'd ever seen.

"You ain't seen nothing yet," Charlie whispered. "Just wait till you see his collections of antiquities and oddball Egyptian stuff, that museum. And the greenhouse, just wait."

I compared this monstrosity to the apartment on Park Avenue. My aunt and uncle had done up their new home in such a lean, spare style that it lacked any personality; it felt nothing like home, and it had no heart. Connor's house was the opposite: an overabundance that spoke of trying to fill a void, for this palace held no more homely warmth than my aunt and uncle's apartment.

My own home, for all its lack of modern conveniences, for its small size and peeling paint and stained wallpaper, it had been a place of warmth and love. Until the war. Until Teddy. Until Pops thought he was missing something, and became angry and bitter, filling his own emptiness with ill-gotten gains. I missed my homely house. I'd rather have it any day, even in the face of Pops's wrath, than the cold and sterile tomb holding my aunt and uncle and cousins, or than the treasure store, the dragon's hoard, that lay here.

But I didn't have long to contemplate this spectacle. Daniel Connor emerged from the room to our right. He nodded his head, and when our eyes met, I felt that I was in the presence of a predator.

He smiled, all teeth, white and straight despite his boxing days. Money can buy almost anything, I thought. His steel eyes glinted; I thought again of light reflecting off water, or off of chains.

He reached for my hand, and my mouth went dry as he took my fingers and bent and brushed them with a kiss. I did not yank my hand away. I had to remember my new purpose: to make him like me. To make him leave Pops and Teddy alone.

"I'm so happy you're here," he said, straightening.

As if I'd had a choice.

CHAPTER 25

LOU

I watched from the upstairs window as Charlie helped her out of the limo. I was just getting dressed. She looked at the fountain and the house, and even from that distance I could see she was pretty knocked off her feet by what she saw.

That was the way I'd felt, when Danny brought me out there the first time. It was right after he'd bought the place. He got it from a rich country-club snob type who had tons of initials in his name but no dough in his wallet. The bum hadn't even stayed to show Danny around, just sold it and took off for France or Florida or someplace. Anyhow, Danny'd finally bought it around 1921, and then he brought me out there, keeping the Algonquin for times in town. He was having to do a bunch of decorating, 'cause the snobby bum had left it just empty and plain. But Danny, he'd started filling it lickety-split, once he had the keys in his hand. Crates were busting out all over the place, crates filled with sawdust packed around these objects Danny collected.

Not that Danny ever went anywhere to do the collecting; he had people for that. The only thing Danny collected himself was me.

Until she stepped out of that car, younger than me and prettier. Sweet and innocent and knocked off her feet by Danny and his house. I saw it all, knew what it was all about. At the time, watching out the window, I twisted the silk sash of my robe so tight I put a little rip in it. Which is what made me cry, when I heard the rip.

I really liked that robe, that pink silk. Danny'd bought it for me just after we met when he took me shopping at Macy's, and I really liked that robe a lot.

CHAPTER 26
MAY 24, 1925

ALPHONSE CAPONE
Second Hand Furniture Dealer
—Business cards printed for Al Capone as he set up shop in Chicago,
1920

JO

Connor wasted no time taking me on a grand tour of his house. But first he dismissed a disappointed Charlie. I turned back and caught Charlie's eye as I followed Connor down the vast hallway that split the house; my insides were squirrely as my only friend— at least, I hoped Charlie was still a friend, even after all this— disappeared when we turned a corner, me with Connor.

I was on dangerous ground now, playing a delicate high-wire act.

We walked through room after room, downstairs, upstairs. I stopped keeping count after a while. They were each different, as if Connor was displaying archetypes of decor. Here was a room decorated in black and white; there was a room with rosebuds on every surface—wallpaper, fabric, carpets—and finished with vases filled with rosebuds. I couldn't imagine the cost of the fresh flowers alone.

As we passed through a second-story bedroom dressed all in yellow (with an arching frieze of golden putti angels fluttering overhead) Connor froze. On the table sat a vase of daffodils, tulips, and coreopsis, but they were wilting, the petal edges brown, and I watched as his face went dark. He picked up the vase, porcelain, gilded, and he strode to the nearest window, opened it, and pitched the entire thing out—vase, flowers, and all. I heard the vase smash on the paving below.

I sucked in my breath. Heaven forbid if I ever wilted in front of Daniel Connor.

Charlie hadn't even come close about the museum, which formed one entire ground-floor wing of the mansion. As I stepped inside, right then I began to see Daniel Connor in a new light. I wasn't sure if he was a genius or insane, but what he did with his money was something else.

The room was huge—about the size of my high school gymnasium—all white, with high clerestory windows to let in only indirect light. There were two sets of huge double doors: the pair through which we entered from the house and a matching pair at the far end of the room. Most pieces were displayed in glass cases on white pedestals. It was arranged, Connor explained, in a particular order, more or less by age from oldest artifact to youngest, with one notable exception at the far end—his most precious Egyptian piece, he said. As I walked through these displays, I thought of all the museum directors who'd love to get their hands on Connor's collection.

Connor had amassed an assemblage of fossils—fish, dinosaur, shell—preserved and labeled. Pottery shards and complete pots had been collected from Mesoamerica; shale flints and obsidian

SIRENS

knife points from the western United States; jasper beads and small onyx statues from Africa. Larger mammal fossils came next, including the intact skeleton of a great ape.

As I paused there, looking up at the skeletal hulk, jaw open in a shriek, great arm incongruously wielding a club, Connor came up beside me. "I understand we are now related to this fellow." He gave a slight laugh.

"You don't believe in evolution?" I asked.

"I don't believe in anything except being on top," he replied. "And at the moment, he's dead, his direct descendants are picking lice out of one another's fur, and we are on top." He shrugged. "But as it happens, I do believe that we have evolved to master all living things, we humans. Some of us have, at any rate."

I had nothing to say.

The next section contained jewelry, ancient and antique pieces from all over the world, pearl, jade, bone. I examined a lapis necklace, heavy and huge.

"I'm thinking of having a replica made." Connor said from behind me.

"It's lovely," I murmured.

"Perhaps I could have it made for you. The color would complement your eyes." He shifted, while I stood frozen in place. "Wait."

He stepped around me as he took a small key from his pocket, then unlocked the case and lifted the glass covering and set it aside.

"Turn around," he commanded.

I turned. I couldn't breathe. Connor lifted the necklace over my head with both his hands, hooking the clasp at the nape of my neck. Hold still. Do it for Pops and Teddy, my inner voice said. Don't shudder or pull away. Sacrifice. Remember Pops and Ma and Teddy. Time stopped.

He took my shoulders and steered me in slow motion to a glass case just reflective enough to catch our ghostly figures, my eyes now lake-wide, my short hair dark as midnight, the necklace a broad collar, his eyes over my shoulder. He smiled, then dropped his hands.

"You see?"

I nodded. We stood like that for what seemed forever, our eyes meeting in the glass, and then I reached up, undid the clasp, removed the necklace, and turned, holding it toward him. I took one step away from him, holding the necklace between us with my outstretched arm, waiting for him to take it.

"Ah," he said, and smiled more broadly. "Not yet, then."

Not yet. Not ever. Not ever?

He returned the necklace to the case. As he locked it he said, "If not a necklace, then why not a position at *Vanity Fair*? I understand they are eager to hire smart young women like you."

I swallowed. "I'll have to look into it." This was what I'd planned, wasn't it? Make Connor like me.

"I can make it happen," he said with a shrug. "Or not. I just need to know about Teddy."

Ma. Pops. And my own dreams, just within reach, just out of my grasp. "I'll think about it," I said. I tried not to let my voice shake.

He smiled.

I said nothing more as we progressed toward the far end of the museum, and I circled the displays, always aware of just where Connor was in the room, aware of the precise distance between us.

Beyond the jewelry was a selection of rare manuscripts—some illuminated; some, from what I could see, one-of-a-kind rarities, hand lettered in a language I could not read—but finally, at the far end of the room lay Connor's treasure: a sarcophagus from Egypt.

It was painted, decorated with the figure of a man reclining, scenes from life or death depicted in miniature around the base that sat on a high plinth; resting on top of the man, as guardian, was a jackal, sleek black, with ears like arrows and white eyes with black pindot pupils.

"The mummy is still inside, still intact." Connor turned to me. "Would you like to see it?" He leaned with his full weight against it and pushed on the lid, which slipped back a quarter of an inch.

I raised my hands and took a step back. "No, thank you."

"Does death make you squeamish, Miss Winter?"

I considered my answer. "No. Not death. Just the thought of a body preserved that way. It's . . . it gives me the creeps."

"Ah. But the spirit—do you think the spirit prevails?"

I remained silent.

"There is a magician, Howard Thurston, who claims to speak to spirits. I understand you are a fan of Sir Arthur Conan Doyle. I believe he's a spiritualist, too. Unlike their mutual friend Houdini, who believes in nothing but the facts." Connor paused. "What do you believe, Josephine?"

What should I say?

Connor went on. "I agree with Houdini. It's all nonsense. There is nothing but this moment." He swept his hand around the room.

"What you see here is the smallest reflection of the history of our planet, which is a tiny inkblot in the universe. The only thing that matters is what we have in this moment, in this life." He looked back at the ape, captured in permanent menacing reach. "What we have. What we take. What we win." Connor raised his clenched fist, echoing the gesture of the naked ape, with the closest thing I'd seen to actual emotion, though his voice was soft and controlled.

I met Connor's eyes, reweighing my earlier question: Was he a genius or was he insane? He smiled at me. "Shall we?" he asked, and gestured toward the door behind the sarcophagus. The white eyes of the jackal seemed to follow me as I moved.

Connor opened the double doors that led into a sunroom in the shape of a hexagon. It was filled with plants and rattan furniture, and featured a small splashing fountain in the center.

"Is this your greenhouse?" I asked.

Connor threw his head back and laughed. "No, no. This is the solarium. There's the greenhouse."

A broad lawn stretched downward away from the house, toward Long Island Sound. The water was still, glinting and shimmering in the morning light beyond a low line of trees and shrubs that framed the end of the lawn. Just before the line of trees stood a large glass-and-iron greenhouse.

"Let's walk down to the water, shall we?"

Connor led me on a winding path that trailed past the greenhouse, through the trees and scrub roses, now fully in bloom, to a slim stretch of rolling dunes that fell to the water. A dock lay in front of us, a small trim motorboat secured alongside. I stopped, not walking past the edge of dunes onto the flat sand.

"You aren't fond of the water, Josephine?"

"I don't mind the water. But the beach . . ."

"The sand, then. Yes, it does get everywhere."

"No. It's Teddy. The last time I was at the beach . . ." Ach! I bit my lip. What was wrong with me? Why did I mention Teddy? Was he a hypnotist, Daniel Connor?

Connor coughed, casual, his eyes surveying the water. "Of course. They thought he'd drowned, isn't that right? They found his clothing not far from here, as I recall. Of course, you and I know better, don't we?"

Oh, yes. I knew where they found Teddy's clothing, all right, since I'd led them there. And I surely did know better.

"He had to hide, I imagine, after what he'd suffered. The war damaged a great many people, including, I believe, your brother. The terrible price of freedom. But hiding is not dying, is it?"

The back of my neck prickled. Burned. I switched subjects. "What did you do during the war, Mr. Connor?"

He looked at me sharply. "I was looking after a good many people. People who counted on me. People from the neighborhoods, those who have little." He paused. "My brother served."

I hadn't heard mention of Daniel Connor's brother before this. "Did he come back?"

Connor looked out over the water, shading his eyes with his hands. "I'd like to show you my greenhouse, Miss Winter. It's time I showed you my orchids." He took my elbow in a firm grip, steering me back through the trees.

Connor took a small key fastened to a long gold chain from his pocket to unlock the greenhouse door.

While the day was sparkling, clear, with pleasant late-spring temperature, the greenhouse was stuffy, hot, dripping. And the scents of the flowers inside were powerful. The combination made me light-headed. The greenhouse seemed even more enormous from the inside: two aisles with tables covered with plants lining both walls and another stretch of bare tables down the middle. It was a radiant jungle, with orchid blossoms dripping exotically over the paths. And water dripping in long beading strings down the glass.

"Look at this one. It hales from South America, from Brazil." Connor paused before a specimen. "Do you see how the stamens and carpals are fused? How it lolls? This provides a platform for insects to pollinate the flower." His hand hovered over the flower, not touching it. "Such a desperate and desirous thing." He walked a few steps farther. "Ah. Look. The color of this blossom. Such a scarlet. What insect could resist?"

"They are beautiful."

He stood still before the blossom, staring into it. "How could anything—anyone—compete with that? Such pure beauty." He wasn't talking to me; he seemed lost. And as I watched him I felt shock: Danny Connor's eyes glistened. His voice dropped to a near whisper. "How could one ever hope to attain such perfection?"

I heard the slow *drip, drip* of moisture, and smelled the must, the heat prickling my skin.

He turned to face me, his steel eyes shining. "They are more than beautiful, Miss Winter. They are as perfect a thing as exists."

I turned away to remove myself from his disturbing gaze and walked down to the end of the row, fanning my face with my hand. "What's this?" I asked, seeing something that looked different, hairy and vaguely threatening.

He laughed. "My one peculiarity: a Venus flytrap." He came to stand beside me. His face was pale and cool, his eyes icy. "It's a carnivorous plant. Would you like to see? I keep dinner at the ready."

I stepped away from the seductive mouth of the plant. "Ah . . . carnivorous?" The heat was stifling. Beads of sweat formed on my forehead.

Without another word, Connor took a bottle from a nearby shelf. Several grasshoppers flopped against the glass. He opened the bottle and removed one of the grasshoppers with a pair of tweezers, clutching it by one leg. The grasshopper came to life, struggling and bucking, trying to wrest itself from the vice grip of the tweezers. Connor leaned forward and dropped the insect onto the moist throat of the flower.

It closed at once, with such a snap that I stepped away again. "Oh!" I clutched at my throat, as if I could feel the grasshopper fighting for its life.

"Amazing, isn't it? It will dissolve the insect over the next day or two."

"Alive?" I squeaked. "It eats it alive?"

Connor shrugged. "A grasshopper has no feelings."

I began to shake. "And you know this because . . ." I found it hard to form words.

He laughed and tossed his hand. "A grasshopper is an insect of almost no brain. Unlike you, Miss Winter. Unlike me. What does it matter? In nature, the grasshopper would succumb just as it does here."

"In nature," I said, the heat rising to my face and my whole body in a tremble such that I couldn't control my voice, "it would have a fighting chance. It wouldn't have spent time stopped up in a bottle, and it wouldn't have been so carelessly and . . . and cruelly helped to its death."

"I know a great many things about having a fighting chance." Connor's voice was low, a faint rumble. His eyes grew brighter still, and he brought his clenched fist to the air between us. "You have to take what you want. Take it. Take it!" His fingers were squeezed so tight his knuckles were white. "I thought you understood that, Josephine."

My skin grew cold, my limbs stiff. He was horrifying, cruel, and selfish. Not a minute ago, the orchids brought him to tears, and yet, this emotion from him now. He hid his cruelty behind a veil of cultivation and seduction.

He collected himself, turned away, and replaced the bottle on the shelf; I watched the remaining grasshoppers batter themselves fruitlessly against the glass. Then Connor turned to me, placing his palms flat on the bench. "You are an attractive girl. But you are too soft."

I took several steps until the end of the table lay between us. "Really."

His eyes were narrowed and hard, focused on me. "I think I've had enough of this dance, Josephine. I would like to know what you know about your brother. About Theodore Winter."

I laughed and repeated, "Really?"

"Yes. What did he tell you before his unfortunate disappearance?"

"Why should he have told me anything?" My smile felt fixed and frozen.

Connor gestured, tossing his hand. "I know that you and he were close. That he trusted you. I happen to know that he confided in you. Maybe even left something with you."

I bit my lip. How could Connor have any idea about Teddy and me, about what Teddy left me?

"Your brother was privy to certain information, Josephine. Information that concerns me. Did he divulge it to you?" He paused. "I believe he did."

I trembled, even in that smothering, stifling greenhouse; but I folded my arms across my chest, defiant, forgetting what I'd promised myself I'd do for the family. Begging such a man would do nothing for us, no matter how much he liked me. "Even if he did, I wouldn't share Teddy's secrets."

He stepped forward and bent over the table toward me. "You are like an orchid, Josephine, as I have already said. Attractive. Difficult. Enigmatic." He stepped away and pulled a pair of scissors from his pocket, then turned to the shelf behind him, upon which rested a small plant with a pendulous fuchsia blossom. With a sharp snap of the scissors he snipped the blossom from the stem and held it to his nose. "And fragile. Like this blossom. Which will wilt and die now in a matter of hours. Such a perfect thing, made for one purpose, and now its purpose is unfulfilled."

My hands were shaking, so I put them behind my back. "Teddy trusts me."

Connor held the blossom between his two fingers. He stared at it a moment longer, then gripped his lapel and shoved the stem into the buttonhole. "I wear this blossom. It does not wear me." He stared at me, and bitterness filled my mouth. "I care nothing about your relationship with your brother. I need what he entrusted to you."

"I can't help you."

"Can't?"

I resolved, stiffening my shoulders. "I won't."

"Then, I'm afraid, the rest of your family will learn, one way or another, about your stubborn attitude." He paused. "And, my dear, you said, 'Teddy trusts me.'"

I froze.

"'Trusts.' Present tense. Most revealing. Your family, Miss Winter, your father in particular, will not thank you."

Teddy. Pops. I was trembling all over now, the heat notwithstanding. I turned and moved as fast as I could for the door of the greenhouse. Connor caught up with me from the other aisle. We reached for the doorknob at the same moment. I yanked my hand away, not wanting our hands to touch. Not wanting to feel the touch of his hand on mine.

"No one walks out on me," he said, his voice soft, those steely eyes on mine.

All the flowers in the greenhouse seemed suspended, their blossoms frozen, even the slipping drips on the windows stilled.

The Venus flytrap shook ever so little. I remembered the overheard conversation between Connor and Pops. The threat, the tremor in Pops's voice, the fear in Ma's eyes. Pops didn't have Teddy's journal; he didn't know that I'd helped Teddy stage his suicide. There was nothing Pops could do to save us.

This was up to me.

"Wait." My throat was thick. "I might have been mistaken."

Connor's eyebrows lifted, those eyes boring into me like blades.

My family might owe Connor nothing if I . . . if I . . . "The orchids are lovely." Sweat dripped down my spine. The skin of my scar chafed and burned. "Your orchids. They are lovely."

"Yes," he whispered. "And?"

"I will . . . Let me think."

He smiled. "Think, Miss Winter. But not for long. I need to know where Teddy is. I need whatever he may have left behind. The clock is ticking. And I like adding to my collections in a timely fashion."

I put my hand back on the knob and turned it, and the door opened, revealing Louie on the other side.

"Danny!" Her eyes flew between us. "It's lunchtime."

His words came out a growl. "I've told you never to disturb me here. *Never.*"

She nodded, but looked back and forth from him to me, suspicious and hurt. "But sweetie, Cook made such a luscious lunch, and it was getting cold; I just wanted—"

The slap was so hard it sounded like the vase smacking onto the paving. My hand flew to my mouth; Louie's hand flew to her cheek, and the tears started to her eyes. I could see her swallow. I pressed my fingers to my lips to keep from telling Connor what I thought of him.

Without a word Connor pulled me outside, turned, and locked the greenhouse door behind us. He pushed past Louie and walked up the grassy slope toward the house, gripping the lapel that held the orchid and pressing it to his nose.

Louie and I stood facing each other. I knew he'd slapped her because I'd made him angry. It made me feel sick. I took my hand from my mouth and reached for her.

"Don't." She stepped back, her eyes snapping. "Don't you dare."

I wished we could be friends. "But Louie . . . why do you stay with him?"

Her cheek was scarlet; mine throbbed in sympathy. She leaned her head toward me and said from between clenched teeth, "I love him. I love him, okay? Fine with you? You just keep your mitts off him, sister."

I shook my head, and spoke past the lump in my throat. "I have no intention—"

"Good. Fine. Then we'll get along just fine."

I watched her as she stared at her feet, then away at the ocean flashing sunlight beyond the edge of the lawn. The breeze riffled the grass, mowed to a perfect height. I wanted her to understand. I reached out to touch her arm. "I'm not going to take him from you, Lou. That's a promise."

She narrowed her eyes at me, suspicious, mouth stiff and accusatory.

I went on, "He wants something from me."

She paused, glancing from my hand that rested on her arm to my face. "What?"

"Information. About my brother."

Her eyes stayed narrowed, but I could sense her softening. "Teddy."

"Yes. And I— I made Teddy a promise. Now I don't know how I can keep it."

She put her fingers up to her cheek and touched the bruise. "Listen. He knows you have something Teddy gave you. And he thinks you know what happened when Teddy disappeared. He thinks Teddy is still alive and hiding out. Or so he's said. In moments when he doesn't think I'm really listening." She glanced sideways at me. "Do you? I mean, it was mysterious, the way Teddy just . . ."

I stepped back, leaning against the greenhouse frame for support, feeling weak. "How does he know?"

"He knows. Don't ask me how; he has his ways." She shrugged. "It's only a matter of time. He'll find a way to get to you. He always does."

"Lou . . ."

She dropped her head, the dark, curling waves of her hair falling across her eyes. Then she lifted her face again. "Come on, doll. There's a really nice spread in the dining room. Danny'll just chuck it out if we don't join him."

It was all I could do to sit at the table and pick at the food; my stomach was in knots. Connor talked almost nonstop about a shipment of orchids due in from South America. Their color. Their rarity. How he'd made a deal to have them smuggled north, and how many people he'd had to bribe. Louie laughed at all of his jokes, oohed and aahed at each of his over-the-top comments, and fawned over him, even feeding him sardines with her fingers and licking them afterward. Disgust crawled over me.

When Charlie appeared at the door, ready to accompany me back to Manhattan, I was so relieved I could hardly move fast enough. Connor and Louie walked me to the door, arm in arm, Connor bending over my hand in farewell.

At his touch I felt ill.

Just as Charlie helped me into the backseat of the limousine, Connor called out.

"Miss Winter! Please give my warm regards to your father. Oh, and to your mother as well."

His words were weighted. I knew they contained a warning.

All the way home I fretted. So much so that, when I entered the apartment and saw Pops standing in the foyer with my uncle, I leaped into his arms.

CHAPTER 27

LOU

After lunch, after she left, I went up to my room. Headache, I said. Splitting, I told him.

I took off my diamond bracelet, laid it out on the table in the square of sunlight until the reflection was ready to give me that headache I'd complained of.

How much? I wondered. How much would it be worth? Would it buy my freedom? Maybe I could hop on a train, head west. If only I could open that safe, get the necklace, the earrings—those diamonds would be enough—and then I'd be free. . . . Or maybe some of that weird stuff in the museum, those big gaudy jewels . . .

Ah, but then I thought about it again. Charlie. I couldn't leave Charlie. Not in the same town with Danny, if I jilted him and stole his jewels. Especially not if I took something from his precious museum. He'd take it all out on Charlie. Believe you me, Danny would've given the business to everyone I cared about.

Okay, so Charlie'd go with me. He could play his music for a bit of dough, for when the money ran out. Yeah, him and me, on the lam, that's what I considered. I even had an okay singing voice, so maybe we could go together, him playing backup; maybe that's how we could make it. . . .

That's when that one big tear rolled down my cheek and landed on the table, reflecting the light like those diamonds.

There was nothing I could do. I was, pure and simple, nuts about Danny. Crazy nuts. So nuts I knew I'd never disappear on him. You don't have to believe me. But I didn't leave him, did I?

I turned my attention to other matters. It was okay for me to hate Jo for bending Danny's wandering eye. That gave me something to chew on, all right, no matter what you might think of me. I didn't care for all her weak protests, that nonsense about her brother; she couldn't fool me. She was dying for my Danny. So what would you expect me to think?

Get rid of her, and Danny would forget her soon enough. Put her in a box and make her disappear, like that Thurston fellow did. Then I'd be the levitating girl.

Yeah. Put that Jo Winter in a box, and make her disappear.

CHAPTER 28

MAY 24, 1925

The darkness was rising, but much was still hidden by the shadows.
—*Sir Arthur Conan Doyle, The Hound of the Baskervilles, 1901*

JO

"You're early!" I said, my voice muffled against his shoulder. "You said a couple of weeks. I'm so glad you're here."

"Now, Josephine, no need for such a display." Pops hugged me and then pushed me away. Then he held me farther back, at arm's length. "What in heaven's name have you done to yourself?" Anger mingled with his surprise. "Only a few days, and look at you. What have you done?" His gaze drifted over my hair and then settled on my knees, exposed beneath my silk slip dress.

I tried to keep tears from forming as I touched the nape of my bare neck. I'd been so happy to see him; now my joy was squashed by his condemnation. Even though I'd known he never would have approved of my hair and clothes, I murmured, "I really hoped you'd like it."

Silence filled the air, thick and unpleasant. My uncle came to my rescue. "It's all the rage, Billy. My daughter bobbed her hair, too. I guess it's easier for the girls to deal with." He gave a halfhearted chuckle.

Pops remained silent. Then he shook his head. "You look like one of those floozie types. I'm disappointed in you, Josephine."

I sucked in air. I shouldn't be surprised; I'd never please him. I wasn't Teddy. "Did you bring Ma with you?"

He glanced at my uncle, his eyes dark. "No. Your ma has left to visit her aunt."

"Why? Is Aunt Elizabeth sick?" My great-aunt Lizzy was as tough as a warhorse, having lived alone on the Montana plains all her life. After Teddy spent that summer working for her, he'd maintained I'd inherited her tough and stubborn nature. "Is something wrong?"

"Not exactly."

My nerves tingled. Pops was hiding something. "Pops. What's going on?"

"What's going on is that you've clearly been disobeying me." His harsh voice cut right through me.

Between the greeting he gave me and the terrible experience I'd had at Connor's I had no patience left. And here I'd thought to defend Pops against Connor, by giving up Teddy—by giving up myself. I folded my arms across my chest, my anger yielding to defiance.

My uncle, still trying to lighten the mood, clapped his hands together. "Well! I guess that's fine then. Jo, your father's here to see me. You'll see him before he leaves. You can run along now."

Distant street noise filled the silence, the honking, rumbling cacophony of New York. Yesterday those noises had gotten on my nerves, frayed as they were from my experiences of the night before. Today New York's glamour shone like a beacon signaling my way to escape from Pops's stifling demands.

Pops turned away from me to stare, down the hallway toward the spare, white living room. "Sure, Uncle Bert. I'll be in my room." Then I paused. "Mr. Daniel Connor just had me out to his estate on the island. It was a pretty swell place. He sent his best wishes."

Pops turned around, sharp. "Connor!"

My uncle's face was fixed in a thin smile, his eyes flitting between Pops and me.

Pops flared. "What have you been doing with Danny Connor?"

Trying to save you and Ma, I thought. Pops had let me down hard, and I was not about to forgive him. "You said I should meet people. He's one of the people I've met."

"Connor is not someone I want you mixed up with, Josephine. I want you to stay away from the likes of him. Bert, I thought you understood that."

"Ah!" My uncle opened and closed his mouth. "Gosh, Billy, I honestly didn't know anything about it. It must have been something Melody cooked up." He blinked and licked his lips. "But after all, Daniel Connor knows a lot of important people in this town. It's hard to get around New York without running into people he knows."

"People he knows?" Pops's voice rose. "I didn't have the likes of Danny Connor in mind when I sent Jo here. Just the opposite. I want to keep her away from . . . Here, Bert, I thought we had an understanding."

An understanding? "Pops . . ."

Uncle Bert's hands flapped. "Jo's a smart girl. She sees right through stuff. I know she can take care of—"

"I want her to find a match. *A good match.* Get her out of this situation. Not find herself in one of Connor's speakeasies with the other floozies." He waved his hand in my direction. "Already looking like one."

"Now, Billy, don't talk that way. Jo's been out with Melody."

"Then tell your daughter not to take my daughter out anywhere she can run into Danny Connor."

My impatience swelled. Pops and Uncle Bert were talking about me as if I wasn't there. My voice shook. "Pops—"

He held up his hand to silence me.

Uncle Bert rocked on his heels and sucked in his cheeks. "Mary and I have been thinking about having a party. We'd host all the best people. None of the lowlifes, I promise you. I can introduce Jo to the best folks in town, cream of the crop, real high-society stuff. Even some of those types who hang out at the Algonquin—those artists and writers. Hey? How about it?" He looked at me. "What about it, Jo?"

I folded my arms, pursing my lips, finally able to get a word in. "Gee. That would be swell."

My uncle beamed, not hearing my sarcasm. "And Billy, I almost forgot! She's already met John Rushton."

Pops nodded, approving. "Now, that Rushton's the kind of man I was talking about. He'd keep her safe and sound."

What was I, invisible? Pops seemed to think I was an object to be bartered over. And Rushton. My anger swelled. "I'm not interested in John Rushton," I said, my tone defiant.

Pops looked at me, his eyes flashing. "You'd be lucky to have someone like John Rushton even pay you the smallest bit of attention. He's from one of New York's oldest families."

"So I've heard."

"He's smart. And he has connections. He's got a big house and a bigger bank account. And he can keep you away from the likes of Connor."

I dropped my arms to my sides, rigid, my fists clenched. "I really don't care. I do not want to be talked about like I have no choices. I told you this before, and I'll say it again: I am not ready to get married, Pops."

He leaned toward me. "You will do as I tell you."

"No, Pops, I won't. That's not what this is about anyway. You didn't send me here to find a match. You wanted me out of the house." I watched the astonishment cover his face. "I'm betting you sent Ma out to Montana for the same reason." I straightened my back. One obnoxious male in my day was enough, and Connor had tried my patience. "And what about Teddy? Connor wants a piece of him. That's the real problem, isn't it? You can take your schemes about my future and toss them in the Hudson River for all I care."

I turned on my heel, marched to my room, and locked the door.

I paced the room, back and forth. As I did, and as my temper cooled, I began to think about everything, and I softened. Pops was trying to protect me—that I knew already. I knew he loved me; he might be hard-nosed and domineering, but he loved me, all right. I'd grant him that. Well, I'd fallen into the danger zone in spite of Pops's best efforts. And it wasn't his fault, any of it, really.

I had to face it. This all started with Teddy.

Whatever Teddy had gotten mixed up in with Daniel Connor

was big. Too big for Teddy to handle himself, and now Connor was chasing the Winter family down one member at a time.

But the expectations. Pops had such ideas for me, like he'd had with Teddy. Teddy had to be perfect, be the hope for the Winters. He had to go to war, return a hero. To go out into the world and lead. And he failed. Pops talked a good line, about how Teddy walked on water, but deep down I knew. Pops had never forgiven Teddy for falling apart when he came home, and he never would. He left us high and dry and sent Pops into bootlegging for Danny Connor.

The stress had to have gotten to Teddy. I knew it did.

And now it was up to me. Up to me to live up to Pops's expectations, to be perfect. And Pops's version of perfect? A nineteenth-century girl who married up and brought her family class and money. Not a twentieth-century girl who worked and lived on her own. Certainly not a flapper with bobbed hair and exposed shins who talked back to her father.

I sat down on the edge of the bed and stared out the window at the thin strip of blue sky that lay squeezed between the high-rises across the avenue. The westering sun reflected in the buildings' windows, making gilded rectangles, like eyes. New York was alive, animal-like, stretching and yawning in the afternoon, and changing its mood as it readied for another evening of glitter and glamour.

Pops was trying to be a good father, but he was still wrapped up in his own thwarted dreams of fortune and nightmares of loss.

I didn't understand what anyone was really up to. But I knew who did.

I opened Teddy's journal to the gap where pages were missing. I leaned back against my headboard to read the next section, hoping

I could make sense of it, even though the gap in personal entries was over a year wide.

March 3, 1921
Daniel Connor, reputed king of the East Side, took me in. Said I could be trusted and he liked that. The paycheck is good, he doesn't ask questions, and I told him I wouldn't do anything underhanded.

He asked me to define underhanded.

I said I'd never kill another person, long as I lived. I'd done enough of that, and I was finished with it.

He said okay.

March 18
I think this'll work out all right. The orchids, they are something else. I wish I could spend every second in the greenhouse. It's kind of soothing. Danny, I think he appreciates that I get it.

I think he gets me.

April 23
I keep going over it all in my head. Rushton was a nice guy. And his brother . . . just a kid. They weren't part of the problem.

Sometimes I think I left pieces of myself scattered in that trench, like I was blown up and didn't know it, pieces of my heart, my brain, my soul. I don't know that I'll ever get them back.

And I sure wish I'd never been a part of . . .

April 29
Danny Connor's all right, near as I can tell.

Danny Connor? Teddy worked for Danny Connor.

I felt as if the wind had just been knocked clean out of my lungs. I'd been right: this did all start with Teddy. But not in the way I'd thought.

No question: I couldn't read on. Something had happened in that year that was gone. I had to find those missing pages. I looked again at the hint: *library lions*.

I buried the journal, wrapped in the scarf, deep in my bottom drawer.

Pops and Uncle Bert were still in the living room. "I'm going to the library," I said. "I won't be long." Uncle Bert gave me a cheery wave. Pops didn't turn around.

It was rush hour, and the streets were alive with traffic. I made my way west to Fifth and then downtown to the library, the tall columns whose steps were flanked by those familiar lions, and I stood on the steps and remembered.

Teddy had lifted me up so that I could touch one great paw, and then we'd made our way inside. I poked around that same paw but knew no pages could be hidden there, in the weather after all this time and in public view.

We'd also gone inside, and Teddy had taken me to the stacks and— Suddenly I knew what Teddy's note referred to.

I moved into the main reading room and made for the stacks, looking for fiction and the author's last name beginning with "D."

There it was: the collection of Sir Arthur Conan Doyle that Teddy had introduced me to that same day, here in the library. We'd checked out *The Hound of the Baskervilles*, the very same volume that sat on the shelf even now. I pulled it out and opened the book.

The smell of the old paper; the feel of the pages; the heft of the volume. Teddy was right there with me all over again; my memory of that afternoon was so strong. He had read the book to me over the next few weeks until we'd returned it to the library.

I flipped through the book, not knowing what I'd find—a sheaf of pages tucked inside, perhaps? But if there had been pages left there for me, they were long gone. Disappointment curled through me like a cold chill.

I checked out the book and walked back to the apartment, pushing through the crowds. By the time I got back, Pops had left.

I retreated to my room, tired and frustrated, opening *The Hound* to random pages, trying to decipher the clue.

The night sounds of the city grew louder through my open window, and I heard snatches of song and screeching laughter and howls and catcalls and honks and slams and tires and brakes and all the relentless cacophony of this island city rising up. All its inhabitants carrying on like there was no tomorrow, because, after all, we lived in the decade when skirts rose and mores dropped and, why, Prohibition was just another rule to be broken, like all the other broken things strewn about the concrete sidewalks of this magic kingdom that we called the city of New York.

* * *

The knocking was soft at first, a quick *thump, thump, thump.* Then louder. Then, "Jo? Jo?"

I sat up, heard someone fumble with my door, and then a key in the lock; in my stupor, I didn't know where I was. For an instant I thought it was my dream—the fire, haunting me—and I was awake in a snap.

My uncle opened my door, the keys dangling from his fingers. "Jo?" And my aunt swept in, my uncle framed in the doorway behind her.

My aunt's hair was tied in a wad of rags; I tried to wrap my mind around what was happening. It wasn't a fire. I took a breath. My aunt sat on my bed, the light from the door silhouetting her face, which I couldn't see.

"What?" My mouth felt like it was filled with cotton. "Aunt Mary?" I flipped on the bedside lamp.

"Jo. Your father's all right. He's fine. He's gone to join your mother." My aunt rocked back, her mouth working like she was searching for words. "They're both fine and far away, now."

"What?" The cotton was gone; now it felt like a thousand icy needles were stabbing me behind my eyes.

"Your house, Jo. I'm sorry. It's gone. Lost in a fire."

"A fire . . . ?"

"Burned, honey. I'm so sorry." My aunt hugged me hard, then pulled back again. "Today. While your father was out of the house, thank heavens. He might've been inside, but he wasn't, he was here. But everything else is lost. Your house was burned to the ground."

Fire.

The scar on my back ached and tingled with remembered pain.

CHAPTER 29

LOU

Did Danny do anything bad with his own two hands? Not to my knowledge.

He might have asked for things to be done. He might've said, "Take care of it." I don't even know that for sure. I am pretty sure he wasn't a killer, at least not from the time we met. He swore that to me, up and down, when I asked, especially after what Cook said that time. 'Cause how could I have stayed with—loved—a guy who pulled the trigger and then came home and gave me a kiss?

Oh sure, Danny was a tough guy, no question. But he didn't need to be the one to take care of things, you know? He had people for that.

Ryan and Neil, I didn't like those two goons. I watched out the window when they came up that day, and they stood around the fountain talking to Danny. He stood there with his hands in his pockets, thumbs out, that Italian jacket smooth on his body, not a wrinkle. Golly, he looked swell. Those other two guys, they might've dressed natty, but they couldn't wear it like Danny could. They always looked like they were about to eat something. Or someone.

So that day they came up, and everyone had this long talk in the driveway. Danny was all control, which was one of the things I loved about him. Those boys were all smiles and winks and nudges. Goons. Then Danny made his way out to the greenhouse while they drove the car around to the side. Show over.

Later on I heard the gardener complaining that he couldn't find the petrol he used for that new machine Danny had gotten for cutting the grass. I figured those boys were up to something, and if they needed petrol, it was something hot.

Speaking of hot, if Danny knew how much I spied on him, my goose would be cooked. But a house like that, with all those rooms and all those windows? And me with nothing to do all day but paint my nails and keep myself looking nice for him, for those times when he wanted me to look nice? What else was I supposed to do?

All I wanted was to keep my Danny. I'd have done whatever it took. So sure, I spied. I had plans for Jo Winter. My hands with those pretty painted nails, I could keep them clean, too, and maybe find people of my own.

But did I? Keep listening, Detective. This is where the story gets interesting.

CHAPTER 30

MAY 25–JUNE 1, 1925

Sure, his hair is red, his eyes are blue,
And he's Irish through and through!
Has anybody here seen Kelly?
Kelly from the Emerald Isle!
—Lew Fields, "Has Anybody Here Seen Kelly,"
from The Jolly Bachelors, 1910

JO

The next few days were a blur. Aunt Mary insisted on dosing me periodically with Wampole's Preparation, as if my drinking an elixir of cod liver oil would bring back my family home and keep them safe.

Uncle Bert made the trip up to White Plains to investigate the ruin; Aunt Mary forbade me to go.

"Your mother is trusting me with your care. She doesn't want you upset by what you'd see there." Aunt Mary's face was gray, and dark circles had formed beneath her eyes. "Besides, it's danger—" She stopped.

"It's what?" My own stomach was in knots. It wasn't only the things that we'd lost that bothered me. Yes, I felt a keen loss for my simple, sweet home, my room with its peeling flowered wallpaper.

Rather, it was like a part of my soul had been stolen while I slept. "What, Aunt Mary?"

She finished the word. "It's dangerous."

"Dangerous." My voice rose. Of course it was. I knew just how dangerous Daniel Connor was. I'd hesitated giving Connor what I knew about Teddy, and Connor had exacted his punishment. At least Ma and Pops had a refuge that was far, far away. At least they would know nothing about my future dealings with Connor.

Because, clear as day now, the only way to stop any further madness of this sort was to give Danny something: Teddy, or myself.

My aunt went on. "A smoldering ruin is no place for you. Your uncle will save anything that can be saved, and he'll make sure that it's all taken care of."

But nothing could be saved. The house had burned clean to the ground, and Pop's small storehouse with it; the alcohol must have aided the fire. Uncle Bert came home after two days, worn-out.

"There's a small insurance policy to be paid out," he said. "The property is still yours." He sat in the living room in his shirtsleeves with his vest unbuttoned, mopping his brow, his jacket thrown over the chair. "But it's all ash. That's all that's left. I tried to find whatever I could. I took a rake to some of it. . . ." His voice dropped away, and I went to him and hugged him, mainly so he wouldn't see my tears. "Your father was lucky not to be home. Neighbors said it exploded in flame. He'd never have gotten out. I'm sorry, my dear. Terribly sorry."

Aunt Mary spoke up. "But you have a home here, as long as you need it."

Uncle Bert looked past me to her, and I couldn't read his expression. I straightened and backed away.

"Isn't that right, Bert." It wasn't a question.

He hesitated before saying, "Yes. Of course." He smiled at me. "Don't you worry, Josephine."

Ma and Pops were safe; that was the true consolation. I could barely keep track of the days, what with fire investigators asking questions and the exhaustion that stole over me. I received a letter from Ma, postmarked from Helena, Montana, about five days after the fire.

> *Your father arrived last night. We're both weary, but Lizzy's place is big and she is grateful for the company. Why, you should see the skies here, Jo. So grand and sweeping, and the blue mountains ringing us like a fortress. I'd forgotten, it's been so long since I was last here. I think your father is overwhelmed. But Lizzy has put him right to work fixing the roof on the henhouse, and I can see already that this physical labor will take his mind off of things and do him good. You stay right where you are, Josephine. You promise me, you'll stay right there. No harm will come to you as long as you rest in the care of your aunt and uncle. Your father made some mistakes, and that's why this happened. So you stay put, please. Be good to your aunt and uncle, as they are being exceedingly generous.*

I didn't have much choice in that. I didn't have much money— only what Melody had slipped me here and there—so I wasn't sure I could even get to Montana, nor could I find Lizzy's ranch, even had I wanted to. I read on:

*Josephine, your father still wants you to consider marriage as
an acceptable way out. Love from us both.*

An acceptable way out of *what*?

I was living on borrowed time. Or at least, that's how it felt.
Ma and Pops thought that by leaving me here I'd be safe; I wasn't.
Here in this Park Avenue apartment, with my kindly but mentally
wandering—and now frightened—aunt and uncle, it was like the
first shoe had dropped, and we all waited on the thud from the
other one.

*   *   *

I closed my bedroom door after dinner a couple of days later,
and my eyes rested on the library copy of *The Hound of the Baskervilles*
sitting on my dresser. I hadn't picked it up since the night I'd
learned about the fire. I opened it and leafed through it once more,
wishing Teddy's missing pages would simply fall out.

And then it came to me in a flash. I had my own copy of Doyle's
story on my shelf. Teddy had given me the volume for my last
birthday before he disappeared.

I pulled the book from the shelf. No pages slipped into my
hand, but as I opened it and leafed through I could feel it—a
thickness at the back cover. The flyleaf bulged.

My hands were shaking as I peeled back the flyleaf, picking the
glue with care to reveal Teddy's missing journal entries. I unfolded
them and pressed them flat, both estatic I'd solved the puzzle and
dreading what I'd find written there.

December 5, 1919
John suggested the upstate house and Uncle Bert
and Aunt Mary agreed, and I drove Melody up there
today. Just in time is my feeling. There's a staff, and
she'll be well cared for. I think John is better than
decent. I wish I could tell him the truth about me,
but I don't think he'd hear it.

January 23, 1920
If I ever lay my hands on the guy . . . At any rate, the
family is coping.

There was a series of entries about John and his brother, about
the work that Teddy was doing for John. I noted that Teddy had
gone from calling him by his last name to calling him by his first.
Teddy seemed to like what he was doing:

March 14
I'm beginning to feel whole again. This is the right
place for me. John's as decent a fellow as one could
wish.

March 22
This stuff about the Irish nationalists is driving me
crazy. Conspiracy theories are everywhere. There's a
"red" under every bush; "Bolshevicks" hide behind
every door. Just because there are a few radicals
out there doesn't mean every Irishman in town is
dangerous.

John and I argue about it. He thinks we ought to close our borders. I know some of those guys now, and while a few might be up to no good, most are decent and hardworking folks. I think the war was bad enough, and we need to move on.

Well, times are good, anyhow. There's a lot of money to be made. The whole country seems to be in for a party.

Drinking even when it's illegal, wild new music, automobiles on every street, money in every pocket, girls in skimpy dresses—yup, we've recovered from the Great War, right?

April 10

That's it. These guys I've been meeting with are too radical for me, suggesting dangerous and destructive things. They've gotten desperate, but that's no excuse. They are true anarchists. I broke ranks with them.

I did learn they had a benefactor—a moneyman—but I don't know who he is.

Maybe John's right in a way. But no, I don't believe that. But I also don't believe in the way they want to handle things. Got to lay low for a while.

May 19

Mel home. Everyone on edge.

July 10
Went to Coney Island for the 4th. Too many
fireworks. Too many memories. Heard bombs in my
head for days. I won't make that mistake again.

September 18
I did make that mistake again. I wish I could've died
because then the nightmare would be over.

September 19
In the wrong place at the wrong time. I can't chase
the horror from my mind. All that blood, all those
bodies, the sound, the sound! That terrible noise
ricocheting around and around the square, and
when I ran outside the building, I was deaf, just like
before. All I could do was fold myself in, cover my
ears, cover my eyes, I couldn't help them.

I couldn't help him. He was lying two feet away
from where I fell, John's brother Frank, and I
couldn't help him. John was shouting at me, but I
was deaf. He shook his fist in my face, but I was
frozen.

Frank was dead, anyway. I know death when I
see it. I wish it had killed me, too. That's twice I
escaped when I couldn't save anyone around me.

Oh, heaven help me. Now John knows what
a pathetic fool I am. How I'm no hero. Now he
understands.

September 20
It's all a mistake, a ghastly mistake. Rushton is not
speaking to me. How could he think I'd do a thing
like that? I was in the wrong place, that's all. But he
won't believe me. I said too many sympathetic things
about the Irish and Italians, and now he won't listen.

He's convinced I did it.

Someone gave them financial backing. I wish I
knew who it was. Then I could prove my worth.

I'd kill the guy. Yes, I would.

October 1
I have to leave Rushton's employ. Bitter and sad. But
of course, so is he.

I leaned back and rubbed my eyes. Teddy took care of Melody;
he worked for Rushton; he was present for that terrible bombing
that happened in September 1920; he had to leave Rushton's
employ. Why would Teddy have removed these pages—I still
didn't understand.

The next entries had him working for Connor. He needed the
work, that much was clear.

May 12, 1921
Danny Connor's all right, but I don't much like
Patrick. Oh, he's a charmer, and that's half the
trouble right there. But he's lazy and likes to pick a
fight and drinks a heck of a lot.

Danny wants to do right by the Irish community.

He spends a lot of his time and money down there.
It makes me feel different about him.

June 16
Patrick and I went at it today, and Danny's boys
had to pull us apart. I'm not much for fighting, but
Paddy had it coming. He's ruined more than one
girl, and I wasn't about to stand by this time.

June 23
A whole shipment came for Danny today, and when
I saw the contents, I had to bite my tongue. Still, I
have to give him credit. He spends a lot of time and
money working for the brotherhood. He's not what
I had figured. Maybe I was wrong about him. And
heck. Everyone's in on the booze. Everyone.

Maybe it's Patrick. Maybe . . . This is something
I don't want to get mixed up in but don't have any
choice.

I have my suspicions. Patrick talks a whole lot
when he's drunk. Says things nobody would say in
their right mind. And what he said the other night
made me think. Was he messed up in that business?
Should I do something about it?

I do think about John.

And heck. There is dough to be made here.
Maybe . . . since I've already lost my honor, who
cares? It could sure make Pops happy. Why not?

July 10

Took Jo back to the Met today. I wonder if she'd
ever understand. How can I make her understand?

Back to the Met. Something about all the trips Teddy and
I took to the Met had bugged me before, and now clearly they
were more important than I'd thought. Maybe going back there,
like I'd meant to the day I'd met Charlie, would help me think
it through. And at the moment a brisk walk would do me some
good. I needed to clear my mind and think about what I'd just
read.

I put the missing pages where they belonged and closed the
journal again, hiding it deep in my drawer, and headed down in
the elevator, pressing a dime into Joey's hand and picking up a
big grin.

The sun had passed overhead as I stood looking down Park
Avenue. The city was alive with afternoon bustle. I hadn't left the
apartment since learning about the fire, and it felt good to be out.

Ed was, as always, friendly, but he stopped me as I was about to
walk up Park.

"I've been asked to keep you from going out, miss," he said. His
smile dissolved into an uncomfortable frown.

"Oh, jeepers." I wasn't angry with Ed, but I thought my aunt
and uncle were going overboard. "I'm only going up to the Met for
a few hours."

"Then would you at least consider taking a taxi?"

I relaxed. The day was warm. Much as I loved walking, I could
indulge Ed in this.

He stepped right out, raising his gloved hand and blowing his whistle with such vigor that his cheeks grew bright pink.

* * *

I loved the echoey marble expanse of the Metropolitan. The crowds trailing in hushed clusters, the reverential cathedral-like atmosphere. Teddy had brought me here a half-dozen times or so after he came back from the war.

I made my way slowly through the vast hallways, up marble staircases, twisting and turning; it was such a huge place, it was easy to get lost. Teddy almost always took me to the same gallery. Now it was up to me to see if I could figure out why, and what it was he wanted me to understand.

We had often lingered before the paintings of Winslow Homer. Boats, the ocean, tropical scenes, beaches, fishing. Placid and restful, in pale washes of sand beige and teal blue, soft clouds, soft features, these paintings were meditative.

I sat now in the gallery for over an hour, thinking about our last visit to the Met.

"I love the water, Josie," Teddy had said.

"Why?"

He'd looked at me. "Maybe I should be more clear. I love these scenes of the water, not just any place." His eyes grew clouded. "I've seen the ocean look very different."

"When you were on your way over there, you mean?"

"On my way back." His eyes still had that gray cast. I wanted to bring back the blue, the blue of his eyes like the blue seas in Homer's paintings.

I took his hand. "I'm glad you're home, Teddy."

He looked at me as if he didn't know me and said, "Sometimes, you know, I can't figure out what's right. I'm just not sure anymore." Teddy stared like he was seeing straight through me. "Maybe someday, Jo, you'll have to do something for me. It'll be the right thing, I promise. Okay?"

I couldn't say anything; I didn't understand. As far as I was concerned, right was right.

And then the storm passed, and his eyes cleared, and he took me for ice cream.

Teddy loved these Homer paintings. Maybe it was just that these scenes seem so peaceful. Was that all it was?

I wandered through the museum until about three in the afternoon or so, and decided there was no harm in walking back to the apartment down Fifth and through the park.

Teddy had been in trouble. When he disappeared, I was the only one he'd confided in. Everyone thought Teddy died, killed himself, drowned in the ocean. Only I was sure—and Danny Connor believed—he was still alive.

I walked in the shade of the trees in Central Park, pigeons cooing around me. It was a still day, silent except for those pigeons, warm but not hot. A soft breeze rustled the leaves above my head; the city noises disappeared; the grass smelled sweet and green. I had stepped into another world, still and calm, like the world in Homer's paintings.

I was down around Sixtieth or so when I saw Melody up ahead, in about the same place I lost her last time, only now she was heading downtown, like she was on her way back to the apartment. I paused.

What was Melody doing, spending every afternoon, as near as I could tell, in or around Central Park?

And then it dawned on me, and instantly I was sure I was right: she had a lover. That had to be it. That was why Teddy took her out of town. Melody was seeing someone, and it wasn't a happy romance or she wouldn't have been so upset all the time. Maybe he was a married man, someone her parents wouldn't approve of. A star-crossed love would explain everything.

I followed her but at a distance. She stopped at the apartment entrance and talked to Ed, and then walked on, downtown and to the east. I was about three minutes behind her.

"Hey, Ed."

He looked visibly relieved to see me. "So glad you're back, Miss Josephine. Did you enjoy the museum?"

"I did." I decided to fish. "Anything new around here? I thought I saw Melody just now."

"Miss Melody went over to Lexington to do a bit of shopping. But there is someone waiting upstairs."

I groaned. "Mr. Rushton?"

"Not this time, miss. It's Miss Louise O'Keefe. I believe she is a friend of Miss Melody's."

"But . . . didn't Melody want to see her, then?" An odd feeling grew in me.

"Miss O'Keefe asked if she could wait for you." Ed's smile faltered. "I hope I did the right thing, letting her in. I didn't see the harm."

"No," I assured him, "no harm. Thanks, Ed."

Louie was leafing through a glossy magazine in the living room. "Jo!" She bounced up as I came in.

"Hi, Louie."

"Sorry about last time, okay? You know, out at the mansion." She watched me, those big dark eyes like searchlights.

"Sure. Me, too." I forced a smile.

"Listen, honey. I'm here on a mission. From Danny."

"Danny?" My muscles tightened.

"Okay, so don't interrupt, I gotta remember the exact words." She paused and went on as if reciting. "He wants you to know that he'll do whatever it takes. He heard about that business, and that's what he said, though he didn't tell me what business. But he said, Gee, it was too bad, that business. And he wants you to know— and this is what he told me—that he's ready to step in. To help you. That's what he said." She paused. "He also said I should tell you that the two weeks are almost up."

I stared at her, silent.

She pushed a curl behind her ear. "I'm just delivering a message, doll." Her eyes didn't move away from my face.

"Fine." I sank into a chair. Danny was threatening me directly. Now that Pops was gone, it was all up to me.

"Fine?" Lou asked. She twisted her pearls around her finger. She hadn't yet removed her gloves; she hadn't thought she'd be staying. I could tell what Louie was asking me, underneath her message.

I tried my most serious, earnest tone. "Lou. Listen. I have no interest in Danny Connor. I give you my word."

She was quiet for a minute before she gave a small laugh. "No problem, hon." Then a smile broadened on her face. "So. Let's go do something, just us gals. Let's go out . . . wait a sec. I know. Shall we go surprise my brother?"

"Charlie?" Now my heart beat a little faster. "Where?"

"At the Algonquin. Waddaya say?"

It was my turn to smile.

CHAPTER 31

LOU

I'm a patient person.

I didn't believe a word of what she said, natch. Who would believe that a girl like Jo could have no interest in Danny Connor? But I was willing to play along, 'cause that would make it easier for me in the end.

When Danny told me to go get her, take her out on the town, I asked him, "Why?"

"I don't need to explain myself, Louise. Sam will drive you in."

I ran the bracelet around and around my wrist. "Sweetie, why don't you come along?"

He looked at me with those stormy ocean eyes of his. "I have things to do here. I'd like you to have an evening off."

I got it. He wanted me out of the house. At least he wanted me out of the house and in the company of that Jo Winter, so I knew he wasn't going sniffing around her back door. "Okay, hon. Do you want me to stay at the Algonquin, then?"

Danny hesitated. "That might not be a bad idea." Then he leaned over and kissed me something wicked. "But I'll miss you."

Oh, my pounding heart. Whoever said love can't kill? I thought I might melt away right there.

I remember thinking, Jo Winter, you watch your step. There's no chance I'm letting you take my man away from me, not a teeny-tiny chance.

Thinking is not a crime, buster, remember that.

CHAPTER 32
JUNE 1, 1925

There was music from my neighbor's house through the summer nights. In his blue gardens men and girls came and went among the whisperings and the champagne and the stars.
—F. Scott Fitzgerald, *The Great Gatsby*, 1925

JO

"I need to change my clothes before I go anywhere," I said. The walk downtown from the Metropolitan had me feeling limp and bedraggled.

Lou shrugged and checked the clock. "No hurry. Charlie's there until five."

She followed me into my bedroom, and kicked off her shoes and flopped across my bed, resting her chin on her hands. The childlike gesture made me pause. I asked without thinking, "How old are you?"

"Me? I'm twenty-one."

I stood, one hand on the closet door, stunned. "Twenty-one! I thought you were at least Melody's age. Maybe older."

She gave that throaty laugh. "Yeah, I know. I look older. Or, more like, I act older. Well, I've seen my share. Our parents died when Charlie and me were kids. I was fifteen. I kind of raised him."

"I'm sorry." Fifteen. At fifteen, I was daydreaming about the romantic heroes of the books I read, like Mr. Rochester or Mr. Darcy. I never thought I'd meet a real Moll Flanders. At this thought, my stomach gave a lurch, and I ached for Louie. For what she must have put up with, or had to endure.

She went on. "It was a little rough. I mean, I had the neighborhood: the old people who sat outside and looked after things, the others who gave us food and whatnot. They were kind of an extended family. We were all Irish in this New York neighborhood, all together. But really it was just us, Charlie and me, until I found Danny. Then he took care of things." She turned over on her back and stared up at the ceiling. "Now Danny takes care of every little thing for me and my brother."

I watched her in silence, chewing my lip.

She turned her head. "It's okay, doll. Really. Now, what are you wearing?"

I pulled a little peach silk chemise from the closet. She nodded and waved her hand. "Go."

I headed for the bathroom. "I'm going to shower. I'll be fast."

"Take your time," she called.

After twenty minutes or so I came out, toweling my hair, dressed. Louie was standing at the closet door. "Nice rags."

"Melody gave me all of these dresses and things. Her hand-me-downs. They are nice, aren't they?"

Louie nodded. She picked up a pair of shoes while I put on what little makeup I had. I watched in the mirror as she wandered to my dresser and began idly opening the drawers. "Mind if I snoop?"

I was there in an instant. "Yes." Teddy's scarf, and its contents, still lay in the bottom drawer.

Louie looked at me in surprise. "Sorry." She shrugged. "I was just, you know. . . ." Her eyes betrayed hurt.

But I didn't move.

She went back and sat on the bed, looking down at her hands. "I'm sorry. I get so little girl time, you know? Danny, he keeps me in tow. I was tickled pink when he asked me to come here." She paused and looked up at me. "I kinda felt right off that we could be, you know, friends." Her eyes, big and round, welled.

I went and sat next to her. "It's just. . . . Don't worry about it." I patted her arm. "I know we could be friends." Did I? I wanted a friend. . . .

She smiled. "Really? Okay. That's great." She raised her eyebrows. "You ready?"

"Sure."

We went down in the elevator together, and when we reached the lobby, I stopped. "Darn! I forgot my purse."

"You don't need money," Lou said, marching toward the door, swinging her own beaded purse from its drawstrings. "I'll take care of all that. Or rather, Danny will." She laughed.

"I just want it, you know," I lied. "It has my lipstick and stuff. Things. Wait here a sec, okay?"

"Want me to go back up with you?" She stopped dead and looked at me, as if she knew what I was up to.

"No, no. I'll be right back."

It took me only a couple of minutes. I made Joey wait—with the door closed—until I finished. I gave Lou a big smile when I got back down to the lobby. I really did hope we could be friends.

It was just that I still had to protect Teddy. I still had to keep my promise.

And I couldn't let on to Louie what was really going on, not just yet, not until I was sure about her. I could not let on that I might still need to play along with Connor.

I knew that Louise O'Keefe might understand that kind of sacrifice. But I also knew she would never forgive.

*　　*　　*

Louie leaned toward me, grabbing my arm, as we walked into the Algonquin lobby and stood gawking. People swirled about us, dressed in the latest and most expensive fashion. A woman with a feathered hat pulled her small dog on a leash through the lobby, the dog in a fast trot. A couple snugged against the concierge desk, and I watched his hand slip along her waist as she pulled closer to him. A man in a hat pushed back off his forehead slouched inside one of the telephone booths, his cigarette bouncing on his lips as he talked into the receiver.

Louie whispered, "Danny got Charlie this job. Danny knows the manager. Okay, so he knows everyone. He's even got a suite upstairs. Anyhow, when Charlie needed something besides his music, you know, something that might really pay the bills, I asked, and Danny answered." I looked at her; she shrugged. "Like I said, he's been really good to me. To Charlie and me. Which is what counts."

We walked toward the dining room. The parquet made a *tap-tap* sound under my feet; the carpets muffled all noise.

"Hello, Miss Louise." The maître d' gave a small half bow.

"How's everything today, Jacques?" she asked. She pronounced it "Jack."

He nodded toward the corner. "Charles is working out just fine. Would you like a table?"

Louie leaned closer to him. "We'd like a table somewhere hidden. You know, where we can spy on him." She looked at me and winked.

"Certainly." He led us to a table behind a square oak column from which we could peek over at the group in the corner of the Rose Room. As we walked by Lou leaned toward me and whispered in my ear that the writers of the Round Table had nicknamed themselves the "Vicious Circle." She giggled, clapping her hand over her mouth and staggering. "Vicious," she repeated. "Don't they look it?"

The Round Table group consisted of all men today, none of whom I recognized from the last time, and they were having a fine time, laughing, smoking, drinking, and looking anything but vicious and all seeming to talk at once. Though it was late afternoon yet, and a public place, I assumed from the gaiety and loose behavior that alcohol was involved in those tall glasses, although it might have been tea. These were my idols. But I had eyes for only one person in the room, which brought my brain to a standstill while my heart galloped on.

Charlie O'Keefe.

He wore his waiter's uniform—white shirt, black pants, a half apron—and leaned back against the wall, his large dark eyes tracking everything that happened at his table, waiting to respond. He reminded me of a cat, coiled and ready. He was strong and capable. I sucked in air.

Lou touched my arm. "Jo?" She began to giggle. "You're not looking at those Round Table types, are you."

I pursed my lips, suppressing a giggle of my own. "No, I'm not."

"Well, I'll be." Louie sat back, a grin crossing her face. One soft auburn curl peeked out from her cloche and met the corner of her lip. "Josephine Winter likes my little brother."

The rush of heat from my throat ran right up into my cheeks. "I guess so."

"You guess so? Honey, I'd say you were smitten."

I shrugged and stared down at my hands, trembling but folded neatly on the white tablecloth.

Louie leaned over to me. "I'm thrilled. Now we can be like sisters." Her eyes shone; I thought about how she feared that I might go after Danny, and I was glad.

I grinned and then looked again at Charlie, who was filling water glasses, moving carefully between chairs. But he sensed my eyes on him; he raised his head and stared back at me and kept pouring, watching Lou and me, until one of the patrons shouted "Hey!" as water topped the glass and drenched the table. Charlie went to work at once, apologizing, mopping, removing offending linens, while Louie and I dissolved into helpless laughter and the Round Table patrons decided it was time to abandon their refuge.

Poor Charlie.

Or, at least, I thought it was "poor Charlie," until I saw that his guests weren't truly upset; one of the men slipped him a folded bill and another clapped him on the back, while a third, passing our table, said, sotto voce, "I'd have dumped the pitcher, too," and tipped his hat to us with a grin, saying, "Ladies."

Once the Round Table crowd left, Charlie's stint was finished for the day, and he changed out of his apron and arrived at our table just as we finished our order of tea and petits fours.

He was flush with good cheer. I looked away as he sat down, pulling over a chair so he could join us. I tried not to let him see my eyes; they'd reveal everything I felt, including how wrong I felt for mistrusting him.

"Hi, Jo!" he said. "What a nifty coincidence."

Louie dissolved into another fit of giggles. I rested my forehead on my palm.

"Have you two been drinking?" Charlie asked, appalled.

"No," Louie answered.

"Of course not!" I replied at the same time. At which point I had to pinch myself to keep from laughing out loud.

Charlie looked bemused and shook his head.

Louie collected herself. "Charlie, Jo hasn't been around town since she's come to live in the city. I'm betting she hasn't seen the real New York with the eyes of a grown-up. I was thinking: let's give her a tour of Broadway. Maybe we could take in a show."

"Excellent!" Charlie said, and he reached over and covered my hand with his own.

My eyes met Charlie's then, and my smile met his, and my heart—well, it's impossible for me to say what his heart did, but mine was thumping like a drum. His warm hand rested on mine for what seemed like forever. I didn't want to believe, at that moment, that he'd choose loyalty to Danny over me.

There were tons of shows to choose from, but in the end we went to a magic act by that magician, Howard Thurston, at Louie's urging.

Right off the bat, I was kind of shaken. The posters showed Thurston holding a skull, surrounded by ghosts and nasty-looking devils, and the question: DO THE SPIRITS RETURN? I thought of Teddy right away.

Which was most peculiar seeing as Teddy was not a ghost. Not dead, really. Only pretending.

Thurston did something astonishing: he made a girl float up into the air, and he invited people from the audience to check her out, to see that she was really floating. Charlie jumped out of his seat and ran to the stage, where he and all the other volunteers were paraded around and around; and he came back, his eyes all on fire, claiming she was really floating there, all by herself.

After which Thurston put her beneath a sheet, from which she vanished, just like that.

Like Teddy had vanished. Though I was the one holding the sheet and making believe he was gone.

Afterward, Louie, Charlie, and I walked down Broadway and stopped in to pick up a snack at the all-night diner. The bright lights above us winked and glimmered red, white, yellow; the crowds leaving shows filled the air with laughter, cabs and autos honked, rumbled, brakes squealed.

Charlie looked over his Coke at me. "You could be on Broadway, Jo," he said out of the blue.

Louie slapped his arm. "Charlie!"

He turned to her. "She could! Look at her. They'd hire her on Broadway to star in a show, just like that." He snapped his fingers. "She's a peach!"

I felt more like a tomato. My face must've looked that red, at least.

"Really, Charlie," Lou said.

"Anyways, Jo looks to me like she could be a star," Charlie mumbled.

"'Anyway,' Charlie. Not 'anyways.' Sheesh," Louie said. "Even if you're right about Jo. Which you are."

I met Lou's eyes. She was smiling, but something about her read sad. Why? It was just Charlie being silly. I shifted. "Listen, I need to get back. My aunt and uncle will be having a fit, not knowing where I am."

We took a cab back to the apartment. Sam was waiting for Louie, the limo double-parked on the avenue. But there were also a couple of police cars pulled up to the curb, their red lights flashing. My stomach clenched.

When Ed saw us, he practically jumped out of his gray double-breasted coat.

"Oh, Miss Josephine. I didn't see a thing. It was just the usual traffic. Nobody out of place. I'm so careful, you know? There was one delivery—flowers—for Mrs. Jacoby. That must've been it. How was I to know? The guy looked legit, and Mrs. J said it was all right. 'Send him up,' she said. So I did. Sent him up the servants' stairs." Ed was sweating; he mopped his brow with his hanky. "I'm gonna lose my job. That's the long and short of it. As I should, for letting that happen. I'm so sorry, miss. I really like your family."

That's when I began to feel sick, but I tried not to show it. I put my hand on Ed's arm. "For letting what happen, Ed? What about my family? Are they all right?"

"They're okay, thank heavens. But the apartment—it was ransacked."

CHAPTER 33

Lou

Okay, so I might have been misdirected.

First off, how could I know that Jo had a thing for Charlie until I saw them together? And then, how was I to know that Charlie felt the same?

I gotta tell you, that warmed my sisterly heart, thinking about Charlie so happy. And then realizing that Jo was not going to come between Danny and me because her attention was elsewhere.

When she heard that news about her aunt and uncle's apartment, though, my sisterly heart turned to lead. I could tell she thought Charlie and me had a hand in it, that robbery. That we had taken her out to keep her away while someone went into the apartment for whatever.

And for all I knew, Danny, my sweet Danny, his long fingers had stretched clean across Manhattan and done the deed. Not him, no, never, but one of those goons of his. Sometimes they did things without him asking. Most times he had a plan.

And then I wondered why he might have a plan, and how that plan involved Jo, and my green-eyed monster self showed its ugly little head once more.

Now, you might be thinking, so it's Danny, not Jo, who's at fault. Danny I should blame. Danny I should be mad at. You would be wrong.

Bottom line: Who was I gonna stand with, I ask you? Sweet Jo, or my one and only? Who do you think?

CHAPTER 34

JUNE 1–6, 1925

I cannot fix on the hour, or the spot, or the look, or the words, which laid the foundation. It is too long ago. I was in the middle before I knew I had begun.
—Jane Austen, <u>Pride and Prejudice</u>, 1813

JO

I was a statue on the sidewalk, at least until my legs began to feel numb and I thought they'd go out from under me. Charlie caught my arm as I began to sink.

I looked at him, and then at Louie. They looked upset—Charlie looked positively horrified—but I pulled back, easing my arm from his. I had only one thought: betrayal.

Louie had enticed me out on the town. She'd wandered into my bedroom while I was showering. I'd left her alone, and though I hadn't thought she'd found the journal in the drawer, she may have, and then tipped off Connor. Or she hadn't even needed to tip him off: maybe the plan was always to take me out, and give them a chance to search for something—anything—of Teddy's.

If so, she was a darn good actor. And she would have broken my heart. And Charlie, well . . . I didn't know what to believe anymore.

He did work for Connor. All my ugly suspicions of Charlie came roaring back, all those doubts, and they hurt, oh, golly. My eyes and throat stung with the hurt.

I couldn't trust Louie. And if I couldn't trust Lou, I couldn't trust Charlie, either. They both belonged to Connor: they owed him their lives; they owed him everything. That's what Lou'd said. Why wouldn't they do what he asked? How far would they go for him?

Because it was Connor—or his men—who'd ransacked the apartment.

"I'm going in. Thanks for the evening," I said, turning away from them.

"Jo!" Lou touched my arm. "Honey—"

I yanked away. "Leave me alone."

She took a step back. "Oh, Jo."

I lifted my eyes to hers. "You knew. You're so jealous, you don't care a thing about what happens to my family or me. You knew what would happen, and you lied to me."

She shook her head, her eyes round; Charlie reached for my hand.

I backed away from him, snapping at him, my insides coiling like snakes. "Don't touch me. Don't. I know what this is about, for you, too. You want Danny to give you a great job at one of those joints of his. Make you famous. You can play your music all you want. Well, good luck, that's all I have to say. Thanks for a swell evening. Thanks for nothing. Don't bother me again."

I left them on the sidewalk, Charlie looking stricken, Lou looking galled. My head whirled, and the snakes in my stomach twisted into giant knots.

As soon as I stepped into the apartment, I knew for sure it was Connor. The only rooms in disarray were my room and the library, too. Which made me feel sick.

Chester sat on a chair in the foyer with an ice pack on his head. My aunt and uncle and Melody stood in a tight cluster. Police in uniform were traipsing in and out of my room and the library, carrying things in gloved hands.

"Hey!" My books, in a disheveled stack, were cradled in the arms of an officer. I grew angry now. "Those are mine!" I spied the Sherlock Holmes; what if there were other clues from Teddy hidden in my favorite books?

"Sorry, miss, but we've gotta check everything. Somebody went through these books, the way they were tossed around the place. We need to find out why. Maybe find fingerprints."

"Uncle Bert, those are my books. Please don't let them."

Uncle Bert came over and put his hand on my shoulder. "Officer, really. Must you? Works of fiction?"

The man looked over at a plainclothes officer who must have been in charge, and who made a face but shrugged. The policeman handed me the books.

"Thank you," I said, as stiff as all get-out. Several officers were standing in the door to the library; I couldn't wait to get in there but didn't want my actions to seem odd. I marched instead to my room, which was in a true shambles.

Every drawer, all my bedding, all the clothes in the closet, all were ripped and shredded and scattered. Knives had been taken to most of it, even the mattress. My underthings littered the floor; the color rose into my cheeks, burning hot. I stooped and tried gathering them in a pile, to hide the most personal items. Even my bathroom was a mess, bottles smashed and broken, including, to my misery, the bottle of Chanel No. 5 that Melody had given me. Its fragrance permeated the air.

"Oh!" The sound escaped me as I sank onto the only chair still upright.

"Miss, you need to leave," said an officer. "We're working, and you're in the way." Still hugging my books, I made my way to the library, my heart in my throat.

It was a mess, with all those leather-bound, mostly unread, books scattered and torn. Leather bindings were snapped; precious volumes lay heaped, pages fluttering. It broke my heart.

But I was at once relieved of another, more pressing, worry. No one, it seemed, not the robber and not the police, had discovered the hidden liquor closet.

I went back out to the hallway and stashed my books on an occasional table. "What happened?" I asked Chester, who tracked the mess of activity with one eye while covering the other with the ice pack.

"I surprised him," Chester said, and lowered his hand so I could see the ugly black-and-yellow bruise forming around his eye. I winced and sucked in air in sympathy. He replaced the ice and went on. "I came in while he was making a mess of the library. But I didn't get a good look at him. He connected his massive fist with my face and took off down the service stairs before I recovered."

I knew that the apartment was empty late at night, if none of the family were at home. In the evenings the servants went back to their own rooms.

"Do you know what he wanted?" I thought I knew, but I wanted to hear from Chester.

He shook his head. "Ow. Got to remember not to move like that. No, I haven't a clue, because as far as I could tell, he was empty-handed. Which is why he could give me such a perfect shiner."

I let go another breath.

The plainclothes officer rounded up his crew, who came out of my room carrying, I assumed, at least some of my clothing, stuffed inside my pillowcases. "Sorry about your things, miss. We'll return them as soon as we can." He turned to my uncle. "I'll put a couple of men on the street for a few days, Mr. Cates. I hate to think what would've happened if one of the ladies had surprised the thief."

Aunt Mary gave a small cry, and Melody put her arm around her mother's shoulder.

The plainclothes man coughed and lowered his voice. "You know, of course, that no other activity can go on while we investigate." Which I took to mean that my uncle would be unable to bring in any liquor for his private stores.

Uncle Bert nodded, staring at the floor.

When the police were gone, the rest of us stood in the foyer in silence, until Melody spoke up.

"Jo will sleep in my room with me. My bed is plenty big. Jo, I have lots of other clothes, and we'll go shopping straightaway tomorrow." She looked at her parents, from one to the other. "Mother, Daddy, it's only things. Just things. No one was hurt. Well, Chester. But he'll be fine in a day or two. And the papers will call him a hero, so he should have plenty of sweet little flappers vying for his phone number."

Melody impressed me, her strength and determination. But as I looked at her parents, I could see what thought had crossed their minds. Neither my aunt nor my uncle would look at me. I'd brought trouble to my own parents. And now I was bringing my trouble into their house, into their lives, into their family.

"Look," I said. "I don't want to be a burden."

"Oh, no, dear, you aren't," said my aunt in an unconvincing fashion.

"It's time we got some sleep," Melody went on, her tone even more firm. "We can talk about this in the morning."

We parted ways for the night—Aunt Mary gave Chester salve and a fresh bag of ice—in a barrage of awkward hugs.

Once I was alone with Melody even her facade slipped. "I'm exhausted. There's a clean set of pajamas in the top drawer. Night." And she lay down with her back to me, an eye mask covering her face, and slept.

I lay in the dark forever. This was an entirely new level of threat. It was one thing for me to leave my home—Pops had chased me out ahead of the storm—and for it then to be destroyed. That was a narrow miss, but still a miss, since no one was hurt. But this was something else. Connor was not just threatening me, he was hurting my family, even my extended family.

I made a decision, lying there, listening to the night sounds of New York—the cars honking, the brakes, the low rumble of movement, always movement, for that was New York, the city that moves endlessly.

I had to leave my aunt and uncle's place. It was too dangerous for them for me to stay. I had no idea where I'd end up. I'd have to figure out a plan first. But there was no doubt in my mind. I had to leave, before someone I loved did get really hurt. Or worse.

* * *

It took three days before I was alone again in the apartment and could get to the journal. I still hadn't figured out where I'd go once I'd retrieved it, but I'd leave as soon as I could. The tension in the apartment had been growing steadily.

And in those three days, I had more time to think through the whole mess. I realized that if Louie had found the journal in my room while I was showering, she would have made off with it there and then. Why wait? And how would she have alerted Connor about the journal while I had been with her all evening? The look on hers and Charlie's faces when we found out about the robbery told the tale. They hadn't known what was going to happen.

I'd misjudged Lou. And Charlie. Especially Charlie. I'd been so sure I was right in the moment. But now I hoped I'd been wrong.

"Melody," I ventured the second evening after the break-in, when she seemed to be in a better-than-usual mood, "how can I get in touch with Louie?"

Melody was thumbing through a magazine as we sat together in the living room; according to the police, the library was still off limits, although it had been cleaned. She didn't look up at me. "Just call Danny Connor."

"What if I don't want Mr. Connor to know?"

Melody shut the magazine and stared at me. "I'm sorry?"

"I don't want him to know I'm looking for her."

Melody watched me, her eyes narrowing but unfocused; I had the feeling she was trying to assess me, or my purpose. "Doll, what's going on?"

I opened my eyes wide in an attempt to play innocent. "I just want to reach her, that's all."

"Right. And I'm the Queen of Sheba. Look. It was your room

they searched, not mine. Not Chester's. And your house they torched. So maybe you could enlighten me a little here as to why you want to avoid Daniel Connor. Or, at least, indulge me with a great lie."

I'd grown fond of Melody. She might be a flapper, she might have her touchy moments, but she was all right—honest, kind, and generous. She'd given me a whole new wardrobe in the blink of an eye, some from her own closet and some from a short shopping spree, and never complained while we were having to share quarters. She was smart—and even better, she was wise.

"I can't tell you everything. Mainly"—and I decided to be honest here—"because I'm not sure about it all yet. I want to apologize to Louie, that's all."

"Apologize! Why?"

"I thought she was a weasel."

At that, Melody burst out laughing. "Louise O'Keefe, a weasel?"

I shrugged. My center had slipped. How could I have misjudged Lou?

She stopped laughing and said, "Honey, honestly, I don't know. Connor is possessive. He knows where she is and who she talks to every darn minute. You might have to wait until we can catch her alone, shopping or checking up on her brother or something. Let me think about how we can manage it."

I knew I could go back to the Algonquin . . . but the thought of going through Charlie, for some reason, made my heart beat hard. Probably because I'd thought he was a weasel, too, and I knew I couldn't have been more wrong. And possibly because, as Lou had assessed quite rightly, I was, as far as Charlie was concerned, smitten.

A day later, in the afternoon, everyone had left for their appointments, figuring at last that I could be trusted to be alone in the apartment.

The library had been cleaned; what books and small things remained were back on their shelves. The broken knickknacks had not yet been replaced, so the room had the air of a public space. The library had been the only warm and cozy place in the apartment, and now it, too, was impersonal.

But the secret liquor closet remained unsearched and undiscovered by the police, although it was still well used by my rattled uncle every evening. I pushed on the sidewall and then slid the panel aside; the smoothly built contraption opened like magic.

I reached deep behind a couple of cases of champagne that sat on the floor of the closet. I felt around with my fingers until I finally touched wool. Then I breathed a sigh of relief—it was still as I'd left it. I pulled out my old dark brown sweater, the one I'd wrapped tightly around my scarf with Teddy's treasures inside.

I slipped into my old room—bare and clean now, but still private—to read Teddy's journal, picking up where I'd left off.

August 16, 1921
He's involved, I know he is. Paddy's a rotten egg.

I made friends with a guy over there, Aldo Giaconni. He had the best sense of humor. Between his accent and his jokes, he kept me going more than a few times. He wanted to be a chef, and talked about his grandmother's cooking in a way that made my mouth water. We spent a lot of time together.

Until he caught the dysentery. Lots of guys died retching and crapping all over the place. I hated that it happened to Aldo, that even his dream and sense of humor couldn't beat back the grim reaper.

I don't have a problem with the Italian guys back here. I don't see why Paddy's so burned. What did they do to him?

August 20

Danny doesn't want to see it. I keep telling him, Paddy's bad news. He's going to bring it all down, but Danny shuts me up so fast, sometimes I think he'll kill me if I take one step more.

August 31

I love the orchids. I started spending as much time as I could out there. It's like a dream out there. I wish I could bring Jo to see them, when they're in bloom.

On the other hand, some guys who have it all— money, dames, power—they still hate anyone who's different. Different accent, different haircut, it doesn't matter. Some guys just don't get it.

I lowered the journal to my lap. I wished Teddy was here to explain this to me. I didn't understand.

I raised the journal again, only to hear the elevator.

My digging would have to wait; I didn't want to be surprised with the journal in my hands.

As fast as I could I bundled everything—the scarf, the medals, the journal—and flew out of the room and down the hall to Melody's room. I heard the elevator door open, and heard voices, and I stuffed everything inside the closet, tossing the old sweater over it all to hide the scarlet poppies, and shut the door.

Then I took a breath.

I went back into the hallway, closing the door behind me and smoothing my hair and my dress. I followed the sound of the voices to the living room.

Uncle Bert was there. And John Rushton.

CHAPTER 35

Lou

So that night, the night of the break-in, Charlie and me walked downtown to the Algonquin, not saying a thing. He thought it was my fault, that Danny had put me up to it. I knew then how sweet he was on Jo, and how he thought for sure he'd lost her. Charlie left me at the hotel without more than a "G'night" and I made my way up to Danny's suite alone.

Knocking around alone in that swell but empty joint meant my brain was knocking around with thoughts about Jo and Danny. Maybe it was just coincidence that Jo's apartment was ransacked while we were out, but my tingly feelings were alive. What would Danny want that he'd find at her place?

I took a hot bath and wrapped myself tight in one of those oversize robes, and then I opened the big windows to the dark and stood looking down Forty-fourth toward the East River. From this high up I had the feeling I could see forever. The lights below and around me and off in the distance twinkled like stars in the sweep of space, and the night was rich with the faint sounds of air brakes and auto horns. I imagined I could smell the river, fishy and rank.

Somewhere across that city Danny was up to something.

I knew something was brewing just before Teddy disappeared. I'd bumped into him in the solarium as he was tending to the plants in there, snipping off dead leaves.

He'd straightened up fast and said, "Hi, Lou."

"Say, Teddy, you're just the fellow who'll know. Did Patrick—"

But he interrupted before I could finish my question. "Don't talk to me about that bum, all right?" And he turned on his heel and left; one hand clutched a bunch of dried-out branches, the other hand gripped his sharp pruners, and he walked out on me just like that.

Well, jeepers. All I'd wanted to know was whether he knew where Paddy had gone. Danny had been pacing around like a caged lion, trying to figure out where his baby brother had made off to this time, and I wanted my Danny to feel better.

As I sat in the Algonquin suite that night, I thought about it. Teddy was up to something, and maybe Teddy'd confided in Jo. And Jo was holding out on Danny.

If Jo stood in Danny's way, it wouldn't be pretty. As in, this suite was high enough in the sky that if someone wanted to make a girl levitate after a fashion, why, he surely could.

I stood at the open window and looked down on all those sparkly, starry lights. And a sneaky little thought did creep into my brain, and this is one thing I'll confess to, Detective:

One way or the other, I didn't think Jo Winter would be my problem for much longer.

CHAPTER 36

JUNE 6, 1925

"Your young men did not fail," he said, "to measure up to the standard of American manhood when the call came."
— "Thousands Honor Heroes of the War,"
The New York Times, May 30, 1921

JO

John Rushton. On the one hand, he was a stuck-up prig. On the other, Teddy had been his friend. And yet Teddy had to leave his employ, and made it sound as if at that point Rushton had hated him.

Talking to Rushton was one way to figure this all out.

As I walked in the room, Rushton said, without so much as a hello, "Josephine, I'm glad you're here. Now. We must talk about Teddy's journal."

"We must . . . ?" I sputtered. "Must?"

"Now, Jo," my uncle said, raising his hands palms out. "Now, now." Poor Uncle Bert. He was more and more incapable with every passing day.

Rushton went on. "I watched your brother write in it the entire time we were over there. And I happen to know that he kept writing in that journal up until he disappeared."

"So why are you asking me about it?" I asked, folding my arms across my chest.

He sighed. "Josephine, when your brother came back from France, at first he worked for me. That is, until he quit without warning. I suspect he left my employ because he was into something and got in over his head. When he disappeared, the journal disappeared with him."

It made me uneasy to hear Rushton say what I already knew. I went to the window that looked out over Park Avenue.

"So," Rushton said. "Can you tell me where it is?"

I faced the men again. "No."

The room went still. The traffic buzzed and droned and honked; sunlight streamed through the tall window, casting a bright rectangle on the floor. I could feel the warm air through the glass at my back. It made my scar itch.

"Why won't you let me have it?" he asked, his voice soft.

I put on my stoniest expression. "Because I don't have it," I lied. "Not anymore. I— I left it at home. At the house that burned down. I assume it went up in the flames."

Rushton must have believed my act; he looked stricken. He looked away, then moved to the window, standing next to me. "That's it, then. We'll never prove it." He put his hand on the window frame, as if to steady himself. "That was my last hope, to find out—"

I felt sorry for Rushton in that moment. "To find out what?"

He turned to face me. "Are you familiar with the Wall Street bombing of 1920?"

"Yes. Chester told me about your brother Frank. I'm sorry."

He winced. "Did Chester also tell you that Teddy might have been mixed up in it? Because I believe he was."

243

I wouldn't accept that. Teddy said he was just in the wrong place at the wrong time. I shook my head. "That's not possible."

"I'm convinced of it. In fact, he as much as told me."

"I don't believe it. No. That wasn't Teddy." He was wrong. Teddy went to a few meetings, and left them behind when he decided they were too extreme.

"I'm sorry, Jo. I'm convinced that Teddy was mixed up in the whole business. Teddy had something to do with moving the money, or the materials, something. That whole summer before he disappeared, something was not right. I could feel it." He paused. "I think that's why he disappeared. He'd been going to meetings with these anarchists; he sympathized with them. I think he disappeared because he was involved. Up to and past the bombing."

I gripped the edge of the window behind my back. "Teddy, an anarchist. Do you really believe that?"

He nodded.

I turned to look out at the street below.

Rushton went on. "It makes sense, doesn't it? Teddy was nervous about something. Maybe he was about to take the fall. But he wrote about it in his journal, I'm sure of that. And there's something else. I've heard rumors that Daniel Connor was involved. I think Teddy uncovered Connor's part in all of it. I'm betting he said something in his journal. If that's true, your brother's words would convict Daniel Connor and would've told me who was responsible for my brother's death."

I stared at the cars and people moving up and down Park Avenue. I could see the limousines from here. Everything looked clean and shiny. The Emerald City. Of course, the workers and the support staff were coming and going. But even they looked polished from this height.

Rich man, poor man.

Teddy hated that. And that's what the anarchists were all about, right? Disenfranchised immigrants and hardworking laborers. They aimed their anger and their frustration at the rich. Then it struck me, the other thing Rushton had said.

"You used the word 'disappeared,'" I said without turning around. "Do you think Teddy's dead?"

Rushton stirred beside me. "I don't know."

"Do you think," I asked, "do you think Teddy could really do something like that? Kill people like that?" My question floated into the room, not really directed at Rushton. I stared down at the street. I couldn't believe that Teddy might be an anarchist, a bomber, someone involved in the murder of innocent people.

"I liked Teddy. He saved my life." He sighed. "But who knows? All I care about is justice. I want to find out who was responsible for the deaths of my brother and all the others."

"And you think that the answer was in Teddy's journal?"

"I think it could've stood as evidence, if he included enough details. I think if he added names and dates, I could begin to string it together. I could build a case." Rushton, next to me, paused, staring into the sunlight, squinting down at Park Avenue. "I've made this my life's work, Jo. I don't intend to stop searching. I'm doing it for my brother."

I almost made a move, then. I almost went into Melody's room to fetch Teddy's journal. Almost. But something stopped me.

Teddy stopped me. I believed that my brother was a hero,

incapable of such a crime. I believed in him too much; it would kill me, would kill Pops, to find out otherwise.

Oh, I was still so sure I knew right from wrong.

My uncle, long silent, coughed. "Jo, your aunt and I have been talking. We think you should join your parents out west. We'll set it all up for you. There's a train in the morning."

I nodded. I wanted to seem agreeable. Of course, I had to leave them, leave the apartment. But I couldn't leave New York now. I had Teddy's journal—and now it was clearer than ever that I had to keep reading it, whatever I might learn. There was much more here than met the eye—more even than John Rushton thought he knew.

And if I left New York, I couldn't unravel this mystery.

A hand on my arm in the dark, here on a street downtown.

I rubbed my arm now, in the sunlight, and thought of the other compelling reason I didn't want to leave New York: Charlie O'Keefe.

I knew what I had to do and where I had to go. "I'll be ready for the train, Uncle Bert," I lied. "Excuse me."

I went to pack a small bag with the things I'd need. But not so that I could catch a train.

* * *

I had to wait until my uncle and John Rushton left the apartment before I could leave. It took me almost no time to pull my things together, just a few changes of clothing—thank goodness it was summer—and the contents of my silk scarf. Then I had to sit stiff and silent in a chair by the door, listening and waiting, because I was packed and ready long before the elevator door clanged shut behind them.

I looked at my watch, and adjusted my cloche and my short

kid gloves. After five minutes, I rang for the elevator myself.

Joey eyed my valise, a small bag I'd taken from Melody's room. "Going somewhere, miss?"

"Just visiting an old girlfriend," I lied. Leaving my family now, money wouldn't flow as easily. But still, I needed Joey's silence. I parted with a precious quarter.

"Thanks, miss!" He smiled, then gave me the sealed-lips sign, and I couldn't help smiling back.

Ed—who had not lost his job, although he had been reprimanded following the break-in—also looked curiously at my bag. "Cab, Miss Jo?" he asked.

"No, thanks. I'm going to walk. It's a lovely day."

"You'll be back later today, then?"

I looked at Ed. I liked him. I'd grown to trust him. "Ed, I won't be back today. Or tomorrow. Can you give my aunt a message for me?"

"Of course."

"Tell her I'm fine. Tell her not to worry."

He tipped his cap a bit away from his forehead. "Yes, miss, I'll tell her that." He scratched his brow. "Is it true she shouldn't worry?"

I forced my lips to form a smile. "Yes." Inside, I was trembling with the lie.

He adjusted his cap again. "Now, I have a bit of money in my wallet, from tips and such." He reached for his pocket.

I put my hand up and lied again. "No, but thank you. I have money. I'm fine." I had very little, in fact, but I couldn't bear to take his. My throat felt a tickle as I thought of the sacrifice he, a hardworking guy, would have made on my behalf. I had to look away.

"When should I say you'll be back, then?" I could tell he was asking as much for himself as for my aunt.

"Say," I hesitated. I thought it would take me a week, maybe two, to unlock all the secrets. Little did I know. "Say two weeks. I'll see you in two weeks."

He nodded. "I'll be watching for you, Miss Jo. You take care, now."

My throat was so full by this point that I had to swallow hard before I could say, "'Bye, Ed."

It was far too early for me to head in the direction I'd planned to go, and the sun beat down on the city streets. I lifted the valise so that I could tuck the strap over my shoulder and headed over to Central Park, where I could at least sit on a bench in the cooler shade and think. I made straight for my favorite spot, near the zoo, picking up a lemonade from a stand along the way.

The park was full of people today. People wilted in the heat, bedraggled in their undone collars and neckties, jackets draped over shoulders, dresses damp with sweat and clinging to backs. Along the edges of the paths I saw scraps of wadded paper, lost hair ribbons, a grimy ball. Pigeons strutted and begged. The grass was filled with the floating seed heads of dandelions waiting on an idle breeze.

I brushed off the seat of a bench, sat down, and ran through everything in my mind. Teddy was not a hero, even though we'd all called him one. He might even have been responsible in part for the deaths of thirty people on Wall Street on that September day. But I didn't want to believe this.

The last time I saw Teddy, talked to him—that hot June day a year ago—he had asked the unthinkable. He'd asked me to lie to Ma, to Pops, in a way that would surely tear them apart. He'd said it was so he could escape. So I did it. I did what he asked, and it tore the rest of us to shreds and now we're all floating in tatters, like the wisps of paper that float around the New York streets in a wind, the ticker tape that lifts and flutters after a parade and litters the park walkways.

I let Teddy go, walk off, leave me to tell them about the beach, the sand, the water, the clothes he left behind; he left me to lie for him. He disappeared, and everyone believes him dead. Everyone but me. And Connor. Teddy was alive, but now with the danger, he couldn't show himself.

Why didn't he talk to me then? Why hadn't he told me everything when he still could?

I stared into the dappled shade of the trees, feeling the soft whisper of a breeze on my neck, watched the dandelion seeds float up and away like ghosts in a mist.

And then I realized Teddy *had* told me. I had the journal.

I opened the valise and reached inside, feeling for the journal, pulling it out and setting it on my knees, picking up where I left off.

September 10, 1921
When I'm not in the greenhouse, I'm at the beach. That's the only place I can find it—peace. It's the water. The way it stretches out to meet the sky.

September 17
Antonio's all right. Lives in Brooklyn, knows his way around the plants, that's for sure. We've started hanging out together for a smoke in the evening before he goes home, walking the beach. He's

younger than me, didn't serve, but his uncle did.
He's got some ideas, Tony does.

That whole time back in '20, while I was working
for John, I thought I understood. I look back on
what I felt then, and it makes me mad at myself. I
never want to think that way again.

October 12
Talked to Pops. He could see what kind of money
there was to be made, running booze. He said some
funny things to me about how so many politicians
got their start doing things not exactly on the up
and up. That kind of stuff.

I didn't want to say anything, but I know he still
thinks that someday I'm going to be some big shot
or other.

It ain't happening, Pops. I don't know what I want
from life, but it isn't being a big shot of any kind.

I just have to look around to see that lots of
folks need help. Maybe I can find some way to help.
Maybe this Prohibition thing is made for people
like me to get rich and help others.

Like Danny Connor's done.

October 22
Pops tickled about the money. Says he's putting it
away for a rainy day. Thrilled with me for getting
him mixed up with it.

So. That's when Pops got involved in the bootlegging. With Teddy's help. I leaned back against the bench. I was weary, deep-down-in-my-bones weary, and sad. That, I'd never guessed.

Beggar man, thief.

I looked at my watch. It was almost one now. I didn't want to read anymore at the moment. My world had already been turned upside down enough today. If I sat here another hour or so, then it would be all right to head on. The sun slipped between the leaves overhead and warmed the back of my neck, and irresistible drowsiness stole over me. I had to close my eyes, had to. I folded my hands around the journal and closed my eyes, just for a second.

The laughter of children woke me. That and a feeling that I was being watched prickling the back of my neck.

I swiveled on the bench, caught the retreating back, the blond hair in sunlight, and thought, Teddy? He vanished into the shade of the trees around a curve in the path as I sat frozen. Teddy. He was here.

My hands still clutched the journal. The nannies had returned with their charges, all gathered in their usual spot, the children running through the grass and shrieking in pleasure, scattering the birds and filling the air with happy noises. I adjusted my cloche and tucked the journal away.

As I lifted my head again, I saw Melody. She was up the path, about a hundred yards or so, sitting on a bench with her back to me as the path curved. I sat still and pulled my cloche lower over my eyes. I didn't want her to know I was spying on her.

She was meeting her lover, I was sure of it. I looked up the path and down again, searching for the likely candidate. An elderly gentleman approached, leaning on a cane. A young man—but no, he walked right on by her, whistling, winking at me. Couples strolled by arm in arm; a woman in a boa walked her dog; pigeons fluttered and dropped. No lovers. I turned back toward Melody.

She was staring at the children. Her head turned as her eyes followed one child in particular. A tow-headed boy who ran headlong across the grass, yelling at the top of his lungs, his legs pumping, his face lit with joy. He had to be about four, maybe five. He had a familiar look, an expression. . . .

I put my hand to my mouth. I knew.

One of the governesses stood and stretched and called, and the boy ran to her, Melody's face turning so that her eyes could track him. The boy reached his chubby arms up for a lift, and the governess hoisted him into the sky as he laughed; then she set him down again and took his hand to walk him home.

I pressed my fingers against my lips as they walked away, retreating, as Melody's head turned so that she could follow them with her eyes.

Oh, poor Mel.

She rose from the bench and walked briskly away in the opposite direction, back toward the apartment.

Melody did not have a lover. She had a child. A child she'd given up. A child she could watch only from afar.

Melody, the flapper, who hid her mistakes behind a veil of pleasure. I felt the tears in my eyes. The reporter from *The Times* had heard the rumors. Now I understood Aunt Mary's concern: she wanted her daughter to give up the child, but Melody wouldn't, not really. And good for you, Mel, I thought. Good for you for loving so fiercely. Melody had a child, and she couldn't let go; her heart held on tight to the boy with blond curls who clung to the hand of a nanny, unaware his mother was only a few feet away.

And the father? Well. That was an open question.

And then . . . someone else greeted the nanny. Melody was long gone. Someone approached from the other direction and greeted the child with fatherly affection.

John Rushton.

John Rushton, who'd been so openly condescending toward Melody. Who treated her like she was his inferior. Rushton, who'd treated Melody like she was trash when he should have been looking in the mirror at the real villain, the villain who stole her heart, her future, and her child.

I felt nothing for him but disgust.

*   *   *

I sat still for a long time, until the sun tilted west and I knew I had to make my way across town or miss my opportunity. My heart broke for Melody. I despised Rushton. And Teddy—he'd known and had tried to help in his own way. This series of revelations was unexpected, so much so that I felt stunned.

But I stirred myself. Now I really had to go. My timing was critical.

I walked down the streets that were alive with midafternoon activity, feeling more nervous with every step. What if Charlie rejected me, turned me away, told me he couldn't help? I had no other options.

It was a long enough walk that I had plenty of time to worry. I stopped in front of the Algonquin and tugged on the ends of my gloves. Well. We'll see just what Charlie O'Keefe thinks of me now.

CHAPTER 37

LOU

So, Detective. Now you see the point, don't you? No? Then keep listening, sweetheart. Remember what I said about coincidence?

That afternoon, after my night in the Algonquin suite, I saw her.

"Hang on a minute, Sam."

I turned right around in the backseat. I figured she wouldn't notice me watching her through the Packard window. 'Cause there she was, like right out of a nightmare, standing in front of the hotel with a suitcase in her hot little hand.

I couldn't help it; my eyes got watery, and my throat sported a lump the size of a baseball.

I'd spent a night in the suite instead of going back to the mansion after a long day of shopping. Danny had sent Sam to fetch me out of the hotel. Sam made it clear that I needed to get a move on, Danny wanted me home.

That was so unusual that as soon as I saw her standing there I was sure Danny was moving her into the suite in the Algonquin in my place.

Okay, so maybe he was putting her there so he could come in and give her the business over Teddy, or maybe she'd gone there to see Charlie. But carrying a suitcase? That meant only one thing, the green-eyed monster yelled in my head. Danny was starting something with Jo, and the baseball in my throat grew to the size of a watermelon. And then darker thoughts began to tickle my brain.

"Let's get out of here," I said to Sam. "And can we take a drive once we reach the island? I want to walk on the ocean side. Put my toes in some real ocean water."

"Mr. Connor, he said—"

"I know, Sam. But I need a walk, first. You'll do that for me, won't you?"

"Sure, Miss Louise."

Good old Sam. Little did he know what I was conspiring, there, in the backseat of the limo.

Yeah, I know, Detective, but like I said. Thinking ain't the same as doing.

CHAPTER 38

JUNE 6, 1925

A woman in the 1920s "knows that it is her American, her twentieth-century birthright to emerge from a creature of instinct into a full-fledged individual who is capable of molding her own life. And in this respect she holds that she is becoming man's equal."
—Dorothy Dunbar Bromley, "Feminist—New Style,"
Harper's Monthly Magazine, October 1927

JO

I made my way through the grand lobby, feeling smaller with every step. I was not here under Louie's wing; the valise I'd borrowed was worn; the dress I'd chosen, a longish dark gray shift with a dropped waist, was about a year out of style. No one was looking at me as near as I could tell, but I felt as though every eye followed me, disapproving, reading my intentions, whispering behind gloved fingers.

How much more disapproving they would be if they knew what I was about to ask of a single young man.

I stopped at the entrance to the Rose Room. It was clear that Jacques didn't recognize me.

"Yes?" he asked, with barely a glance up from his worksheet.

"A table for one, please."

"You are here for lunch?"

"Tea. And something to eat."

He looked me up and down, his eyebrows raised in disdain, then escorted me to a table, leaving me at once to attend to other matters.

Charlie was in his usual spot, but I couldn't see him well, as I'd been seated at the far side of the room and two fat pillars stood between the Round Table and me. I ordered tea and cakes and kept my eyes and ears open; I couldn't afford to have Charlie slip away.

I worried that I was there too late, but after finishing what I'd been served I saw that I'd eaten too quickly.

"Anything else, miss?" the waiter asked.

"No," I answered.

"I'll bring the check straightaway."

Then I would have to leave. Long before I could get to Charlie. "Wait," I said. "I'd like some soda water."

He nodded, looking troubled, then leaned forward. "We don't allow alcohol here, miss," he whispered.

"What?" I was stunned that he'd thought I wanted a drink.

"In case you've got a flask." He pointed at my leg, and I realized he thought my long skirt might hide a garter with a tucked-in flask. Asking for soda water was the cue, as Melody had told me.

I pulled myself upright. "I have no flask," I said, trying to keep my voice steady.

His eyes widened, and he said, fast, "Sorry, miss. It's just, you know." He nodded his head toward the Round Table, again populated by all men, who again were jovial and, I wagered, drinking alcohol. "We're not supposed to let it happen, but there are certain types who can get away with . . ." His voice trailed off, and he left to fetch my soda water.

"Certain types." I had a clear feeling that "certain types"—men—could get away with just about anything. But that a woman alone was suspect. Despite the suffrage, despite the rise of the flapper, despite the fact that women could work, could live independent lives, despite our being able to fling off corsets and adopt comfortable clothing, despite all our modern conveniences, not much had changed for women. Melody, in her rant of a couple of weeks earlier, was right. Nothing had really changed.

Melody had to give up her child. Louie had to give up her soul. What did I have to give up?

In a way, I realized, Pops had the right idea. Marriage, a good marriage, was still the only option available to girls like me. Ma, Aunt Mary, they'd made their marriages their careers. For a girl who didn't marry, at least not straight out of high school, what other prospect was there?

Something shifted in me in that moment. I'd always been so sure that if I thought something through I'd be right, and I'd always thought I knew which side to choose—the right side. But everything came in shades of gray. Everything and everyone. The guys Teddy met and lost in France. The immigrants with their dreams just off the boat. Pops and his desire for riches. John Rushton and his brother. Melody and her child. Lou and Danny Connor.

Even me, Josephine Anne Winter. My life was not planned clear and simple; it was not written down. There were no magic formulas to follow. Adding "a" and "b" would not necessarily lead to "c." If I was to get anywhere in this life, I would have to take risks; I'd have to face the fires. I'd have to be willing to be wrong.

I had to ask Charlie for his help, but I wasn't going to be ashamed of it. Maybe a flapper wasn't just a "floozie," as Pops would say.

And maybe I was turning into a flapper, and that was just fine. Maybe a flapper was a girl who could stand up for herself and admit she didn't know it all.

When the waiter came back with my soda water, I stopped him. "I need to get a message to my cousin," I said, nodding my head in Charlie's direction. "I have to meet him when his shift is over."

The waiter relaxed into a smile. "You're Charlie's cousin? Why didn't you say so? Sure. What's the message?"

I told him and watched as he crossed the dining room, watched as he whispered in Charlie's ear, watched as he pointed in my direction. Charlie's face lifted toward me, and my heart did a little fluttery dance as I met his dark but unsmiling eyes.

Then I sipped my soda water slowly, feeling both relief and a new kind of anxiety at what Charlie would say.

* * *

He wasn't done until after five, and I'd depleted much of my meager stash of money ordering a second soda water. I hadn't dared take out the journal and read it in public, now that I knew what it might contain. Charlie came and sat down at my table.

"Your cousin, eh? Well, I guess that's better than being your enemy." He was tense but not unkind. "Let's go. We can sit in the lobby—there's a nice quiet corner."

The corner was occupied by two great soft chairs pulled close. Our conversation was muffled by the thick carpeting and drooping potted plants. Charlie and I sat facing each other, knees just touching. He leaned toward me. "Okay, Jo."

"First of all, I'm sorry. I thought you had something to do with it. With the break-in."

He smiled almost at once, relief flooding his features. "Oh. Okay."

"I thought you were in Danny Connor's pocket."

He tensed again. "I'm not. But . . ."

"What?" I felt my mouth go dry.

"I thought you were gone for good."

I swallowed. "I'm sorry," I repeated.

"Sure." He looked at his hands, flexed his fingers. "I tried to put you out of my mind. I asked Connor for help."

I couldn't speak.

"So he did. He got me a job. A big one. Full-time musician at a place that pays big. I'll be a headliner."

"Oh! That's great, Charlie. Really. That's what you want."

"Yeah." He looked at the floor. "Trouble is, it's in Chicago."

"Oh," I said again. And again, "Oh."

Charlie looked at me. "But now you're here."

I swallowed hard.

"You came back. I thought you were done with me. You know, because I'm just a waiter . . . trying to be a musician . . . just some guy. Some guy you thought had double-crossed you."

"Charlie," I started.

He interrupted. "Look, I leave at the end of the week."

The end of the week. "You're not just some guy to me, Charlie. I like you."

He lifted his face, and his dark eyes bored into me. "You do?"

I nodded.

"Really?"

I nodded again.

"Because you, you're better than me, you know."

I shook my head. "No, I'm not, Charlie. I've been all wrong about things." My cheeks felt like they were on fire. "So wrong I need your help."

Something flicked across his face, but then he said, "What do you need?"

"I need help finding a place to stay."

His eyebrows shot skyward. "Why? What's going on?"

"I had to leave. I was afraid for my aunt and uncle and cousins. My being there, it put them in danger." I hadn't told Charlie about the fire; now I related the whole story.

"Jo—why didn't you tell me about this sooner?" He looked angry.

"It wasn't until the break-in that I really began to believe it all wasn't an accident. That I might be the target."

"Why?" His eyes searched my face, and his hand reached for mine.

I hesitated. I had to trust him, but I still told him only part of it. "I have something of my brother's that everyone seems to want."

"I see." He searched my face. "Can I ask what it is?"

"His journal. Charlie, it may have some information that Danny Connor won't like."

Charlie leaned back, pulling his hands away. "Won't like because . . ."

"I'm not certain yet. But John Rushton thinks Teddy might have implicated Danny Connor in the 1920 Wall Street bombing."

Charlie let out a low whistle. He leaned his head back and studied the ceiling. Then he shook his head. "You said 'might have.' Do you know for sure? Have you read the whole thing?"

"Not yet."

He leaned forward again. "I can't believe it. Connor's no angel, that's for sure, but that bombing? Nah. No way."

"But Teddy did work for him. And Teddy was a believer, at least for a while."

Charlie nodded. "I remember when I met Teddy. It was when Louie took up with Danny." He pursed his lips. "I was fifteen, and kind of not connected with the real world. One day Louie and I lived in a pretty bad place downtown. The next we lived in this hotel, and then in the mansion, the one you've seen, out on the Island." He looked down at his hands, working his fingers together. "It wasn't real clear to me what Lou had to give up for me, you know. I didn't get it back then. She made sure I kept going to school. She had to grow up way before—"

"I know, Charlie. She's told me. She's all right with it."

"That's because she loves Danny. She believes in him."

"But that doesn't mean he's a good guy. That doesn't mean he isn't involved in the bombings."

"I don't buy it. You know, I think he's too worried about his reputation to get mixed up in that. He wants to be seen as the Irish savior."

"All I know is he and several other people want to get their hands on this journal, and that makes me a target. So I need to find a place to stay." I looked at my hands, knotting them together in my lap, with my knees pressed tight. "My own home is gone, and I don't know this city as well as you do."

Charlie leaned forward again. "I've got a great idea. Trust me."

I looked up into his dark eyes.

He smiled. "Trust me, Jo. I'll treat you with respect like I would my own sister. Even if I'm glad you aren't."

* * *

Charlie walked me straight to one of the ladies-only hotels in Midtown, saying he could vouch for it. He pressed a twenty into my palm and wouldn't take no for an answer. Then he waited outside while I went in.

The matron looked me up and down, and I could hear the word "flapper" hanging in the air, but I paid for a week up front, gave her my best schoolgirl smile and polite speech, and she let me take a room. It was spotless and right next to the bath.

I settled in for a few minutes, then found Charlie outside. He was leaning against a lamppost. At the sight of his wolfish body my heart gave a quick leap, and when he saw me and smiled it did a little dance right in my chest.

"Now what?" he asked.

"Now I've got to read some more of Teddy's journal. Find out what he was trying to hide. See if there's something in there about Connor."

"Would you consider having dinner at my place first?"

My face burned a hot pink. "At your place? At your apartment?"

"I swear, Jo." He raised his hands. "I'll bring you right back here. Eating there is a lot cheaper than going out. And I like to cook. And it might be one of the last times, you know, before I take off for Chicago."

My heart slowed down, way down, as I thought about Charlie leaving.

Charlie and I took the bus downtown. From a vendor on his block we bought roast chicken and vegetables and cheese and bread and apples—and a cheap bottle of bootleg wine the guy slipped out in a brown wrapper from behind the bottom door of his cart. Charlie's apartment was a couple of rooms in a tenement on Christopher Street, with a kitchen tucked in one corner of the larger room.

Charlie was tidier than I'd imagined, especially since I was an unexpected guest. There were a few dirty dishes in the sink, and he ran into the back room to yank some laundry from his makeshift line and throw the coverlet up over the bed. But the floor was swept and the icebox was clean.

I stood awkwardly in the middle of the room as Charlie bustled around me, tucking things in place and talking a mile a minute about how the apartment was nice and quiet and the landlady pleasant and the rent so cheap he could squirrel money away for the day when he could move to a bigger place uptown. Assuming he stayed in New York. He started in on the vegetables, scrubbing and chopping and setting them to roast in the oven.

"Shoot," he said. "Forgot something. Can you watch the vegetables for a few minutes? I'll be right back."

He left, and I was alone. I took off my gloves and hat and placed them on a small table close to the door. I moved to the window. Charlie's apartment was on the third story, and it was in the front, so I had a decent view up and down the street. I shifted the sash up high enough so that I could lean out on my forearms into the warm June evening. It seemed as if all of New York congregated below. Organ grinders; movable vending stalls piled with fruits and meats and dry goods; kids running into the street after hoops and balls; couples strolling; mothers dragging children; cars, wagons, honking, shouting; the stench of humanity, of horse sweat, of dung, of rot, of fragrant cooking . . .

New York was alive. Or maybe I should say, this part of New York was truly alive. Lights flicked on in the windows of an apartment down the street. Someone shouted from a fire escape to my left at a person hanging laundry from a fire escape across the street. The tenements here stretched five stories up, and for several blocks all I could see was life going on and on and on.

Above the street hung a sky of evening blue, that thick, deepening blue that pressed like a soft weight, that spoke of the promise and threat of night. I sucked in the air, dirty and rich.

I'd never known this side of New York. Teddy had never shown me anything like this. My aunt and uncle and cousins lived a rarified, sheltered, and sterile life. I'd been shielded by a comfortable home. Now here I was, in the grit and grime of lower Manhattan and I felt, I felt . . . I felt I'd come home. I closed my eyes and listened, just listened.

Children and music, shouts and whistles, the clatter of pots, the sound of water running through the pipes, the *flap, flap* of the hanging laundry.

Then a *click* behind me, and I turned as Charlie stepped in. I made to close the window, but he stopped me.

"No," he said. "If you don't mind, I like the air."

I smiled and then saw that Charlie had bought fresh flowers. Yellow coreopsis, white daisies, blue larkspur.

He held them up, a bit sheepish. "Some lady who'd driven a truck in from the Island grew them in her yard. They looked, I mean, it seemed to me that it's kind of a special occasion. You know." He turned such a deep red I thought he might faint.

I took them from him. "Do you have something we can put them in? Like a glass?"

He went to the cabinet and produced a drinking glass. "Will this do?"

"Perfect." I smiled, and we set to having dinner, and for the moment I forgot about Teddy and the growing mystery and my worries. Instead, I concentrated on how much Charlie was growing on me, first as a friend, and now, I hoped, something more.

*   *   *

It was around nine when Charlie dropped me back at my hotel, on his way to his nighttime gig. The narrow-eyed matron reminded me about curfew, but I assured her I was in for the night. In, and ready to read more from Teddy's journal. I pulled the easy chair close to the table with its soft-glowing lamp, next to the open window.

November 3, 1921
I about strangled Patrick today. I can't believe he'd get Danny mixed up in that business. What with everything else we've got going, what does he think? Danny just blew it off—his kid brother, being stupid—but I can see what'll happen if Paddy gets caught. We'll all land in prison, and Danny and me with a noose around our necks.

November 20
Paddy's hanging around, down at the speak. Boys have seen him. He's real hot under the collar, ready to come for me, but I don't care. I don't like this whole business.
Let him come.

January 10, 1922
Danny has a real sweet girl. Louise O'Keefe. The
only thing is, she's pretty young. She acts all mature,
but I can tell. She's not much older than Josie.

Paddy hits on her. I've stepped in, but it's only
a matter of time. That idea makes me sick. More
than once I've almost said something to Danny, but
held my tongue.

February 3
At least Danny's treating Louise right, near as I can
tell. And she seems happy. She seems to really care
about Danny. Maybe she's good for him. Charlie,
her kid brother, he's enrolled in school. Danny
supports them both.

Sometimes I do think Danny's okay.

April 12
I can't believe it. Paddy's telling everyone when he's
too drunk to keep his mouth shut. If it's true, I'd
like to kill the guy myself. Right from the get-go I
knew he was bad news. I can't believe Danny knows,
or he'd have done something. God forbid he should
ever find out.

And Aunt Mary and Uncle Bert can't find out,
either. Never.

What's next? I'm worried that Danny will . . .

And there, again, a gap. I made a fist, pounded my leg. Honestly!

Pulled-out pages, just like before. I wanted to scream. If only I'd seen the gap sooner. Another wild-goose chase, another wait until I could find out what Teddy had hidden.

I turned back and forth, looking for the hint. It had to be there, somewhere.

I found it about two pages further on, buried on the bottom of a page that tallied expenses for the month of May. Small cramped handwriting in a different ink:

That last visit to the Met. That statue.

The message was for me, but like the first one it was a puzzle. What secrets could the statue hold? Teddy must have truly felt threatened to make this such a problem for me. And it was only for me—no one else would have been able to decipher the clues the same way I would. I took a deep breath and thought it through.

That last visit to the Met—to see the Winslow Homer paintings once again. To talk about the ocean, the cool grays and blues of Homer's scenes, sitting on the marble bench. Teddy seemed so distant and sad. As we left the museum his walk was a shuffle like that of an old and broken man. My heart was broken, too. I still felt it, such sadness, and when he paused in the last gallery before the statue, so different from the Homer.

That statue. So different. I sat upright. I had to take another look at the statue in person, and discover what clue it held. More pages, like the Sherlock Holmes? I could only hope.

CHAPTER 39

LOU

By the time I got home Danny was fit to be tied.

"Where have you been?"

I shrugged. I wasn't ready to give him an inch. I was all suspicious about what he wanted from Jo, so I wasn't going to play nice. "I took a little walk on the beach."

"Beach? We have a beach right here. I told Sam to bring you straight home."

"This isn't the ocean, Danny. This is the Sound. I wanted to hear the waves." I had my back to him as I removed my gloves and hat. "Did you miss me that much?" I turned around.

He was chewing his lip. "Sometimes, Louise, you try my patience."

He was in a funny mood. Dark, like he'd seen a ghost or something. It reminded me of how he looked after Paddy took the fall. That insecurity he buried deep inside that he almost never let on about. His sadness made me feel bad. Maybe I'd misjudged him about Jo. I put my hand on his cheek and his stormy eyes met mine. I said, "I'm sorry, honey. There's something about the waves, you know?"

He hesitated just for a beat. "All right, Louise." Then he kissed my fingers and turned and walked away.

CHAPTER 40

*Taking everything into consideration, the most interesting things I have
learned about people are their love of mystery . . . and, most strikingly of all,
the wish to believe the supernatural, especially in some evidence of life after
death.*
—Howard Thurston, <u>My Life of Magic</u>, 1929

JO

The next morning I headed uptown to reach the Metropolitan
Museum as soon as the doors opened. A long line formed at the
museum entrance, and it was all I could do not to barrel through
the crowd. Once inside, I had to restrain myself from running up
the broad marble stairs to the first gallery on the right.

The Egyptian prince was still there.

It stood in an alcove, lit from above, looking exactly as it had
looked over a year earlier. He was worn almost featureless by
weather, yet the proud prince still stepped out with his right foot,
held a staff in a firm grip in his right fist, and fixed his eyes on
some distant point way above my head and way back in time.

Teddy had stopped there on our way out, mesmerized. And said,
"Look at that, Jo. Will you just look at that."

"What, Teddy?" I had been confused. "Look at what?"

"Why, he's the spitting image . . ." and he'd stopped. Looked down at me. Had a twinkle in his eye for the first time in months. "He's the spitting image of Uncle Bert."

I'd looked back at the Egyptian prince, said, "Um . . ."

And Teddy had laughed. So I had, too, because it was so good to laugh with him.

"Nah, just pulling your leg. But Aunt Mary must think so." I was even more confused by that comment. Clearly, the memory stuck. Mainly because Teddy had been happy, something I hadn't seen in so long.

Now I stood looking up at Mentuhotep II, who looked nothing like my round-bellied uncle. I glanced over my shoulder; the only guard was looking away, watching a group of noisy schoolkids. I drew closer. A rope guide draped around the base. If pages were hidden, they were out of sight. I'd have to slip under if I was to search behind the striding prince. Maybe he'd slid them between the wall and the prince.

I took a chance and moved fast. A two-inch gap between the statue's base and the wall revealed . . . nothing. And then, "Hey!"

The guard was at my side in an instant.

"I'm sorry," I said, using my best high school French to feign an accent. "I dropped my guidebook." I pointed down behind Mentuhotep.

He narrowed his eyes, but when he bent to look behind the statue, I ran.

"Hey, now!" he yelled after me, but I pushed through the school crowd, ducking, and plowed down the marble staircase and out into the summer sunlight.

And then, bending double to catch my breath in front of the

Met, it came to me, why Teddy had stopped before the prince.

I walked as fast as my legs could carry me back down Park
Avenue and stood sweating in the shade of a building across the
avenue from my aunt and uncle's apartment.

Ed was there, rocking on his heels, moving to the door when
someone went in or out. I watched him for about half an hour
before I screwed up my courage, then crossed the street just as
a cab pulled to the curb and Ed went to grab the door handle. I
slipped behind him into the lobby and found Joey sucking on his
cheek and staring at the ceiling.

"Joey?"

He looked like he'd been caught red-handed in a theft.

I folded a whole dollar into his palm, which burned his cheeks
crimson. "Is anyone in the apartment?"

"Just the help, miss."

"Take me up?"

"Yes, miss. Right away, miss."

When we reached the foyer, I turned to Joey, bending almost to
one knee. "I'll only be a minute. You wait for me, okay?"

He looked at me, then at the crumpled bill still in his palm,
likely the biggest tip he'd ever had. "I'll be here, miss. Right here."

I could hear noises from the kitchen, but since Ed hadn't
called up on the intercom, neither Malcolm nor Adela made an
appearance.

I slipped down the hall and into the library, shutting the door
softly behind me. There it was, the miniature prince. The statue
was an exact replica of the one in the Met, standing on a high shelf,
from where it had survived the break-in. I must have glanced at it
a hundred times, and I'd never made the connection, despite its

being the only old-looking thing in the apartment. I had to pull a chair over to take it down from its lofty spot.

It was hollow, made of some kind of clay. I peered into the hole in the bottom.

The pages were wadded deep inside, so there was no help for it. I smacked the prince against the brick back of the fireplace, scattering the broken fragments all over the hearth. I hoped it was not too valuable a replica, but I had no time to worry over it. I opened the door; Joey was hissing.

"Miss! Miss!"

I ran down the hall clutching Teddy's missing pages.

"Someone's buzzing me from the lobby!"

"I'll take the servant's stairs, then."

He nodded, wide-eyed, and I made for the service door, thinking that by breaking the statue I wasn't much better than whoever had ransacked the apartment and given poor Chester his shiner.

The servants' entrance opened into the back of the lobby, hidden by artfully placed palms. I opened the door a crack. Ed stood outside on the sidewalk with his hands clasped behind his back. Joey was letting Melody into the elevator.

I felt terrible. Melody was my friend, but I couldn't risk being trapped. And I was afraid she'd realize that something was different with me, now that I knew her secret. I waited until the door clanged shut behind her and the elevator groaned up.

And Ed. I couldn't get him into trouble. I waited until he went to whistle down a taxi before I slipped out through the big doors and made my way along the sidewalk, my face hidden beneath my tightly pulled cloche.

It was about noon when I finally got back to my hotel room. I barely had my hat and gloves off before I collapsed with Teddy's bunched-up pages and began to read.

June 22, 1923
I'm so angry I can't stand it. I actually quit today, but Danny wouldn't hear of it. Said he'd never forgive me, and then gave me that look that says, You'd better listen. But he still excuses Patrick, that moron. I don't care if they're brothers; Paddy's a lying bum.

June 25
The investigation is thick around us. Even Connor sees it's better to slow down on all activity for a time. Just lay low. Draw no attention.

June 27
The reward is $20,000. That's a lot of dough. Pops would sure be delighted. He could quit the business, buy a big house, heck, he and Ma could move into the city, into a swanky place near Uncle Bert and Aunt Mary.
      All I have to do is be a snitch.
      I've already cheated once. Why not? Patrick deserves it.

July 10
I destroyed all the evidence. It still ticks me off that it was here, all this time. It's been years. What if they'd found it?

I couldn't believe I hadn't found it earlier. He'd
buried it but good, and I was too busy to notice
something underfoot in the greenhouse. Only
because I had to rebuild the tables did I make the
discovery, the wooden crates. They were stamped,
dated: summer 1920. I knew.

It made me feel ill, the whole business, the people
who died, and for what? He didn't get to any of the
powerful men, just the everyday workingman and
workingwoman, and John Rushton's brother. And
I heard there were a couple of other young runners
in the crowd, just kids. What's the point? Didn't we
go to war for this?

Just death, for no good reason. I couldn't believe
Patrick could be such a fool. I was too upset even to
tell Danny, and then I figured maybe that was wise.
Why mix him up in the problem at this point?

I carted the stuff—the boxes of fuses and
explosives—in the wheelbarrow down to the Sound
and disposed of it. Probably took me eight trips.
I thought I'd sink the boat with the weight before
I could get out deep enough. And had to do it on
a moonless night so no one saw. Took most of the
night. I'm exhausted but can't sleep.

What an idiot that Patrick is. One of these
days . . .

I put the pages down. The investigation. Teddy must have found
the bomb materials. And how that finding implicated Patrick.

I finished the removed pages; the entries now picked up again in the journal.

July 12
Ran into John. I can't even write about it now.
It feels bad, holding this all in, holding myself together. The only time I can think now is out in the greenhouse, when I'm alone.

July 17
I stood in front of the police station for over an hour. Had to move on when I feared someone would get suspicious.

What Pops could do with that $20,000. I keep thinking about Ma and Jo, dressed nice. About Jo getting a real education, going to college, even.

But Danny would know: that's what I'd be afraid of. And then we'd all be in danger. No, it's no good.

July 21
John thinks Danny was involved in the business. Naturally, I tried to fend John off. The last thing we need is to invite suspicion.

Danny's a good guy, working for his people, trying to help. How could he be involved? Still, it's probably a good thing I didn't tell Danny about what I found. I tried to persuade John that Danny was just a businessman, but John is obsessed. And me? There's a real danger that if—

And there it was again. Another set of missing pages. The last set, as this was where the journal ended. I leaned back and the chair creaked, and I was back in New York, with cars honking and engines accelerating, and brakes squealing, and the smells of grease and dust and frying food. Just as I was so close, another missing section.

Teddy was not involved in the bombing. But Daniel's brother, Patrick, he was another matter. He was the bomber. And that, *that* was what made trouble for Teddy, for me. He knew the truth, and that's why Daniel Connor was not letting any of this go.

But Teddy was not involved. I leaned forward until my head rested on the table and breathed a sigh. I hadn't realized how worried I was until I felt this relief. I thanked all the stars that Teddy, my Teddy, could still be good.

*   *   *

The knock on the door startled me so, I almost dropped the journal on the floor.

The matron peered around me into the room, suspicious, then straightened. "You have a phone call. You can take it in the corridor."

"Thanks," I said.

"Young men are not allowed in the hotel," she said over her shoulder.

I picked up the receiver and said hello, then heard the operator click off before I heard Charlie ask, "You okay?"

I thrilled to his voice. "I'm fine."

"Want to meet me for dinner? I got a big tip for my booking last night. It's burning a hole in my pocket."

Charlie was practically grinning through the phone line. I

grinned back, hugging the big black receiver to my cheek. "Sure. Where and when?"

"Would you mind taking a cab down to my place, about six? I've got something special in mind."

I hung up, still smiling.

I took a hot bath and pulled out my one nice dress. It was a soft green rayon with little woven branches running through the fabric, making a raised pattern, the thread of the branches of a darker green. I knew it must have looked good on Melody, but I had to say, as I looked in the bedroom mirror, it suited my darker coloring and blue eyes to a T. And with the dropped waist with its fat loopy dark brown ribbon, it sure was the style. It came with a long skinny brown jacket to cover it, and I'd brought the only jewelry I owned, my grandmother's pearls, which I fastened around my neck.

Maybe all that preparation paid off, because when I arrived downtown and Charlie opened his door, his mouth dropped open so far I thought his jaw might touch his knees.

"Wow," he said. "You look . . . You're a knockout."

I started to giggle and drew both hands over my mouth so I wouldn't look foolish. I swallowed hard and said, "Thanks."

He stepped aside so I could enter. Feeling sheepish, I gestured at the dress. "It's Melody's. Everything I have, I got from her."

"Well, she has nothing on you. I mean, she's nice enough. But . . ." His voice trailed off. Then he squared his shoulders. "Someday I'm going to be rich. I'll be a hit cornet player in a hit band. You wait. Then if you want a pretty dress, why, you can just ask, and I'll take you to the finest place in town." He paused. "Maybe it's all gonna start when I get to Chicago."

All sorts of thoughts went through me then, and they went

through my mind so fast I could scarcely keep up. The first thought was, Why, Charlie was willing to buy me pretty dresses sometime in the future, which meant he wanted me in his future. That gave me such a thrill it went right up my spine. The second thought was, Good for you, Charlie, for having a dream.

And the third? It was a contradiction, not a question. The third thought was, Why should you have to pay for my dresses, Charlie O'Keefe? Why shouldn't I be ready and willing and able to buy my own pretty things, whenever I want, with money that I earn?

"It's really sweet of you to say, but I can take care of myself."

I regretted the words the minute they were out. Charlie's face grew dark, and he turned away.

"I knew it," he muttered.

"Knew what?" My stomach was all twisted up now.

"Nothing, never mind."

"No, Charlie, tell me—"

"It's that . . . that you're better than me. Smarter. You come from a better class. I've been waiting for you to throw me off. You probably think this place"—and he cast his arm around the room—"is pretty shabby."

"No, Charlie, no. That's not what I meant."

He stood there, hulking, his broad back to me. "I thought you might want to come to Chicago, maybe, after I get settled. I guess not."

I sighed. "Charlie, that's not it. I want to be independent, that's all. I want to be on my own, making my own way. Pops wants me to get married just for the sake of it. He doesn't believe in me. And he certainly doesn't think a girl can do things, make something of herself. Please, Charlie. And I'm not smarter than you. And you've got such a talent." I hesitated. My words came out small and squeaky. "I meant what I said before. I really like you."

His shoulders drew back a little.

"Honest," I said.

He turned toward me.

I said to him, "You've been so nice and all. I'm sorry I said anything. I was wrong."

Our eyes met, and we stood there for a long moment before he smiled. "I guess it's no secret that I like you, Jo Winter." He raised his head. "I hope you're not playing with me. I want to believe you. And I do believe in you."

I felt a flutter of happiness at that. "The only thing is . . ."

His smile sagged, and his lips formed a thin line.

"I just don't know that I can come to Chicago. I hadn't realized it before, but I think New York is where I belong."

Even as I said the words, I knew it to be true in my heart—that the crazy, busy, clamorous island of Manhattan had grabbed my heart, just as firmly as this boy had. I wanted them both. But I might have to give one of them up. "Charlie, I do like you. I'm just trying to follow my heart. And you have to follow your heart, too. If you need to go to Chicago to make music, why then . . ." My voice broke.

"I want to make music," he said. "But now I know I want to make music with you around."

We stood, the two of us, in awkward silence, looking anywhere but at each other.

"I like you, Charlie," I whispered.

His voice was gruff, low. "I like you, too, Jo Winter. Really like you." He worked his hands. "Maybe Danny'll help get me a booking here. It's not like I want to leave." He shook his head. "I've got a few days. Something'll work out."

Oh, how I prayed for that to be true. Even as I grimaced inwardly at the mention of Danny.

He smiled. "Right now I'd like to show off this pretty girl I'm with. Show New York what a star really looks like. Okay with you?"

I nodded, and we stepped out into the June evening, with my whole being singing like an electric wire in a high wind.

* * *

The street was alive with activity. The vendor carts still carried the day's fresh produce, and women were out buying for the evening meal. Old women in black from head to toe, the old style, complete with shawl and button shoes and skirt to the ankles; younger women in shorter skirts but still handmade muslins with white linen shirtwaists, certainly not flapper fashion, and usually these younger ones had a child or two or three in tow. The alleys were festooned, from one balcony to the one across, with lines of laundry that could be winched back and forth. Shirts flapped like flags, sheets billowed like sails.

What men were around were hawking—or pickpocketing. One such, a young guy, younger than me, bumped up against Charlie, who stopped and seized the boy by the shoulders.

"You'll not be doing any of that here, if you know what's good for you," Charlie said, his voice a low growl.

The boy slunk away, melting into the crowd.

Charlie took my hand in his, mine feeling so small and delicate in that big maw of his that I felt insignificant. But happy.

To our left was a storefront whose sign was in Hebrew; to our right was one that sold nothing but handkerchiefs. We had to walk down the middle of the street, dodging autos and horse-drawn wagons, because the sidewalks were stuffed, all the way to the curb, with pushcarts holding goods to be sold.

Charlie's building had one telephone in the hallway outside the landlady's apartment. It was ringing as we stepped outside; seconds later she came running down the street after us.

"Mr. Charlie! Telephone call for you. Important." As we followed her she said to Charlie, "I hope your cousin"—and she narrowed her eyes while looking at me—"is getting on well, being newly arrived from the old country, and all."

Charlie raised his eyebrows at me, mouthed, I lied.

I smiled and nodded, trying to look like Charlie's cousin, and keeping my mouth shut, for there was no way I could feign a brogue.

"Thanks, Mrs. Daly," Charlie said. We walked back to the tenement and up the steps; Charlie lifted the dangling phone. "Hello?"

He was silent, listening, and he turned away from me so that I could not see his face. The tinny sound of the voice from the receiver filled the air: a woman's voice. I guessed it must be Lou.

"Uh-huh . . . okay . . . yes . . . right." Charlie hung up and turned toward me, his expression solemn.

"What?" My belly clenched.

Charlie nodded toward the landlady's open door, took my elbow, and steered me back out to the street. We faced each other on the busy sidewalk. "The problems for your family aren't behind you. Leaving them didn't change anything."

"What? What do you mean?"

"That was Lou. She's just heard from Melody. Someone roughed up Chester. Picked him up in a speak last night and gave him a real going-over. He's in the hospital, Jo. This isn't over just because you wish it was."

Chester. I clutched Charlie's hand. "What can I do?"

What could I do?

CHAPTER 41

Lou

It was in '23, when Danny figured out about Melody, that things got ugly. Sure, Teddy and that John Rushton tried to hush it up, but Danny, he has his ways. He didn't find out until too late, of course, but that didn't matter. Danny blamed everything on the Cates and Winter families. And that made them all his enemies.

Danny, he went about revenge in his own sweet way.

I met Melody not too long after I met Danny, when her pop and Danny started doing banking business together. I told Danny privately that I had some tingly feelings about that Cates family—they were pretty upper crust, and there was something else I couldn't put my pinkie on— but Danny brushed me off, and besides, I liked Mel.

So I started to spend time with her. I told Danny he'd have to let me have girlfriends, 'cause a girl needs other girls, you know? Sometimes guys can be just too dense. And besides, who else can a girl talk to about *la mode* and such? And how else could I keep an eye on things?

Mel is the perfect flapper. It's as if Scott Fitzgerald writes his stories about her. She has the body and the face for it, which does make me a little jealous, since I'm a curvier type. Danny, he liked me that way, but it isn't the fashion. So I'm always on one diet or another, trying to make myself skinny like Mel or Jo. And Mel, she's got the attitude, that nothing-is-really-important attitude. Although sometimes I do worry about her.

Sometimes I think she's more like Eugenia Kelly, that rebellious party girl of, gosh, ten years ago, and I worry that Mel will end up in the same bad way. Melody had some deep secrets, but she didn't let on, not even to me. I've had to figure it all out strictly on my own.

It wasn't until a couple years after we met that I figured it out. And really, that might've been when Danny had his first inklings. When they brought Patrick back, all broken, Mel was visiting at the house. I could see right off she'd known him from somewhere. From before. I could see it, and my tingly feelings about exploded when I watched her watch him.

I could tell she would've used those sharp red-painted nails and killed Patrick herself, if he hadn't already been dead.

CHAPTER 42
JUNE 8–9, 1925

The past and the present are within the field of my inquiry, but what a man may do in the future is a hard question to answer.
—Sir Arthur Conan Doyle, The Hound of the Baskervilles, 1901

JO

All my pleasure at being with Charlie vanished. I asked, choking, "How 'roughed up'?"

"Someone got the jump on him. They wanted to know where you were. When he said he didn't have a clue, they took it out on him."

"But he's okay?"

"They broke a couple of ribs, did a number on his face. Threatened him. I guess he's pretty banged up."

I covered my mouth with my hand. I might not like Chester, but he didn't deserve that business. I hoped I wouldn't be sick right there on the sidewalk.

"He'll be okay."

"This is my fault," I said. "I've got to take care of it. Now."

Charlie looked at his hands. He looked up at me. "It's Connor, isn't it?"

I nodded.

"Do you know what he wants?"

I swallowed. "Teddy. And if he can't have Teddy, then he wants Teddy's journal. And now I know why." I paused. I had to trust him. "There's actual evidence in the journal that Danny's brother was the Wall Street bomber."

"His brother, Patrick?" Charlie had an odd look on his face.

I nodded again.

"Well, that's not a problem then."

"It isn't? Why not?"

"Because Patrick's dead."

Dead! I felt a sweep of relief. "So nothing will come of it if I give Connor the journal, right? It's useless to the police if Patrick is dead."

Charlie rubbed his chin. "I guess that's one way to look at it."

I spoke fast now, sure that I was right. "Danny Connor wants it so his brother's name won't be sullied. He must want to destroy it so no one ever discovers his brother was involved. There's nothing there for anyone else to worry about, if the bomber is already dead." I paused. "Danny's just protecting his family's reputation. Right?"

"Right, I guess." Charlie pursed his lips.

I reached for Charlie. "There's only one way to put a stop to this. I need to see Danny Connor. Can you arrange it?"

Charlie shook his head slowly. "Jo, that's too dangerous. No. I won't put you in that kind of danger."

I spoke fast, again without thinking. "It's my choice."

His eyes grew sharp. "I can't even protect you? What kind of guy do you want me to be? Some good-for-nothing, lazy bum?"

I wrapped my hand around his arm, which tensed as I touched him. "Charlie, I wish you'd understand."

"Well, I don't. It's not how I was raised. I was raised to take care of a girl, to keep a girl safe. I was too young to take care of Lou, and now you won't let me. . . ." He chewed his lip hard. "This isn't right. You putting yourself in danger and not letting me protect you. You won't let me do anything for you."

I tightened my fingers. "Yes, I will. Please help me set this up. We'll meet in a public place. If you help me, you could be there. I'll be fine in a public place. Danny Connor wants the journal, and I'm going to give it to him."

"I don't know. . . ." Charlie's eyes were dark, and he still wouldn't look at me.

"I'll give it to him. and that'll be that. You'll be there."

Charlie looked down the busy street.

"Charlie, no one else knows I'm with you, right?" And my insides twisted as I wondered whether Charlie was hiding something from me. "Louie doesn't know where I'm staying, does she?"

"You think Lou would tell Danny?"

"I don't know. It's best if she doesn't know anything. She loves him." Who knows what someone might do for love?

I only wished I had time to read the rest of Teddy's journal. But that couldn't be helped now. I was sure that what I had read was all I needed to read.

Charlie placed the phone call. When he came back outside, his face was hard and ashen.

"Okay. I don't like it, but I won't fight with you. For better or for worse, Connor's meeting you tonight."

We made a stop at my hotel so that I could pick up the journal;

I tucked all the torn-out pages inside where they belonged. I knew there was still one set missing, but it couldn't be helped. I needed to keep my family safe.

And to keep them safe I had to give Danny Connor Teddy's journal.

Because I had only one other thing to give away: me.

* * *

The joint was quiet when we got there, since Charlie had to set up with the band. He seated me at a corner table with a reserved sign on it so I wouldn't be bothered. Connor was to arrive around nine.

But long before that, Charlie gave me a tour of the place, showing me the layout of the club, and in particular how I could get from the ladies' room to a door leading to the alley. Then he handed me a ten spot, despite my protests.

"In case of a raid," he said. "Exit and cab fare, plus. That's all I need to worry about, you being arrested."

I smiled but felt a pang, because he was not smiling back.

Just before he went onstage to warm up, Charlie sat me at the table. As he started to move away, I grabbed his arm. "Wait."

He turned back and stared at me with those great dark eyes. I pulled his arm, tugged him toward me, and as he moved toward me and took both my shoulders in his hands, I leaned to meet him. He kissed me, just a soft kiss but on the lips, like he was caressing his cornet, just ever so soft. Our first kiss, my first kiss. I let my eyes close, and when he pulled away again and I opened my eyes, he was smiling.

"Jo, you're a mystery that I'm trying to understand," he said, shaking his head.

"Please keep trying," I whispered.

Charlie took the stage, and I ordered soda water and waited.

The place was dim, and soon smoke wreathed the ceiling as patrons gathered by twos and threes. The music started and filled the air, competing with the thrilling laughter, with the ice clicking in glasses; flappers paraded in and dapper swells glided by in black tie. Someone popped a cork, and the table exploded with surprise; couples began to dance, her beads flying, his hands snapping. A flapper with a feathered headband and a long cigarette holder sat with her back to me, her beau fingering the sequined fringe on her sleeve, while she did her best to pretend to ignore him.

It was a warm place, but I felt a growing chill.

I held the journal in my lap. In the semidark I thought I'd better recheck one last thing. I'd read it earlier, but it was still a puzzle. I opened to the last gap of missing pages. Nothing followed them except a small note:

It's written not in but underneath the stars.

Underneath the stars? What could Teddy mean by that?

The band was still in its first set when Connor came in, early. Charlie, playing with his eyes closed, had no clue Connor was there. As Connor slid into the chair opposite me, his gray eyes met mine, and once again I felt the seductive power behind those eyes, once again I couldn't help staring at him.

Charlie, I thought. Charlie was right around the corner. Sweet, kind Charlie. I could leap into his arms in a few long strides.

"Josephine. So happy you've changed your mind." Connor leaned forward and took my free hand, lifted it, and brushed my fingertips with his lips. I cringed.

I cleared my throat. "Where's Lou?"

He waved his hand. "She's somewhere else." His eyes didn't leave my face. "You have something for me?"

I pulled the journal from my lap and placed it on the table between us. Connor's eyes slipped from my face to the journal and back. He smiled. "Have you read it?"

I nodded.

His eyebrows lifted. "And?"

"There's nothing here to worry about, since your brother is dead."

Something flickered across his face, something I couldn't read. The smile vanished. "I should like you to come back out to the house, Josephine."

"I'm sure I shall."

"Now."

I froze inside. "No, thanks."

"Surely you aren't meeting someone else?" Connor's eyes traveled away from me for the first time, moved to the stage where the music was in full swing, where Charlie was playing his heart out, lost in his music, unaware of anything around him.

"No, of course not." I spoke loud, to pull his eyes away from the stage, away from Charlie. The thought of Chester, beaten, in the hospital, filled my mind. "But . . . I'm enjoying the music."

He turned back to me. "You may believe you're right about many things, Josephine. But understand, I'm not giving you a choice."

Then I saw them, those two thugs, Ryan and Neil. They were over by the door, one on either side. Charlie, his back to me, was oblivious.

I had to do this by myself. I had to keep Charlie out of this, if I could. My family was bad enough. If I crossed Connor now, I might condemn them all, including Charlie, to something worse than Danny'd given Chester. The question was, What could I do?

Connor took out a cigarette, tapped it against the case, and lit it, the lighter flaring. I held as still as I could against the flame. He exhaled a stream of smoke, then said, "It doesn't have to be this way between you and me. We don't have to remain enemies. Not any longer. We could become good friends." He leaned over and touched my arm.

I felt a chill but didn't move.

"You see, I may have the journal, but I need to be sure that none of this information will ever find its way out into the world. You, for instance, have read the journal. And Teddy is still out there, isn't he?" Connor smiled, all teeth. "So you understand that our friendship—that I'm assured I can trust you—that is paramount."

"I see."

"I could even make you a star, in return for your friendship. As you have seen, I like to surround myself with beautiful things." He paused. "What is your greatest wish, Josephine? What do you want more than anything in the world?"

"I want you to leave my family alone," I whispered.

"And for that you are willing to . . . what?" He took another drag, exhaled, his eyes never leaving my face.

"What do I have to do?"

A smile crept across his face. "Become such a good friend of mine that I can rest assured that neither you nor Teddy will ever betray me."

"Good friend," I echoed.

"Come out to the house, Josephine."

I had no choice. He gave me no choice. I tried to smile, but it was a brittle attempt. "All right."

Connor's steel eyes kindled, and he placed his hand on my arm again. It took all my strength not to pull away.

"But I'd better hit the ladies' before we take a drive." I held up my empty glass.

He nodded, then took my wrist. "Don't be long."

"No," I said. "No." I tried not to let on that my mind was racing.

In the ladies' I splashed water on my face. Danny Connor frightened and repulsed me. I couldn't go with him, not ever. I prayed that what I did next would not make everything worse for those I loved.

I was in the alley inside of three minutes, made a fast loop to the nearest street, and hailed a cab. I looked back as we pulled away, and a figure stood on the curb, a man, staring after us.

I thought for a moment it was one of Connor's men, but I'd moved like lightning. Or was it Teddy? Blond, with that stance . . . I almost stopped the cab, but we lurched away from the light and he was gone.

Teddy and I, together we could maybe take on Connor. But alone, I was not prepared for this. I pressed my fingers to my forehead. Maybe, like Teddy, I would have to disappear.

* * *

When I woke up, the sun was streaming through the windows of my safe room in my hotel. As I washed and dressed, I tried to figure out what to do next. Charlie would be worried sick about me, so I needed to let him know where I was right away.

I remembered the exchange number at Charlie's building. I told

Mrs. Daly that I was his sister Lou since I couldn't play the Irish country cousin over the phone. When Charlie picked up, I could hear the relief in his voice, even as he whispered. I pictured Mrs. Daly hovering behind her partly open door.

"Where are you? I've been out of my mind."

"I'm at my residence. I'm fine. Thanks to you and the ten bucks and the escape route you showed me."

"Thank heavens. Can you meet me at five at the Algonquin?"

"I'll be there."

"What happened?"

"I'll tell you when I see you."

After I dressed I went downstairs to the lobby and sat for a few minutes, gathering my thoughts. I watched the other girls—not much older than me, most of them—heading out to work. They seemed ready to take on the world, some in neat, pressed, and belted suits; some in dropped-waist dresses with slouchy sweaters, neat-as-a-pin hats, gloves, clutches, hose, heeled shoes. All with an air of responsibility and livelihood. Maybe they had boyfriends. Maybe not. It didn't matter—they had lives.

That could be me. I could be a working girl in New York City. And why not? I just had to slip into a new life, away from Danny Connor. The way Teddy had managed to do.

I returned to my room and packed my valise and gave the scowling matron a healthy tip to make up for my sudden change in plans.

I had tons of time before I'd meet Charlie, so I left the hotel and walked. And walked. New York on a fine day in early June was alive, stretching, growling, hissing, and belching; steam rising from holes in the street; the ground rumbling under my feet as the trucks and buses thundered past. I window-shopped and stopped for coffee and a doughnut at a cafeteria. I watched the passersby and tried to find myself in the crowd.

Tried to discover who I was. Tried to discover who I could be.

Josephine Winter, teacher.

Josephine Winter, secretary.

Josephine Winter, scribe.

In the few weeks I'd been in New York, I'd adopted a new style of dress, a new set of friends, and a couple of new addresses. But what about me, inside? My own journey had been lost in a flurry of confusion and danger surrounding my family, all because of something that began with Teddy.

Because of Teddy and his journal, and maybe what he'd done, everyone he cared about was in some kind of peril.

I bit my lip. I'd never thought about Teddy that way before. Like he'd been haunting me, but not in a good way.

No, I didn't mean it. Thinking that Teddy might not be my guardian but my plague, as if the thoughts alone would bring down evil. No. Teddy had always been there for me.

I'd always have Teddy.

"Miss?"

"Oh, excuse me!" I'd stopped walking, was standing still in the middle of a crowded sidewalk, halting traffic, stopping the progress of one pleasant young man, who tipped his hat. I searched his face, thinking for a moment that I saw Teddy there, in such similar blue eyes, such a similar swatch of blond hair, such a similar expression. I knew I must've looked startled, to say the least.

"You all right, then?"

"I'm fine." The color crept up my cheeks. "Thanks."

He tipped his hat again and went on his way, that not-Teddy, as I moved to the nearest shop window, where a flapper ensemble was displayed, from dress to cloche to bobbed hair to full red lips. She was carrying a valise.

And then I realized. It was my reflection I saw, not a mannequin.

Who are you, Josephine Winter? Where are you going?

I walked farther until I was at the corner of Madison and Forty-second. Suddenly, I knew. It was written not in but underneath the stars. The stars!

I was going to see the stars.

CHAPTER 43

Lou

She could've been a star. Another Clara Bow. She had the looks for it. And the smarts.

That's what scared me, that with those looks and brains and long legs and that sweet innocence she was Danny's type. Younger, prettier. If Charlie was in the way of Danny, God help him. If I was in the way . . .

Danny didn't know that I'd taken the other car that night. That I'd followed him. That I saw them together. Saw him smile at her. Saw him touch her arm. Saw that look in his eye.

I would've killed her right there, if I'd had a gun in my hand.

So you can see why I did what I did. I made up my mind that I was going to hang on to Danny one way or the other. Charlie, he didn't know I'd turn snitch when he mentioned the journal. But then again, he didn't see that look.

⌀IRENⱾ

If that Jo Winter proved to be a problem, well, honey, as I said to Danny when we first met, I'm willing to manage anything.

Including making someone disappear.

But hang on. Don't go thinking the wrong thing, Detective. The story ain't over yet.

CHAPTER 44

Apparently the diagram was placed on the floor and thence copied to the ceiling. It might have been better if the artist had held the diagram over his head and transferred it, as it were, by looking through it.
—"Constellations Reversed," <u>The New York Times</u>, March 23, 1913

JO

I stood there, looking up at Grand Central's ceiling, trying to puzzle it out.

Okay, so the constellations were backward; that didn't tell me a thing. I tried to recall our conversation, Teddy's and mine, but that meant nothing to me, either. I walked from one end of the station to the other, lugging the valise, thankful that I hadn't tried to bring any of my books, but nothing I could discern about these stars made any sense.

Perhaps I was wrong. Perhaps these weren't the stars Teddy meant. Maybe it didn't even matter now that Connor had the rest of the journal.

But no. Something in my gut told me that this was just what he meant and that I needed to find those pages if I could. I set the valise down and looked up at Orion with his three-star belt, shading my eyes with my hand.

Bang!

The noise made me jump out of my skin. It echoed through the high-ceilinged hall, a shattering gunshot.

I froze, expecting to see chaos, to hear screaming. Looked down at my own body as if I expected to see my lifeblood oozing from a wound.

That's when I realized that no one else was disturbed by the noise, and then I saw why. It wasn't a gunshot: a man had just slammed the door to a locker, one of those metal lockers that lined the walls of the station to hold travelers' parcels and suitcases while they waited for their trains.

A locker. Words from his journal: "not in but underneath the stars."

If Teddy had put his final pages in a locker . . .

But which one? And where was the key? Where would Teddy hide something meant for me?

A train had arrived at the platform behind me, and passengers streamed past where I stood. Women with flowery dresses; flappers giggling and clutching at one another; men in business suits; a young man in uniform. A young man with blond hair and blue eyes who reminded me so much of Teddy that my heart stood still for a moment.

As he passed me, he smiled, and I smiled back, a frozen smile, my hand reaching for his arm, and I said, "Teddy?"

His smile broadened. "Sorry, miss. Name's David. But Teddy's one lucky fellow." And he saluted and moved on past, as I caught a glimpse of the medals on his chest.

One was shaped like a star.

I practically ran to the ladies' bathroom, where there were benches and I could open my valise without displaying the contents to the world. I found the scarlet poppies and unfolded the scarf to expose three small boxes.

In one of the boxes was a Silver Star.

I wrestled the medal out of the box; it was attached to felt wrapped over cardboard. As the medal and the cardboard popped out of the box, something else fell out and hit the floor with a metallic ring.

A key. I had to smile, though it was a sad smile. A key with the number 77. Of course, Teddy's "lucky" number.

It took me a few minutes to find the locker and a few fumbling tries with the key, for the lock was stiff and hard to work, but then it was open, and the smell hit me first. I stepped back, and that's when I could see it.

There were no pages inside this locker. Only a decaying blossom, putrid, oozing. The blossom of a Venus flytrap.

*　*　*

I entered the Algonquin lobby a full hour before my rendezvous with Charlie, so I sat in the corner, trying to make myself disappear.

The shadows were long. A tired bellhop pushed a luggage cart, one wheel squeaking. Someone at the front desk argued with the manager. A harsh laugh erupted from the dining room. I was drained and frightened.

Connor had gotten to the locker ahead of me.

He'd pieced the puzzle out from the journal, and he'd figured out which locker to open. Danny surely knew Teddy's military history. He would've known about the Seventy-seventh. He was a far better sleuth than I was. And he'd forced the locker—probably why I'd struggled with it—and he had Teddy's last pages. I did not.

That dying flower in the locker was a message meant for me.

My entire plan had collapsed. My family would not be safe, not until I solved the problem of Danny Connor. Or until Teddy came back and helped me take care of our family.

A shadow fell across me, and I looked up, thinking it had to be Charlie. I started to reach for him, except it wasn't Charlie.

It was Danny Connor.

"Let's go," Connor said.

*　　*　　*

About five years ago on a hot July afternoon, Pops had taken Ma and me on an excursion down to Coney Island, where Teddy joined us. It was one of the last times we were all together as a family, and happy. It took Teddy a full hour to persuade me to take a ride with him on the Wonder Wheel, which had just opened. As we went around the Ferris wheel and then stopped with our basket swaying from the highest point on the turn, I felt as if I'd left my stomach somewhere on the ground 150 feet below.

Teddy took my hand and steadied me, and pretty soon we were laughing together, and then he and I went back in line three times, even though each time we rode the wheel I felt that my stomach had to play catch-up.

That was how I felt as I sat there looking up at Connor, at his expressionless face, and then at Lou, who hovered behind him, and whose face twisted and worked with emotions I couldn't read.

"Where?" I asked.

"To where we can have a conversation," Connor said.

"Like the kind of conversation you had with Chester?"

"I didn't speak with Chester. I believe that was an overzealous Neil." Behind Connor, Badger Face Neil sneered. Ryan and Neil, both there. The two goons grinned at me, the kind of grins that I imagine wolves make before their evening meal. Connor shrugged. "Your cousin's face was a bit too pretty. He needed a new nose."

"You're nothing but a bully," I said, rising out of the chair. And then I reeled. "How did you know where I was?"

He smiled.

Charlie? Charlie had betrayed me? It was the only possibility. The gorge rose in my throat. I stared Connor straight in the eye. "I hate you."

Connor's eyes sharpened. "Careful, Miss Winter." He nodded toward the door. "Let's go."

My heart beat hard. "I could just say no. I could make a fuss, right here in the lobby. So you'd have to leave me alone."

"Please," he said, but it wasn't a request; his tone was disparaging. "This is 1925. Anything goes. No one will pay the slightest bit of attention. If you insist, we could go upstairs and have a conversation in my suite. It has a nice view of the city, from a high floor, with a lovely tall window that opens quite wide."

My stomach took another turn on the Wonder Wheel.

"Tell your friend to get a move on," Connor said to Lou.

Louie reached her hand for me. "Come on, doll," she said, her voice tight. "Don't make this difficult."

I paused and said to Danny, "You've got the journal. Why take me? Why now? I'm not going to reveal what I know. Besides, your brother is—"

He interrupted, eyes flashing, "Like Teddy? We know better about Teddy, don't we?"

I pressed my lips together.

Then he waved his hand. "You've read it." It wasn't a question. "But not the entire journal. Because some pages were missing, weren't they? Locker number seventy-seven."

"So what?"

"The thing is, Miss Winter, I can't take the chance that Teddy might have revealed things to you in person. Since we both know that you helped him stage that little episode on the beach a year ago . . . Teddy's journal can be destroyed, but I'm afraid we still have to deal with you."

"But," I began, and I hesitated. What should I say? I didn't know what was in those pages. Teddy had kept every secret.

"And frankly, I'm not of the same mind about you as I was. I don't need to add to my collections." I knew what he meant. I'd lost my opportunity to make myself a bargaining chip. I glanced at Lou; her eyes were cold.

Connor barreled on. "Let's go—I've had enough of you and your family. And there's something else, if you resist." He paused. "My brother Patrick, unlike Teddy, was never good at keeping secrets, especially when they involved his lady friends. So I know that Patrick was responsible for your cousin Melody's predicament."

I froze inside. Patrick was responsible. I'd thought John Rushton . . . but then . . . "How . . ."

Connor said, "I've been very good to a couple of maids in various households. You already know Adela. And one of John Rushton's maids is a sweet little thing who talks too much. Rushton is caring for a young boy, Leo, who is of special interest to Melody." He paused again. "I've been thinking of inviting little Leo out to the mansion. What do you say?"

"Leo?" I asked, my voice breaking.

Connor smiled. "Your cousin's child. My nephew. His name is Leo."

Leo. Melody's little boy. I'd assumed he was Rushton's. I'd been so wrong.

"Perhaps you didn't know all the details. Leo is Melody's child—and my brother's. Leo is my nephew, Josephine."

"Your nephew?"

The Ferris wheel feeling came back then. How stupid I'd been to assume I knew everything. I'd been so, so wrong. I'd misjudged Rushton. But more importantly, I'd underestimated the danger Connor posed. He knew about Melody's deepest secret: Leo. And Leo was his nephew. I might have given myself to Connor and, maybe, kept him away from them all—especially little Leo. But now it was too late.

Danny's cold glance told me all I needed to know. "Let's go," he said again.

The guys moved aside so that Lou and I couldn't help but walk between them. I looked around, frantic, wishing that anyone was looking at me. But Jacques stood impassive at his podium, staring down, and the columns blocked my line of sight into the Rose Room. Besides, who was I looking for? Charlie had betrayed me—betrayed my whole family—to Connor. My heart broke, and I swallowed hard against grief.

No one else in the lobby of the Algonquin looked in our direction, either out of curiosity or concern. As we moved through the doors, I saw the doorman I'd seen on that first day. Pete. Maybe

SIRENS

I could make him see I was in trouble. I gave him a big smile.

But Pete had eyes only for Danny Connor. "There you are, Mr. Connor, sir. Kept your car waiting like you asked, yes, sir, even put a little polish on it for you, there." He reached for the back door of the limo, held it open. Danny gave Pete a wad of folded bills as he slipped into the back of the car. "Thank you, Mr. Connor, sir, much obliged."

I tried to catch Pete's eye, but he was fixated on getting the bills from his hand into his pocket. Or maybe he'd learned to ignore girls like me when they were in the company of Danny Connor.

Then I hoped for a minute that Sam would be behind the wheel, but he wasn't. Ryan took the wheel and Neil climbed in beside him. I sat next to Louie in the back, facing Danny.

"Where are we going?" I asked.

Danny Connor smiled. "Why, home, of course."

I looked out the window as Ryan eased away from the curb, wishing I could send a message to someone, to my aunt and uncle, to Mel, hoping I'd see the Algonquin again, but fearing I wouldn't.

And that was when I saw Teddy. It was a quick flash, the briefest out of the corner of my eye, but I was sure. So sure I leaned toward the window, my mouth open, almost ready to cry out before I caught myself. So sure that tears welled in my eyes, and then Teddy was a blurred image. But it was Teddy, standing on the sidewalk watching the limo pull away, watching me through the window, mouthing something to me, something that maybe I imagined, but held on to that whole ride, hoping against hope.

Teddy, my hero, my guardian; he said, *I'll find you.*

307

CHAPTER 45

LOU

At that point it wasn't like I had a choice. Not anymore. How was I to know what was inside that stupid book of Teddy's? Danny, he held his cards close to his vest.

I had my doubts, in the car. She was just a kid. Not much younger than I was when I met Danny, remember? And I had believed in Danny, had believed that he wouldn't do anything really awful. But my heart was thumping something wicked, because I wasn't sure what was in that book, and what it meant to Danny, and what he might really do if he was shoved into a corner. I'd seen Danny shoved into a corner only once or twice, and the results weren't pretty.

And what he'd said about the little boy. Mel's little boy.

I knew now Jo wasn't a threat to me but to Danny. And I began to feel sorry for Jo Winter.

And I began to look at my Danny in a new, not-so-nice way.

⌒IRENⱾ

Somewhere on the drive out to Great Neck we passed the sign, the billboard, peeling and faded, from one of the shows. I'd seen it a million times before, but now I saw it. *Really* saw it. I mean, it was a sign. A sign, get it?

HOWARD THURSTON: THE WONDER SHOW OF THE UNIVERSE! SEE THE YOUNG LADIES DISAPPEAR! SEE THEM LEVITATE! DO THE SPIRITS RETURN?

That's when I had the idea. The disappearing girl, the girl who floats away. Of course! I got that tingly feeling right up my spine, and you know what that means. The idea that popped into my head, that was it.

At that moment I reached over and took hold of Jo's hand, and our eyes met, and she got it, too. I had to hold tight to Jo's hand so she wouldn't float away premature, if you get my drift.

Yeah, Detective, that's when it all started to shift inside me. From Danny to Jo.

309

CHAPTER 46

But above the gray land and the spasms of bleak dust which drift endlessly over it, you perceive, after a moment, the eyes of Doctor T. J. Eckleburg.
—F. Scott Fitzgerald, *The Great Gatsby*, 1925

JO

It was dusk when Ryan closed the gates behind us and steered the car up the long drive with its gargoyle ornaments. The fountain in the court danced, and the lights were on under the water, shining up through the spray, creating shadows that shot up and made those cupids look like dancing devils in the growing dark.

Connor opened the door and gave his hand to Lou, who clutched me with her other hand. When we were all standing on the cobbles, Connor said, "Take our guest up to the Rose Room, Lou. Find something for her to wear. We'll dress for dinner tonight. Formal. Neil"—and he nodded at Neil—"you'll stand guard at Miss Winter's door."

Louie led me up the front steps, Neil right behind, carrying my valise.

"Neil!" Connor's shout froze us all. "No one is to touch her. You understand me? Ryan?"

"Yes, sir," the men chorused. Lou squeezed my hand tight.

"Come on, doll," she murmured. "It'll be all right."

The Rose Room was a self-contained suite, with a bedroom, bath, and dressing room on the third floor, and with only one entrance. Louie left me to fetch some clothes while I went to the window.

Three stories in this place made a Wonder Wheel height. I remembered how the porcelain vase had smashed on the paving.

The only good thing, as far as I could figure, was that the windows overlooked the front of the house: the driveway, court, and fountain. I could see who was coming or going. There might even be a way for me to signal someone, as long as Connor and his men had their backs turned. A decorative cornice ran along the underside of the windows; I figured it would be enough for me to balance on if I could get a grip on the bricks above. There might be an open window into a room down the way. Maybe I could try during the night . . . as long as no one patrolled or looked up.

I tried to open the sash, but the window wouldn't budge. I moved to the other window, but it, too, was tight. Then I saw why: the windows had been screwed shut. I looked at the screws. Without tools, it was hopeless.

Connor thought of everything, I had to give him that.

Louie came in, carrying an armful of clothing. "Danny said we'd dress for dinner. That'll be fun." She dumped the clothes on the bed. "I bet Danny's asked Cook for something special. I've got this sweet rayon number in green that'll hug your slim little figure like a dream. . . ."

I grabbed her hand, interrupting. "Louie. What am I doing here? He's keeping me prisoner."

She wouldn't meet my eyes. That auburn curl of hair fell across her cheek. "Sometimes Danny gets these ideas, that's all."

I backed away. "Ideas! This is one heck of an idea."

"It's my fault. I was jealous of you," she murmured. "I wanted you gone. As in vamoose. Scram. Disappear."

"What?" I sank down on the bed.

"I thought Danny had a thing for you. I was jealous. I thought you'd see what a sweet life I have and you'd try and take it from me." She smiled, her head still bent. "I was so happy when I saw how you felt about Charlie, and how he feels about you." She met my eyes. "But I still couldn't let it go. That Danny might want you. So when Charlie slipped and said something about you showing up today at the Algonquin, I told Danny. To stay in good with him, see?"

I couldn't find any words.

"Now I get that it's all about that stupid book of your brother's. What's in there anyway?"

"Nothing that explains this kidnapping."

"Kidnapping!" Lou laughed, but it was halfhearted. "Honey, he just wants to talk to you. I'm sure that's all."

She turned back to the task of sorting out clothes and hanging them up. She pulled a lime-green rayon floor-length sleeveless gown from the pile and held it up, over her arm like a shopgirl. It had a draped neckline and was bias cut, gorgeous, silky, and slinky. "I think this'll look wonderful on you. It'll match your

eyes. Got shoes to match. I wish Charlie could be here to see you."
She spread the dress out on the bed.

I reached for her arm once again, laying my fingers on her, and
said softly, "Danny may not be what you think, Lou."

Her eyes burned at me and she pulled away. "Don't. Don't even
try. I still love the bum, even though . . ." She bit her lip. "I like
you lots, and I'm gonna take care of you, Jo, but don't you say
anything bad about Danny." She moved toward the door. "Danny
likes to eat at eight sharp. Cocktails at seven. Neil'll escort you
downstairs." She shut the door, and I heard the lock click.

* * *

Neil carried a gun. Just a pistol, in a shoulder holster, but he
made it clear he was armed by removing his jacket and hanging it
over the back of the chair that was sitting in the hall outside my
rooms. When he knocked on my door at seven and I stepped into
the hallway in the lime-green rayon, he raised his eyebrows and
lifted the jacket off the chair, ever so slowly.

I walked down the stairs, him trailing me, lifting the gown so that
I wouldn't trip. From below I heard phonograph music—something
classical. When we reached the bottom, I followed the sound.

The drawing room had a double-height ceiling and extended the
length of one wing. Neil stopped at the door and shut it behind
me. The glass doors overlooking the terrace were open to the
night, which was warm enough that I didn't feel the need of a wrap
over my bare shoulders. Danny and Louie were down at the far
end: Connor standing before a small and unnecessary fire, Lou
slouched in an armchair in a black floor-length gown with cap
sleeves. She leaped to her feet when I entered the room.

"How often do I have to tell you?" I heard Connor, his voice a growl. "Don't be so unladylike."

She stiffened and turned to him. "Sorry, hon. I forget, you know?" She simpered; I could feel it all the way across the room. She reached her arm to him. "I'm sorry."

That seemed to appease him. But when I reached them, he looked at me. "As part of your training, I wonder if you remember who wrote this piece of music, Louise."

He was looking straight at me, those steel eyes narrowed to slits.

She took a step back and clasped her hands together. "Oh, I know this one. We listened to this one last week, didn't we, sweetie?"

"Yes, we did. What is it?"

"Oh," Lou said. "Oh, I know this." She paced a little, working her hands into knots. "Um . . ."

"Louise?" Connor's eyes never left mine. "You see, Josephine, I'm proud to be Irish. But I disdain ignorance. If we are ever to prove to the world that we should be treated with respect, we must become educated in all things." He paused, his eyes narrowing. "Louise, you are taking an awfully long time recollecting." I'd never witnessed such a cruel exchange. It made me sick. I drew my hands into fists. "I would wager that your friend knows this composer."

I did, but I wasn't about to give him the satisfaction. I shrugged, though my hands were still clenched. "Mozart?" I asked.

His steel eyes flared, then he turned to face the fire. "It's Bach, Louise. The *Brandenburg Concerti*."

"It was on the tip of my tongue! Bach! Of course!" Lou said, and put her hand on his shoulder.

Sirens

His hand flashed and caught her on the lower part of the chin. She staggered back, her hand to her face. When I moved toward her, she shot me a look that I took to mean, Don't. So I froze.

But my insides boiled. I saw what it meant for him to think that he was right, that he alone was right. And I cringed at my own sense of rightness.

Lou pressed her hand against her chin. "I promise, sweetie. I'll remember next time."

"I believe you should offer our guest a drink."

"Sure! What would you like, doll? We've got a super bottle of champagne on ice right here."

"That'll be lovely," I said through clenched teeth.

Louie poured me a glass. I took it, looked at it, and downed it in a gulp.

I wasn't certain whether I was trying to fortify myself, drown my troubles, or prove something to Connor, but drinking the champagne like that was a mistake, as I could sense almost at once.

Louie's eyes grew round as I held out my glass for a refill. She mouthed at me, Watch it.

This time I held the glass up before I drank. "A toast," I said. The room swam a bit around the edges.

Danny turned, his eyebrows arched.

"To Teddy," I said. No one else moved. "For bringing us all together," I said, and took a sip.

"Oh!" said Lou. "I'll drink to that." She took a sip, her eyes darting between Danny and me. He did not lift his glass.

"Josephine," Connor said, his voice a slow drawl, "if you think that Teddy, or his journal, will help you now, you are mistaken."

The room swam at more than the edges; the whole place seemed to shrink around me, constricting like a tight-focused telescope. I put one hand on the high back of the chair next to me.

"Your brother betrayed me," Connor continued. "He lied. And he was responsible for Patrick. . . ." Danny paused, as if something caught in his throat. "I won't tolerate deception. I will not forgive. My dear, you are here as bait."

Bait. Hooked, that was for sure, even now when I fought him. And then . . . the swirling thought . . . deception?

Danny went on. "You see, I'd asked Neil and Ryan to take care of Teddy. To get rid of him, last year. There was some confusion, because you came out with the discovery of his clothing, the presumption of his drowning."

Yes, I did. Teddy had asked me to. He had to pretend to be dead, that's what he told me. So I helped him pretend, even knowing the pain it brought our parents. Such pain. Oh, how this room swam around me.

"Neil and Ryan found him not long after that, Josephine, or so they've assured me. Found him alive and then—and I do find this ironic—dumped him alive in a weighted sack into the Sound, right out here, not far from where you said you found his clothes."

Now the room swam with a vengeance.

"The problem is, they never made certain Teddy was dead. They left. And now all these odd coincidences . . ." Danny moved toward one of the tall doors and stood staring out into the dark, toward the Sound. "I'm certain I've seen Teddy. I think you have as well. I believe he may have made it out of that sack alive."

I gripped the chair back to steady myself.

Connor continued. "He's a Houdini, your Teddy. He wriggled himself out of one thing or another, slick and sure. He got out of the war alive. He missed being killed on Wall Street in 'twenty. And he squirmed out of the sack my boys stuffed him into. Since he's alive I'm quite sure he'll come for you. And when he does, I intend to kill him. Along with everyone else who betrayed me."

Lou sucked in air, a sharp, short breath.

I gripped the chair back with both hands now as the room grew fuzzy and dim, my fingers clenching the plush fabric. My words came out in a croaked whisper. "Why did you burn down my family's home?"

"Neil and Ryan ransacked the place looking for the journal. They cleaned up after themselves." Connor shrugged, then pressed on. "The fact that you've read most of your brother's journal makes the rest of this easier. I imagine you know how I handle problems. Yes"—Danny leaned over and picked up the journal and held it— "over the last few hours, I've been doing my homework. Unlike my sweet Lou, who cannot remember Bach from one week to the next because she does not do her homework." Connor put the journal down and then placed his hand on the back of Louie's neck. I watched her eyes widen as his fingers tightened on her.

"Homework?" My words were slurred.

He picked up the journal again, turning it in his hands. "You're here because your presence will bring Teddy." He moved to the fire and tossed the journal into the flames.

I moved fast toward the fire, stumbling, my champagne glass cracking on the fireplace brick, and Lou reached me just in time, wrapping her arms around my waist and pulling me back before I reached into the flames.

My scar burned, my mind burned with hatred for Connor, as I watched the journal burn, as I'd lied to Rushton about his journal burning with our house, as I felt myself burn, as I felt my scar burn with shame. I felt the tears well, but as I swallowed them down my burning throat, as I watched the solid piece I had of Teddy for sure die, watched the flames consume his past, his thoughts.

I straightened and shook off Lou's embrace, then turned to face Connor, my mind churning with thoughts of hatred and revenge.

He said, "Everything I did, everything I've done, I've done for my brethren. So that they would love me. And so that I could rise above."

I seethed.

"I don't expect you to understand, Josephine. How could you?"

I couldn't.

"Ah, but don't be too sad. I do have the last pages. The ones you haven't read." He reached into his breast pocket and pulled out the final pages from Teddy's journal.

I staggered, reached, but Connor pulled his hand away, fluttering the pages. "I don't think so. These are for me," he said. "I believe Cook has prepared salmon. Louise, would you lead the way?"

She came and took my hand, then led me down the room, which seemed all unbalanced and tipsy, turning and twisting. Again, as in the car, Lou closed her fingers around mine and squeezed.

The memory of that squeeze was the only thing that sustained me through a long and silent dinner.

And this. This sustained me all through the evening, through everything. That I truly had seen Teddy in front of the Algonquin, that it hadn't been some trick of the imagination, some illusion. Daniel Connor believed Teddy was alive, just as I did. A Houdini, that's what Teddy was. Teddy was alive.

And coming for me. Just as Daniel Connor wished.

This knowledge made me sick, and at the same time it filled me with joy.

* * *

I had no other alcohol that evening, but I slept as if sedated. Luckily, I'd managed to make my way into my own bed. When I awoke, the sun was streaming through the open curtains and the room felt hot, my mouth sticky and dry.

I dressed, and when I tried to open the door, there was Neil, waiting on the other side, unlocking it so I could make my way to breakfast. I was alone, and ate under the silent stare of Neil, with only the slow, sonorous ticking of the tall clock—a rare early American antique, collected from some family farmhouse, where it had lived for centuries, only to be sold to Connor by a poor farmer who probably didn't know its worth—in the corner of the dining room to keep me company. That and, with incongruous disdain, an empty suit of antique English armor.

When I finished I asked if I could take a walk, Neil shook his head, his mouth twisting into a sneer. "You're to stay in your room." He lifted his hand and gestured at the stair.

"Where's Lou?" I asked as we ascended.

"She went into town."

"And Mr. Connor?"

"In the greenhouse." Neil pointed, moving me up to my room, and I went inside and heard the door lock click behind me.

I went to the bathroom window. It was higher than the others, the windowsill about four and a half feet up, but I was delighted to find that it was not screwed shut. I pulled a chair over and pushed up the sash. The wind lifted the curtains, bringing in the smells of new-cut summer grass, the brick warmed by the sun, the salt and seaweed of the Sound. There was rain on the wind now, too, as low clouds gathered from the west and the sun flitted in and out.

I looked up and down the drive and lawns for any sign of Ryan or Connor before I leaned my head out the window. The height of this window made the cornice below a dangerous six-foot drop. But I could see how the bricks were laid and that I could hang on with my hands, and that once I made the cornice I could plant both feet and scoot along. I leaned out farther, hanging on to the window frame tight. A terrace, a small balcony, with French doors, hung to my left maybe twenty feet away. I tried to remember from my tour which room those doors led into, but the place was so huge all my memories were jumbled.

But the thought that I had an escape route gave me hope.

I leaned out once more and saw that below the balcony thick vines were trained up the side of the bricks. Perhaps a trellis perched underneath the ivy; perhaps the ivy itself would bear my weight.

If I had no other choice, I would risk it.

I heard a noise out front. A car pulled up the long drive; I could see it weaving through the trees. As it turned into the court I saw that it was Connor's limo. I ducked my head inside and went to the fixed windows of the other room.

The limo pulled to a stop by the fountain, and Ryan got out from the driver's side. Lou opened the back door and stepped out, and my breath caught. Charlie followed her.

They stood talking in the driveway. Ryan walked back around the house and out of sight. Lou, in a soft gray chemise, gray hat, long gray sweater, looked like a dove, her hands fluttering as she spoke. Charlie wore an argyle vest over his white shirt; the vest made him look young, collegiate, like he was home for the weekend from Yale or Princeton. My heart thumped.

Was Charlie involved? Lou said that she'd told Danny about my meeting with Charlie. Did Charlie know what was going on here? And, oh my sinking heart, did Charlie belong to Danny Connor?

Lou looked up and saw me and quickly shook her head, which I took to mean: Get back.

I stepped away from the window and went to the door, pressing my ear against it, listening as the front door opened in that great hallway below and Louie's voice floated up. I couldn't hear words.

Then I heard her coming up to my room and a minute later heard the door unlock.

I'd hoped Charlie would be with her, but she was alone. She closed the door and put her finger to her lips.

Then she said, loud, "Danny wants you to stay here." She waved me to the other side of the room so that Neil couldn't hear us. "I went and got Charlie," she whispered.

"Does Danny know?"

She shook her head. "I figured that there's strength in numbers."

But that made me queasy. Would having Charlie here really stop Danny Connor from doing something terrible? I doubted it.

"What if Danny—"

"He won't," she whispered, but I read the doubt in her face.

"Lou, can I trust Charlie?" Could I trust her? She'd already betrayed me once.

Her eyes grew round. "Yes. Yes."

"Because, Lou. If I can trust Charlie—if I can trust both of you— if he's not in Danny's pocket, then he's Danny's enemy. And you know what he does to his enemies."

"He would never hurt Charlie." The tears welled in her eyes. "Danny, he, he might be bad, sometimes, but he loves me, he does, I know it. . . ." Her voice trailed off.

"Lou. Oh, Lou."

The tears spilled then, and she looked at the floor. It had all been a mirage, a trick, an illusion, that Danny was good and kind; it was something he'd done to win her. He'd played it to the hilt, the best of showmen, until now. I wrapped my arms around Louie and hugged her hard as her shoulders heaved. We stood that way a long time.

When she pulled away, I knew she'd turned a corner. I could see it in the lift of her chin, how she squared her shoulders, how she dried her eyes with purpose, smashing those tears with her palm. If it was Charlie or me against Danny, I knew now where she'd stand.

Lou wasn't Danny Connor's moll any longer. She wasn't anyone's possession or plaything or victim. She was Louise O'Keefe. I loved her like a sister.

Then she said something that made me fearful all over again.

"Charlie and me, we thought we saw, just as we were turning in the drive . . ." Her eyes met mine.

"What?" I clutched her arm.

"Someone was out there. I think it might have been—"

"Teddy?" My heart pounded.

"I don't see how. But still . . ." She added, "Ryan didn't see him. He was busy with the gate."

If Teddy was here, then Connor's trap was working. As much

as I wanted Teddy to come save me, I needed to get out of the mansion so that Teddy wouldn't try to reach me.

"Danny says you're to stay here. He'll send food up. Charlie and I will be in the house, Jo. We won't leave you."

Lou hugged me hard and then, just before she left, she reached into her pocket and handed me an envelope. After she left I heard the key turn in the lock.

Inside the envelope were the pages from Teddy's journal. And a note from Lou: **Stole them out of his jacket.** I sank onto the bed and read.

> August 12, 1923
> So. It wasn't Mel's fault. I should've known; Patrick was the lowest kind of scum. When he threatened to go get the boy, I snapped. I wasn't going to let the likes of him go after Mel's little boy.
>
> I don't like it, but it's done. He deserved everything he got. I'm glad I took care of him.
>
> That's right, world. I killed Patrick Connor. With my own hands, I beat him to a pulp. Yes, it sickens me. Yes, he was the worst. But that doesn't excuse what I did.
>
> I'm no hero, just a murderous beast.

Oh, Lord. Teddy, you killed Connor's brother? Danny wanted revenge, and no wonder. I read on.

> Now there's only one thing left. Family comes first, that's the way of it. I have to protect Melody. And if

it means I have to protect John Rushton once more, that's what I'll do. He's the only one who can look after Mel's boy . . . and since that's what he's been doing.

Thank the good Lord John agreed to take Leo in.

Maybe Mel can make peace with it one day.

September 2

Danny will be after me now. I've made my bed. John and Leo and Mel will all be safe. But with Danny's eye fixed firmly on me and my whereabouts, he won't be looking at them. I'm a dead man. I just have to keep Danny's gaze from lighting on any of them, including Pops and Ma and Josie.

Josie.

But that other business . . .

I lowered my hand, unable for the moment to read on. Patrick was dead; Teddy had killed him. Danny Connor was bent on revenge for his brother. Teddy was a murderer.

But Teddy was a hero. I didn't care what it looked like. I didn't care what he'd had to do. As far as I was concerned, Teddy was a hero.

I lifted the remaining pages.

September 4, 1923

Danny knows I killed Patrick. It's all over.

September 5

I can't believe what I just discovered. Why didn't I figure this out sooner? When I confronted him, he admitted it. Admitted he was as good as the cold-blooded murderer of Frank Rushton.

All along, Daniel Connor has been fronting for Patrick and the others in that business. All along, Danny was the benefactor. He was supporting the anarchists. He was responsible for Wall Street, 1920. All along, He was the one supplying the money for the explosives. He's the one responsible. All this time.

I figured it out when he asked me to balance the books. Because I knew the numbers on those crates I ditched, I knew what was in them. I knew he'd bought and paid for the explosives. Others along with Patrick carried it out—maybe those Italian guys but maybe not—but Danny was the moneyman.

By having me balance the books, Danny Connor handed me the key to his prison cell.

He can't ever read this journal, but someone must. I won't be able to escape. I have to find someone who can set things right.

I'm an accomplice, just for hiding the evidence. That's what he said when I faced him down. He's holding that over me to keep my mouth shut. That

and Ma and Pops and Josie. He said he'd take it out
on them.

On Josie, sweet Jo.

I can't ever let him get his hands on this journal.

But it might help them. Might help her.

Teddy. Oh, my.

Now I understood why Danny Connor wanted the journal. Now
I understood why he'd never let me leave this house in one piece. If
I didn't get out of here, I'd draw Teddy right into Danny Connor's
trap, and he'd kill us both.

I tucked the journal pages together with the scarf that was tied
around the medal boxes and hid everything under my pillow.

I set my alarm for four A.M. I didn't wear pajamas, but slim black
pants and a black long-sleeved sweater so that I wouldn't have to
dress. It would still be dark at four, and I imagined sleep would
even take Ryan and Neil by that time. I planned to make an escape
out the window, and then . . . well, I hadn't thought further.

I hadn't thought about the rain.

CHAPTER 47

Lou

It happened so fast and so hard it was like hitting a wall at a hundred miles an hour.

One minute Danny Connor was the center of my life, and I would do anything, *anything* for him. I would do anything to keep him. I would've even done something awful to Jo.

There. I said it. Okay?

The next, Danny was like that old story, the kid's story, you know the one? Where the emperor has no clothes? He was exposed. I saw everything he hadn't wanted me to see. I'd been bewitched, or something.

It took Jo Winter to lift the spell.

When I heard him say that to her—"I intend to kill him"—that was the start. Well, I thought, Danny Connor, if you can be so cold-blooded as all that . . . Except the cold blood was running through my veins, let me tell you, 'cause I knew the kind of stuff he was really capable of. I'd just chosen until that moment to look away. That's when I decided to steal the pages for Jo.

But it really hit me when Jo hinted about Charlie. When Jo hinted that Danny might hurt Charlie, why, that was the last straw. I had to choose.

And what do you think? Who would you choose? Family? Or the guy? I've made some bad choices, brother, and this time I went the right way.

It hurts, it hurts, oh, unless you've been there, you can't imagine what a choice that is. My heart about splintered into a thousand pieces.

And then I thought about Charlie, and I took those splinters and sharpened them to knife points. To use on Danny.

That's right, Detective, just what you thought all along. Not Jo, Danny.

CHAPTER 48

JUNE 10, 1925

He believed that men lived many lives, coming back to earth again and again as children return to school after a summer of play.
—Fulton Oursler on Howard Thurston, *The Sphinx*, May 1936

JO

The crack of thunder woke me from a sound sleep. A minute later came a flash of lightning, so bright it filled my room, and then another rumble. Rain slashed against the windows. I squinted at the clock ticking at my bedside: midnight.

Cursing, I slipped from the bed and went into the bathroom, pulled the chair over, and opened the window. Rain hammered my face as I leaned out, trying to see my route. I could not make it to the cornice, which was slick with sheeting rain, unless I wanted to break my neck. No escape for me from this room as long as the storm raged.

I pulled inside as another stab of lightning illuminated the lawns. And my breath caught. There. There!

The rain blinded me. I rubbed my face, but it streamed over my eyes and I still couldn't see. But I had to; I had to be sure.

I jumped from the chair and ran back to the bedroom and pressed against the window glass, felt the thunder shake the house, tried to see through the rain. I was so sure I'd seen him, there at the edge of the trees. . . .

Another flash, and, yes! Teddy.

My Teddy. Teddy, so solid, standing there staring up at the house, in that same old beat-up jacket he wore back from France, I knew it was him, looking for me, and I wanted to cry out and warn him but also gather him, bring him back, bring him back firmly and forever from the dead, I missed him so much. Teddy was also wearing that look of astonishment and determination that I so loved because I knew it was meant for me.

I ran between the two windows trying to see, but without the benefit of the lightning it was dark as pitch. Another flash—but he was gone now, and I almost broke down in tears, so helpless as I was. Was he a phantom, or really here?

I sank down onto the floor with my back against the bed. Maybe I could wait out the rain that now poured in through the open bathroom window. Maybe . . .

Another great streak and almost simultaneous clap of thunder, and I heard buzzing and arcing, as if the house had been struck. I leaped up again and then I saw it, the electric pole by the drive, by the side of the garage, burning like a torch from the lightning strike. It flamed to the sky, brilliant. I turned on one of the lamps: nothing. No electricity.

I ran to the bathroom window and pulled myself up again. Even if I broke my neck, I had to try. The electric pole burned bright, bright enough for me to see the cornice, the bricks, bright enough for me to see . . .

Teddy.

I saw a figure, a shadow on the cornice onto the balcony of the room next to mine. Joy filled me, mixed with fear over the flames now shooting skyward as the creosote-covered pole torched.

I pulled on shoes and ran to the door of my room. Shouts came from the hallway. From behind me the red firelight of the burning pole created a rosy pall, and the shadows leaped against the walls of my room, dancing. I heard the chair in the hall scrape as Neil pushed up, heard his footsteps in the hall, heard him curse about not being able to see, heard him yell down, "Get me a torch! I'm blind up here!"

I tried the door to my room. It was not locked.

Ah, Teddy. He'd come in and unlocked my door.

I opened the door, and as I did the door caught Neil's chair and knocked it over so that it hit the wood floor with crack, then I heard Neil's surprised shout and awkward flail as his feet tripped and danced and then I heard him tumble down, down, falling over and over down the broad steps to the second-story landing.

And a shadow, a man's shadow, followed Neil down the stairs, running all the way down.

Teddy. Had Neil stumbled, or had Teddy pushed him?

My heart pounded. There were shouts from downstairs now, but they didn't make sense, coming first from one side of the mansion and then the other, and no one seemed aware of what had just happened to Neil. From far below I heard the crash of some great glass and wood thing falling.

Then I heard a gunshot, short and sharp and heard Louie scream once, clipped, which gave me the courage I needed. Louie, Charlie. I needed to get to them. What was happening to them?

I crept out into the hall and clung to the railing. It wasn't until the next flash of lightning that I saw what had happened to Neil, how he lay crumpled, distorted, on the landing, his head thrown back at an unnatural angle that made me shiver all over.

I slipped down the stairs, gripping the banister. When I reached the landing, I hesitated. What if Neil wasn't dead? But the next flash of lightning told me there was no question. His eyes were open, staring, vacant; his mouth, the blood . . . I swallowed bile and slid past him, careful not to touch his twisted body.

The shouting had stopped, and I paused halfway down the next flight of stairs. The storm raged as if it had stalled right over the house, thunder and lightning crashing and bursting; through windows that faced the front of the house the red light from the burning pole cast an odd glow.

Teddy was there in the dark somewhere. He'd come to rescue me; he was trying to find me. I could feel him.

I reached the main floor and went to one of the two tall windows that flanked the front entry. The pole still burned, and the fire had spread to the garage now, the garage being made not of brick but of wood, and it must have been dry wood at that, from the way the fire flared through the roof. Wires lay arcing and spitting on the ground across the drive. The cupids in the fountain at the center of the court, made lifeless by the lack of electricity, reached skyward with grinning, mocking mouths, streaked by the rain that seemed unable to quench the fire. It was unnatural. It made my skin burn, my scar tingle. I wanted out of the house, away from the fire.

I had to find Charlie and Lou.

My eyes had begun to adjust to the dark. With each flash of

lightning, I had to pause now, as if someone had flashed a bulb at me, and I saw stars for a few seconds until my eyes adjusted again to the blackness. I slipped from one room to another on the main floor, pausing at each doorway. The servants had gone for the night. As far as I knew it was only Danny, Ryan, Charlie, Lou, and me in the house. Now that Neil was gone.

And Teddy now, Teddy was here, too. Somewhere, looking for me.

I moved along the wing that splayed toward the Sound and opened a door; I'd reached Connor's odd museum. Beyond it lay the small sunroom that led out across the lawn to the greenhouse. I slipped inside the museum and closed the door behind me.

I remembered the museum layout. The fossils were arranged first, bones and impressions and petrified pieces. The intact skeleton of the ape. Then came the jewelry and small artifacts, the books, then the antiquities. All in order of age from oldest to youngest except that one, the pride of Danny Connor's collection, the one that made me so squeamish. The sarcophagus.

The sarcophagus lay at the very back of the room, just before the doors. Upon it, that jackal sat watch with its white all-seeing eyes.

Against the white walls, even in the darkness, the skeletons stood out in relief, all teeth and claws. Another flash of lightning bit the dark, and in that room with those white walls and the high clerestory windows I was blinded. I threw my hand over my eyes and stopped moving, my other hand on one of the display cases. Stars shimmered behind my eyelids for almost a minute before I could open my eyes again.

I left my hand on my forehead, shading my face, in case there came another blinding flash. Past the artifacts, past the necklace that Connor had wanted to copy for me, past the books. Into the antiquities: prehistoric, Egyptian, Greek, Roman. Then the last, the jackal guarding its brilliantly painted sarcophagus.

A coffin. That's what it was, a coffin. An old, decorated coffin. According to Connor, still holding remains.

Someone had pushed on the lid. The lid was ajar, a two-inch-wide black crevasse open along the side closest to me.

My spine tingled with fear. I had no choice but to go around it, right around, in order to reach the doors on the other side. I slid to the wall, pressing my back right against the wall, feeling that those white jackal eyes—eyes that shone in the dark as if they were lit from within—followed me. I reached the door to the sunroom and put my hand on the knob. Which turned under my grip, from the other side, a complete surprise.

I scuttled back, my heartbeat quickening to a gallop, and dropped to my knees behind the plinth.

The door opened, and someone stepped into the museum from the sunroom, and I could tell at once, by the way he carried his broad shoulders, by his wolfish gait.

"Charlie!" My voice came out a harsh, whispered croak.

He turned to me as I reached him, and he clapped a hand over my mouth. Then he dragged me back through the door and into the sunroom and shut the door behind us. My heart pounded in my ears; I couldn't breathe.

I struggled against him, fighting Charlie, as he wrapped one arm around my waist and kept his hand over my mouth while he dragged me across the sunroom, and fear and confusion and tears of pain and misery welled up.

And then he pressed his mouth to my ear.

"Sssh. It's okay. No noise."

When I relaxed, he lifted his hand from my mouth.

I whirled to face him. I was so mad I was ready to slug him—but instead, I reached both hands up to his face and kissed him hard on the lips before pulling away. And I knew. Because he reached for me and kissed me back, equally hard, drawing me against him and wrapping me in his strong arms, strong but gentle as his kiss softened and melted into mine, and then both of his hands lifted as we pulled apart and he cradled the back of my head and touched his forehead against mine, and I knew. I knew.

He mimed not to speak but to follow him. In the far corner of the sunroom, Louie sat huddled against the wall, her face, when the lightning revealed her, drawn and pale.

I crouched down with Charlie and Lou, and we put our heads together, Lou reaching for my hand and taking it in one of hers. She was trembling, badly.

"Danny?" I whispered. "Ryan?"

"I was fighting Ryan," Charlie said. "We fell against that big bookcase, and it came over. I got out of the way in time, but Ryan didn't. He may be dead. Sure looked it."

"Neil is dead, too," I said.

We all exchanged looks.

"Neil fell down the stairs," I said. "But Danny?"

"Don't know," said Charlie. "But . . ." He looked at his sister. She lifted what I now saw was a folded sweater from her shoulder, and I saw the blood.

"He stabbed me," she whispered. "And he has a gun."

I sucked in breath, reaching for her.

"I'll be okay," she whispered, cracked.

But it was a lot of blood, soaking her shoulder, the sweater, a swelling dark stain. "We've got to get you out."

"There's someone else here, Jo," Charlie said. "Someone came down the stairs and grabbed Danny just after he stabbed Lou. He moved so fast . . . I couldn't see who it was. And Danny fired at him. I thought it was Neil, but that doesn't make sense now. Who is here?"

Then we heard it. A noise from the other side of the door. From inside the museum. The crack of something, glass, or maybe porcelain, followed then by a clattering that went on and on. I imagined one of the skeletons, maybe the ape, in pieces, scattering across the marble floor. Instinctively, the three of us drew together, Charlie pulling me tight against him and turning so that he was protecting both Lou and me.

In all the pain, the tension, the worry, the fear, I felt his warm body against mine, his arm around me, and now I smelled his sweet musky scent, his aftershave, and I pressed into him, fitting into him like a key into a lock, pressing my cheek to his shoulder.

Another noise, a scraping, and then the door from the museum flew open and someone fell into the sunroom, tripped, then ran to the other side and flung open the door that led out into the lawns and the night. The wind howled through the room, throwing both doors from side to side, slamming them back and forth in a rage, cracking glass and wood. In the confusion I thought I saw someone else run through the room and out into the dark. Then I realized that the rain had stopped but the wind still shrieked and now scattered sparks from the fire in all directions. The burning garage met the house just outside this sunroom, and the entire garage was all at once in flames, the old wood popping and bursting into red tongues of fire. I grabbed Charlie's arm and pulled him and pointed at the fire that was licking up the outside walls of the house.

Fire and flames. My heart pounded in my chest like it might explode.

Charlie turned and picked up Louie, lifting her like a child, as she stifled a cry. He made for the door with me right behind him just as the wood-frame windows of the sunroom exploded in flames.

I felt the heat on my back, my scar, and I held my hand tight over my mouth so I wouldn't scream as I pushed through the broken glass, following Charlie and Lou out of the burning building and into the night.

CHAPTER 49

Lou

So you think I did it, don't you? Well, get a load of this. Danny stabbed me. I didn't stab him. All I could think then was that if I didn't die from loss of blood, I'd die of a broken heart. That's what I wanted, anyhow.

He stabbed me in the shoulder, the big jerk. He should've put the knife in a little lower. One pain to replace the other. End it all as it should end.

So there, Detective. Danny Connor was the love of my life. Just keep that in mind and have a little pity.

CHAPTER 50

JUNE 10, 1925

The high, thrilling song of the Sirens will transfix him,
Lolling there in their meadow, round them heaps of corpses
Rotting away, rags of skin shriveling on their bones . . .
—Homer, <u>The Odyssey</u>, Book 12, 50–52

JO

I fell to my knees on the wet grass. Ahead of me Charlie stumbled, then knelt so that he could let Louie down. I heard her moan.

Behind us, the sunroom exploded into flame. I turned. The mansion was burning, flames licking the walls of the museum, striking high into the air with ash and sparks and smoke. It was only a matter of time now. Every treasure there would burn, and then the house, all of it. I felt the heat on my face: an all-consuming fire.

"It might collapse. We've got to get farther away," I said to Charlie, trying to control my shaking voice.

He bent and picked up Louie. She cried out. "She's bleeding pretty bad," he said, short of breath as he struggled to lift her.

Down the slope the greenhouse loomed, its glass reflecting the light of the flames. The wind still whipped around us, fanning the flames and driving a fine cold mist, and neither wind nor mist could be good for Lou.

"Let's get to the greenhouse," I said.

"Greenhouse!" Charlie turned. "But Connor . . ."

"Yes. He could be there. But—" I couldn't tell Charlie about Teddy; I couldn't tell him what I felt. "It's shelter. We've got to get her inside."

We stumbled down the slope. As we reached the bottom we saw a flash—not of lightning this time, but of a gun, and the report just after, both coming from the dock that jetted out over the Sound.

Charlie and I stopped dead, but no noise came from nearby; from below, on the water, we thought we heard something . . . voices? They were drowned out by the explosive sounds coming from the mansion behind us, as the fire whipped from one end of the house into the middle, destroying everything in its deadly path. I turned. The whole lawn glowed ghastly pink. Flames rose into the sky as if whipped by the devil himself. As things inside combusted they created small explosions, like shots, and the cracking of glass and crashing of wood echoed through the dark.

I turned back to Charlie. "The greenhouse!" I said.

The door was locked. I saw that as a good sign; I didn't think Danny Connor would be inside with the door locked. The door had small glass panes. I stuffed my fist deep into the sleeve of my shirt and hit the glass door once, twice before one of the glass panes broke. I reached inside the door and unlocked and opened it, then stepped inside; after listening for a few seconds, I beckoned Charlie in.

The center table was meant for propagating, and sections of it were bare. I swept my arm over the surface to clear a space large enough for Lou. Charlie laid her down. Even what I could see of her in the darkness that was illuminated only by the burning mansion was not comforting.

Louie was sheet white, and semiconscious, moaning softly. The sweater that now lay loose against her shoulder was saturated with blood.

"Charlie, someone has to go for help. Otherwise, she'll bleed to death right here."

"What about the phone?"

I shook my head. "Even if there were a phone out here, the power and phone lines were certainly strung together."

"But I can't leave you."

We looked at each other. I lifted my hand and touched his cheek. "It doesn't matter. The one who stays takes one risk. The one who goes takes another."

He put his hand up and took mine and pulled it to his lips and kissed my palm. From my hand through all of my body I felt that kiss, running down my arm and into my gut, into my soul. I closed my eyes so that I could feel the damp press of Charlie's lips on my palm. And then he pulled me toward him, a single fluid movement, so that his lips were now on my lips, and he pressed his body full against mine, soaking into me as the rain had soaked into the ground around us, the heat from his lips like the fire coursing through the house.

It lasted only a moment, then he pulled away.

"I'll be back as quick as I can. Look." He pulled a pistol from where he'd tucked it into his belt, placed it in my palm. "Found it on the floor next to Ryan."

I looked at the gun, silver and menacing, then I nodded. Charlie touched Lou, and she turned and groaned, and then he was gone, closing the greenhouse door, and loping with that wolfish gait across the lawn, past the burning house that now lit up the sky, running toward the road.

I looked at Lou. She was unconscious now. Our only hope lay in the fire—that the flames brought help out to the mansion and that Charlie intersected that help on the road.

The greenhouse held its humid warmth tight, its musky earth smell close. Except for the glow from the fire, there was no light. I went to the greenhouse door, intending to lock it, but something stopped me.

Fear. Somewhere out in the dark Connor still lurked. Somewhere down by the dock. Teddy was there, too, I believed, but I couldn't be sure which of them prevailed. I had to know. I had to know who would be left. And whether he would save us, or kill us.

I went back to Lou; I could do nothing for her. She was deathly pale but breathing. She was cold. She was still. She needed blood, and that I couldn't supply. I took her hand between my two and held it.

"I'll be right back," I whispered. "I have to make sure he won't come back for us." I touched her cheek; she was so cold. I placed the gun on the table, next to her right hand.

I went to the door, opened it, and stepped back into the night.

The front had brought cold air, and I shivered. The mansion burned in front of me; it would burn for days. But it wasn't the mansion or even the fire I cared about now. I turned toward the dock.

The grass gave way to rough sedge and then rocks as the shrubs closed in around me, a thorny thicket; I pressed my way through until the water glinted ahead, and I knew I was close to the dock.

The dock was a massive rectangle that pushed out into the sound. Even in the dark its shape stood out. Cold wind whipped my hair, which I tucked back behind my ears. Branches tossed by the wind flashed back and forth between me and the open dunes that led to the dock.

I'd remembered it, the small boat tied to the dock, the last time I was there. But now there was no boat.

At least not along the length of the dock that I could see by the light of the buoy, which swept past at thirty-second intervals, illuminating dock and water around. On the second sweep, I scanned again, thinking I'd missed something. On the third sweep I saw them out on the water.

Shadows—two figures, in a boat, standing. Wrestling. The boat rocked, and then nothing. Dark.

I ran down to the dock. The water, stirred up by the storm, washed in a noisy *slam, slam* against the dock and the beach, and drowned out all other noise.

I watched the buoy; the fourth sweep of light approached, coming, coming . . . the boat again, but only one man standing, looking down, straightening, lifting his head, and then darkness.

Oh, Teddy. Or was it Connor?

My heart slowed as it counted the endless beats while the light moved over the restless water. The wind whipped cold mist against me, the waves pounded the dock, and then the light back again, again, and . . .

Nothing. Empty water. I ran to the end of the dock, chasing the light that swept past, over black water that chopped and washed over the piers. The next light. Nothing. And the next and the next after.

Had I dreamed it? One had gone under as surely as one had won.

But then, where was the survivor?

I turned and ran back up the dock, and back through the brush to the lawn and the greenhouse, and thrust open the door. Lou was still breathing shallowly, still lying like death, but not yet dead, and I clasped her hand. I feared for her and for me if I should lose her. She was so far gone. I wanted to bring her back. I leaned over her so that my lips almost touched her ear.

"Danny Connor won't hurt you anymore," I said, even though she couldn't hear me. "Teddy got rid of Danny. I think we're all right."

I had to believe it, but I was wrong.

The door opened behind me and I turned, and it felt like slow motion, like I was in some moving picture. Jo Winter, star.

"Is she dead?" Danny asked, pointing at Lou with the muzzle of the gun.

"Almost," I said, my voice cracking. "Thanks to you."

He grunted, and then he stepped inside and closed the door behind him. He was soaking wet from head to toe. His clothes were muddy and torn, and his nose was bleeding and swollen, broken. He was a wreck. Behind him, the fire reared up, flames leaping.

"Where's Teddy?" I asked.

"Gone." His voice was raspy, his steel eyes brightened. "No one breaks Daniel Connor's nose and gets away. No one."

My heart sank, and tears filled my throat. "The water? Is he in the water?"

Danny sounded puzzled. "I was in the water."

"But . . . what happened?" I had to know about Teddy. "Is he dead?"

"When she"—he pointed the gun toward Lou—"when she began to bleed, I didn't know what to do. And then I saw him and I ran to the dock. Where I last saw him."

"Saw who? Teddy?"

Connor drew up. "Stop saying his name." He turned and I caught the expression on his face. I thought, He's insane, completely insane. His eyes were bright and blank and wide, and his face contorted with rage and fear.

Oh, heavens. Connor had gone mad, and he had a gun. The other gun lay at Lou's side, just far enough to be out of my reach

"Why don't you go away and leave us alone?" I said in a whisper, my voice trembling.

"You don't understand," he said. His voice took on that familiar tone of haughty disdain. "Which makes you such a mystery, Josephine. That you could be so sharp and yet so dull, all at once."

My back went stiff. I turned to face him fully, my left hand still tight around Lou's, my body protecting hers. "Then please, Mr. Connor. Enlighten me."

"I possess her, don't you see? She's mine. And therefore, I can dispose of her as I wish. And you."

My stomach was in knots. "And me, what?"

"Ah, Miss Winter. Jo. Revenge is sweet, as they say. You are Teddy Winter's sister. And he was disloyal to me. He killed Patrick." Connor swallowed hard. "Your brother took something very precious from me. It's only fair that I return the favor. And he would've turned me in. When I gave him everything." He sighed.

"I would've given you anything." Connor waved the gun in the air. "And now, look," he said, and turned toward the house so that now I could see in the firelight the tears that streaked down his cheeks. "Look. You've destroyed everything. Everything that meant anything to me, you have ruined."

"I didn't start the fire, Danny," I said, my voice quiet. "Lightning struck the electric pole."

He smiled, but it was a twisted smile. "You did start the fire, Jo, just not that fire. I possess you just as I possess her." He gestured toward Lou.

My body went icy with fear. "You don't own me, Connor."

"No? Pity. Because I'll have to kill you." A great crash came from the house as part of the interior collapsed. He turned, and I heard his intake of air. "You did this," he whispered. "One way or another." The madness again, consuming him as the fire consumed his entire world. "You and your brother. You, siren, you bewitched me. And Teddy still haunts me. It's time to put an end to it. It's high time I made you both pay." He turned, raised the gun, and aimed it at my heart.

I would've died trying to defend Lou, but instinct made me lift my hands in a fruitless gesture.

Danny Connor went rigid, his eyes widening with horror, and he backed toward the door of the greenhouse, his free hand groping for the knob. I was fixed on the gun in his hand that now waved wildly.

"No," he said in a whisper. "It's not possible. I've killed you. With my own hands! Stay away from me!"

Gripped by madness, he looked past me, past Lou, into the darkness.

And then I sensed Lou, who lifted with inexplicable strength from the table behind me, and held the gun I'd left for her in her shaking right hand, pointing it past me, just past my shoulder, aiming at Danny, the gun wobbling so that I grabbed her hand.

I grabbed her hand and lifted it, because in that moment I knew what was not right. It was not right to kill Danny. He didn't see us there, right in front of him in the greenhouse. He wasn't aiming at us any longer. He was aiming at the ghosts of his own making.

It was not right to let her kill him.

I knew that and lifted her hand so that when she fired, glass shattered around Danny's head, breaking the bleeding light from the burning mansion into a million burning, crimson, starry fragments.

Danny stumbled wide-eyed, backward out of the greenhouse, into the wet grass, toward the mansion. From deep inside came a thunderous crack, as if an explosion, and Danny turned and raised his hands and ran toward the house, dropping the gun as he ran. And then he fell to his knees, kneeling before the burning ruin, and he keened, a high wail that, despite whatever I felt about him, despite all his offenses, broke my heart: Daniel O'Banion O'Connor grieving the loss of something he loved more than his own life. All his possessions, all that collection of things that told the false story of who he was, that made him something, that gave him a history and a purpose. And when the wall tilted in a slow sway and then fell, full, onto the miserable figure of Danny Connor, I gasped, "No!"

The flames seemed to spring out of the grass.

But I saw something else through the flames. The house was in ruin and beyond it, in the court, before the mocking cherubs

347

that frolicked in the fountain, there were trucks spouting water and men running and shouting, moving this way and that, and I thought, Charlie. Charlie had come back for Lou and me.

I turned back to Lou. She lay pale and still, far too still. I touched her cheek, and it was cold. She was dead, I was certain, and the gun had fallen from her hand to the floor.

And then something moved just out of the corner of my eye, in the shadows at the back of the greenhouse.

Teddy?

Then Charlie was there by my side, and others, too, and they lifted Louie onto a stretcher and out into the night before I could react. Charlie had his arm over my shoulder and was leading me out of the greenhouse when I stopped him.

"Wait. One second."

I turned and ran to the back of the greenhouse.

"Teddy?" I whispered into the darkness.

Nothing.

Then a rustle from my left, and I spun.

But it was only the Venus flytrap, swaying a little, its gaping mouth open, waiting, hungry, beautiful, deadly. And beneath it, a poppy.

Not a living flower, but a silk scarf with red poppies, wrapped and tied around a bundle in a shape so familiar that I put my hand to my mouth and found it hard to breathe. A French silk scarf with a poppy pattern, wrapped around three boxes of medals. I'd last seen these things in my room in the mansion that now flamed and smoked and smoldered on the other side of the lawn. I had no idea how they would have gotten here, like this.

And folded and inserted into the knot of the scarf, a single sheaf of journal paper. A single last page.

"Teddy?"

It would have taken a multiplicity of actions so brave, so right, they could only be accomplished by a hero.

"Jo?" It was Charlie, come up behind me.

I picked up the scarf. "Something I forgot," I said, my voice breaking.

How could I tell him it was Teddy? Would Charlie understand? Maybe someday, but I didn't think he'd understand today.

I peered into the dark recesses of the greenhouse, as if the plants could tell me, but I saw nothing. Just the Venus flytrap, mouth open, nodding.

And then I thought about Louie. Dead, I was certain.

I clutched the scarf and its contents tight to my chest. "Let's go after Lou," I said. "She needs us."

CHAPTER 51

Lou

It was while I was dead that I realized that I was the levitating girl.

And I was the disappearing girl. Not Jo.

I found that very funny, and I tried to laugh, but laughing was impossible in my state. Unlike levitating, which seemed more possible with every passing moment.

Now, Detective, I think you can see why I couldn't be a suspect. I was dead when it happened.

I thought this story was all about her. All this time! I thought it was Josephine Winter, Star Girl. Star of my brother's life. Star of something, that's for sure. All this time, and the story is about me, Louise Moira O'Keefe.

Why me? You may not believe it to look at me now, buster, but I'm a nobody. I'm just an Irish girl from the Lower East Side who found a guy and became his moll. I don't have what it takes. Not like Jo. She's smart, I could see that right off. She has that magic that sends out waves, and people believe. People will flock to her like she's some kind of siren.

And Teddy. Why, he was the nicest guy. He was there the whole time, letting me know it was all okay, that help was on the way, but even if it didn't get there, that was okay, too, you know? Teddy was a bit of a puzzle, but that was Teddy.

Which was why, while I was dead, and realizing all this stuff, I made the decision, and said as much to Teddy. I was levitating all right, but so what? I decided. I was not about to disappear.

No, sir.

It was quite a day for me, the day I died. First, that I wasn't someone's any old possession. And then, that I wasn't gonna disappear.

CHAPTER 52

JUNE 10–11, 1925

Thurston's trick of levitation . . . is a particularly uncanny piece of work. . . .
—Review of Howard Thurston's magic show, <u>The New York Times</u>, September 9, 1919

JO

The hospital was white, white and quiet, after all the dark and flames and noise. Charlie and I sat in a bright, white hallway, waiting, watching the nurses with their squeaky, squishy shoes walk by, their overlong crisscross-strap pinafores over blue uniforms and thick white cotton stockings exuding old-fashioned comfort.

I leaned against Charlie, my head nodding despite the light and the hard wooden chair, exhausted by the combination of too little sleep and too much emotion. Every time the double doors at the patient end of the hall opened I started, until Charlie wrapped his arm around me so that I could nestle my head in the crook of his arm, filling my nose with his scent, soothed by the warmth of his body against my cheek.

I clutched the poppy scarf and its contents.

I must have been dozing when the voice woke me. "You're the one brought in Louise O'Keefe?"

A nurse with gray hair pulled back tight under her cap stood in front of Charlie.

"How is she?" he asked, his voice husky. He cleared his throat.

"She's doing fine, now. You got her here in the nick of time."

I shifted, and Charlie stood. "Can I see her?"

"Are you family?"

"I'm her brother," he said. He pointed at me. "And this is her cousin."

I nodded, biting my lip and standing.

The nurse narrowed her eyes slightly. But she didn't question. She studied a clipboard and made a note, and then said, "All right. Follow me. But she's sleeping, and I don't want her disturbed."

We trailed the nurse down the white hall to a door that opened into a ward with large windows at the far end that let in the pale natural light of early morning. There were maybe twenty beds in the ward, all but a few filled with still-sleeping patients; Lou lay in the bed third from the end.

Her auburn hair framed her face like a cap and her eyes were closed, but I could see that the color had returned to her cheeks and lips and she was breathing softly. Her left arm was bandaged up and over the shoulder.

"She lost a lot of blood," the nurse whispered, "but the wound was clean and should heal nicely."

Charlie wrapped one arm around me. As I watched Lou's chest rise and fall I thought about what Danny Connor had done to her. About what girls like Lou suffered for the security of a relationship, or for what they thought was love. About what Melody had said about a girl's choices today: that we still had no real choices; that if we step too far out of line, somebody's going to yank us back.

Now that I knew where Melody was coming from, why she said that, and now that I knew how much Louie had been willing to sacrifice, I had to rethink. Is a girl's—a woman's—new liberation in this wild decade—our freedom to wear what we like, our freedom to party all night, our "flapperness"—is it real freedom? Did we expand our choices, or have we just changed the shape of our confinement?

Louie. This is your story. You survived Danny Connor. You did what you had to for Charlie, sure; you thought you were in love, sure. But when the time came, you made the right choice.

The nurse tapped on Charlie's shoulder, signaling that it was time for us to leave.

She stopped us in the hall outside the ward. "Because it was a stab wound, the police need to speak to you. Someone's been waiting down at the front desk."

Charlie nodded. His white shirt was stained with Lou's blood, and then I realized that my black pants and sweater were covered with dirt and ripped in places. I longed for a hot bath and sleep.

We made our way down the stairs to the main entrance of the hospital. A man in a suit leaned against the front desk, chatting with the nurse. When he saw us, he straightened and pulled a pad and pencil from his pocket.

"I'm Detective Smith," he said. "This is more excitement than we usually get out here in Great Neck."

He asked questions, glancing back and forth between Charlie and me, mostly questions about how long we'd known Daniel

Connor, why we were at the house, what had happened. I told him I was Connor's guest; Charlie said he'd done odd jobs for Connor for several years. Did we know why he'd stabbed Louise? No, perhaps a lover's spat, Charlie ventured. What about the fire? I saw it start, I told him, from a lightning strike.

He asked about the men—Neil Shaunnesy and Ryan McMann—and for the first time I realized I'd never heard their last names. Charlie said he thought they'd been lost like Connor, fighting the flames, inside the house, that that's where we'd seen them last.

We told Smith the truth, for the most part; we just didn't tell him everything.

Detective Smith seemed satisfied, although he warned us he might have to ask more questions at a later date, and he offered us a ride.

Charlie and I looked at each other. "Can you take us to Manhattan?" I asked.

Smith glanced at his watch. "I'm off duty anyhow," he said. "Sure. Where to?"

I turned to Charlie; he shrugged. "What about your aunt and uncle?" he asked.

I pursed my lips. "There's something I want to do first."

I gave Smith the address, and he seemed surprised. "Pretty classy neighborhood." He looked us up and down.

"He's an old family friend," I said, with no hint of irony.

On the drive I asked if the police had found anyone else on the property. Any unidentified man, alive or dead.

"What do you mean?" He glanced at me in the rearview, his eyes sharp.

Charlie squeezed my hand, but I pressed on.

"During the storm, while the house was burning and we were trying to get out, I thought I saw someone, another man, outside the greenhouse."

I know I saw Teddy. I was so sure.

Smith was silent for a minute. "No one mentioned that. But I'll check into it." He paused. "You say you saw the lightning strike the pole?"

"Yes."

"So you don't think someone set the fire? Someone like this man of yours?"

"No, no, I don't."

"Okay, I'll check it out." We drove for a time, then he glanced back at me again. "Hang on. Your name's Winter. You aren't related by any chance to Theodore Winter?"

My heart skipped a beat. "I'm his sister."

"Oh, boy. This is a coincidence." He shook his head.

"What do you mean?" Now my heart was beating hard; Smith had pulled the car over, into a parking lot off to the side of the road.

He cut the engine, then turned to face me, one arm over the backseat. "Your brother's been missing for a while. About a year, right? His clothes were found down on the beach there, but no body. Everyone said it was suicide, being he was a vet and all."

I nodded.

"You found those clothes, didn't you? His sister. That's what I remember. You found the stuff down on the beach. You reported how depressed he'd been and all, so everyone thought suicide."

I tightened my grip on Charlie's hand.

Smith sighed and ran his hand over his head. "I'm real sorry to tell you this now, Miss after all you've been through."

I waited, not breathing.

"We found your brother's remains a couple, three weeks ago, just down from Connor's place. He'd been tied up, in a weighted bag, and dropped in, looks like about a year ago. Some lobsterman pulled it in from where it had caught on his traps. We've been trying for the past week to find family, but your house in White Plains is gone and your folks disappeared. We located your aunt and uncle a few days back, but they didn't know where you were. And here you are, showing up here, just like that."

We all sat there, waiting, as if the car was suspended in thin air, floating.

Then I whispered, "Are you sure it's him?"

Charlie leaned forward. "He's been gone a whole year. How can you be sure?"

"We got the dental records." Smith's eyes searched my face. "Looks like murder, now. He was tied up but good."

I stopped breathing.

"Yeah." Smith scratched his chin. "The signature of a gangster hit. Prohibition's brought out the best in everyone, you know? Guy makes a mistake, they knock him out, stuff him in a sack with rocks, toss him overboard."

"Murder?" I whispered. "Teddy's dead?"

"Yeah. Likely we'll never catch who did it." He removed his hat, rubbed his balding head. "Something else you want to tell me? About your brother? About what he might have been doing before he disappeared?"

I shook my head, while Charlie squeezed my hand tight. I'd

been wrong. I hadn't seen Teddy; I couldn't have. Not once in all that time.

Teddy was dead. Had been dead for a year.

"I'm real sorry," Smith said, shaking his head again. "What a coincidence."

*　*　*

When we arrived on Fifth Avenue, Smith pulled up at the curb, gave a low whistle. "So just the one guy lives here, huh?"

"More or less," I said. I was as exhausted as I'd ever been.

We thanked Smith, and he gave us each a card with his name and phone number. "In case you think of anything else. About your brother, about anything." He looked at Charlie. "I'll need to ask your sister some questions, once she's recovered. Need to close the books on her deceased boyfriend."

He watched us from the car as we rang the bell. I wasn't sure whether Rushton's butler would even be awake—it was just getting on seven in the morning—or that he'd know who I was or that he'd let us in. So I was taken aback when the door was answered by John Rushton himself, already dressed for the day.

He looked us up and down and then stood aside to let us in. I still clutched the scarf and its contents in one hand; Charlie held the other, squeezing my fingers tight.

We followed Rushton down the hallway, past several large rooms, and stopped in a smaller sitting room at the end. There he turned to face us.

"I know all about it. I have connections with the police, who've been watching Danny Connor for a long time, at my request."

"Detective Smith didn't know much," Charlie said.

Rushton smiled briefly. "My connections are a bit higher level." He paused, then his eyes met mine. "I know you're looking for answers. But the explanations could take some time. I suggest we wait until you've had a chance to rest."

I was having difficulty keeping my eyes open. I was having even more difficulty keeping the tears from spilling over. But it couldn't wait.

"No. You need to know about Melody. You need to hear it."

Rushton raised his hand.

"Don't shush me. Don't!" I had nothing left but emotion. "I know about Leo. I know where he is, and who his mother is, and who his father was, too."

Rushton rubbed his eyes. "Can't this wait?"

"No. No." I leaned into Charlie.

Rushton said, "Fine. All right. It was Teddy. He made the request, the only one he ever made of me, and after he'd saved my life, I couldn't say no. He asked me to take the boy in. I lost Frank, so Leo became everything to me." He paused. "Leo is my family now."

"Teddy? Teddy asked you to take in the boy?"

"His only favor. Well, that and assisting Melody during her time. Supporting her. Keeping her away from Patrick and Danny. I owed Teddy. I told him as much, and I make good on my debts." Rushton paused, looking at his hands. "Besides. It was for Melody. I would do anything—" He stopped. "Teddy had to protect his family." Rushton stared at his hands, flexing them, examining them. "That's something I understood."

"Why not give the child back to Melody now, then?"

"She doesn't want Leo." His voice shook. "And I'm attached to him."

"No, you're wrong." I was beginning to understand the real meaning of right and wrong.

He lifted his hands. "Melody's a flapper, enjoying herself. Doing what flappers do." He was lying to himself. Now I could feel it. He was dismissing her because he was protecting himself. "She just wants to be out partying, having a good time. I've been watching, but it's clear to me. She's like all you other . . . well." His eyes were bright. "You've made it clear you don't think of yourself in that way, and I'll respect your comments. But Melody spends her nights on the town, in speakeasies. Just the reason a cad like Patrick Connor could take advantage of her." He looked at the floor. "I'm not certain she'd make a good mother for Leo."

"You couldn't be more wrong," I repeated, trying to keep my seething anger in check. "She's suffering because she can't take care of him. Because she can't be with him."

"Nonsense." He waved his hand and turned away.

"I just spent the past forty-eight hours with nonsense," I said, my voice rising. "Danny Connor was nonsense. I've watched Melody watch Leo. I've watched Melody drink to try to forget. I know she loves him."

Rushton turned, and his face had sagged. "But I've had him so long. . . ."

"Are you blind?"

As I watched him then, all his arrogance slipped away. He seemed vulnerable and lost. "I can't give up Leo. He's the only family I have now. I've kept him safe. I took him in. Melody doesn't want either one of us."

My heart broke for him. His arrogance and haughty manner were a defense. He was as damaged as Teddy, from his past, from the war, and then broken further when he lost his brother. He'd done something generous by helping Mel and taking Leo in, but he'd acted out of his own self-interest, too. And I knew then how he truly felt about Mel.

"You need to talk to her." I looked at the floor. "She has a crush on you anyway," I said, shrugging, looking up again. "She's in love with you, for pete's sake."

"What?" His eyes searched my face. "Miss Winter, I'm hopeless with people. I don't understand them. And I've certainly never understood Melody. So please don't tease me."

He cared for her, despite all the things he'd said. "I'm not teasing, John. She's in love with you. Go talk to her."

He looked at me, his eyes suddenly bright with hope.

"One last thing. Patrick and Danny Connor were involved in the bombings. Patrick helped pull the trigger, so to speak. But Danny, he gave his brother the money."

Rushton stiffened.

"I suspect Connor financed the bombings because it was one more way for him to get in good with the Irish community. It was all he cared about, that he had their respect, even the anarchists'. But you can lay it to rest now, because both the Connors are dead." And, I could have said, the proof is at the bottom of Long Island Sound.

"I knew it." Rushton said. "Thank you—thank you for, well, everything."

Charlie put his arm over my shoulder, and I leaned heavily against him.

Rushton had his driver take me to my aunt and uncle's apartment and take Charlie to his place.

In the car, on Park Avenue, Charlie kissed me. "Can I see you later?"

"In a day or two. Yes."

I watched that dark cloud creep over him. "Jo . . ."

"Wait, Charlie. I really like you. Really and truly. But there are some things I have to sort out." And then I kissed him, holding his face between my hands. "Okay?"

He nodded, and I loved him for understanding. Loved him. So I kissed him again, full on the lips, letting myself melt against him, right there in the limo, his strong arms wrapping around me, his full sweet lips pressing hard against mine. I pulled away slowly, touching his cheeks, his dark hair, brushing the curls from his forehead. I touched his lips with my fingertips, gazing into his soft black eyes.

And then I opened the car door and left.

CHAPTER 53

L o u

Well, I wasn't about to die and let Jo ditch my baby brother, now, was I?

Plus, there was all that other stuff to clean up. John Rushton and Melody and little Leo. Jo's future. Charlie's future.

My future.

Teddy let me know I'd better get a move on if I was to straighten it all out, and I liked Teddy.

Who knows? Maybe he and I . . . heck. It's kinda hard to get stuck on a ghost, even if you've already been there yourself.

CHAPTER 54

JUNE 11–12, 1925

No—Gatsby turned out all right at the end; it is what preyed on Gatsby, what foul dust floated in the wake of his dreams that temporarily closed out my interest in the abortive sorrows and shortwinded elations of men.
—F. Scott Fitzgerald, *The Great Gatsby*, 1925

JO

Sleep is a wondrous thing.

But first, Ed. I don't think I've ever been as happy as I was when I stepped out of Rushton's Daimler, all torn and ragged and messy, to be hugged by the likes of Ed the doorman. It was like having Pops, a happy Pops, back with me.

And Joey—even he gave me a hug, and I told him on the way up in the elevator that starting in the next week I'd be tutoring him in his letters in his spare moments. To which he replied, wide-eyed, "Yes, miss. I'd like that, miss."

Aunt Mary and Uncle Bert were both there, both looking awful, which made me feel awful. But they were so relieved that I was all right that after hugs and tears they ushered me into my bedroom— my bedroom, tidied and neat—so that I could rest.

"How's Chester?" I asked.

"He's fine," said Uncle Bert. "Nose like a boxer, but, well, it's made him a little more humble, in fact." My uncle cleared his throat.

"And Melody?" I asked, trying to stifle a yawn.

Aunt Mary shrugged. "Asleep. But she hasn't been out carousing around since you left. She's been talking about getting a job. Maybe something you said . . . ?"

I shook my head. "Not me, Aunt Mary. Mel's got a mind of her own."

I wanted to take a bath, and I thought I might read that single last page of Teddy's journal, that page I still clutched tight in its scarf bundle; but when I sat down on the bed, thinking, I might just rest my eyes first, I fell into a deep sleep before I could move again.

*   *   *

When I awoke it was late afternoon, and I stood at the tall window of my room and watched the city that never sleeps match my yawn and stretch. I saw the buildings across the street reflect the late-day coppery sun. Saw the deepening blue of the sky beyond as I looked east, out over the east side of the island toward Long Island Sound.

The Sound. Where Teddy had died.

I sat on the windowsill and spread out the last page.

> September 12, 1923
> If you're reading this now, Josie, it means I'm dead.
> I'm sorry, sweet Jo. If I was there, I'd be saying
> stuff like, I miss you, and how can this be, so I
> can only imagine what you're thinking as you read

this. 'Cause I know you'd never have opened this journal—you'd have kept your promise—unless I was dead.

Danny Connor is going to come after me, and I have to keep him from going after you and Ma and Pops. So the outcome may not be what I want.

But here's the thing: I'll protect you for as long as I can. I won't rest until I know you're okay. Happy and safe. That's what I gave up my soul for, and until you're safe I don't get it back.

Now that you've read this, you've got to do me a favor.

I was never a true hero. Never felt like one, never liked the whole business.

So I'm going to ask you to . . .

CHAPTER 55
SEPTEMBER 1925

So we beat on, boats against the current,
borne back ceaselessly into the past.
—F. Scott Fitzgerald, The Great Gatsby, 1925

LOU

That's the way it happened, I swear. You guys have been swell listeners.

Lemme add a few things here. If it hadn't been for Jo, I'd be dead. If it hadn't been for Jo, Mel wouldn't have gotten her little boy back—and bagged a guy like John Rushton in the bargain. If it hadn't been for Jo, Charlie would never have been so happy.

Now I've got a job, and Jo's got . . . well, I'll let her tell you. And we've got the apartment—our nice cozy little place in the Chelsea Hotel—thanks to Jo standing up for us and hitting the street. We're not swimming in dough, but mine's a decent job, and we're sticking together. When Jo's got her feet planted solid on the ground, that's when she'll consider taking Charlie up on his proposal. I admire that—she wants to make it herself and not depend on a guy, even a good guy like my brother, to make it for her.

We kind of joke about how she thought she knew right from wrong but she really had no clue.

Sometimes, when Jo doesn't know I'm watching, I see her staring out there from our apartment window, out and up into the night sky, and what's really spooky is she talks to herself. Actually, I think she's talking to Teddy.

So okay. I talk to him, too. You got a problem with that?

I wonder. What does it mean to believe in yourself so much that you don't let some guy push you around? What does it mean to believe in something, the way Jo does, something so big and powerful that you can't let it go? What does it mean when Jo says, "Everything comes in shades of gray, Lou. Just when you think you're right, you find out something that sends it spinning backward."

I'm still trying to figure that one out.

Well, Detective, I've got nothing more to add. You can see what really happened. I'm guilty of a lot of things, but nothing you can arrest me for.

Am I free to go?

* * *

JO

This window from our living room looks west. I like that; I'm more of a sunset type than a sunrise. There's something about knowing New York is about to wake up for her nightlife and watching the lights go on and the stars come out, all that stretching and yawning and preparing; something about hearing the music that swells up from the street, smelling the toasted bitter of chestnuts, leaning out into the chill evening air, something about a New York night that makes me feel alive.

And now I'm back in school—they let me in, up at Barnard

Women's College, a work-study thing, after I wrote about what I'd been through this past summer in a story that they said showed "promise." I bit my lip not to laugh. Since I know a bunch about promises.

I know Lou thinks I'm a little crazy. Maybe I am. I have Lou and my family. I have Charlie, and that thought makes me smile and warms me from my toes right on up. The little crazy part is that I also still have Teddy.

It was when I went to the dock not long ago, that cold air, that icy water, those stars, when I let go of those medals, when I pitched them into the water, that's when I felt it. Like a sigh, from me, from him, like the release of all the bad things Teddy thought he'd done and all the bad things he really had done, and I knew I'd freed him at last. Knew I'd really kept that promise anyhow. And now I have Teddy new, the golden-haired brother who loved me with a pure heart.

But mainly I have me, Josephine Anne Winter, who has no clue what mysteries might spring up, and who still doesn't know what it takes to be a true hero and is not always sure about right and wrong, but who is ready to find out. I'm ready to chart my own course, and whether I'm a flapper or not isn't the point.

My future is very much up in the air, an open book, an unfinished story. I get to write my own ending. I get to find all the characters and the plot. And I believe it'll turn out okay now.

I'm guided by the stars.

AUTHOR'S NOTE

There's no question that the Roaring Twenties hold a mystique for contemporary readers. I think the reason for this is that there are many parallels between the 1920s and today: the excessive "anything goes" lifestyle, the emergence of wondrous new products, the search for spiritualism, and even the social and political tension that led to a Wall Street bombing. Veterans who had returned from World War I were as damaged as those who returned from Afghanistan and Iraq. In the 1920s flapper fashion ushered in a radical new style. The automobile ushered in a new physical and psychological freedom. Advertising and product development made their first appearances. And, of course, Prohibition is an endlessly fascinating subject, with its clandestine "speaks"—which encouraged the emergence of jazz and the blues and the rise of the gangster.

A number of resources gave me insight into the 1920s. Frederick Lewis Allen's *Only Yesterday: An Informal History of the 1920's* was first published in 1931, which gives it the air of immediacy. Joshua Zeitz's *Flapper* is a fascinating look at the women's liberation movement that truly began in the '20s. And Lucy Moore's *Anything Goes* is a colorful examination of the nuances of life in the 1920s.

But I confess I was most taken with the spiritualism movement, and three of its intriguing figures, who also happened to be close (if argumentative) friends: Harry Houdini, Sir Arthur Conan Doyle, and Howard Thurston. Thurston, in particular, fascinates me, and I learned much from Jim Steinmeyer's biography of Thurston, *The Last Greatest Magician in the World.* Here was a man convinced of the reality of reincarnation, who yet thrilled the masses with his fakery and magic craft.

We resonate with history's repetitions: the reckless 1920s and 1990s, followed by the belt-tightening 1930s and the first decade of the twenty-first century. I love the resonance of history, and I hope I've given you something to savor of New York in 1925.

ACKNOWLEDGMENTS

Jen Bonnell, my amazing editor, you have done it again: pared my prose, focused my rambling, and helped me find the right words to build a world. It has been a true pleasure to work with you.

The luckiest day of my life was the day I met my agent, Alyssa Eisner Henkin. You are not only my agent but also my friend. Thank you always for your willingness to support me, to defend or console me, to instruct me. I love our wide-ranging chats but more importantly I value your guidance.

I have a new critique group here in Montana—how could I get so lucky again? You guys read the entire first draft of this novel (when it was huge, and all over the place) and you dissected it and advised me and set me on the true path. Sandra Brug, Kiri Jorgensen, Bailey Jorgensen, Maurene Hinds, and Linda Knox: you are all amazing and talented and really, really, *really* smart. Thank you so much. We are missing one member of our group who also gave me great advice and insight: Elaine Alphin. We think of you all the time, Elaine. There's a chair at the table waiting for you. And chocolate, too.

My friend Michele Corriel read an early draft of *Sirens*. Michele, you were right every step of the way (second person address—gone!), and I value your terrific feedback.

I am enormously indebted to those in Speak/Puffin/Penguin who have supported me and believed in my work: Kristin Gilson, Eileen Kreit, Greg Stadnyk, Pat Shuldiner, and Nora M. Reichard.

Finally, to my sweet and ever-patient husband Jeff and my understanding and sometimes impatient but richly imaginative son Kevin (yes, you do have the best ideas): thank you both. You are willing to be my beta readers, willing to put up with my late nights, willing always to be there for me. How lucky can one girl get?

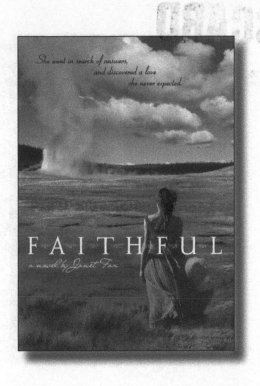

She went in search of answers,
and discovered a love
she never expected.

FAITHFUL

a novel by Janet Fox

Sixteen-year-old Maggie Bennet's life is in tatters. Her mother has disappeared and is presumed dead. The next thing she knows, her father has dragged Maggie away from their elegant Newport home, off on some mad excursion to Yellowstone in Montana. But when she arrives, she finds herself drawn to the frustratingly stubborn, handsome Tom Rowland, the son of a park geologist, and to the wild romantic beauty of Yellowstone itself. And as Tom and the promise of freedom capture Maggie's heart, Maggie is forced to choose between who she is and who she wants to be.

"Fox combines mystery, romance, and a young girl's coming-of-age in this satisfying historical tale." —*Booklist*

"Yellowstone is lovingly and beautifully depicted. . . . Thrilling episodes sprinkled throughout will engage readers." —*School Library Journal*

COUNTY LIBRARY
DISCARD
TILLAMOOK, ORE.

She had to unlock her heart to
discover the true meaning of love.

Forgiven

JANET FOX
author of *Faithful*

"Absorbing, exciting, and romantic." —Nancy Werlin, National Book Award
Finalist and *New York Times* bestselling author of *Impossible*

Kula Baker never expected to find herself on the streets of San
Francisco, alone but for a letter of introduction. Kula soon finds
herself swept up in a world of art and elegance—a world she hardly
dared dream of back in Montana. And then there is the handsome
David Wong, whose smiling eyes and soft-spoken manner have an
uncanny way of breaking through Kula's carefully crafted reserve.
Yet when disaster strikes and the wreckage threatens all she holds
dear, Kula realizes that only by unlocking her heart can she begin
to carve a new future for herself.

"Absorbing, exciting, and romantic."
—Nancy Werlin, *New York Times* bestselling author of *Impossible*

"Kula's story comes to a heartbreaking, bittersweet conclusion that will leave
readers satisfied." —*School Library Journal*

PO #: 0003245204